YANKEE
MISSION

JULIAN STOCKWIN

YANKEE MISSION

HODDER &
STOUGHTON

First published in Great Britain in 2022 by Hodder & Stoughton
An Hachette UK company

1

Copyright © Julian Stockwin 2022

A CIP catalogue record for this title is available from the British Library

Hardback ISBN 978 1 473 69913 7
Trade Paperback ISBN 978 1 473 69914 4
eBook ISBN 978 1 473 69915 1

Typeset in Garamond MT by Palimpsest Book Production Limited,
Falkirk, Stirlingshire

Printed and bound in Great Britain by Clays Ltd, Elcograf S.p.A.

Hodder & Stoughton policy is to use papers that are natural,
renewable and recyclable products and made from wood grown in sustainable
forests. The logging and manufacturing processes are expected to conform
to the environmental regulations of the country of origin.

Hodder & Stoughton Ltd
Carmelite House
50 Victoria Embankment
London EC4Y 0DZ

www.hodder.co.uk

To my friends across the Atlantic
who have themselves answered Neptune's call

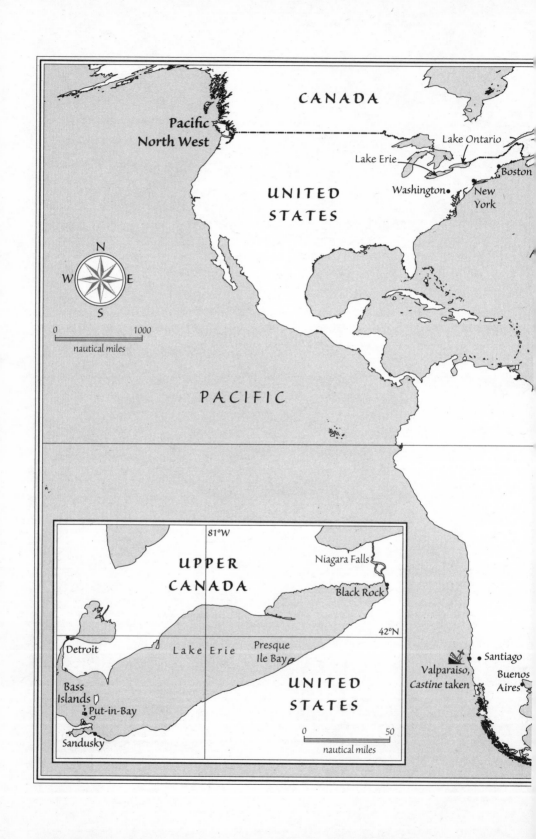

CANADA

Pacific
North West

Lake Ontario

Lake Erie

Boston

UNITED
STATES

Washington•

New
York

N
W E
S

0   1000
nautical miles

PACIFIC

81°W

UPPER
CANADA

Niagara Falls

Black Rock

42°N

Detroit

Lake Erie

Presque
Ile Bay

Bass
Islands

UNITED
STATES

Put-in-Bay

0   50
nautical miles

Sandusky

Valparaiso,
Castine taken

Santiago

Buenos
Aires

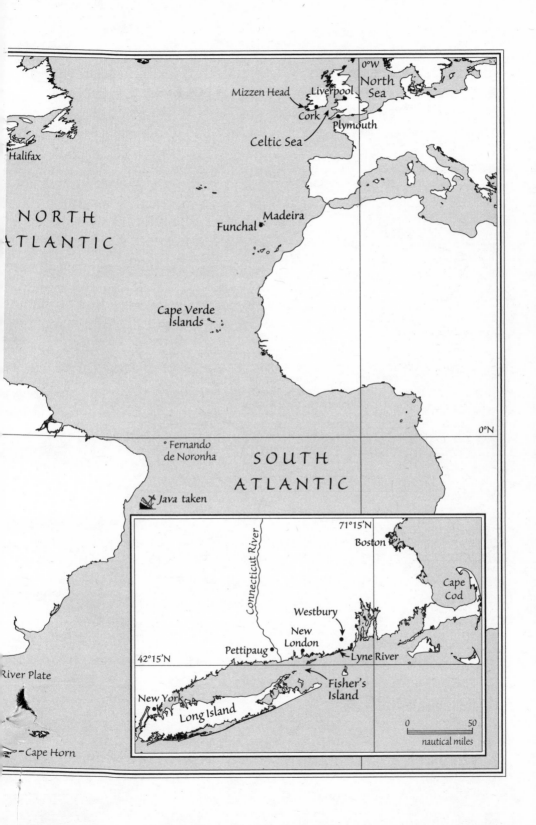

North Sea

0°W

Mizzen Head

Liverpool

Cork

Plymouth

Celtic Sea

Halifax

NORTH ATLANTIC

Funchal • Madeira

Cape Verde Islands

0°N

° Fernando de Noronha

SOUTH ATLANTIC

Java taken

River Plate

Cape Horn

Connecticut River

71°15'N

Boston

Cape Cod

Westbury

New London

Pettipaug

Lyne River

42°15'N

Fisher's Island

New York

Long Island

0   50

nautical miles

Dramatis Personae

* Indicates fictitious character

Ships' companies

Barclay	Commodore, HMS *Detroit*
*Binard	Kydd's manservant
*Borden	Master's mate, USS *Prospero*
*Bowden	First lieutenant, HMS *Tyger*
Broke	Captain, HMS *Shannon*
Chads	First lieutenant, HMS *Java*
*Davis	First lieutenant, USS *Kestrel*
*Denby	Second lieutenant, HMS *Active*
*Gindler	Officer in United States Navy
*Halgren	Coxswain, HMS *Tyger*
*Hanson	First lieutenant, USS *Castine*
Hollett	Surgeon, HMS *Rattler*
*Joyce	Sailing master, HMS *Tyger*
Lambert	Captain, HMS *Java*
*Parnall	Boatswain, HMS *Active*
Perry	Commodore, USS *Lawrence*
Poole	Captain, HMS *Rattler*

Riordan	Captain, HMS *Maidstone*
*Rollins	Temporary surgeon, HMS *Rattler*
Robinson	Sailing master, HMS *Java*
*Stirk	Gunner's mate, HMS *Tyger*
*Tyler	First lieutenant, HMS *Active*
*Wiley	Boatswain, HMS *Whippet*

Others

Alleyne	Comptroller of the Clerks-in-Office, Office of the Inspector General of Naval Works
Andrews	Commissioner for the auditing of public accounts
*Appleby, Mrs	Housekeeper to the Kydds
Bell	Designer of *Comet*, first steamship to ply freely for passengers
Bentham	Inspector general of Naval Works
Brunton	Inventor of studded link chain cable
*Burrowes	Captain of militia, Mustauk county
*Craddock	Kydd's confidential secretary
Dewey	Port admiral, Plymouth
*Gardner	Office of Board of Ordnance
Goodrich	Mechanist to Office of the Inspector General of Naval Works
*Harper	Major of militia, Trowton
Hislop	Lieutenant governor-elect, Bombay
*Godfrey	Kydd's clerk
*Jackson	Hunter and militia sharpshooter
Meade	Governor of British administration of Madeira
Melville	First Lord of the Admiralty
*Phipps	Midlands ironmaster
*Pinckney, Anne	Fisher-girl

Popham	Gifted but controversial admiral
Tecumseh	Shawnee chief and ally of Britain
Trevithick	Cornish inventor and engine-smith
*Tucker	Clam digger in Connecticut river
*Upjohn	Fraudulent designer of water distillation plant
Walker	Aide to Governor Hislop
Warren	Admiral of the Blue, in command of all forces in Western Atlantic
Wrights	Brothers commissioning first ships in steam

Chapter 1

Winter, 1812

HMS Java, *off the coast of São Salvador de Baia, Brazil*

'Do pass the salt, dear fellow,' Lieutenant General Hislop asked affably. Energised by the cool morning breeze drawn into the great cabin by the ship's progress through the tropic seas, he was enjoying a hearty breakfast of devilled kidneys.

Henry Lambert, *Java's* captain, complied politely. It was advisable to keep in humour this high-ranking gentleman who was being conveyed to India to take up the post of lieutenant governor of Bombay.

The 38-gun frigate was crowded with men destined for crew-starved ships on the distant station and laden with much-anticipated naval stores, including some all-encumbering copper sheeting and much military impedimenta.

It had been a hard voyage so far, the clamping winter bluster causing several false starts before they met better weather in the horse latitudes, and after a mercifully rapid transit of the doldrums, they could now expect a good run to the Cape and on into the Indian Ocean.

'So we're on course for India in, what, a month or so?' mumbled Hislop, through his toast.

'Assuming we don't meet with contrary winds, which doth signify Neptune's displeasure.'

'Or the enemy,' interjected Major Walker, one of the general's aides and an incorrigible pessimist.

'The enemy? I don't suspect any of Boney's finest here, this far from home. We've swept the beggars from the seas, you'll allow.'

'None other? Dutch – or American, come to that.'

'What would any of them be doing in these parts? Waiting for us?' Captain Lambert's slightly nettled tone was the only hint he was at all concerned that his high-placed cargo was in any way at hazard.

Chads, the young first lieutenant, remarked, 'Sir, the Yankees have some big brutes when it comes to frigates and—'

'We've lost a couple of frigates to them only? Are you then affrighted, Mr Chads?' The words were barbed.

'Not really, sir. After all we're Royal Navy, they're not. But . . . but . . .'

'Yes?' The hard-faced Lambert leaned across the table, glaring at him, challenging.

'Sir, *Java* is only a 38 to their 44s, and with a ship-of-the-line's scantlings and armament they're bound to cause us vexation. I'd be happier once we're away off the American half of the world.' As first lieutenant, Chads had responsibility for the rating and assigning of men to their stations for storm and action and knew only too well the difficult situation *Java* was in. Two-thirds of her ship's company were temporary, a larger portion than usual being pressed men and those destined for transfer, the rest in this new commission unknown and untested. And counted in their numbers were twenty or more boys of eleven or younger, midshipmen and volunteers.

Hislop said nothing but his now-grave expression indicated that he wanted assurances.

Lambert replied strongly, 'We're here, Brazil under our lee and far from their—'

'Ah, I've wondered,' Hislop said quietly, 'why I'm treated to the sight of the southern continent out there so close. Surely a more direct route to India is to be desired, rather nearer the African shore.'

'The winds, sir. We obey the reigning winds, which come from the north-east in the northern hemisphere and quite another direction in the southern. We ride them to best advantage. We decrease our time on voyage at the cost of distance by making rendezvous with the east tip of Brazil before putting our helm up for a course across to the Cape of Good Hope to take up the monsoon to India.'

'I see. Then if—'

A distant hail was heard, answered from the deck. The naval officers looked at each other questioningly, and shortly there was a polite knock at the door and a midshipman messenger appeared. 'Foretop lookout reports square sail to the sou'-west, sir.'

'Thank you,' Lambert said. 'Let me know when we discover more.'

'You're staying on course.'

'Yes. Very likely to be a coastal craft, possibly a Portuguee trader. We shall finish breakfast, I believe.'

Amiable conversation was taken up again, but before the table was cleared the midshipman reported back gravely, 'Mr Buchanan's respects, an' vessel is full-rigged and standing athwart.'

'I'll be on deck presently,' Lambert grunted, finishing his coffee. 'A juicy prize, perhaps?' He winked at Chads.

Anything under square-rigged masts had to be of interest but it would be some time before it was visible from the deck.

'Well, Mr Buchanan?' Lambert enquired, once he'd made his appearance.

'It seems he's altered away, sir.'

'Running? Sign of a bad conscience, General.' Next to him, Hislop accepted a proffered telescope but confessed he could understand little.

'To the east? Odd,' muttered Lambert, retrieving the glass. 'Takes him further out to seawards. I'd have thought it more to his advantage to close with the coast.'

From the deck the ship was still only royals up at the horizon and fine on the bow.

Then the sails changed relationship to each other. 'Hello – the beggar's putting about . . . and now he's by the wind and heading our way.' Lambert snapped the telescope shut and handed it back to Buchanan. 'Rouse out our private signal. He has to be one of ours. I've not heard of any in these waters. Wonder who he is.'

An hour later there was no doubt this was a frigate, and a large one. There were frowns on the quarterdeck and animated talk among the seamen on deck.

'Hmm. I think we should be prudent, Mr Chads. Clear for action in slow time, if you please, just in case, then send the hands to an early dinner.'

'May I?' Hislop began.

'Yes, General?'

'If this ship is an American, should we in all prudence be considering an engagement, at all?'

'Why, sir! If it flies any flag with which His Majesty is

opposed I will do my duty. Any other course is dishonourable and a derogation of trust.'

Hislop pursed his lips and said quietly, 'Sir, I'd be remiss should I not remind you that you have your duty to convey myself and others to India in accordance with your orders.'

'You might remind me, sir, but I see as my higher obligation that of upholding the best traditions of the Royal Navy in taking battle to the enemy wherever I see him, not fleeing before him.'

Hislop harrumphed. 'Then of course you have our approbation and support should you see fit to move against this vessel.'

'Thank you, General.'

They were closing fast and Lambert caught the sailing master's eye. 'I'll trouble you to keep safely to windward of the chase, Mr Robinson.'

So it was now a chase, Chads saw. The captain was not about to let it go.

Java shaped course to conform to the larboard tack of the other, near a mile downwind. When settled on course she hoisted her red ensign and at the same time threw out the private recognition signals. The other frigate seemed to hesitate, and then a flourish of colour appeared at its mizzen-masthead.

'She's American!'

The United States jack flared out at the foremast and another ensign fluttered into life at the driver gaff leaving no more room for speculation.

'An' she's a commodore, b' all that's holy!' one sharp-eyed seaman blurted, noticing a broad pennant at the main.

'Quarters for battle, Mr Chads,' Lambert ordered crisply, and for the first time on their voyage, the martial thunder of a marine drummer was heard at the hatchways.

He then turned to the army officers. 'Gentlemen. The next few hours will be busy and dangerous. I advise that you will take shelter below decks. Mr Buchanan, if you'll . . .'

'Captain,' asked the general, quietly, 'pray where will your own officers be during the action?'

Lambert looked at him curiously. 'Beside the guns, the masts. Why do you ask, sir?'

'And you?'

'I will be in command at my post here on the quarterdeck, with the first lieutenant, my ship's clerk and—'

'Then that's where we shall be also,' Hislop came back.

'But—'

'Sir, do allow that a general officer's duty includes that of sharing a battlefield's dangers with his men, as does yours.'

It was now the age-old stealthy manoeuvring, the probing into strengths, weaknesses and deceptions with which a frigate duel opened and so often ended with a battle-winning move by the wiser.

Both ships took in their courses, the big ocean driving canvas, to leave topsails, the traditional fighting sails in close combat, hoisted.

Tensely, Chads watched as the two men-o'-war edged towards each other, like prize-fighters shaping up for a brutal onslaught. Before long it became clear that *Java* had the edge in speed, a vital advantage, enabling her to keep to windward and therefore dictate the pace and direction of the inevitable clinch.

Men stood motionless by their guns, eyeing the big frigate with expressions ranging from scorn to apprehension. They were an untrained, scratch crew who had not yet fought together, and with the American showing willing, they were in for a fight for their lives before very long.

Lambert volleyed out orders and sail was trimmed – there was no sense in careering past the enemy – and then Chads saw the deeper intent. By falling back *Java* would be in a prime position, on the enemy's weather quarter, to open the battle with a murderous raking into the American's stern.

As if surmising what was intended, the whole length of the enemy's larboard side erupted in smoke and blast, heavy shot pluming and skipping close to *Java,* most in line and well-laid.

That one act informed much and Chads felt his belly turn cold. As well, the disciplined rolling broadside from aft to forward told of a strong, numerous and well-trained crew. That it happened well outside the range of their own guns and with a heavy concussion also spoke of the twenty-four-pounders carried by the Americans. They were comprehensively out-gunned and couldn't yet reply with their own long eighteens. In close combat this weight of metal would tell, possibly fatally.

He continued to pace slowly next to the captain. 'A brave showing from Cousin Jonathan,' he said lightly.

'So far,' Lambert said quietly. 'There's naught to be gained by standing off. I mean to close and grapple with the villain.'

The American emerged from the smoke of its broadside and in a further savage crash another was unleashed.

This time *Java* felt hits and the wind of iron shot but she was far from being daunted, closing until she had the range, then unleashing her fury in a crashing broadside, which told visibly on the American decks, and throwing a-flutter her flying jib. In an act of supreme bravery a crewman swung out into the fore-rigging and among the storm of shot whipping by he passed a stopper, restoring the ship's manoeuvrability.

Swinging in, *Java* attacked with all she had, her eighteens, carronades and, when close enough, marine musket fire in a deafening chorus of violence. It was returned with a vicious sleeting of shot, both ships taking punishment.

Throwing free more canvas, *Java* pulled ahead with deadly

intent: to hurl herself across the bows of her slower enemy to loose a raking broadside into its unprotected fore-parts.

Her helm went up and a broadside smashed out simultaneously with her opponent, and the space between was abruptly choked with towering gun-smoke. By the time it cleared it was apparent the American captain had saved his ship. Hidden by the smoke, in an instant he'd thrown over his helm and worn about to leeward, leaving *Java* to race on ahead. Not to be caught so easily, Lambert bawled out orders that had his ship wear about as well, in chase of the American but implacably keeping on to windward.

The battle went on, this time hauling to westward, the two now locked in ferocious combat in a furious hell of noise and death.

And the smaller ship was getting the better of the fight. Using her speed she pressed ahead then suddenly her captain bawled, 'Hands to wear ship!'

In a daring move she put about, letting the bigger frigate surge ahead – and *Java* was in position for a devastating rake across the stern of the American frigate.

Lambert didn't hesitate. 'Fire!' he blared, and a merciless avalanche of shot smashed into the heavier frigate's stern-quarters, gun after gun crashing round-shot into the pretty windows.

Chads touched his arm. 'You see that?'

'What?' snapped Lambert, distracted.

'Her name – *Constitution*. Which did for *Guerriere*.' A frigate such as theirs – and in the process had turned a world that believed the Royal Navy invincible on its head.

Sudden shrieks and the sight of flying splinters, flung bodies and their opponent's helm smashed to pieces, brought a pandemonium of cheering from *Java*'s men, and she swept past, crossing the wake of *Constitution*. But the larger frigate made

8

no move to retaliate. Instead it kept on a steady course eastwards on its way out of the battle.

'You'll disengage, sir?' General Hislop had crossed the deck to stand beside the captain. His features were composed but the fierceness of the conflict had plainly affected him.

'Why should I do that, sir? My ship is whole. Our only chance is to keep within range of our own guns.'

'To finish the job.'

'Quite so.'

Chads's mood lightened. *Java* was prevailing over her larger and better-armed opponent and he knew it would hearten both the Navy and the British public to hear of a victory.

'Wear us about, Mr Robinson.' The east-north-easterly wind was light and playful, and there was no spirited pirouette when *Java* wore about for another raking shot at the steadily retreating *Constitution*, only a ragged ripple of firing at the now distant target.

Lambert swore and ordered his frigate around in chase. At this range there could be no more attempts at a rake across the stern but with her superior speed she could overhaul the big frigate rapidly and, when past, throw over the helm to cross its bow for a lethal rake.

As she began to overlap, an astonishing thing happened: in *Constitution* the big main and fore-courses dropped from their yards and with their added impetus *Java*'s onrush was nullified and the two plunged on side by side a mere two hundred yards apart.

And then Chads understood. *Constitution*'s helm had been wrecked, yet she'd kept straight on her course until a jury tackle at the tiller had been rigged, even at the cost of making it seem she was abandoning the fight. Now *Java* would pay.

The American had timed his move well, and the smashing match could begin.

Flame stabbed and blasted from the muzzles of scores of weapons, a hurricane of shot exchanged across the space between them. The din was amplified by the facing sides of the ships, a fearsome assault of iron into timber that splintered and disintegrated, finding cordage and masts, carvings and bulwarks, gun carriages and human flesh.

Men slaved at their guns, muscles bunching, eyes reddening, backs a nest of pain.

Officers paced their quarterdecks while sharp-shooters took aim, and all the time iron missiles extracted their lethal due of the men who served so nobly opposite each other. Powder monkeys in their race from magazine to gun saw the corpses of their shipmates but stumbled on, some to meet their own end in a brutal impact and welter of blood.

And then the tide of battle turned. This time against *Java*.

The twenty-four-pounders of *Constitution* reached out and, with a resounding snap above the infernal din of battle, took away *Java*'s bowsprit and with it most of her head-sails. Seeing this, *Constitution* pulled ahead and in the smoke of her own broadside wore around to catch *Java* in a merciless rake.

Lambert realised the intention and roared out the orders to tack about to avoid it but the loss of head-sails meant *Java*'s manoeuvre was thwarted, she could not lever herself through the wind's eye. She hung in irons.

Constitution did not hesitate: surging past she slammed a terrible broadside directly into her stern then came up on *Java*'s starboard side with all guns ablaze.

The havoc was indescribable, wreckage raining from aloft, guns overset with hits, rigging parted by chain-shot, all punctuated by inhuman shrieks as seamen paid with their lives for the madness of war.

'Should we not withdraw?' Hislop muttered, as the broken body of his aide was dragged away.

'Be silent, sir!' Lambert roared. 'I still have the advantage!'

'Sir?' Chads said, unable to see one.

'We go in to board! With our "passengers" we must outnumber even the Americans.'

It could work! Still to weather of the foe, they had this advantage.

'Lay me aboard the American, Mr Robinson,' Lambert threw at the Royal Marines officer. 'Have your men in position, if you please.'

'Sir, the master has been taken below.'

'Do it!'

Lambert eyed the gap and urged his boarders forward in readiness. They snatched up cutlasses, pistols and tomahawks from their chests and massed together on the fore-deck in a cheering, raucous crowd, wild to get to their tormentor. In *Constitution* seamen roaring out their defiance crowded together to repel boarders as *Java* swung towards its bow but at that moment the American frigate got away a full broadside squarely into her bows. And with an appalling, rending crack a round-shot took *Java*'s foremast just beneath her fighting-top and, like a tree felled in a forest, it came down, rigging, head-sails, along with the men in the top. It crashed down, splintering the bulwarks and crushing boarders, to end draped over the side, a dead weight of wreckage trailing over her beakhead and side bringing her lunge down to a crawl.

Constitution shot ahead but could not avoid the spearing remnants of *Java*'s bowsprit catching in her mizzen gear, the heavy ship drawing the other around until the British vessel, bows on, could no longer reply to the savage point-blank raking fire that was gutting her. Eventually she tore free but lay unmanageable, giving the American opportunity to take her time in circling around for another killing rake.

If sail of any kind could be bent on to the remains of the

foremast there would be some chance of defensive manoeuvres, and seamen fell on the wreckage with axes, knives and cutlasses to cut it away. As they struggled, *Constitution* crashed in another broadside, this time aft. Unable to miss at this range, the mizzen topmast took fearful damage, the driver and its gaff tumbling down over the side, and *Java* came up uncontrollably into the wind.

The big frigate began circling, like a carnivore about to put an end to a wounded beast, but *Java* stubbornly refused to give up the fight.

'Just let me grapple the once,' Lambert ground out, pacing slowly. But *Constitution* would never let it happen and wore about to pass clear. The remains of *Java*'s foremast teetered and fell. The mizzen was brought down in a tangle of rope and canvas and, encouraged, *Constitution* loomed near to give her marksmen in the tops a closer shot. She passed slowly down *Java*'s starboard side, where so much of the wreckage from aloft was draped, guns thundering out again and again in a hideous blast of noise.

Defiantly, *Java*'s remaining gunners fired back but the blast caused the canvas to catch flame, a deadly threat, and her returning fire slackened as seamen left their weapons to douse it.

Chads knew that the end could not be long delayed but, taking strength from his captain, paced on. Then, with a choking grunt, Lambert spun around and fell to the deck, a bloody chest betraying his death wound. Chads dropped to his knees beside him but there was nothing he could do except motion for men to take him below.

He was in command now and bleakly he looked about the charnel house that was *Java*'s upper deck. Piled corpses beside the guns, blood trickling down the scuppers, sprawled wounded against a gun carriage breathing their last. The ship's company had given their all and it was not enough.

In a choking rage he saw how *Java* had been mercilessly savaged, now all three masts brought down, leaving her a riven hulk. He raised his eyes to see *Constitution* making off in a wide circle, seeing to her own hurts, but she would be back. Was now the time to give in? To hand a third defeat of a Royal Navy frigate to the Yankees? Centuries of tradition, years at sea, hammered in on his senses – he would fight to the last, as Lambert would wish it.

'Sir, we've taken a deal o' shot in the hull as is set fair to sink us,' the exhausted carpenter reported.

'An' we've less'n half our guns fit f'r service,' the gunner said, 'even if'n we can man 'em which we can't.'

The boatswain, bandaged and in visible pain, hobbled up. 'If ye likes, sir, I can rig a staysail on what's left o' the foremast, but 't won't be much.'

How could he yield the ship when he had men like these?

'We'll not give in, men. Do your best,' Chads said gruffly.

Their ensign, before proudly aloft, now flew from the stump of the mizzen-mast, and as the men laboured Chads looked out to where *Constitution* lay off, working on her own repairs. With an inevitability that was so unfair, as evening approached so did their nemesis. Cautiously, in a careful and methodical manner, she came on until it was indisputable what was going to happen.

The big frigate was taking position for the final act – to lie across the helpless *Java*'s bow to batter and crush her to death.

Chads gulped. All options, all moves, every chance of striking back, had narrowed to one choice: to yield or futilely end the lives of his brave and resolute shipmates.

He hesitated for a brief moment only, then crossed to the makeshift halliards and, with tears streaking his face, he lowered *Java*'s colours.

Chapter 2

Knowle Manor, Devon, England

'Well, who's my big boy, then?' Sir Thomas Kydd RN, captain of the line-of-battle ship *Thunderer* cooed, not at all noticing the dribbling that had begun to decorate his full-dress uniform, which in his hurry to make acquaintance of his first-born he'd forgotten to change.

The pink scrap of humanity wiggled uncertainly, staring fixedly at him, warmth radiating through its swaddling. It was an incredible, mind-scrambling thought that this precious new life was his, that his name would be carried forward by this tiny creature, who would look to him for a steer through the rocks and shoals of life before maturing into a splendid youth and young man who—

'Sir, an' you're holding him all wrong!' Mrs Appleby, the housekeeper, scolded, reaching for the infant and making much of positioning it in the approved manner.

Behind her Kydd's infinitely precious wife Persephone looked on indulgently, and while the child was being seen to, he snatched another fond kiss.

'There, sir. Now you try 'un.'

Gravely he accepted the tiny morsel but its face reddened and wrinkled in objection and a loud squalling began. He hastily handed it back.

'He'll be used t' ye, by an' by,' Mrs Appleby consoled, rocking it into quiescence.

They were shortly to have their first-born christened Francis Powlett – after the doughty Elizabethan mariner, and the captain of *Artemis* frigate, under whom, as a lowly seaman, Kydd had served on an epic voyage around the world.

'You didn't say how long you'll have with me . . . us,' Persephone said, her eyes on his, never leaving.

'Oh, er, some time, I'd think. *Thunderer* is to rest after the Danish hurricanoe and her men must take their liberty ashore.'

'How . . . long?'

'She's in good hands under survey in Portsmouth and no doubt they'll let me know if she needs any repair.' At her look, he added, 'Darling, I'd think at least a month or even more will be granted us.'

'So little? It's quite unfair,' she whispered brokenly. 'Dear man, you've done your duty and they owe you—'

'My love,' Kydd answered gently, 'the world's on fire and no man knows the end of it all. Just now it's my duty to serve – as I must.'

The days dissolved into a delirium of happiness. Along with the choice of special touches for the nursery there was much discussion on the baby's christening and formal entry upon the world.

But in a brace of weeks only, one morning it came to an end. As usual they rode together into Ivybridge to the London Inn. It was invigorating exercise and as an excuse they awaited the mail coach for any post.

A note was handed over, from Dewey, the port admiral at Plymouth. The first lord of the Admiralty, newly arrived on his visit of inspection, had expressed a desire that Kydd do attend on him – did the nominated date and time suit?

Kydd reasoned that it was probably only a polite request to make his acquaintance while in this part of the realm, but any summons from the highest in his universe was sufficient to cause concern and he accepted without delay.

Two days later he was stiffly seated in the smaller drawing room of Admiralty House on Mount Wise, gingerly accepting tea and dainty cakes from the admiral's lady.

'Why, so handsome of you to come,' Melville, the second viscount of that line and an increasingly effective new first lord of the Admiralty, said, as he entered with Dewey, extending his hand. 'You've had a more than entertaining time in your ship-of-the-line in your first commission it seems.'

Kydd scrambled to his feet. 'It has to be said, sir.'

'I'll see you later, Robert?' Admiral Dewey asked.

'You shall, old fellow,' Melville answered amiably. 'Captain Kydd and I have a trifle to discuss.'

Excusing himself, with but a single glance at Kydd, Dewey left them to their privacy.

'I would wish for more time together, Sir Thomas, but these days I'm unconscionably pressed by tedious matters politick.'

Kydd tensed. This was not the youthful and retiring Yorke of the previous administration but a person of large presence, a man of the future, whose devotion to his situation as head of the maritime defences of England was fast becoming evident. This was no casual reacquainting. 'I understand, sir.'

'Then you'll forgive me if I find myself cast in the character of the purveyor of bad news.'

'Sir?' Kydd responded, with a degree of wariness.

'You've grown attached to your wooden world, I've heard.'

'As fine and noble a barky as ever I've sailed in, yes.'

'Then I fear my news will be anything but welcome. Sir Thomas, *Thunderer* was taken to survey and I've been asked to acquaint you with the fact that in the great storm and previous she suffered more than was suspected. The master shipwright has allowed that only a middling to great repair will see her put to rights. And finding a sum for it from this year's vote for, um, a no-longer-young vessel would have to be justified before the Board or . . .'

The saintly sorrow on his features did nothing to soften the blow, and at the same time Kydd felt an increasing uneasiness. Why should the first lord of the Admiralty himself pass this on, a devastating but entirely routine notifying? Especially as a Board-level decision on *Thunderer's* fate was not normally within his notice.

'A sad blow to me, my lord,' he murmured, his eyes pricking.

The implication was that he'd lost his command and almost certainly they had something in mind. If it was a shore appointment, say as equerry to the Prince Regent, it would be an unbearable fate for an active sea officer.

'I will do all I can for you, Sir Thomas, but as you will be aware, the times are not favourable.'

Kydd remained silent – there was nothing he could say, only wait for the substance at hand.

'On another matter, you've heard that the Americans have had the gall to take a third frigate?'

'I'd read something of the kind.'

'*Java*. A French-built 38, and carrying important passengers. A bloody enough encounter off Brazil a few weeks ago and the Yankees are even now crowing their victory to the masses, you'll believe.'

'Sir.' Kydd was sympathetic but it was the other side of the world and really had little to do with him.

'The country is furious and demands redress by any means, restore the balance in a world gone mad, punish the impudence kind of thing. The prime minister and cabinet are taxing me with my impotence and I'm hard put to conceive of anything that might satisfy both.'

'A reinforcement of the North American station, sir? I've heard there's only one sail-of-the-line and a handful of frigates there.'

'I can't. Bonaparte is retreating from Moscow but losing a single battle doesn't by any means allow us to believe he's finished, certainly not with his entire fleet still in existence. No, what is more needed is a flourish of some kind, a demonstration that we still rule the waves no matter what upstarts do to challenge us.

'Yes, I'd conceive that this would answer. What do you think, Sir Thomas? We put down one of their heavy frigates in return? Not with overwhelming force, which would make them martyrs, but one to one, a fair fight, frigate upon frigate.'

'Possibly, if it could be arranged as such.'

'I rather think it could be,' Melville ruminated, stroking his chin. 'If I send a legendary name of laurels in frigates, it will meet all three demands.'

'All three?' Kydd asked.

'The public will be mollified that one of their heroes is being dispatched to deal with the Americans, my colleagues at the Admiralty will applaud my parsimony in the matter of reinforcements, and of course it will be of inestimable value to His Majesty's arms that the Yankees be shown their place in this way.'

'Do you have any name in mind, my lord?' Kydd asked carefully.

Melville raised his eyebrows. 'Why, your own first comes to the forefront. Do recollect that you are without a ship at this time, *Thunderer* being destined for . . . that she is no longer fit for command, and you are therefore immediately available for special service, dear sir.'

'A frigate. Will this not be in the nature of a degradation in rank, sir?'

'Merely temporarily, I would have thought, a month or two until the job is done,' Melville answered smoothly.

'In a borrowed frigate,' Kydd said, in a brittle voice.

'You refer to the time needful to raise her crew to your exacting standards. I can understand that, you may believe, Sir Thomas, and that is why I offer you a solution. Shall we suppose that *Tyger* frigate be made over to you – purely on a temporary basis? I understand her crew are still intact from your recent relinquishing of her command. Kydd of the *Tyger*, hmm?'

A jet of hope and pleasure came and Kydd hid its presence with a cough as he struggled for a cool mind. All those oaken faces he'd so missed – restored to him! But they were of the past. The future was in *Thunderer*, now lost to him. But as soon as the thought came to stifle his joy he had an answer. Dare he press his advantage on the person of the first lord?

'My lord, you've answered any objections I might have in the most handsome manner. There is one last assurance I crave – that I be restored to rank after my duty is done. And what better security that this is in prospect than that *Thunderer* is given the repairs she deserves in readiness for my resumption of command?'

There was a glimmer almost of amusement in Melville's expression. Far from being offended by the demand he seemed entertained by the effrontery.

'Umm. I fancy I shall need to carry the Board with me but, yes, this is possible.'

'Sir?'

'You have my word on it, sir. And in writing in due course. Then . . .?'

Kydd's broad smile seemed to satisfy.

'Very well. *Tyger* will be recalled – she's in the North Sea at the moment. You shall be receiving orders to attach to the North American station, Sir John Borlase Warren, new-appointed. He'll have orders to allow you to cruise freely off the coast to tempt the Yankees to try their honour upon you.'

'Sir.'

'And to release you once the deed is done. Agreed?'

'I will endeavour to satisfy, my lord.'

'Oh, one last thing – do keep this to yourself, old fellow. No sense in warning off Cousin Jonathan. We keep announcements until after we've got a scalp, agreed?'

Meaning that if perchance *Tyger* was added to the lengthening list of American frigate victories it could the more easily be disowned, Kydd mused cynically.

Chapter 3

Knowle Manor

'I understand, darling,' Persephone said, with a visible effort, then looked away and did not catch Kydd's eye. 'Do your duty, dearest, and know that . . . that . . .'

Kydd held her fiercely. 'I'll be back to you and the younker in a month or two, and that's my promise!'

She didn't reply, staring away woodenly.

'What is it, Seph? I've been away to sea above a dozen times before – this is no different.' It must be the same for all married officers: a little one arrives and its mother's fears are multiplied beyond the usual. But what could he do about it?

Persephone raised her eyes. They were wide and troubled. 'Darling, you'll think me a silly, but I've not a good feeling about your going to America. They're a proud and unforgiving race and their frigates are accounted huge and unbeatable. Even with all your bravery and sea cunning it'll be—' She broke off with a sob.

Kydd kissed her. 'My love, perhaps you're forgetting something?'

'Oh?' she said, in a small voice.

'I'll be in *Tyger*, the tightest barky that ever swam – and not only that but her complete crew as I took into battle at Lissa. I can't ask for a better lay than that, my love.'

She was not to be consoled and only earnest discussion on warm clothing against the American winter and the adequacy of coverings in a captain's cot could raise her spirits. Kydd, whose experiences as a young officer in Halifax included the remembrance of the snuggling warmth to be won from a hammock and bearskin, allowed himself to be fussed over until she was more like her old self.

Before the end of the week a stiff but respectful letter arrived from the Plymouth admiral advising Kydd that *Tyger* was on her way and to hold himself ready to assume command. His attention to promptness in the matter would be appreciated as it seemed that, for various reasons, a degree of discretion was being advised and the handover would take place only after she'd been provisioned and watered for immediate departure on the voyage across the Atlantic.

Kydd gave a twisted smile. Her captain – Faulknor, wasn't it? – would be more than mystified at the sudden orders and couldn't be blamed if he took a dim view of the proceedings and the apparent haste. Kydd hoped he would accept it in good part or it would be a difficult time.

He sent a letter to Lucius Craddock, his friend and former confidential secretary. Harry, as he had invited Kydd to call him, was now back with the family business in the north, but there was little chance he could be there in time and would therefore have to miss the opportunity of setting foot on the continent of North America. But Binard, having loyally followed him out of *Thunderer* to become an admired butler and major-domo in Knowle Manor, would accompany him.

The man made much of listing requirements of the voyage, to Kydd's quiet amusement. Having served on the French side in *Volage*, raiding the shipping lanes of the North Atlantic, Binard was no stranger to victualling in a frigate and Kydd knew he would be right royally looked after.

The summons came in days. Kydd lost no time in setting off, turning in the carriage and treasuring his last sight of Persephone carrying their little one and forlornly waving him off.

It shouldn't be as bad as she was dreading. He'd get the true situation from local sources, the captains who'd been on station in Halifax throughout the first six months of the American War. Even Borlase Warren, the new admiral, should see it in his interest to have a reversing frigate victory under his command and would not be obstructive. As for the Americans, he doubted they would hazard any of their precious heavy frigates in combat with a first-rank British ship, when they could hurt their foe much more effectively by falling on their ill-protected and vital convoys.

No, it was much more likely they would keep from any confrontation and then the question would be: how long should he spend sailing fruitlessly up and down the coast, flaunting himself?

He arrived at Mount Wise and was cautiously welcomed by Admiral Dewey.

'I've assurance from *Tyger* they are ready for sea, lying in Cawsand Bay. Captain Faulknor will be here presently. He hasn't yet been informed. Sherry?'

A little after eleven the flag lieutenant announced the presence of *Tyger*'s captain and Faulknor entered. With a polite nod to Kydd, he announced to Dewey with suitable gravity that *Tyger* was now ready for sea on her confidential mission, whatever it might be.

Kydd felt for him. How many times had it been that he himself had entered into the lion's den in trepidation hoping to receive orders for an action against the enemy, a chance for distinction, prize-money – excitement after the tedium of convoy escort or other duties?

'Very good, Captain Faulknor. I have some pleasant news for you. I herewith grant you two months' leave on full pay. How does that suit you, sir?'

'B-but *Tyger*'s just now ready for sea, um, not in repair or . . . or . . .'

'The purpose, sir, is to allow Sir Thomas the temporary use of your ship while he conducts a particular operation against the Americans. He will return your ship to you within the time specified.'

'Then I should—'

'A form of handover *en petit* would be all that is expected of you. I shall turn over to you both this office for a period of time to this object, after which Sir Thomas will be conveyed on board in your barge, while you are then free to proceed on leave.'

To his relief, Kydd found Faulknor both understanding and respectful. It was a given that Kydd knew his ship from truck to keelson and her company equally well. That 'Kydd of the *Tyger*' was needed at this time, an officer with inside knowledge of the United States Navy from his time in *Tenacious*, was reason enough to yield up his command. As it happened, for family reasons a decent spell of leave would be more than welcome.

The undertaking that Kydd would fall in with Faulknor's ship's standing orders, his rating of men and a continuation of accounts under signature was all that was needed to complete the process.

'You'll take care of her, sir? I've grown a mort . . . fond of the old girl, if you see what I mean.'

'I do, and I shall. Have a fine leave, Mr Faulknor, and *Tyger* will be waiting for you when you return.'

Chapter 4

It was time for Kydd to take possession of *Tyger*, to read himself in but more to see her for the first time since his grief in watching her put to sea from Plymouth Sound under another's hand. He knew the way to Stonehouse Pool and stepped out, a pair of dockyard workers behind with his baggage in a cart. He gave an inward smile: who would it be in the boat's crew? They'd apparently been told that a temporary captain would be appointed for the period of Faulknor's leave, and very shortly they were due for a surprise.

His sudden appearance in all the splendour of a senior post-captain had the barge crew scrambling to their feet on the jetty. Kydd approached briskly, and from one, then another came disbelieving cries.

A massive figure shouldered himself to the front. 'Cap'n Kydd, an' it's rare good an' all to see ye!' Halgren tentatively held out a hand – his right, the other adorned with an iron hook, the penalty for heroism at Lissa.

Almost speechless with feeling, Kydd shook the hand of his former captain's coxswain, mumbling something. The others snatched off their caps and came up: the bluff and steady Moore, then the Irishman with an unruly temper – who was it now? McHeaney. Another – Skellig, a dour character from Skye, and . . .

'To *Tyger*, Halgren,' Kydd said gruffly.

'Sir – then you're the temp'ry cap'n?' The incredulity was not feigned.

'Yes. Do get me to *Tyger* and you may hear all about it.'

It was a short pull only to Cawsand Bay and there she was – just as his precious memories had it.

As they headed towards the ship, his searching eyes picked out the individuality and beauty of her lines, here and there the scars of battle, which brought to mind the time and place she'd suffered them. Much had passed since last he'd paced her quarterdeck and now—

'*Tygerrrr!*' Halgren roared deafeningly, at the challenge from the watch-on-deck, signifying the captain of the named ship was in the boat.

Kydd saw a side-party smartly assembling, clapped on his gold-laced hat and prepared to board. But there was some sort of disorder on board, men racing along, faint shouts on the air. Should he slow and give time for the officer-of-the-watch to take charge of it?

Then he saw what was happening. His eyes stung. He'd been recognised, and the side-party of half-a-dozen midshipmen and petty officers was turning into an ever-increasing lane of men, ready to welcome their old captain.

He began mounting the side-steps and, as his hat appeared above the level of the bulwarks, Herne, the boatswain, piped him aboard, loud and clear.

There was nothing for it but to move forward through the double line, now stretching across the deck to where the officers stood. He did not follow the usual procedure and go directly to them to be welcomed aboard. Instead he paced slowly, meeting the eye of every man, a murmured word here and there until he reached the officers.

'Mr Bowden,' he said softly, to the first lieutenant, whom he'd known since the young man was a midshipman. 'How does it go?'

'M-main w-well, s-sir,' Bowden blurted. Kydd was touched that this was the first time since the man's youth that he'd been caught in a stutter.

'That's good. And, Mr Brice, you look chipper, sir.'

The third lieutenant, introduced as Matthew Harland, he didn't know – the replacement for Maynard, the promising seaman who'd died at Lissa.

There was no time to be lost and he turned to his first lieutenant. 'Clear lower deck, Mr Bowden, to lay aft ship's company by divisions.'

He stepped aside from the rush and bustle, standing by the wheel and taking inward delight in recognising features and quirks of nautical dress until, with commendable alacrity, a sea of faces looked aft expectantly.

And there, muscling to the forefront, was a knot of seamen he'd know anywhere and whom he'd rather see than a hundred pressed men.

They were led by a hard, almost piratical figure, whose dark eyes glittered under a red bandanna, the dull gleam of his earrings marking him out as a seaman of an older navy. Gunner's mate Toby Stirk, with his long-time crewmates, quartermasters Doud and Pinto.

As his gaze passed over them, from a completely expressionless face Stirk gave a slow wink, acknowledging the restoring as shipmate the raw young lad pressed into *Duke William* so many years before.

Kydd took hold of his feelings – his real home was *Thunderer*

28

and she would need him. At this moment, however, there was a job to do and he would do it.

He waited until he had silence. 'I have to tell you that it's with very great pleasure I come aboard my old ship to be greeted by so many of my past shipmates.'

A rustle of appreciation passed through them, nothing so unseemly as giving vent to shouts or cries of feeling.

'I'm your captain, but only for a short time. I can now tell you why. It is . . . an important mission for which *Tyger* and her company and I as her captain have been especially chosen.'

He looked about significantly. 'You've all heard of the shameful loss of three of our frigates to the Americans, which has sent Parliament and country into a fret. It's now our task to go over and teach the Yankees a lesson by taking one of theirs. To undo the shame, put the Royal Navy back as ruler of the seas where it belongs!'

A bellow of voices showed he had their loyalty and resolution so he went on strongly: 'It'll not be easy – their frigates are bruisers and well manned and it's going to be a hard-won fight. But we've faced worse and prevailed, and all England will glory in our victory.'

He was drowned out by bursts of cheers. Kydd nodded in acknowledgement, raising his hat to bow this way and that, then waited pointedly for quiet.

'And so I have only these last words for you, Tygers all.'

They subsided quickly.

'Hands to your stations – unmoor ship!'

A boat brought last-minute dispatches along with Binard, importantly guarding cabin stores of undoubted necessity, which were summarily hoisted inboard, and His Majesty's Frigate *Tyger* put to sea.

The traditional first-night-at-sea gunroom dinner was a

roaring success. With Binard taking charge over an astonished and aggrieved officers' cook, the cuisine delighted, and *Tyger*'s officers set to with a will. Later, over old port and cigars, Kydd heard of *Tyger*'s adventures since he'd left: a modest affair against a Dutch inshore convoy, a bombardment of a truculent fort in the Frisians, but nothing to match what they'd achieved together in earlier days – not the fault of their captain at the time, whose virtues were reviewed in discreet detail.

In return he briefly mentioned *Thunderer*'s escapades as Bonaparte marched into Russia but, to the barely concealed satisfaction of these frigate officers, dwelled at length on the tedium and daily sameness that was the lot of a ship-of-the-line, uncomfortably aware that after this mission he would be returning to such a world.

He heard which characters remained and who of the Tygers had moved on and been replaced. These were few: a new master's mate, Stukely, well thought of; another midshipman, Gower, whose connections ensured a degree of wariness, and a number of seamen. In effect he had his old *Tyger* back.

'Sir – tip us a tune!' Brice demanded, his brandy well tasted.

The roar of acclamation that went up made it impossible to refuse.

> '*Ye mariners of England!*
> *That guard our native seas,*
> *Whose flag has braved a thousand years,*
> *The battle and the breeze!*
> *Your glorious standard launch again*
> *To match another foe!*
> *And sweep through the deep*
> *While the stormy winds do blow!*'

Kydd turned in disgracefully late, lulled rapidly into sleep by the familiarity of *Tyger*'s easy sequence of creaks as the long Atlantic swells passed by under her keel.

Chapter 5

The approaches to Halifax, Canada

They raised the Sambro light in the early hours through a damp mist, placing them within a dozen miles of the entrance, and Kydd gave orders to shorten sail in order to arrive only after first light. He'd been to Halifax many years ago in his first ship as a raw young officer the year after the frigate *Tribune* was lost with all but twelve men not far north of Sambro. He was not seeking similar immortality.

The pilot came on board soon after a wan, sunless daylight put in its appearance, allowing the bleached grey-white granite headlands to stand out from the dark carpeting of endless forest, a bleak and stern prospect in the early-morning chill.

Kydd shivered and his thoughts turned to when he had last been there. It had been a formative time for him, finding his sea-legs as an officer after years before the mast. And becoming involved with the formation of the new United States Navy, which it was his duty now to challenge in war.

He wondered what had happened to Lieutenant Jasper Gindler, the upright and patriotic officer who had ended proving a friend when most needed. Of one thing he could be certain: if there were more like him his task in any confrontation would be no easy affair.

'York Redoubt coming abeam,' reported Brice, lowering his telescope. There wasn't much to see, for the fortification was set well down, its battery thus protected, but with McNabs Island it marked the entrance proper to Halifax, and Kydd snapped to a professional alert.

Past the end of McNabs Island the channel opened up to Halifax harbour, and more memories came flooding back for Kydd.

He could see that the town had grown remarkably, some of the landmarks now near hidden in urban growth. If he got time he would step ashore and revisit his old haunts.

Thankfully he noted ahead the North American squadron at their moorings, the 74, *San Domingo*, prominent, with its admiral's pennant indicating the presence of the commander-in-chief, and there was the old 64, *Africa*, which Kydd remembered from his time at Copenhagen. There was another, rather untidy sail-of-the-line and a gaggle of frigates, but nothing to suggest a battle fleet.

A dispatch boat hailed up for *Tyger* to moor with the frigates and within the hour *Tyger*'s captain was being piped aboard the flagship and into the presence of Sir John Borlase Warren, Admiral of the Blue and in command of all naval forces in the Western Atlantic from the Arctic to the Caribbean – such as it seemed they were.

Rather stout and possessing a formidable nose, he could be intimidating to some.

'So, Kydd of *Tyger* – whom I last recall as a new-minted sloop commander in the Med learning his trade.' It had been years before and Kydd was surprised he remembered something that had meant a lot to him at the time, the dismissing of an alleged charge of abandoning his station without leave.

'Sir. You have been advised of my mission?'

'I have. Which I must say directly contradicts my prerogatives as Flag in these waters.'

Kydd hesitated. 'Um, might I enquire in what way, sir?'

'You've been sent here to trail your coat off the Yankee's ports to entice out one of their frigates to slay with your no doubt excellent *Tyger* frigate. You should know that for the last six months our orders have been to let 'em be, leave 'em in peace to give 'em time to come to their senses and end this foolish clash at arms. Do bear in mind, sir, that they declared war on us in June and only in the middle of November have we responded in kind.'

'But, sir—'

'I'm aware what your orders are, Captain. But further to my last, know that by the very dispatches I've just received, I find I'm to blockade the Delaware and Chesapeake. God alone knows with what vessels I can do this,' he finished bitterly.

'Sir, I can hardly expect to lure any out if they perceive a blockading ship-of-the-line or two in the offing,' Kydd said stiffly.

'Then might I suggest you get on with it before my plans are complete?' Warren said, with heavy patience.

'I will. Er, the nature of my existence here . . .' Kydd began delicately. If he was under Warren's command he would require his written orders, but if he remained under Admiralty direction his would be an independent cruise – if at the cost of being denied support of any kind including a line of credit for stores and victuals.

Warren gave it thought. Then, picking up a pencil, he

announced, 'I find that you have been attached to my squadron – you will hoist my colours directly.'

'Sir.' So he was going to be part of Warren's blockade plan.

'However, you are herewith detached from the squadron on special duty. My orders to you coincidentally will have the very same wording as that of your Admiralty mandate. Happy?'

It was handsome of Warren: desperate for ships and having a patrol line along some thousands of miles of coast the temptation to co-opt Kydd's valuable ship must have been considerable.

'I am indeed, sir.'

'Then do ready your ship for sea, and you go with my best wishes for what's to come.'

'Sir.'

'Oh, and it might be worth your while to make your number with my senior captain, frigates. He's been long on the coast and knows how the land lies, so to speak.'

Chapter 6

Tyger was brought alongside the wharf at the Halifax naval yard for her furbishing and storing, estimated at no more than three days. Liberty was granted to both watches in turn and Kydd set off to visit the senior captain, frigates. He was to be found apparently, as always, in his ship, the 38-gun frigate *Shannon*.

Her captain, in very ordinary working rig, met him on the quarterdeck. Kydd had been careful to shift out of his dress uniform for he'd heard something of the sensitivities of this unconventional officer.

'Captain Philip Broke,' he introduced. 'And . . .?'

'Sir Thomas Kydd for my sins,' Kydd answered, not sure how to relate to a man who was said to live and breathe for his great guns. 'Come to enquire of the state of the war in these parts, as advised by our admiral.'

'Then you're joining my band of few?'

'Well – yes and no.' He went on to explain, but tailed off at Broke's expression.

'As you're sent in over our heads to make a hullabaloo at our expense?'

'No, not at all.'

'Sir. Know that I myself have endeavoured to the same end and will not rest until I have a Yankee frigate under my guns. But for my other sea duties it would have been before now, I can assure you.'

Kydd saw the tenseness, the glowing eyes. 'I'd be much obliged should you tell me more of this station,' he asked mildly.

Broke regarded him for a moment then loosened, inviting Kydd below.

When they were sitting together in the sparsely furnished cabin he began. 'They're a scurvy crew, the Americans, but I still can't put a reason to why they want a war. Near all their revenue is from acting the innocent neutral and playing both sides with freight in their bottoms for either. They buy contraband French goods in the United States, then sail to France arguing that the cargo is theirs, only to sell it on to the villains on arrival, but we're fast catching on to their knavish tricks. They stand to make a hill of treasure, but they must see that all that's now contraband to us.'

'They're making much of our boarding and pressing American seamen.'

'American – hah! With the going rate for a United States protection on the Liverpool waterfront not over a guinea, what English seaman would shy at double the wages and no war thrown in?'

Kydd stirred uncomfortably. After his early experiences he knew that Americans were by no means a foolish people and felt there had to be another reason. 'Could it be they think a French battle-fleet might be expected at any time to help an old ally, we being sore distracted by Bonaparte's affair in Russia? It has to be said it wouldn't take so many to clear us from the seas, this side of the Atlantic.'

'Yes, what with two-thirds of our number permanently away on escort duty. You're right – it's a rank mystery why there's no alliance even, like the last time there was an American war.'

'True enough. Er, could you oblige me with a tour of your ship, sir? You're reputation goes before, as it were.'

'Indeed, old fellow,' Broke said, suddenly energised. 'You look like a gunnery man as will appreciate my small improvements.'

Kydd chuckled. 'Graven on my heart – increase your rate of fire and you double the number of guns!'

'Ah! I'm on another tack entirely, Kydd. I say – increase your accuracy and you double the execution.'

It was an education for Kydd. Gun sights of novel design, dispart fittings that allowed for the incline of the piece from breech to muzzle, and ingenious techniques to make precise elevation and gun-laying.

'I exercise guns every forenoon and not necessarily running 'em in and out. They're to practise on targets and not your cask and flag – the smaller the better.'

'Smaller?'

'Of course! This way they learn what accuracy means and by this, in action, I can select a mast to bring down, sweep away the helm – even smash a gun-deck gun by gun, just as I please.'

Kydd's interest quickened. Not for Broke was it the traditional brute battering of the foe, this was a methodical reduction of one's opponent's ability to fight.

'A fine notion indeed,' Kydd said warmly. 'And I'd take it kindly if one day I might witness a practice.'

There were bare days before he left. Kydd thought of those he'd known in his previous service on the station. The King's son, Prince Edward, the former commander-in-chief, with his mistress Julie, had moved on to become governor of Gibraltar, taking with him much of the glamour of high society but leaving a colonial town a provincial city of stone and parks. Greaves, the commissioner for lands, was now an attorney general and infirm, while Kydd's uncle, if he still lived, would now be getting on, and the old backwoodsman would probably not be appreciative of a visit from a distinguished name.

Instead he made the most of laying his hands on the charts and coast pilots that would give him insights into the American sea world. The frigates could be anywhere – Boston, Baltimore, other seaports down the coast – and he had to know something of the hazards.

Broke was helpful, sharing freely his experience, especially of the myriad tiny havens between the larger deep-sea trading ports and their individual oddities.

Kydd's peg-legged sailing master, Joyce, had some knowledge of these waters but years ago in the War of Independence and he felt dubious about any inshore working. As this was exactly what Kydd had in mind – a provocative cruise close in with the coast – it was not going to be an easy mission.

Chapter 7

Kydd wasted no time and put to sea with no fuss or flourish. *Tyger* stretched her wings for the south: her orders to tempt one of the American heavy frigates to sea for single combat. As yet Kydd had no plan to achieve this – it was going to be hard enough to find out where they were lying, let alone oblige one to come out and fight.

At least winter had loosened its icy clamping on these northern parts, and even if there was snow and ice in the continental interior, all harbours were now ice-free and his quarry could be anywhere, fettling for the upcoming season of predation. From Broke he knew their names: *Chesapeake*, *United States*, *President*, *Constitution*, others. Their captains, too – Samuel Evans, the short-fused Stephen Decatur, John Rogers and Isaac Hull. All blooded and capable. Which one would eventually find *Tyger* under its guns?

He reviewed his choice of ports: New York and Baltimore were the major ones, and in the Delaware and Chesapeake, further south, those that were to seaward of Washington and Philadelphia. Time was of the essence, therefore all those south of New York were beyond his cruising endurance, which left Boston and New London.

There he would make known his presence – but not before he'd thoroughly exercised his gun crews to a pitch he'd seen before only in Broke's *Shannon*. There was neither the time nor the available parts to experiment with the new techniques Broke had developed. That would come later. For now he would face the Yankee frigate with the traditional virtues of brute courage and skill at arms.

The exercises proved *Tyger*'s mettle and he stood back as his crew threw themselves into their practice, and by the time the first outlying islands of Boston Harbor came into sight he had his plan.

There were two main entrances to the capacious interior harbour a couple of miles apart. Everything under sail must pass through one or the other. If he stood off and on directly to seaward he'd achieve two things: a watch on Boston that could not be bettered and at the same time he was trailing his coat before the forts and batteries that no doubt stood in defence on the islands. The presence of an English frigate of size flaunting its colours so close should stir some action.

It was almost too good to be true – no sooner had *Tyger* settled on her casting to and fro across the entrance than the masthead lookout shouted, '*Deck hoooo!* Fine t' larboard – frigate, an' under full sail athwart!'

Visible from the deck, Kydd saw that it had been obscured by a rugged island, and on sighting *Tyger* had quickly altered course to close.

'Quarters, Mr Bowden.'

Was it nothing but chance or the grim unfolding of Fate that had brought them to a confrontation so soon?

Automatically Kydd sniffed the wind. A north-easterly, with

the other coming down fast in its eye, its colours end on giving away nothing.

Tyger was under easy sail across its course, and Kydd immediately brought her around, hard to the wind, to sail her nearer and, more importantly, bring her broadside to bear in a first exchange – a raking onslaught into its bows.

There was no deviation in its course directly towards them, the act either of a supremely confident captain or a madman arrogantly contesting *Tyger*'s right to trespass into American waters.

'Stand by the starb'd guns,' he growled – and then everything changed.

As if sensing Kydd's action the frigate abruptly slewed to present her own broadside and in so doing her colours were revealed, the blue ensign of Warren's command, a Union Flag at the fore.

It was *Maidstone*, one of the older craft of her breed, shabby with sea-worn timbers, probably token of an icy winter on this station.

Kydd, tensed for a bloody encounter, had no sympathy and roundly cursed the ship and her reckless commander. Only now could her signal flags be seen.

'Heave to, Mr Joyce,' he snapped, and to the signal crew, '*Maidstone*'s pennants: captain to repair on board.'

Riordan was youthful for a post-captain, years younger than Kydd, and trod warily into his cabin. 'Sir?'

'Sit. And I'll know why you acted as you did, sir.'

Affronted, the younger man replied stiffly. It wasn't anything more culpable than inexperience and the sudden appearance before him, after an age of tedious patrol, of an unknown frigate and, moreover, one that did not reply to his challenge.

'If you were a Yankee, sir, you'd be hearing my guns by now. I wasn't going to risk you slinking away.'

Kydd sighed. Any hope of luring out an American was dashed now it was clear that two British frigates were waiting outside, and who knew how many more?

'What are you doing here, pray?'

'This is my station per orders of Admiral Sawyer,' Riordan replied primly. 'To watch for movements of the enemy.'

It seemed *Maidstone* had not yet returned to Halifax to receive orders from the new admiral regarding Kydd's mission. It made no difference: it was now a waste of time for him to linger in these waters. Kydd let him go.

Chapter 8

New London was the next port south, around the 'corner' of Cape Cod. It was just inside the lengthy finger of land, Long Island, which originated in New York and extended a hundred miles or so along the coast.

Kydd was aware that time was slipping by before Warren's Admiralty orders had him beginning his blockade and making it near impossible to lure out any American, who with their few frigates had everything to lose by engaging against superior numbers.

Tyger passed Cape Cod well to seaward before shaping course around: here was Nantucket and the whalers but he had no quarrel with them. As far as he was concerned he had only one objective. The common citizens of America and the sea would remain untouched by him.

They proceeded overnight under easy sail. To be spotted at first light squarely and arrogantly across the narrow harbour entrance should be enough to set things in motion. After a last brisk exercise at the great guns it was hands to dinner and grog, and Kydd to his last-minute concerns. He'd done as much as was possible to prepare for the contest, and *Tyger* was in as fine a shape as she'd ever be. When they joined battle, he'd have to manoeuvre such that they were well to seaward of the islands and above all the notorious offshore rock ledges. At the moment the weather was holding.

There was little to be gained by useless worry and he slept well.

At first light *Tyger* raised the twin points of land that marked the approaches to the Thames River. New London was a few miles up, in a near-impregnable deep-water defensive location, but there was only the one entry point so, conversely, it was also a near-perfect prison.

There would naturally be fortifications on the headlands but these would not trouble *Tyger* for she had no intention of running the gauntlet up-river. Their role was to alert New London that a defiant Royal Navy frigate had taken position across the entrance and showed no inclination to leave. All Kydd had to do was wait.

The morning haze fined to nothing and a shy sun presented itself, tentatively warming and promising a pleasant day. Aboard *Tyger* routines continued, decks scrubbed as though never to be running in blood, the forenoon gun practice undertaken with gusto, and an intensity of purpose that was most pleasing.

The day wore on. Cautiously Kydd allowed hands to dinner, for it was not possible to predict when their flaunting of colours would produce a result.

He ate alone, sparingly, thoughtfully. The steady north-westerly would favour the emerging American but it wouldn't matter. He would promptly head out to sea with the Yankee in pursuit until they had sufficient sea room, and then he would turn and fight with all the cunning and ferocity a lifetime at sea had given him.

'Will you be having evening quarters drill?' Bowden wanted to know.

'Um, no. Let 'em have their supper in peace,' Kydd answered absently. No American would put out into the early fading light of the winter evening to begin a combat probably lasting some hours.

And then came another thought: a shrewd captain could use cover of darkness to slip by and take up position to seaward. In this veering north-easterly he would win the weather gage and be in a prime situation to crowd *Tyger* against the coast with all the additional advantage of local knowledge.

'Mr Bowden!' he bellowed, knowing his first lieutenant at this time would be just forward by the conn.

Bowden hurried back. 'Sir?'

'I want a row-guard across the entrance after dark. One boat, and they're to instantly let fly with a rocket should they sight the American frigate.'

Darkness arrived and *Tyger* kept her station all night. In the cold grey of dawn, tensely closed up at quarters, all that could be seen was an empty sea.

It was something of an anticlimax and as the hours went by there was no sign of any answer to his challenge.

Another day slipped past. It was galling but the fact remained there had been no response. Broke had been insistent that this was a favoured lair of the big frigates and at least one should be present. Either there was none or they were not inclined to pick up the gauntlet. How long should he stay here, endlessly waiting?

One more day passed.

Should he try the same posturing off nearby New York? But that had at least two major entrances with all its complications.

On the third day a brig came into view from behind the

three-mile-distant Fisher's Island. It hoisted the correct private signal and made for them.

'*Rattler* brig-sloop, Cap'n Poole,' reported the signals team.

She brought to around *Tyger*'s stern and Kydd hailed her captain to report.

In *Tyger*'s great cabin Poole, a lined and mature individual, accepted Kydd's offer of a restorative hot rum negus with gratitude.

'Are you aware of my mission in these waters, sir?' Kydd began.

'Aye, I am that, sir.' The voice was low but pleasant and held the lilt of the Highlands. 'To lay a Yankee by the tail and show the world we're not yet done wi' them.'

Kydd nodded agreement. 'This is why I'm here, sir. And why I'm asking if you have any intelligence bearing on the matter, Cousin Jonathan being a trifle shy in his appearing.'

To his surprise it brought what could only be described as a wicked grin.

'No mystery there, Sir Thomas. See here . . .' He fumbled in his waistcoat and pulled out a newspaper, smoothed it and found a page before handing it over. 'Read that.'

'*English frigate hero disappointed!*' ran a headline at the top of a column. '*A plot unravels!*' the sub-heading underneath smugly declared, and in the story following Kydd read: '*We have it on the highest authority that a preposterous conspiracy was hatched by London, a desperate scheme to respond to their humiliation at the hands of the United States Navy.*'

So he'd been noticed as had always been intended, but not quite as planned.

The article continued,

Our correspondent in Boston uncovered the sly plot when fishing by Spectacle Island. Not noticed by the lordly Sir Thomas Kydd in his legendary Tyger, *our man looked on as it arrogantly flaunted its colours in the very approaches to our proudest seaport. The intent was clear: to spark resentment at his presumptuous tres-passing in our waters such that any US frigate captain would in all honour feel bound to demand a meeting in the open sea. Unhappily for Mr Kydd and his plot, our man was able to observe behind the scenes as another British frigate crept up to join him, no doubt to be followed by others. If the trap had sprung then our own gallant frigate would have quickly found itself surrounded and outnumbered. As it was,* Tyger *was seen to have slunk away, no doubt to try his luck elsewhere on our coast.*

Damn it! Now no true-blood Yankee would blame one of their own for preserving his vessel by staying safely in port in the face of such dishonourable contriving.

'Thank you for this, Mr Poole,' he said heavily. 'I may have to think again on my plans.'

Time was being wasted in vain manoeuvring to bring about a single-handed combat that his opponent had no intention of coming out to indulge in. Just how long should he continue in this?

'Ah, well, there's no help for it. I'll see you over the side, sir.'

Kydd stood to go but Poole remained sitting, his features thoughtful. 'Do excuse, Sir Thomas, but there may be a way to stir 'em along.'

'Oh? Do tell.'

'They won't come out on account of a flaunting o' colours – but they may to defend their own.'

'Please explain.'

'Do something not seen in these parts since the last war. Close with the coast near here and bombard a village. They must then—'

'This in all conscience I cannot do, sir.' Memories returned from his earlier time in America of the tight-knit community of Exbury, not so very far from where they were now. He couldn't in all humanity visit the terrors of war on such people.

'You have your duty, sir,' Poole said softly, 'and this is a sovereign cure for their skulking.'

'As may be, but I'll not—'

'Sir – am I to understand you wish to make distinction between citizen and soldier?'

'As any who places value on human life,' Kydd snapped. 'Therefore I—'

'Then shall privateers – a citizen navy – be held sacred?'

'Sir! If you wish to top it the philosopher kindly do so at another time. I've other things to concern myself with at this moment.'

Poole gave a thin smile. 'Sir Thomas. Not far from here is a harbour. Pettipaug. It lies safely up a river and may be reckoned a prime refuge for your privateer. Should you make descent on them in their hideaway – to their entire surprise and mortification – I'm supposing it will be in the nature of intolerable to our shore-bound friends.'

Kydd hesitated. 'This lair of privateers, if its existence and so forth is known, why hasn't a move been made against it by us before now, pray?'

'The difficulty of its approaches, is all.'

'Defences, I presume.'

'No, sir. As far as I'm aware it has none to speak of.'

'Mr Poole. You are being far from clear. Are you suggesting I attack this pirates' nest or no?'

'The reason it has been left alone is that it lies six miles above the river entrance, which is itself guarded by a sandbar of monstrous dimensions, passable only by those with local knowledge and at certain states of the tide. Entry of a man-o'-war is not to be countenanced.'

'Have you that knowledge?'

'I regret I have not, sir.'

Kydd sighed, but Poole continued, 'I bring it to notice only as it answers your difficulty. It may well be your superior experience leads you to a course of action that results in success in the venture.'

It was an attractive prospect. Not only would he be able to strike a blow at the accursed privateer vermin but surely it would be sufficient to jolt a response. All he had to do was overcome the natural hazards.

'You were right to make me aware of this, Captain. I've a notion it will serve – if I can conjure a scheme of attack. But without charts . . .'

'I have one of Long Island Sound as includes this place.'

'Get it, if you will, sir.'

It turned out to be a clutch of several, and Kydd keenly took in the situation. Pettipaug was, as Poole had said, some six miles up the Connecticut River in an elaborate cove-indented bend. Careful inspection of the estuary revealed soundings that were anything but favourable for a vessel such as *Tyger* – her twenty-five-foot draught couldn't even think to try to enter the mile-wide entrance, which had depths marked of less than half that. Nowhere was there indicated a deep-water channel and it was becoming clear that the small, shallow-draught privateer schooners must feel perfectly secure in their cosy retreat.

Kydd looked again. This situation was begging one solution: a boat-borne cutting-out expedition.

Six miles. A devil of a long way to pull. And so few boats.

'Mr Poole. Are there by chance any more of your kind in the Sound – on patrol or other?'

'Umm. *Goree* and *Recruit*, both 16s.'

'I've an idea we could deal with a parcel of privateers using boats mounting carronades, but we need more boats than we can muster between us. You have my orders to intercept and bring 'em here if you will. You have two days.'

It would give him time to refine his plans but, above all, to reconnoitre. How this was possible was not immediately apparent. On the one hand he had to establish that privateers *were* at Pettipaug and, if so, how many, and on the other, discover the lie of the land.

Chapter 9

As soon as *Rattler* had got under way, *Tyger* shook out sail and headed down the coast, making much of poking into likely bays and river mouths, as if winkling out coastal prizes.

In the late afternoon the Connecticut River opened up. Kydd slowed his ship and carefully quartered the shoreline with his most powerful telescope.

No fortifications were visible on either side, and a small wooden lighthouse and keeper's cottage nestled on the nearest point. He could see up the river some two or three miles to where it narrowed considerably. That could be a problem if it boasted defence positions. Apart from that, all seemed somnolent and innocent, with very few buildings visible in a dense covering of woodland, a mosaic of different shades of hard, dark green.

This was not sufficient information on which to base a plan of attack, let alone risk men's lives. However, since the entire reason for sending himself and a valuable frigate across the Atlantic was to provoke a confrontation, it had to be accepted that risks could be taken. He himself would set foot ashore.

As dusk drew in, Kydd had his gig in the water around the eastern side of the river, out of sight of the lighthouse a couple of miles on the opposite side of the entrance. With him were four seamen. Kydd's plan required the boat to slip around the point and head upriver to get a feel of the country.

Tyger soon vanished out to sea and the boat was left to creep inshore and around a flat, marshy point of land.

There was little to fear: without fortifications there would be no military to challenge them, and the seamen stretched out in a comfortable rhythm.

'Sir!' the bowman hissed urgently, as they emerged from beyond a dune. He was pointing to a lone dark figure well out on the tidal flats.

'Oars!' Kydd ordered, and the rowing ceased while he tried to make sense of what they'd seen, a regular bending of the figure this way and that. 'A clam digger.' He chuckled, then had a thought.

'He hasn't seen us. I mean to take him prisoner,' he whispered theatrically. If the man was sufficiently unnerved by the sudden appearance of the British in this quiet backwater he might well be persuaded to reveal what Kydd wanted to know.

The boat nosed silently inshore and Kydd motioned to two seamen. 'Quietly, and don't bruise the fellow.'

They squelched ashore and loped along the strand until opposite the figure, then gave a shout and beckoned vigorously. The man was pinioned and brought to Kydd, who knew that if he had to let him go the news that the English were abroad would quickly spread.

'I do apologise for your treatment, sir,' he said soothingly, as the boat was shoved off again. 'I can only plead necessity.'

'Why, don't worry yer noggin about that, mister. Ain't been

53

for a donkey's age as I been called "sir", I havta say.' The voice was reedy and tremulous with drink.

'Sir Thomas Kydd, captain of His Majesty's Frigate *Tyger*, and . . .?'

'Not *the* Kydd o' the *Tyger*, as is in the *Advertiser*?'

'Er, yes.'

'Well, no prizes fer guessin' what you're doin' here.'

'You are . . .?'

'Josh Tucker, an' what about m' clams?'

'I'm afraid you're our prisoner now – but you'll be fully compensated for them,' Kydd calmed him. 'Two dollars?'

'Why, that's right handsome in ye, Mr Kydd,' he said, astonished and then added awkwardly, 'An' I has t' wish yer well in yer doings.'

'Why's that, Mr Tucker?'

'Jus' that since I was fallen on hard times the folk over at Saybrook took agin me, won't pass the time o' day on any account. Good t' see 'em taken down a piece.'

'I don't want to war against the common people, Mr Tucker, only the privateers. It would be a fine enough thing should I find one willing to point 'em out to me.'

'Ha! Don't look at me, Sir Kydd. I'm a right true American, can't bear a hand agin my own.'

'A pity. For any who help will walk away afterwards with a right generous bag of dollars.'

'How generous?'

The cost of setting a couple of privateers afloat? Kydd said it slowly: 'One thousand dollars.'

'Damn! I never heard anyone in this county wi' that kind o' rhino! Er, jus' what does yer man have t' do to lay hands on it?'

Within the hour the business was concluded.

Tucker was a local sea captain fallen victim to drink and

now scraped a thin living scrabbling for clams, earning the contempt of honest townspeople. That he was a man of the sea meant he knew the secrets of the bar and the channels leading upriver to the privateer mooring ground. Once he had been assured of his eventual reward he was free with his information.

As for the reconnoitring he would see to it that a pair of horses was hired from a nearby farm and then they would ride by back trails to a spot he knew overlooking the township.

The next morning Kydd found himself concealed in the woods waiting for Tucker to bring the horses. He didn't fear betrayal – the man knew he wouldn't see a cent of the reward until after a successful operation – and soon a slight jingle of harness announced his arrival.

'Not so far, Cap'n,' he said, handing over the reins of a restless bay, and they rode off down a disused woodland trail that wound through the hills for some miles. At one point Tucker dismounted and motioned Kydd to an overgrown footpath. A few yards further on, the vegetation fell away and he saw that they were on a bluff overlooking the river. Below them, at a point where the river was constricted to less than half a mile wide, there was a fort . . . and was that another on the opposite bluff?

Tucker winked conspiratorially at him as they returned to the horses. 'Saybrook Point, the lazy buggers.'

They rode on through lowland marshland and up again into a thickly wooded rise. Quite suddenly Tucker reined in. 'Here you is, Mr Kydd. Pettipaug town,' he said triumphantly.

At the fringe of the woods Kydd saw that they were looking across the water of a cove to a township that occupied the length of a short peninsula. Both alongside and out in the stream were the unmistakable rakish lines of privateers – he counted twenty in plain view alone. This was worth any risk:

to destroy some would rid them of that number and surely trigger a wrathful response.

He scanned the scene, committing it to memory. One thing stood out: the main street of Pettipaug ended at the seafront and any reinforcements must stand at that particular place.

'Well done, Mr Tucker. I think we'll return now.'

Back on board, *Tyger*'s seamen entertained Tucker while Kydd drew out his charts again. With the priceless addition of his shore reconnaissance he could visualise what shape his descent on the privateers might take.

But there were twenty at the least. How could he, even with several boats and surprise on his side, hope to take more than a few before the rest either rose against him or quit the anchorage? Like a fox among the chickens, he could hope to end only with one or two.

Unless . . .

The next day first *Recruit* and then *Goree*, closely accompanied by *Rattler*, made rendezvous and Kydd was ready with his plan. It called for a total of six boats, each mounting a carronade in the bows capable of round-shot, grape or canister as required, a hundred or more men to be embarked in them, with boarding pikes, muskets and cutlasses. Five marines in each boat in their distinctive red coats would be armed with bayoneted flintlocks, along with an officer apiece with sword and pistol.

With the tide on the flood they'd be carried forward upriver and possibly down on the ebb, sail to be used where it could be. And they had the priceless boon of a local pilot.

Having all the advantage of complete surprise by making the passage at night, Kydd would be satisfied with a privateer destroyed for each boat deployed, a very respectable result if it were achieved.

For once the moon would be in their favour. Full darkness a little after seven and the moonrise at some time after ten, giving three hours or so to passage time – quite adequate even if pulling the whole way.

There was no point in delaying.

Chapter 10

They put off in the near impenetrable darkness, Kydd in the lead in *Tyger*'s launch. A night breeze picked up a little from the south-west so the boats lost no time in hoisting their lugsails, and silently entered the wide Connecticut River estuary.

'Keep t' the left if 'n ye wants a channel,' whispered Tucker, peering out into the gloom with its darker shadows of hilly inshore features. 'Closer, Cap'n.'

Kydd brought the line of boats nearer to the shadows and a few hundred yards further on noticed the black solidity of a headland.

'Quiet, now . . .'

Kydd's heart was hammering.

'Saybrook Point. The fort.'

If they were spotted by the sentries of the fort this close not only would the alarm be raised but they would almost certainly come under fire and—

'Into the bank!' he hissed, at the following boat, and silently they nudged into the shallows on the near side of the bluff.

Kydd waited until they were all in and whispered sharply, 'Mr Clinton?' The Royal Marines officer gave a low acknowledgement from the anonymous shadows in the second boat and came over.

He understood immediately what was needed. Under cover of darkness his task was to create a diversion on the inland side of the fort while the boats slipped past.

There was a path upwards and the marines quickly disappeared. Minutes later, with a rustle of foliage, Clinton emerged. 'Sir, the place is deserted. Not manned in any way, even the guns left covered.'

The gods of war were on their side! They'd managed complete surprise.

The boats put out again but as the river narrowed and took a left bend, the wind, this far inland, became fluky and veered northerly, obliging sail to be struck and muffled oars to be shipped in the crowded boats, reducing their progress. As well, the moon appeared, fitfully illuminating the scene as clouds came and went. Any eyes on lookout would see them now and Kydd felt his skin crawl.

'Around there, Hayden's Point,' muttered Tucker. This was the place they'd taken their fill of the view of the town.

Kydd understood the man's nervousness. If things went against them and it was found he'd led the British up the river, he would be shown no mercy.

In short order their objective was spread out before them. It was about three in the morning and ghostly still, but in the wan moonlight it was plain to see privateers by the dozen, most moored out in the stream but some alongside. A few only showed lights, but what caught Kydd's attention was the peninsula on the left that was the township of Pettipaug. Along its length there were points of light but he was straining to see its end, where the main street met the river in a substantial collection of piers and wharves. There were lights – and they were moving.

In that moment he had to take a decision that could make it a success or failure, cost men's lives or send them forward into victory.

'All boats!' he called. 'Stretch out for the landing place.'

As they closed in, there was a sputter of musket fire from the shore where they intended to land. Kydd's force was in no way threatened for, in the darkness, proper aim was impossible – but the firing told him they had been spotted. The question now was what defences the Americans were going to put up against them.

Nearing the jetty he gave orders for two of the boats to open fire with their carronades into the general area where they would land. At the sudden ear-splitting blast and blinding gun-flash of the balls' rampaging passage, the firing of the defending troops fell off immediately and did not resume.

The first wave of marines clambered ashore in practised motions, covered by the second, and once firmly in possession of the wharf area, the rest of Kydd's men scrambled up.

'Well done, Mr Clinton,' he told the marine, and looked about. Only sounds of fleeing footsteps could be heard and he gave a satisfied smile. This was precisely what he had hoped for and now there was every reason to press on.

He'd turned the tables on the privateers. No one ashore would have any idea of what was happening. At the sight of the red coats of the marines they'd no doubt assume that the British had chosen their snug little town for a raid or even invasion, possibly to the extent of burning it down or worse. The prudent thing would be to flee as fast as possible into the interior and this would include the crews of the privateers.

Kydd gave his orders. Every privateer was to be boarded

by five men and set afire. Hay and firewood were lying about, and the Royal Marines would protect them while they were at it.

'Away the burning parties,' he snapped, then had a thought. 'And if you'll form up your jollies, Mr Clinton, I've a job for them.'

A marching column of redcoats, led by a single fife and drum, was soon stepping out with fixed bayonets up the main street of Pettipaug in defiance of all that the Yankees could do.

Curtains twitched and scurrying figures showed the news was spreading of the unbelievable sight in the middle of the night of the British on the march in their town. Sooner or later the nearest military would be alerted and they would then be in trouble. There was no time to be lost.

A few hundred yards into the town Kydd brought them to a halt. 'Mr Clinton. That tavern – the Bushnell, is it? I'm to make it my headquarters ashore.'

The two-storey building seemed unoccupied and the front door was unlocked. The upper rooms would provide an excellent view of proceedings and serve as a central reporting post.

With a handful of Royal Marines detailed to act as sentries, Kydd sent the rest off with the burning parties.

A number of privateers were alongside, others moored further out. One by one the flames leaped and crackled from blazing vessels up and down the shoreline, vivid and terrifying in the darkness. Boats shoved off from the jetty and the flaming pyres spread out in the darkness, reflecting luridly on the water.

Pettipaug was waking up to a nightmare. Inhabitants stared from their windows at the fearful sight and frightened groups emerged onto the street to stare.

Eventually a small body of men stepped forward. Kydd felt they had a right to be heard and went down to them.

'You're the colonel in charge, sir?' one began.

'Captain Sir Thomas Kydd, sir.'

'Obadiah Mason. Sir, I have to ask it – will our town be burned?'

'This is war, Mr Mason. A war that your president provoked and declared. What else should you expect?'

'Cap'n Kydd – these are the common folk only. They've not set a foot agin you an' yourn and you're goin' to burn down their homes an' places 'o work t' leave 'em all in poverty?' In his nervousness his hat passed from hand to hand. 'I'd say this is more'n a mite hard t' bear, sir.'

'You call the harbouring of privateers a harmless activity?'

'Why, we don't—'

'I'll make a bargain with you, sir. My war is with privateers, not blameless townsfolk. Should you refrain from firing on my men in the course of their duty your town will be left to you. Otherwise I will not let one house stand after setting it entirely ablaze.'

It was what he had intended all along but this made it vastly easier to keep control over proceedings.

'We won't be the first t' fire, Cap'n.'

'Very well, so let it be,' Kydd replied seriously. 'Only the privateers harmed – and their stores confiscated.'

By now there were five or more bonfires ablaze along the shore and out in the stream to be seen from Kydd's 'headquarters', along with the suggestion of light beginning to banish the shadows of night. With it would come the greatly increased danger of attack when pluming smoke would warn the world of what Pettipaug was suffering.

On the other hand while he held the town there was no reason to stop the good work and when daylight came they could go faster. The light strengthened in the east, and as visibility extended, it revealed coves and reaches into the distance, each with a privateer or two snugged down.

With Royal Marines guarding the road, the only highway into town, and seamen watching the river, he should have enough warning of relieving columns when they must evacuate immediately.

Full daylight brought still no sign of retaliation.

Kydd took a slow look about the harbour and came to a pleasing conclusion. If he delayed a few more hours he could destroy all twenty privateers and search out nearby havens where others must be safely moored to wait out the winter season. Not only that: ships at their moorings mid-stream were quite sizeable. This was something he could do to reward the seamen industriously setting fire to what in normal circumstances would be their hard-won prizes – he would choose a couple of the larger vessels, sparing them from the flames, take possession and return with them.

After all, he thought defensively, what better retreat than to have them tow the boats out?

Two suggested themselves: a stout brig of some size and a rakish, hundred-foot-long schooner, clearly a new-built privateer.

'Spare those two – they're ours. Bring 'em alongside and rig them for sea,' Kydd ordered, and anxiously resumed his lookout.

Now a full dozen vessels were afire, sending up pillars of spark-wreathed ugly smoke, surely to be spotted from far away, but nothing had been seen of any move to oppose them. It couldn't be this easy! A ghost of uneasiness crept into his soul but, as if to promise them a safe departure, a distinct north-easterly breeze picked up and, with the tide on the ebb at ten, it was looking encouraging for their retreat.

Rattler's first lieutenant returned. 'Burning parties all reported back safe,' he said, with satisfaction, his face and uniform smeared with grey ash.

'Muster the men on the jetty. Mr Clinton, please draw back your outposts. And where's Mr Tucker?'

Nobody seemed to know until one of the seamen offered, 'Stepped off when the jollies went marching away. Got hisself into that there West Indies warehouse an' said to leave him there.'

'Go and get him,' Kydd ordered irritably. 'He's got to pilot us back.'

Two grinning seamen went to the wooden storehouse on the jetty and after some jovial shouting from inside, emerged, dragging an unconscious Tucker. 'He knew where the rum for y'r deep-water voyages was kept an' thought t' help himself.'

Kydd swore savagely under his breath. The last thing he needed was a betwaddled pilot in the last stage before the open sea and safety.

The two prizes were made ready and all the boats roped together for towing by *Young Anaconda*, the brig. The schooner, *Eagle*, would follow in their wake.

At last they were on their way back – and not before time. Seeing the English boarding their boats and leaving with their redcoats, first one then another sputter of musket fire came from the woody shoreline. Kydd ignored it: at that range there could be no pretence at accuracy. More important was keeping the little flotilla together and moving.

He tried to bring to mind their inward passage but it was near hopeless to remember passing seamarks seen only like phantoms in the darkness. Tucker was propped up against the bulwarks, snoring loudly and no amount of snarling threats brought him to, or even a savage sousing with buckets of water.

Common seamanship had it that in a river bow the deepest

water was to be found on the inner side and Kydd had the long ash tiller put over accordingly but it did not respond. The clumsy vessel took a devilish long time to answer her helm and he soon saw why. With the river's natural flow seaward and the draining ebb tide it was being carried along bodily, the rudder having little bite. The breeze was fair for the moment but if it veered, as it had the day before, they would be in difficulties.

The firing from the shore now increased as they made their precarious way around the first of the major forelands, Hayden's Point. They had to keep in with that side of the river and it now narrowed to less than a quarter-mile across to a marshland shore opposite. It got worse as they rounded the point, then slackened as the shore flattened into bare mudflats and no cover.

But into the river proper came a change in the breeze as it shifted to funnel along the river. Half their advantage was now gone, as the two prizes under sail were obliged to make increasingly shorter tacks against the wind, their advance over the ground cut considerably.

Kydd's calculation gave it as a four-hour transit to reach the open sea even under oars, but if the firing worsened, or if a field piece was brought up, this could change.

Then with a graceful retardation *Young Anaconda* let it be known she would not be going any further. On her last tack she had run into one of the many mud shoals and slewed across the river flow to end immovably stuck fast.

Kydd felt a knot in his stomach. How long could he spare to haul the weighty brig off the mud on an ebbing tide? The firing meant that unseen enemies were closing in.

The towed boats were now being jostled and crowded against the bluff stern, and beating in on him was the realisation that they should abandon their handsome prize.

65

'Heave out as much valuable gear as you can, stow it in the schooner,' he said sorrowfully.

It was asking a lot to require men to be exposed to hostile fire as they did their duty, but in the boats the carronades opened up with canister in the general direction of their tormentors. The fire slackened considerably.

'The prize, sir?' asked *Rattler*'s first lieutenant, pitifully.

'Leave her – and set her a-fire.'

Clinton moved over to speak to Kydd. 'Not wishing to alarm you, sir, but there's a sight I'd not wish to see at this time.'

He handed Kydd a small telescope and pointed. A mile and a half in the distance there were two opposing bluffs, not over a quarter of a mile apart, which they must have passed in the darkness. The activity on both sides could only have one meaning. 'Field artillery being dug in, Mr Clinton?'

'I'm desolated to have to agree with you, sir.'

It changed the situation entirely. They had now to fight their way through against a force whose size was unknown but military authority plain. This was why Kydd's taking of Pettipaug had been so uncomplicated: the enemy had used the time to good effect. While the British were finishing their business, guns were being hauled along to bring up and have in place as a grand surprise for them.

Kydd's boats were full of men. The craft were completely without protection and their carronades were not designed to compete with field pieces, fully dug in. It would be nothing but cold slaughter, were he even to attempt to take them through. Against these odds he was helpless.

He hesitated. 'Can we . . .?'

'No direct assault would succeed, sir. They are there by design, they will have taken precautions and their numbers are not known. I regret that . . .'

'Spoken by the very foremost of the breed, Mr Clinton. So I must consider my position, I find.'

One thing was certain. If they defied the guns and tried the passage they would never survive. Close range round-shot from on high would smash the boats to splinters in short order and the river would be dotted with the sad remnants of his men whom he had commanded to suffer so.

He couldn't do it.

And then . . . there was one possibility, and that a long chance: wait for darkness before making their break.

It was about eleven. It would be dark at about half past six, fully night at seven. Could they sit here in idleness for seven, eight hours while the enemy was free to bring up yet more guns and even closer?

At least at this place it was road-less marshes opposite, and on the nearer side the land had been cleared for farming. No guns could be brought up across such terrain and it would be a rash commander who looked to come against his boats with their carronade armament. They were safe for the moment.

Time passed with agonising slowness.

About midday a light rain began, once turning to sharp points of snow before easing away. At two the last share-out of rations took place, hard tack and cheese. And then at three the monotony was broken when a boat under a flag-of-truce was seen approaching.

'Cap'n Charles Harrison. Are you the officer commanding, sir?'

The young man was in an unfamiliar uniform bearing stars on the shoulder.

'I am, sir. Captain Sir Thomas Kydd.'

'Then I'm commanded to deliver this into your hands, sir.'

He reached into a satchel and handed over a folded message.

Kydd smoothed it open and read:

> *To the Officer Commanding His Britannic Majesty's*
> *Marine forces in the Connecticut River*
>
> Sir
>
> *To avoid the effusion of human blood is the desire of every honorable man. The number of Forces under my command are increased so much as to render it impossible for you to escape. I therefore suggest to you the propriety of surrendering your selves prisoners of War and by that means prevent the consequences of an unequal conflict which must otherwise ensue.*
>
> *Marsh Ely, Major commanding the forces at Lyme & Saybrook*
>
> *NB an immediate answer is expected per hand Captain Harrison*

Kydd kept his feelings to himself and said mildly, 'Sir, while I'm sensible of your humane intentions, we set you at defiance in your power to detain us.' He folded the message carefully and handed it back.

Harrison looked confused. 'So that is your reply, sir?'

'It is.'

The knot of onlookers began muttering among themselves as the essence of the message became known. Kydd gave a bleak smile. 'I would think it wise for you now to make your way ashore, sir.'

Red-faced, the officer re-embarked, and as the boat headed inshore it was sent on its way with round after round of tumultuous cheering. Kydd's heart lifted. With men like these, how could he think to submit?

There were just three hours to prepare for any attempt to break out. Their opponents would know it, too, and would be waiting with guns primed for that critical first hour of darkness knowing precisely where the British must pass on their way to freedom.

It was becoming more obvious by the moment that their remaining prize would not go with them.

The afternoon wind was staying sulkily in the south, which meant that, even with its fore and aft rig, *Eagle* would have to tack about on short boards to win clear of the river. In a constricted waterway in utter blackness, it was asking the impossible.

Kydd waited patiently. Full darkness was essential for their breakout and when it came he fired the schooner and by its lurid flames formed up the six boats, Kydd in *Tyger*'s launch again in the lead. Almost immediately there was a burst of firing from ashore, including at least one nearby cannon. They'd got away just in time but so close had the gun been hauled that at near point-blank range its ball slammed into one of the boats bringing a shriek of pain.

The men bent to their oars and stretched out for their lives away from the flame-lit pool of light – and nearer to the guns and men lying in wait for them.

At a mile distant Kydd gave the order. Oars were quietly un-shipped and brought in and the men lay down below the level of the gunwales. He'd noticed while they were waiting that the tide had turned to the ebb and the river current had noticeably increased, fairly certainly augmented from snow-melt in distant mountains. It should be enough to float them silently along at, say, two to three knots.

He drew his sword and tapped a gunwale with it. 'If anyone gives even a sneeze, I'll spit the beggar!' he growled.

In absolute quiet they drifted slowly on in the blackness towards the narrowest point in the river and their rendezvous with death – or life.

At first there were hesitant shots as soldiers fired at what they thought were the English, but in the pitch-black dark their silhouettes would look anything but warlike, boats with redcoats at the oars, and the firing gave out. Still drifting lazily the boats came on, nothing to give away their presence.

Then with a thunderous crash and leaping gun-flash the first field gun opened up. It sounded like a six-pounder, but this was more than enough to turn a ship's boat to kindling wood. Another gun answered from the opposite bank and for a while the guns hammered out in frightful chorus, slamming shot back and forth in a frenzy of violence, but without result. It was not difficult to understand why: the flash of firing in the blackness had destroyed their night-vision and essentially their aim was pure guesswork, driven on by a furious desire not to allow them to get away.

In the dark below the gunwale Kydd couldn't help a grim smile. Their furious firing from both banks must be causing casualties on their own side for no result.

At one point a huge detonation split the night, probably the accidental touching off of powder barrels kept too close to the cannon by inexperienced gunners. Anything could happen in the dangerous ballet that was loading a weapon in pitch darkness.

The pieces kept up their demented bombarding, but even as they fell astern the drifting boats were now faced with the fort at Saybrook Point, which they had found unmanned before. Without doubt it would now have its share of guns.

But here the river was wider and the current carried them past without incident while the guns continued their futile cannonade.

And then they were through.

Chapter 11

Aboard Tyger

It wasn't a record bag but it must come close to it, Kydd reflected. A grand total of twenty-seven of the vermin put down, a butcher's bill of only two killed and the same number injured. It was gratifying, but at the same time it could only be accounted a side-show, a tactical victory in a strategic goal. Would the Americans now send a frigate storming out in revenge to meet *Tyger* in mortal combat? Or reserve them for the far more damaging assault on England's convoys and leave him with futile gestures his only weapon?

All he could do was continue to flaunt his colours up and down the coast and see what happened. *Tyger* herself was untouched by their engagement and, not having fired a shot, was in prime condition for the contest, her crew with tails high. But the clash when it came would be brutal and near-impossible to call. All he knew was that his fine ship, dear to his heart, would acquit herself heroically.

Unconsciously his hand strayed to the ship's side and brushed it in a caress. She had been his intimate in so many adventures, had stood by him in uncountable perils and now looked to be torn to pieces in a great sea-duel.

In the celebration dinner it had been taken for granted they would prevail, for what ship could possibly challenge *Tyger* on equal terms? He knew, though, that chance was as big a factor as any in a clash of arms at sea, but kept his feelings to himself, touched by their stout hearts and faith in their ship.

He released the sloops and cutters whose men had contributed so much to his recent success and set *Tyger* on course for the Thames River and New London. The weather was dreary, cold and grey with a sullen slop to the seas, but this suited Kydd better than bright sunlight. Gunners disliked trying to lay a gun into the sun's eye. But there was no sudden sighting of a big frigate making its way down the river to meet them. The only sign that they'd been noticed was the total emptiness of the horizon, the sea cleared of every vessel.

Days later, after closing as near as he could to the dangerous estuary of the Thames, it became obvious that his stratagem was not working. Not sure whether to be downhearted or pleased that *Tyger* was being spared a rough handling, he abandoned the strutting and headed back for Halifax around the tide rips off Fisher Island, thereby not letting it be known that he'd left the area.

Not far on the other side, still within Block Island Sound, sail was sighted but it was only the brig-sloop *Rattler*.

Kydd took the opportunity to tell those still soldiering on in these waters that for now he'd given up trying to lure out the canny Yankees and was returning to base. Poole waited for him to finish, then lifted his speaking trumpet and hailed back, 'Sir Thomas, for your information I can tell you I lately gave chase to a deep-water merchantman, a China trader, I believe. It went to ground not far off – Westbury, I'd think, which is up the Lyne River.'

All along the New England coast, rivers discharged into the sound with sheltered harbours inside, ports of refuge for ships beset by foul weather or English predators, much like Pettipaug or larger. A trader inbound from China would make a valuable prize and was worth going after, for its cutting out and capture by the same frigate as at Pettipaug would make for an intolerable provocation.

'Thank you for this, Mr Poole. Stay within hail while I consult my charts.'

To take a merchant vessel on the high seas was no hard task for a man-o'-war, but if it was secure under the guns of a fort or safely alongside in a sizeable harbour it was another matter. Looking at the charts he could see why Poole had not been able to crown his chase with a capture. Westbury, four miles up, was a small town on the shores of a semi-circular indented cove. And, praise be, a deep-water channel all the way. *Tyger* could probably sail in, and with unassailable gun-power cover any cutting-out expedition, presuming they could get past any forts across the entrance to the river.

'I believe we'll make an attempt on the fellow, Mr Poole.'

They met in Kydd's cabin, Poole with a chart he spread out on the table. 'A mite old but has any detail we'd want,' he murmured.

It was indeed old – 1752, to be precise – but while not of the rigorous standards of the Admiralty of their day the cartouche indicated that it had been drawn up by a full captain RN and might be relied upon.

The Lyne River did not have a bar, and while its many bends were well populated by small islands, it wound purpose-fully through an uninhabited wilderness, its wide progression indicating that winds anywhere in the western quadrant could see them both there and on return.

'So. A half-day in, cut the villain out, less than that out with the current,' Kydd grunted, with satisfaction. 'Just the one worry.'

'Sir?'

'If our Yankee cousins have in fact been sent to lay me by the heels and find *Tyger* there, she'd be trapped like a fly in a bottle. I desire you'll mount watch and guard here at the entrance. Should you spy any such you're to fire a minute gun in groups of three as will be my warning.'

'Aye aye, sir. Understood.'

'Then I see no reason why we don't make our move at first light tomorrow. Sir, do you care to dine with me tonight?'

Chapter 12

After a comfortable repast, Poole left early for his ship. Kydd sat back in his armchair and reflected. Tomorrow would be a straightforward, even undemanding action. Since the dawn of their nation the Americans had not had to defend their land and now, only months into the war, had many lessons to learn. The British had so far refrained from the kind of warfare common in Spain and the Mediterranean, sharp and hard-fought with, on the one side, sail-of-the-line, and on the other stone fortresses, no quarter given. After what he'd heard from Warren, his blockade would be stern but limited, but when it became more serious the kind of incursions Kydd had begun would be commonplace and it would no longer be so easily done.

As long as it stirred at least one of the big frigates to emerge – otherwise this had to be the last throw of the dice.

The morning dawned calm and grey – too calm, with a very gentle west-south-westerly barely lifting the sails. It would strengthen as the morning wore on – it always did. But then, before they parted off the entrance, it changed. Instead of the morning mists lifting to the tiny warmth of the winter sun they stayed and thickened. A fog-bank was advancing from the interior.

Kydd was not sure whether to curse or bless his fortune that it was upon them. Their position was fixed by bearings on the twin points of the entrance with small forts on either side as the chill dankness and impenetrable dull white silently enveloped them.

By compass he could set a course that would take them in unseen from the forts and surprise would be complete. On the other hand, once he was inside it was a very different story. In this fog, orientation among the islands was near impossible without sight of the distant leading marks provided for in the chart. If *Tyger* pressed on she could run afoul of any one of the shoals, and in these parts it wasn't the gentle mud of Pettipaug but rock skerries in sand, stray boulders, reefs. There was nothing for it but to anchor and wait for the fog to lift.

An hour passed. Another – and the longer they stayed where they were the greater the chance of discovery. What Kydd needed was another Tucker, with local knowledge enough to take them through. Like the Cornish lobstermen of Fowey who could find their way in anything.

'Mr Bowden!' he called, as soon as he got on deck. 'A line of boats across the channel, stop any fisherman you chance across and bring him to me.'

Even if he ended paying well over the odds for the piloting it would be as nothing compared to the value of a China ship.

The fog was thicker than ever when a low cry indicated that Bowden was back. He hurried down to Kydd alone. 'Sir. I have a fisherman but . . . but . . .'

'Well, show him in!'

It was a young woman, probably not yet in her twenties. In seamanlike boots, canvas trousers and leather smock with a cumbersome sweater, she gave a shy smile as she looked around the great cabin with wide blue eyes.

'Er, this is your fisherman, Mr Bowden?'

'The only one in the boat, sir.'

'It's your boat, then, Miss . . .?'

'Oh, Annie, sir. Annie Pinckney o' Tawville. An' the boat sure is mine, as m' gran'pappy left it to me seein' my brother got hisself lost at sea.'

'Well, I'm Sir Thomas Kydd of – of England, and this is my ship, His Majesty's Frigate *Tyger*.'

She blinked. 'So it ain't yourn, it's really your king's?'

Hiding a smile, he replied, 'As he lets me be captain from time to time.'

She whipped off her Scots-style knitted cap and said eagerly, 'Is there anythin' I can do for you, Mr Kydd? You stopped me to buy some fish? I've had a good catch o' prime flounder this mornin'.'

'We may, Annie, but I'm here to offer you a bargain. I'll wager you know every inch of these waters and upriver too?'

'I go out on 'un every morning after anythin' what swims, I should know it,' she answered smartly.

'Then I'm not wrong in my estimate. If you pilot me up to Westbury I'll give you a sack o' dollars as will make you stare.'

She started in surprise, then said guardedly, 'Why don't you conn it y'self? S'only a four-, five-mile run.'

'I've a deep draught ship, Annie.'

'Not really, Cap'n. Twenny, twenny-five? I've taken up blue-water merchant jacks at more'n thirty feet,' she said, tossing her hair.

She was a river-scamp who'd known her nauticals from

childhood. Just what was wanted, but the other side of the bargain was whether she knew or cared about what was going to happen.

'Annie. This is an English ship. Don't you object to helping us?'

She looked away for a moment, then turned to him, her face set. 'I guess I should at that. But keep your dollars – I'll have you know my folks were loyalists in the War of Independence, an' right now my pa said as how this war is the craziest ever, an' that it'll finish real quick. An' after the English have done Boney down they'll come an' claim their colonies back. I wanna be on the right side when it's over.'

Kydd sat back in delight. They had a pilot – and a right dimber one at that. 'If you do, I'll see you squared off in the way of a reward, Annie.'

After she had left the cabin Bowden voiced his doubts, but Kydd brought out Poole's chart. 'Don't concern yourself, Charles. We'll follow every helm order, course and so forth on the chart – just to be sure.'

After buoying her little boat, *Tyger* was made ready for the expedition. Under topsails only, the anchor was hove in, and with Annie by the conn, they paid off to leeward.

In sure tones she called the right orders – helm down to avoid a suspicious swirl in the water before it came into sight; ease sheets forward to take advantage of the currents around another island; keep close aboard the shore at this point where the deep-water channel ran.

Kydd relaxed, able to spy out the country. It was flat, with the occasional rise of yet another island, well-forested but with no sign of cultivation, a wilderness of countless islets wound through by the Lyne River.

He glanced up at Bowden at the chart. He nodded reassuringly as his pencilled-in course extended. Another couple of hours and *Tyger* would go to quarters.

A straight stretch opened up, and Annie fell back in curiosity to see Bowden's chart. She studied it for a few minutes, then stood back and gave a short laugh. 'That's one ole map, Cap'n, wouldn't trust it. See here – gives the channel on this side, an' since I was a girl we got a pile-up 'o great stones come down when the Lyne changed course.'

A stirring of unease stole over Kydd. He knew about such matters and it didn't seem right with that depth of water further upstream, given that the Lyne was so placid. But what advantage could she hope to gain by throwing out an untruth?

The girl looked at him, then gave a broad smile. 'Don't you worry y'self, Mr Kydd. I'll see you through – as you does exactly as I say, o' course.'

All the same, it was unsettling. Here he was, back in dear old *Tyger*, trusting her to a stranger – a young woman at that. Was his desire for another victory blinding him to dangers?

He tried not to look at Annie Pinckney too closely but sensed in her nervousness, tension. Was this because of the responsibility she was taking on in the conning of a king's ship – or something else?

She called another order that had *Tyger*'s bowsprit tracking to the left of an invisible island, which only loomed out of the fog as they passed it.

Bowden was clearly worried. He was trying to plot their motions but without bearings triangulating them along he could not be sure.

'Sir, I'm not happy about our course,' he whispered to Kydd. 'As I lost track half a mile back. We could be anywhere.'

'Hold steady, old fellow. This is the only way we're going to make Westbury in this, and it gives us perfect cover to spring our surprise.'

'This point,' Annie called, indicating the dim shadow of land slipping by to starboard. 'We're going around it, an' – mark me well – at the end when I tell you, helm hard down, or you'll finish wi' a bunch 'o rocks down y' throat.'

'You have that, Quartermaster?' Kydd asked loudly.

'Aye, sir. At the order, wheel hard over.'

Annie went to the side and peered down into the depths. Kydd had lookouts at the cathead doing the same but guessed she was probably looking for something in particular. Every so often she would flick up her gaze to the dim shadow of the shoreline, then look intently down again.

Attention was drawn forward to the lookouts, peering out to see what fearsome hazard she was saving them from.

Suddenly Annie froze, staring at a progression of split and jagged rocks protruding from the shore, like a cock's comb. 'Now! Hard over – go to it, y' lubbers!'

Kydd spun on the quartermaster, who stood over the helmsman as he whirled on turns as fast as he could.

Like the thoroughbred she was, *Tyger* swept around, tight to the shoreline, which opened into the white nothingness beyond. They'd made it.

Annie was still at the side and unaccountably threw Kydd a look – beseeching, distorted.

Taken aback Kydd couldn't understand. Then, utterly without reason, she tore off her seaboots, flung her sweater to one side and took a neat flying dive into the water, stroking manically for the shore.

Cries rang out in confusion but in a flash some primeval instinct had him bellowing hoarsely, 'Hard a-larb'd for your life!'

For a fateful moment the helmsman paused – was the captain taking the deck?

With all the inertia of a thousand tons, the frigate drove

on to the black granite ledge with a long-drawn-out grinding of riven timbers and sub-sea protests, on and on until she came to a shuddering stop with an ominous stillness.

'Get all sail off her!' Kydd rapped. His mind roared at the betrayal, but at the same time he had to acknowledge the quickness of mind and bravery.

His intellects steadied with near inhuman concentration. 'Carpenter to sound the wells, bosun to rig preventer stay tackles. Mr Bowden – a quick sighting of the condition of the ship fore an' aft.'

He knew the worst already: they were hard and fast on an unknown offshore reef. They had gone in with the flood tide and it must be near high water. The ebb would see them high and dry until the next tide.

On the other hand there was one boon granted them: no masts had been toppled forward by the sudden deceleration. They were absolutely vital if they were ever to get off.

And hanging over them in their helplessness was their probable fate if the fog lifted and they were discovered. They'd gone from contemplating another triumph to catastrophe in the blink of an eye.

Chapter 13

Bywater Island, Connecticut

A duck punt at the water's edge was a prime place to sit
and contemplate and take one's fill of the sights and
sounds of nature. Lieutenant Jasper Gindler, United States
Navy, stretched out lazily, his fowling piece ready in its
brackets, along with a bite or two in a basket and a well-
thumbed book, to see him through the morning.

He liked this seasonal fog, its sound-deadening mystery
causing strange effects. It was not his fault that while his
country was at war with the greatest naval power afloat he
was denied a post of honour at sea. Not, it had to be said,
as a consequence of some professional deficiency but the
result of political in-fighting and personal rivalries in a small
service.

He had no desire to join in the factional disputing and
strife for they came from the very politics that had split the
nation from top to bottom.

Hamilton's Federalists regarded the value of trade with
their biggest partner, Great Britain, of far more importance

to the young but rising country than aggravations at sea and other irritations. These could reasonably be regarded as business costs resulting from their position as neutrals trading with both sides in a wider war. But the Federalists were not in power.

President Jefferson of the Republicans, in the name of smaller government, had done all he could to reduce the size of their navy and army, even going so far as to forbid any building of vessels larger than small coastal gunboats. His Republican successor, Madison, was going to war with nothing much more than their six frigates of an earlier administration and the gunboats, now mostly rotting at their moorings on rivers. As for an army, the Republican belief was that they didn't need one: state militia would flock to the colours in time of emergency, a military force that did not need costly maintenance at all times.

If anything, Gindler was a Federalist with no standing in a Republican world and could not bring himself to curry favour with Paul Hamilton, secretary to the Navy who, it was said, had a name for the utmost reliability – he was invariably drunk by lunchtime.

Gindler had interest from none of the existing captains of ships of significance and found himself superfluous to requirements, given indefinite furlough on half-pay.

This would no doubt change eventually, as the need for a blue-water navy had been dramatically demonstrated in the victorious frigate actions that had roused the pride of a nation. But for now he was occupied in immersing himself in this most beautiful and lonely part of the country, waiting for the call.

In the thick bushes nearby there was movement and a small sea-duck hopped into view. With its black and white contrasts and flash of green iridescence it had to be a Bufflehead, hungry after a hard winter. Gindler hastily reached for his flintlock but paused. Its pert, cheerful optimism touched him and he sat motionless, simply watching the creature.

Suddenly there was a disturbance in the undergrowth, and with a whirring of wings it was off. Gindler frowned. There were no large animals roaming these islands or farms so what the devil was—

A figure wet through and daubed with mud burst into view. Gathering his wits, Gindler saw that it was someone he knew. 'Miss Pinckney! What . . . your boat . . . Has there been a . . . a . . .'

Wild-eyed and shivering uncontrollably, she dropped to all fours. 'Mr G-Gindler, I h-had to f-find you.'

He found a blanket and wrapped it over her. 'Now, what happened, my dear, that leaves you like this?'

There was the briefest of smiles. Then she said proudly, 'I'se been in battle wi' an English ship, an' I won.'

'Please be serious, Annie. You—'

'In the end I sent it smack-wham up on Black Point, where it's at now.'

'You—'

'Mr Gindler, you're a Navy officer. You'll know what to do, but if'n we don't move fast it'll get free on the next high tide an' they'll be mighty angry, I reckon.'

Something in her manner gave him pause. 'You really—'

'I did 'n' all, I swear it! Come an' see for yourself.' Before he could speak she boated the grapnel anchor and took up the scull, pushing them clear of the bank and bending into it like a veteran, heading to the opposite side of the island.

They landed cautiously. 'Stay here!' Gindler told her.

'No! I'm coming with you.'

After securing the punt the two set out across country. Bywater Island was uninhabited with no roads but was ridged with granite. Reaching the last rise, they cautiously looked over.

Gindler saw through the swirling whiteness the unmistakable silhouette of a ship's rigging. And there were three masts – a ship-rigged vessel, a large sloop or, glory be, a frigate.

It was a frigate and it was English. It had no business there but there it was. Gindler watched her crew hard at work, her captain prominent in his uniform pacing impatiently on its quarterdeck. The vessel had by this time settled on its stony resting place with a marked list to port. It was going nowhere until the tide rose.

Carefully he quartered the sight of the stranded ship, taking in as much as he could. The canted vessel was at a fine angle to the shore, her starboard broadside able to bear on any who dared an assault from the land, while her larboard guns could take care of anything coming in from seaward.

Of medium size, her armament would be something like long eighteens, far heavier metal than anything that could be brought to bear from the land and no doubt with a good fit of carronades. From what he could see they were lightening ship by landing stores and water, and the heavy cable being run out of her stern-port would no doubt be made to take a kedge anchor, carried to seaward by boats, then let drop. It would be hauled in by the main capstan when the time came to warp the ship off into deep water.

Its captain was playing it calm and professionally, doing the things Gindler would do in the same circumstances, and in a way Gindler felt sorry for him, brought to such a pass by trusting a girl.

'Annie. You've done a great thing and I admire you for it. Now we've got to do something about it.'

'What?' she asked, with big round eyes.

'Call out the militia.'

The nearest settlement boasting a unit was Mustauk, on the other side of the river several miles away. He recalled that the next high tide was not for another ten hours, and therefore this was the amount of time they had to bring up forces in numbers enough to delay the ship sufficiently that one of their own frigates could come up and put paid to the helpless vessel.

Returning to the punt, he plied it like a fury, heading for his own little cottage, some way ahead. Perspiring, he finally reached its boathouse and, with aching muscles, glided the punt inside.

Annie stood uncertainly so he took her inside, threw open his tallboy and panted, 'My dear, for God's sake, clean up and find some clothes.'

'I'm goin' with you!'

'Only if you're ready in time.' He had a horse and trap at the back. A track joined the road to the horse ferry and Mustauk. If he was quick . . .

He fumed at the wait but knew it was necessary. She was a native of these parts, he just a visitor. After the loss of her father and brother she had kept her widowed mother and two sisters with her work as a fisher-girl and was respected by the community.

'Right.' She'd made cunning use of a pair of his trousers, rolling up the legs and securing the waist with a belt over her petite frame.

The trap set off at a smart trot, Gindler unwilling to wind the horse, an elderly roan. They made Mustauk in an hour and he tied up his rig outside the only store.

'Mr Benson,' he asked the shopkeeper, 'who's in charge o' the militia and where might I find him?'

Astonished, the man replied, 'Now, what would you be wantin' of the militia, Mr Gindler? The English comin'?' He smirked.

'I asked you a civil question, my friend.'

'Well, then, an' that must be Jed Burrowes.' He pulled out a large fob watch and consulted it ostentatiously. 'And at this time I reckon you'll find him at the Blue Goose with his cronies.'

The taphouse was small but had a cosy fire going and half a dozen men with tankards, who stopped their conversations and looked up in surprise at their visitors.

'Miss Pinckney,' said one. 'Youse taking to drink, now?'

'No, Mr Calhoun.' She frowned. 'It's much more important'n that. Tell 'em, Mr Gindler.'

'Mr Burrowes?'

A corpulent man nearest to the fire looked up. 'That's me. Who's asking?' he said defensively.

'Lieutenant Gindler, United States Navy. I understand you're in charge of the local militia.'

Burrowes looked about him in wry deprecation. 'I guess that's me right enough. Call me Captain, if it amuses you.'

'Then, sir, I have to inform you of a situation that requires you call out the militia.'

'What did you say, Lootenant?' he asked, in astonishment.

'Cast up on Black Point, sir, is an English frigate. In all respects unharmed save she does not float.' Gindler ignored the gasps and went on crisply, 'At the next high tide she'll be enabled to refloat and carry on her evil work. Should a body of armed men invest the frigate closely she'll be unable to take the steps necessary to haul herself off. I would think an immediate call to arms would suffice, sir.'

'Ha!' Burrowes grunted, a smile breaking out. 'For a minute there you had me going, sir. An English frigate halfway up the Lyne! They'd never—'

'I'm in earnest, Captain Burrowes. You'll turn out your men or answer for it to the nation.'

Burrowes picked up on the seriousness of his tone and replied quietly, 'Not so fast, Mr Lootenant. It's not as easy as all that. Who's goin' to pay for all this tomfoolery? Certainly, send out the call but where's the coin as will give 'em pay, victuals, arms and—'

'Sir, you're the officer-in-charge in this district,' Gindler snarled. 'It's your damned responsibility to—.'

'Not so, Mr Lootenant. You did say an English frigate?'

'I did.'

'Then in my capacity as your officer-in-charge, dammit, I'm saying that makes it all Navy business, wouldn't you agree?'

As a rumble of comment rose, Annie's waspish comment cut through. 'No, I wouldn't, Mr Jed! You don't want t' go up agin them cos you're makin' too many dollars in the grain trade over t' Spain and the British there.'

Burrowes went red but before he could reply another voice entered, troubled and low. 'Miss Pinckney, you knows we're few an' without guns as can take on a battleship. Is it worth our lives jus' to make a brave scene?'

Another added, ''Sides, it'll only bring 'em down on us somethin' cruel. Let the beggars in Providence deal with it.'

'Are you saying you won't turn out against the British?' Gindler said cuttingly.

'I guess you heard right,' Burrowes said comfortably, lifting up his drink for another pull. 'Hadn't you better be off an' telling your Navy all about it?'

Gindler couldn't trust himself to retort and stormed outside.

Annie caught up with him and pulled him round urgently. 'Mr Gindler – these are naught but a bunch of – of— We can get back across the river an' go to Trowton. They have a big gun. I know, I seen it.'

'How far?'

'An hour or so.'

'We go.'

Chapter 14

Approaching Trowton along a well-forested road down to the plain, Gindler was struck by the quiet. Larger than Montauk, it was tucked within a river bend but with the main street deserted of people it had a defiant, obstinate feel about it. Had everyone left hastily on hearing of the British frigate in their midst?

They'd nearly progressed through the empty streets when a mighty roar erupted from ahead, somewhere out in the country. Gindler tooled the rig towards it, and in a sizeable meadow a substantial crowd was gathered.

It was a fair, and he saw that the focus of attention was a shooting match. Two men, both in a uniform he didn't recognise, were in a standing firing position, taking an offhand shot one after the other at a tree some fifty yards distant. Their concentration was intense and the crowd's murmuring fell away.

One fired again and a figure from the side ran out to the tree, then signalled, by crossed arms, a hit, followed by an outstretched arm thrown out to the left.

Once more the crowd howled their glee. The two shooters shook hands and, amid much applause, a be-medalled officer stepped forward and presented a silver cup to the winner of the tenpenny nail driving. It seemed this was one Quincy Jackson, a thick-set and darkly sun-touched individual, whose loose-limbed carrying of his long-barrelled flintlock spoke of an up-country woodsman.

Gindler pressed forward to the officer, who now held a glass of wine. 'Sir, you would oblige me by pointing out the officer in command of the militia.'

'If b' that you mean the 17th Regiment, Rhode Island Detached militia,' the man replied with ponderous gravity, 'then I can do no better than introduce m'self. Major Jesse Harper, at your service on this fine day, sir.'

Returning his elaborate bow irritably, Gindler snapped, 'Lieutenant Gindler, United States Navy. And I have grave news that you will no doubt act upon as the situation demands.'

'Some wine? No? You appear out of uniform, Lootenant, a shame on our Oakapple Day, sir, the Grand Parade and so forth.'

Gindler looked about at the quantities of men in all manner of dress for their parade – if these were militia possibly they could be mustered and set to marching. 'No, thank you, Major, time presses.'

A small crowd was gathering, their curiosity at an out-of-towner plain. 'Sir, what if I were to tell you that an English frigate lies helpless up the Lyne River, caught out in a raid and wanting only an infantry siege to dismay its crew to abandon ship?' Gindler went on.

An excited ripple of interest came from the cluster of onlookers.

'Why, after Pettipaug that is a concern, sir. East bank or west?'

'West.'

'Then our action is very clear.'

90

'Which is?'

'Stand fast nobly, sir.'

'You . . . you . . .' spluttered Gindler.

'Which is the only act I might contemplate, matters on that bank being firmly within Connecticut and my men being sworn as a condition of their service not to cross state lines.'

'Well, Major! It's the English an' I want a crack at 'em,' whooped one of the young men in uniform. 'Jus' like m' paw at Brandywine Creek!'

'Nye Meiklejohn, hold your peace, you don't know what you're talking of,' Harper spat.

'But he's right, Major,' burst in another wild-eyed youth. 'Ain't every day the British oblige us wi' targets this far up the country!'

He was howled down by others, the arguments loud and ugly with drink.

'Major Harper – are you saying as you're going to make no move against the British?' Gindler said thickly. 'None at all?'

'Well, Lootenant, what do you expect of me? To call out the militia on my own account? It's not within my power,' he added theatrically, with a deprecating gesture. Noticing Gindler's expression, he added, 'But I can do somethin' for you.'

'Do it!'

Harper pulled out a notebook. 'I'll let 'em know at head-quarters. Fast horse should get to 'em in the day. They'll sort it out, right enough.'

'Hey, Major!' The shout came from deeper in the crowd and Harper looked up.

'What is it, Henry?'

'What about them there gunboats? Bin sitting here all this time.'

Gindler stiffened. 'Show me,' he demanded. This was another matter entirely. The previous president, Jefferson, had been against a deep-water navy and instead had gone for coastal gunboats. They had not proved successful in this war but had one big advantage. They were not state but federal assets.

'Take me!'

Led by a substantial crowd, Gindler was escorted to the river and to a large shed along the bank. Inside, two of the craft had been drawn up out of the water, apparently with all of their gear in racks next to them.

Loudly he declared, 'As a duly commissioned officer in the United States Navy I'm herewith taking these vessels into service.'

He had no idea if he could do this but there was one other requirement. 'Where's the Register of Nominated Crew?'

It was a list of men who'd taken a federal subvention in return for making themselves available when the time came.

A coxswain and a gunner were the minimum trained men needed – the gunner to take charge of the twelve-pounder mounted in the bows, which was its reason for being. Low, squat and with two lugsails that could be rigged to give relief to the oarsmen, gunboats were perfect for the job in this unusual situation.

The coxswain recoiled in disbelief. 'You goin' to take a itty-bitty boat like this agin' an English frigate?'

'Sure am, Mr Clay,' Gindler replied, with a wicked grin. 'And I'll tell you how.'

He knew he held an unbeatable trump card: the frigate was hard and fast aground – it could not manoeuvre either to turn on its enemy or to escape. All he had to do was approach the wounded beast from directly ahead and astern and no gun could bear on them. And then between them pound away until either the ship was in ruins or the captain capitulated.

'So what's it to be, you men? History or . . .?'

Chapter 15

Aboard Tyger

The de-storing was going agonisingly slowly. The half-tide rocks shallowed unpredictably and, lying some thirty-five yards offshore, there was little in the way of deeper channels for the big launch to make its way to land, heavily laden. Kydd was well aware that their visible presence on the naked foreshore would betray the fact that *Tyger* was hard aground and lightening ship – and therefore helpless.

It was now only four or five hours to the top of the tide and the ship had to be cleared of anything movable in order to float off. Yet even with her hold empty there was no guarantee she would. With the inertia of speed she'd piled up crazily high. So far there'd been no sign of the enemy, but it had to be assumed that the girl had woken up the countryside. In a way she'd helped Kydd by taking them up this remote waterway to be cast away, out of sight of passing river craft.

Kydd knew he had to make decisions. His plan had been to retrieve the stores and water casks once afloat. It would take as long to bring them back aboard as it was doing to land them. For all he knew a strong army field force was on its way, and if it had artillery, it would be all over very soon.

So, as of now any stores not landed would be thrown over the side without hesitation.

But if, despite all their efforts, they did not float off, what then?

Sombrely he faced the facts. If they were still on the rocks after another tide without doubt the enemy would have brought up what land forces it could muster, and almost certainly a ship of consequence. *Tyger* would need all the defensive gear she had, but there was an unanswerable dilemma. If she could not float with everything movable off the ship the last act of any captain of a stranded vessel would be to jettison his great guns. And thereby render himself defenceless.

A cold premonition settled in the pit of his stomach. From adversity through calamity to tragedy, he couldn't remember a worse plight. And dear *Tyger*, it would be the end for her. She and her loyal crew would inevitably be taken by the Americans, a disastrous fate that would resound across all England.

Even if—

Urgent, muffled cries reached him. Without stopping to find his coat he bounded on deck. Two gunboats had rounded the points of land ahead and astern, perfectly placed for the kill.

They'd been found and the Yankees had made their move.

Although these were only two, they had wicked black guns in their foreparts that they were preparing for a steady battering against bow and stern.

An officer stood erect in one, urging on the rowers. When safely off *Tyger*'s bow, at the correct range and perfectly aligned, a small anchor splashed down and the boat's crew rearranged themselves into battle readiness.

This was not the first time gunboats had attacked a motionless Royal Navy vessel. The masters of this form of sea warfare, the Danes, had made it their own and, no longer possessing a navy, had taken advantage of the summer calms in the Sound to lunge at helpless convoys and escorts. It had taken the British some time to find the answer but they had, and it was simple: arm ships' boats with heavy carronades and fight back directly.

Kydd had the pinnace and cutter out rowing guard. They came into view, a gunner visible in the bows already aiming unerringly for the gunboat at anchor, caught by its own preparations for a static cannonade.

The pinnace opened up first, a distraction shot, which, under a half-charge to encourage ricochets, skittered its roundshot towards the officer's boat, just missing to one side. The Americans found their frantic attempt at getting in the anchor of little use and their own gun was impossible to train. A gunboat was designed to aim with the boat itself: its weight was ungainly when compared to a sleek ship's boat, which could nimbly dodge the slow-fire of its cannon.

With not a single offensive weapon along its side its crew sensed imminent destruction. Some flung themselves into the water before the next ball came. The officer remained standing, shaking his fist at the pinnace, which obliged with another shot.

It took the gunboat squarely in the stem and its strakes flew apart in a shower of splinters. The iron weight of its gun ensured that it disappeared rapidly, gurgling down with finality and throwing its crew, thrashing, into the river.

The other gunboat had seen their doom approaching and lost no time in abandoning their craft, leaving it to the mercies of their nemesis. The pinnace made for the figures splashing about forlornly off *Tyger*'s bow and hauled them to safety, bringing them in as prisoners.

Kydd gave instructions that the officer be brought down to him in his cabin.

'Sir – the Yankee officer.'

He was curious to see what kind of man he was and recoiled in shock.

'Sir, my name is Gindler, Lootenant, United States Navy and—'

'I know . . . Jasper.'

Gindler stopped in astonishment, peered at Kydd and burst into awkward laughter. 'Well, an' I never did! Tom Kydd – as was.'

He stood back in admiration at the star and finery. 'So what must I call you now, old friend? That is if it can be said we still are.'

Kydd felt a jet of warmth at the long-ago memories and quickly got to his feet to shake his hand. 'Let's get you out of your wet togs and then we'll talk. My bedplace is in there. Take what dry gear you need – so long as it doesn't sport any gold lace at all.'

Binard knew what to do and when Gindler emerged there was a hot calibogus and rolls waiting.

'Then what's your tally now, your honor?' Gindler mumbled.

'A long story, Jasper, very long – but Sir Thomas Kydd is what folk must call me now.'

'And a frigate captain, it seems.'

'Another long yarn but this is the borrowed article. A ship-of-the-line is my usual address.'

'Good God, Tom – but you've done damnation well for yourself!'

'As I own that I've been fortunate beyond the ordinary, Jasper,' he said uncomfortably. 'And yourself?'

'Ah. In a small navy that hasn't grown in a dog's age, politicking on all sides, which I refuse to be part of – this is why I'm still a lieutenant and on the beach.'

Kydd felt the bitterness of his words and tried to sympathise. 'Once this unpleasantness is put aside, I'll wager the first thing your president will see to is a navy worth the name as will never have you in this—'

'You think I'm a fool, coming at you like I did.'

'No, Jasper, I don't. I see an honourable man doing what he must for his country. We've been taught by the Danes what to do with gunboats, but you're not to know that. I'm sorry.'

'Tom – sir. I regret this war exceedingly, a more foolish, hare-brained enterprise I've yet to hear of. But, dear friend, my duty is to my country, you'll surely understand.'

'I do, Jasper.' He hesitated, then said, 'And you must understand that, for now, I must go through the motions of making you my prisoner. Here in my cabin, of course, old friend. But a sentry on the door and so forth.'

'You have to do it. This I understand, Tom.' He gave a boyish grin and held out both his wrists. 'Manacle away!'

'Nothing like that,' Kydd said, in embarrassment. 'Pardon me if we must part for now but I've a mort of things to attend to. If there's anything you need, ring the silver bell.' He left quickly and Gindler heard a brief mumble of voices outside and found he was left alone.

Chapter 16

Still weak with reaction Gindler took an armchair and closed his eyes.

With *Tyger* off the rocks and a sound hull she'd be heading for Halifax within the hour – and to his imprisonment as a prisoner-of-war. There was little he could do about it, but he knew from those days past that Kydd was true north and would regretfully but firmly hand him over.

The same remorseless logic dictated that he should do his duty by his country first. After all these years they were friends still, he was happy to find, but this could not be allowed to take precedence over duty. If he saw a seacock unattended he knew he must open it and sink the ship – Kydd's ship. It was unlikely to come to that but . . . if he could try for one last time to rouse the militia before they re-floated he would do it.

So – he must escape. And betray his friend's trust? If it had come to that, so be it.

Energised with the resolution he sat up. Kydd's servant was in courtesy elsewhere. No one other than Kydd was expected to enter his private quarters. On the other hand there was an armed sentry outside the only door forward, leaving him to his privacy – and at the same time confinement.

He remembered the bedplace with its eighteen-pounder long gun hauled inboard and secured. His heart beat faster: where there was a cannon there would necessarily be a gun-port, a prime escape route.

Then his pulse slowed. If he was discovered missing it wouldn't take long to discover how, and the boats on row-guard would be alerted. Then how could he conceal his exit?

It would be dark soon. That must count for something, but what? In a flash of inspiration he realised how it could be done.

Ships varied little in their construction evolved over the centuries, and Gindler knew what he was looking for: the captain's stores locker, a secure place safeguarded by the sanctity of his cabin, a trapdoor set into the deck to a compartment below.

He swung it open and grunted in satisfaction. A vertical ladder led to racks of condiments, spices, bottled delicacies and, of course, at the base, the coolest part, cases of wine.

Not wasting a moment, he pulled over a wooden chair by its leg and scrambling down the ladder at the last moment threw it across the cabin with a loud clatter, swiftly pulling the trapdoor over him.

With a fierce grin he heard the hurried footsteps of the sentry entering, a few moments of bewilderment, then urgent shouts as he left. Others came crowding into the cabin, muffled cries of anger turning to puzzlement, more hails with random scrapes and bangs as a furious search was conducted.

He clung to the ladder, at length hearing the bedlam subside and a commanding voice shouting an order. Then all fell quiet.

99

It was working! He grinned again as he pictured their astonishment and incomprehension as they tried to make sense of what had happened. The stern windows would all be shut, no gun-ports tampered with, yet Lieutenant Gindler had made an escape from his locked cage. He pitied the sentry, for it was the only rational conclusion that in some way he'd passed the man on his way out. They must by now be putting the rest of the ship to a search.

And he had a priceless reward: with his proven absence from the captain's cabin it was the one place that would not be searched, and with Kydd on the upper deck somewhere in a place of command at this time, he would not be going below to his cabin to rest.

He lifted the trapdoor a fraction and listened. Only far-off shouts and the thump of feet.

Easing himself up, he carefully closed it. If there was any time to make his break it would occur while attention was focused within the ship. Now.

He'd hurry to the bedplace, un-reeve the training tackle from the rear of the gun and free the gun-port lid – but he hesitated. Even though it was a foolish move he took off the clothing Kydd had generously lent him and, laying it neatly on the bed, hastily put on his own damp gear. At least Kydd's clothes would be spared a soaking.

He passed one end of the training tackle line around a trunnion and rapidly pulled it through to match the length of the other. It was twilight outside and he eased the gun-port lid upward without securing it. He was in luck – this far aft was where the swell of the counter partially hid his exit. Silently letting the two-piece rope out of the port until it hung suspended from the gun trunnion, he eased his legs through and rotated, clinging to the doubled line until he met the water, cold and spiteful. Wryly he reflected that this was as Kydd must have found when he made his courageous one-man attack on the French privateer those years ago.

Once fully in, he pulled at one side of the doubled line until it unravelled from the trunnion and slithered down. He let it go, hearing the gun-port lid thump home above him. There was now no trace of how he'd made his escape.

With an unhurried breaststroke he disappeared into the gloom.

Chapter 17

'Well, look who it ain't!' The taphouse fell silent at the appearance of the bedraggled figure.

'Mr Gindler!' shrieked Annie, running to him. 'I was so worried about you. You're back!'

'An' lost the fight!' chortled one toper. They'd heard about the attempt from one of those who had fled the other boat, and weren't about to let it rest.

'Pay no mind to 'em.' Annie snorted. 'At least you gave it a try – not like these rats, skulking away while y' took the war right to the English.'

Another said lazily, 'What you goin' to do, Mr Lootenant, now you hasn't boats nor sailor swabs?'

Gindler glared at them. 'As you should be ashamed of yourselves, you useless farmers. What would old George Washington make of you? Too damned slothful to defend your own soil against—'

A thick-set man crashed to his feet and waved his pot at Gindler. 'Watch yer words, cully! This here is Madison's war, not ours, an' I'll thank you to keep your Republican opinions to y'rself!'

'Yeah! Hear him!'

Annie leaped to her feet and shook her fist passionately. 'Leave him be, you varmints. If we're going to win this war, he's the one who's goin' to show us the way.'

'Oh, yeah? What's he goin' to do next? Pull the bung on every English battleship as lines up agin' us?'

The hilarity spread until the taphouse was in a general uproar.

Gindler, sitting with his pot, turned dangerously white and waited for the mirth and cat-calls to subside, then stood up suddenly. By degrees the room fell quiet while he pointedly stalked out.

With a murmur of disquiet there was a general movement to see where he'd gone.

He was standing alone in the early darkness, a supernal calmness in his expression. He turned to the crowd that spilled out of the tavern and raised his gaze to the flag that flew above. The flag of the United States of America. Reaching up he plucked the staff free and faced them.

'I take the "Stars and Stripes" – and I will not rest until I plant it on an English quarterdeck. If I die in the attempt that's my destiny – but I'd happily go to my fate if it's in the company of countrymen of like patriotism. I go now! If there's noble hearts who will be at my side, let history record their names.'

With the utmost dignity he turned and began marching – nobly, pathetically, alone.

'I'm with you!' cried Annie, racing to be by his side. 'Give me the flag. You're done for.'

Gindler surrendered the honour and the girl proudly accepted, bearing the Stars and Stripes to the fore while, gloriously, men hurried to fall in behind the flag and numbers swelled.

More and more – some with flintlocks, others with hay-forks. From the ranks a familiar refrain sounded:

> '*To meet Britannia's hostile bands*
> *We'll march, our heroes say, sir,*
> *We'll join all hearts, we'll join all hands;*
> *Brave boys we'll win the day, sir.*
>
> '*Yankee doodle, strike your tents,*
> *Yankee doodle dandy,*
> *Yankee doodle, march away,*
> *And do your parts right handy.*
>
> '*For long we've borne with British pride,*
> *And su'd to gain our rights, sir;*
> *All other methods have been tried;*
> *There's nought remains but fight, sir.*
>
> '*Yankee doodle, march away,*
> *Yankee doodle dandy,*
> *Yankee doodle, fight brave boys,*
> *The thing will work right handy.*'

It lasted until they were deep in the scrubby woodland, still some miles to go.

'We halt,' ordered Gindler, near delirious with fatigue.

Their numbers continued to increase as the news of their mission spread out across the land, and he later woke to find his force in the hundreds.

'On your feet, heroes!'

It was still in the dark of the night when they staggered upright to press on – they had to, in order to take position behind the ridge before dawn or be picked off as they did so in daylight.

Gindler held one objective above all others. He'd seen all he needed of *Tyger*'s plight and knew she had to come off at the top of the tide, soon after sunrise. If she missed that tide the ship would be pinioned by the rocks for another twelve hours and by then Major Harper's raising of an alarm must bring results. Delay – that alone would seal the vessel's fate.

'Nearly there, Mr Gindler,' Annie prompted softly.

In the half-light at the break of day he thought he could make out the mast and spars of the frigate above the woodland and halted the band. 'Not a sound. Hunker down behind the ridge you'll see ahead and load up. As soon as the crew get going in daylight I want you to let fly, send 'em back below decks. If they can't shift their stores overboard they can't get the barky to float. Signal to be my opening shot. Understood?'

The company crept up to the ridge, in awe of the massive man-o'-war less than a hundred yards distant, heeling to seaward and unmoving, her colours barely lifting in the still dawn air.

Faintly over the cool morning came the piercing sound of boatswain's calls and men started to come out on deck.

Chapter 18

Kydd was still fully dressed, having fitfully dozed in a chair, when worry and futile thoughts had let him, but with the boatswain's calls cutting through, he roused himself and went out to join the men. There was no need to drive them: every one of them was aware of their grave situation and would put in the utmost effort to free *Tyger*.

He knew what he had to do: watch the tide like a hawk, and when it reached its highest point, order all hands to heave in at the capstan on the warps secured to the kedge, sheet anchors out in deeper waters, and pray that enough weight had been shifted to set *Tyger* free. If it had not, he must get rid of the guns without a moment's delay – and all that gave point to the character and purpose of a man-o'-war. Then a tail-between-the-legs return to Halifax and—

A single musket shot rang out. Kydd registered that it came from the ridge inshore, the puff of smoke drifting upwards in the morning stillness betraying its position in the centre. Then the entire length of the ridge opened up in a blazing volley of musketry.

'Down!' bellowed Kydd. The very worst had happened –

the American commander had saved his fire until now, high water, knowing that if he drove Kydd's men from their posts there could be no attempt at pulling the ship off. An intelligent, professional move.

Mercifully the ship was canted over to seaward – if it had been towards the shore not a soul could have lived on her bare decks.

The thuds of bullets against her naked hull were like a hailstorm of venom, allowing none to stand upright. Kydd's mind scrabbled for a course that would take them clear of peril but there was none he could see.

How to stop the deadly fusillade just for the time needed to haul off? If they were prevented from this, *Tyger* was destined for capture.

There was one small mercy. If the Yankees had artillery of any kind they could in a very short time hole the ship but it would have been brought into play from the first.

'Sir?' a hard voice growled by his elbow.

'Yes, Mr Stirk?'

'Our guns. Why doesn't we—'

'I've considered that. We can't depress enough to reach 'em.' The canting deck that was saving them from direct fire was now working against them.

'I was a-sayin' that a broadside at thirty yards might send 'em flying f'r the hills like good 'uns.'

These country folk would never have seen or conceived of the raw fury of a warship's broadside at close quarters – it just might work.

'Toby – the pieces are loaded. Get the gun-captains out of sight with their lanyard high and on my command . . .'

With a thunderous crash, and billowing gun-smoke pierced with stabs of flame, the fierce howl of eighteen-pounder shot fell on the attackers. The pop-pop of muskets ceased instantly and Kydd saw agitated movements ashore. Was it a success? If measured by the number of muskets still in play it seemed it was.

Inland a trumpet bayed, and again, the same tune. Were they fleeing?

Then once more the single musket opened fire, in the same place in the centre of the ridge. Two or three shots later it was joined by others and later more. Within minutes they were under the same attack as before.

Kydd's heart sank. He couldn't in all mercy order his men to reload – they would be cut down as they plied their rammers and cartridges. Any idea of jettisoning their guns was now a lost cause and, with this last act to refloat denied him, there was nothing left but . . .

'Bejabers! Sir – it's *Rattler*!' called one seaman, down on the deck full-length by the hatch coaming. The sloop under cautious sail was edging into view from around the far point, a breath-taking relief.

'He heard our broadside and came a-looking,' Bowden threw, from where he was hunkered down in the lee of the thick bulwark.

Kydd's spirits rose. He slid down the deck to the seaward bulwark, out of the storm of musket shot and watched as *Rattler* took in the situation. While closing on *Tyger* she opened up with a thunder of carronades. The musketry fell away at once as the ridge was swept by canister, hundreds of musket balls sleeting in on target.

'Sir Thomas,' hailed Poole, with a speaking trumpet from *Rattler*'s quarterdeck, his anxiety plain. 'How may I help?'

Kydd thought furiously. But as each idea presented itself he saw difficulties. It would not be practical to think he could now jettison his guns under cover of *Rattler*'s fire – there would be only so many salvoes of canister in her magazines, not nearly enough to last the hour or so needed to lever the guns out. Neither was it worth thinking of towing off the big frigate, not by the little brig-sloop, and in any case the men on her would suffer more while they were laying out the tow because they hadn't the canting of a deck to conceal themselves.

Even wilder schemes passed through his mind but an inevitable conclusion made its way to the fore. It was only a matter of small time that an artillery piece would be brought up. Just needing a couple of horses to haul it, and another for the limber of ammunition, it could in short order render *Tyger* hopelessly unseaworthy with shots into her hull.

The frigate was as good as done for, finished, no longer defensible. Or worth the sacrifice of valuable lives in forlorn schemes.

Tyger. To lay her bones here after what they'd been through together! It was the cruellest of fortunes and tore at his reason. However, one thing was certain: he was not about to let her crew share the same fate.

'Captain Poole. The vessel is fast aground and that on shale and rock and may not be recovered. I desire, therefore, that she be evacuated. All boats conformable to safety under cover of your canister.'

'Aye aye, sir.'

Rattler closed as near as she dared and swung out her boats, her carronades blasting past along the ridge length-wise, with *Tyger*'s men hauling in and manning what boats were left to the frigate after the sudden chaos of assault.

'The Tygers, ahoy – abandon ship! All hands – abandon ship!'

There was nothing more he could do for them now, but his eyes stung in unfathomable grief as her ship's company tumbled into the boats with their pathetic bundles of possessions and pushed off for *Rattler.*

Chapter 19

'Cease firing!' shouted Gindler. 'Stay down. The barky is ours, damn it! Let 'em go, and afterwards we'll take the carcass for ourselves.' There was no way he would admit that the real reason was to cease the blood-letting on both sides when there was no longer any reason for it.

Growls and low cheers met his words. At the Blue Goose later there would be a famous celebration. All they had to do was wait a little longer.

Chapter 20

Kydd blinked until the tears passed, then looked about. 'Mr Stirk?' he called softly to the big man, as he emerged from the hatchway, his earrings glittering, an inevitable bandanna around his head.

'Aye, sir?'

'I've a last duty, as needs your help.'

At first Stirk said nothing, his black eyes sombre. Then he muttered gruffly, 'You're t' fire the old lady.'

'I am. I needs you to set the makings over the fore magazine. When the ship's clear of men I'll touch it off.'

'You, sir? Y'r own ship?'

'Yes, Toby,' Kydd said quietly. 'It has to be done.' The thought of *Tyger* under a foreign flag – an enemy flag – was too much to bear. 'But before I do, I need to know all her company has quit her.'

Without a word Stirk slipped away, leaving Kydd to his thoughts.

Oddly, there was barely a shot from behind the ridge, even at the stream of boats pulling briskly between the two ships, and by degrees the press of men on the frigate's deck diminished.

Some little time later Stirk slithered up beside Kydd. 'Ship cleared o' men, sir. An' I'll get the last boat alongside ready f'r ye when you've—'

'Thank you, Toby. I'll do it now.'

With a lump in his throat, Kydd made his way forward and down the well-remembered fore-hatchway to its base where he saw Stirk had piled inflammables over more substantial materials. A lanthorn had been left next to it and all he had to do was open its panes to let its flames flare and catch – and bring with it the death of his dear *Tyger*.

In rough motions he did what he had to, knowing that if he hesitated for a moment he'd be unable to continue.

The flames leaped up, fed by the train oil that had been sprinkled liberally about, and he saw it well under way before resuming the deck, tears streaking his face.

'Boat's ready,' Stirk said, touching his forelock in salute, something he'd never do in normal circumstances, and Kydd gravely returned the gesture. He turned to leave – but then stopped. With something approaching a visceral hatred he stood tall to take in a last sight of the wretches who had condemned his *Tyger* to this.

Chapter 21

'They've near all gone,' Gindler declared, with satisfaction. 'Nye, take some men and get hold of that pinnace.' It was one of the English boats set adrift, now aimlessly nuzzling the foreshore. He'd use it to board the frigate and claim her as a prize of battle. Obediently Meikeljohn gathered his men and loped off to secure it.

Up and down the ridge prone figures were now recovering their boldness, for they knew the two-master wouldn't bother lingering to fire at them.

But then further along the line one of the men gave a satisfied grunt at something he saw. 'I'm a-goin' to get me an English officer first, friend.'

It was Quincy Jackson, the winning sharpshooter from the fair, and his cross-legged sitting position and burnished long rifle owed much to his long days hunting.

He raised his gun, sighted quickly, then carefully squeezed off the shot.

'Dang me an' I dropped the bastard in one, Ferdie!'

Chapter 22

'Don't show y'self so, Mr Kydd,' implored Stirk – but it was too late. With a meaty smack and pain-wrenched cry Kydd had been flung backwards, rolling to the scuppers where he lay, writhing in spasms of agony.

'Tom!' gasped Stirk, slithering down to him. 'Where's you hit, mate?'

Kydd turned his head back and forth wildly as he tried to control the pain. Ominously a puddle of blood began rapidly collecting under him, a serious or perhaps mortal wound. Stirk scrabbled to locate it but Kydd's lower body was quickly encrusted with blood, dark and shining. Tenderly he explored the area, finding a long tear in his outside thigh instead of a neat hole, scarlet pulsing visibly from it.

'Toby . . . get . . . away,' Kydd said, through clenched teeth, his eyes rolling uncontrollably. 'She'll . . . blow . . . soon.'

'Stay still, cuffin,' Stirk retorted, tearing off his bandanna. 'Not lookin' s' good,' he muttered, as he peered at the torn flesh and began doggedly binding it. The tear ended abruptly and it was obvious the bullet was still in there.

'T-tell . . . Seph . . . I . . . tried,' Kydd gasped.

'Who's that, mate?' Stirk leaned closer to hear.

'P-Persephone, Toby. T-tell her . . .' But Kydd was losing his grip on the world.

'I will, Tom, I will that, mate.'

Kydd's body twitched and tensed, then fell limp.

Gulping, Stirk cradled him but gradually became conscious of figures looming over them.

'Prisoners, sir?' a hard Yankee voice came.

Stirk twisted up to see them and snarled viciously, 'God rot y'r bones an' ye've slaughtered the most true-hearted cap'n that ever trod a deck!'

Gindler dropped to his knee beside him. 'Does he live, still?' he asked softly.

'What do ye care, y' Yankee murderer?' Stirk spat, clutching Kydd tighter, then put his ear to Kydd's chest. 'As he ain't long f'r this world,' he choked.

'Sir.' The first voice was insistent. 'Take 'em prisoners? Show 'em in a cage, like, in Trowton?'

'No,' Gindler said, with infinite sadness. 'We let him die with his countrymen.'

Stirk hesitated, then said gruffly, 'An' as ye show charity to him, I'll even up the score.'

He looked up steadily at the grouped figures. 'If ye wants t' save y'r skins, get off the ship an' don't look back. There's a fire atop the fore magazine as will blow y'all to kingdom come, and that right soon.'

Chapter 23

Aboard Rattler

'Clear these men away, if you please, Mr Poole,' Hollett, *Rattler*'s surgeon said testily. The still form of Sir Thomas Kydd was laid out on the upper deck of the brig and *Tyger*'s crew had gathered round to catch a glimpse of their wounded commander.

Space was made and Hollett got to work. The wound was all too apparent, a ragged tear in the breeches in the outer thigh extending as a full eight inches of ploughed flesh before it stopped abruptly to continue its hidden path into the body. Hollett tentatively pressed around the ugly hole, watching Kydd as he did so, but to no effect. He searched for an exit wound but found none – the bullet was still inside him. A speculum at the mouth showed Kydd still breathing in shallow gasps and a weak pulse was detected.

Hollett got to his feet, shaking his head sadly. 'I do most regretfully fear that the life of this distinguished officer must soon meet its end, gentlemen.'

Waiting for the horrified gasps to die away he added

self-importantly, 'The missile is too deep and we may be sure it has carried with it noxious particles into the flesh, to end in the corruption of sphacelus, which is invariably fatal. Loblolly boys, do carry Sir Thomas down to the cockpit for—'

'Belay that, you two,' Poole snapped. 'My cabin. If he's going to give up the ghost, a man like he deserves a better place for it.'

The two men lifted the litter awkwardly, causing Kydd to give an agonised whimper. Stirk pushed forward angrily and thrust himself into place at the front end. 'Out of it, ye cow-handed looby,' he snarled at the outraged loblolly boy, and gently steered the litter down the companionway into the captain's great cabin.

'You,' he barked at the servant hovering at the door. 'Rig the captain's cot. Now, blast y'r eyes!'

'Not at all, you ignoramus,' Hollett said, with venom, appearing suddenly from behind him. 'Anyone who knows their Paracelsus from a pilchard comprehends the need first to dress the wound. Kindly leave.'

Stirk tensed, advancing on the older man menacingly. 'If all the pintle-taggers in the fleet lined up together t' tell me that kind o' catblash I'd give 'em the same answer – I'm stayin'!'

'Very w-well. Do keep out of the way.'

A sponging with oxycrate, a water and vinegar mixture tinged with wine, left the flesh beneath pale and hideously torn. When the caked blood was washed away and a cataplasm of plant roots and leaves was fixed in place, Stirk tenderly lifted Kydd into the cot and tried to rearrange him. Kydd's eyes rolled and he gave a pitiful mewling now and then.

Stirk had seen many gunshot wounds but none that had resulted in a strong man being reduced to . . . this. Some had made light of their wounds and recovered in days; others had been bright and fettlesome but then had, with a weak cough, lain back and expired. That Kydd had been given such a protracted end was particularly distressing, and with a sinking heart he did what he could for his shipmate.

'Mr Hollett, how's he doing?' The question came from a dozen voices as the surgeon entered the gunroom where the officers were taking their supper.

The man wore a grave expression and didn't speak until he'd assumed his chair.

'Doctor, Sir Thomas – is he any better?'

'Gentlemen, I've already given my opinion. If nature takes its course as it will, I should expect life to be extinct at best some three, four days hence.' He helped himself to the baked fish.

'By God, you take your profession coldly, sir,' a lieutenant said, with feeling. 'What we want to know is how Sir Thomas is in himself at this time!'

Hollett raised a languid eyebrow. 'Really, sir, how am I to know? He exhibits syncope to a degree and therefore cannot be expected to communicate.'

'Syncope?'

'A periodic loss of consciousness occasioned by loss of lifeblood. Do light along the greens, if you will.'

Bowden quietly interjected, 'Doctor, I'm exercised to know just why you've made no attempt at removing the bullet. I've heard tell none are seen to survive when it—'

'Then do cease your conjectures, sir. I will tell you. We in the medical field do swear an oath, the foremost part of which is the *primum non nocere*, "First, do no harm." Meaning that the patient is to be respected before considerations touching on an ardent desire to practise our profession according to the latest fashion prevailing. Sir, we have here a perfect exemplar of such. The bullet is at rest within this officer's body at an unknown locus. And given the grievous character of his wound the outcome is therefore fore-ordained. Why then should I inflict the atrocious pain of a bodily rummage for the offending article when he might otherwise be permitted to pass his remaining hours in as much peace as may be allowed?'

'Thank you, Doctor, for taking the trouble to explain your position.'

A morbid silence followed while the gunroom digested the information.

Gunner's mate Stirk kept faithful vigil at Kydd's bedside. Bathing, rearranging coverings where they'd been thrown aside, settling, easing. It was all he could think to do for his old shipmate.

He stayed through the night, occasionally seeing Kydd's eyes open, wide, staring. He'd bathe his captain's forehead and in a low voice carry on with a dit. 'Well, Tom, as I was a-sayin', you should have bin there, cuffin. Ned Doud on one side, Pinto on t'other, both betwaddled t' the gills an' haulin' on the goatskin. Mr Brice sees us, a right good hand is he, tells us sharp-like t' get it off the ship, or . . .'

Kydd's wild look would ease, and his eyes close, and he'd drift back into whatever nightmare he'd briefly left.

In the stiff north-westerly, *Rattler* made Nova Scotia handily. Poole had his gig swung out and in the water before the sloop had come fully to rest.

He was shown into Admiral Warren's office without delay. 'Sir. My news is unhappy indeed. In the course of an engagement in a fog the frigate *Tyger* did become cast ashore.'

'It has been known to happen on this coast, Mr Poole.'

'Taken at the top of the tide she was unable to get off, and when I came upon her she was under attack by the Americans. The only action open to me was to take her people off as they fired the ship, during the course of which her captain was struck with what I fear is a mortal wound.'

Warren stiffened. 'Do you mean to say Sir Thomas Kydd? Where is he now? Speak up, man!'

'He lies in some pain in my cabin. Sir, I believe we have a physician to the fleet?'

'Yes. This is most unwelcome news. You knew Sir Thomas was here on a particular mission?'

'I did, sir.'

'If he fell gloriously against a Yankee frigate it would be something to offer the English public. I don't suppose . . .?'

'No, sir. He was in a river trusting to find some privateers or similar in order to provoke a retaliation.'

'Which was no business of his to undertake. Still, we must make of it what we can. The physician – Professor Dr Norcombe Gibbons as teaches here – I'll rouse him out to give another opinion. Who knows? He might turn the tide on the poor fellow.'

Gibbons boarded within the hour and was gravely welcomed, his two assistants encumbered with chests of instruments. The professor was a slight-built, intense individual with sharp features and wearing plain dress.

'You are very welcome aboard this vessel, sir,' Poole said, with a bow. 'You should be aware that our patient is well known to the public, having—'

'Yes, yes. I shall make examination as I would any other, of course.'

'Oh, and this is our surgeon, Mr Hollett.'

'Ah, Professor Gibbons,' the man said, with an ingratiating smile. 'A distinct pleasure to make your acquaintance sir, even if your visit be brief – the patient will not be overlong in departing from us, I believe.'

With a sharp glance in return, Gibbons replied irritably, 'As I shall make my own judgement in the matter. So where is the patient?'

Kydd's strong face was sallow, ravaged, and he looked curiously shrunken, seemingly not aware of the entry of a stranger.

The site of the wound was now ugly and inflamed, the course of the bullet contused, flecked with green and violet and ominously oozing purulent matter. The livid redness of erysipelas extended far down the leg and had begun a deadly creeping further up the thigh – it appeared that the end was not far off.

Gibbons lightly traced the course of strike from where it had sunk below the skin and stopped at the sight of a barely visible bruise. Palpitating carefully he nodded in satisfaction even as Kydd gave a piteous yelp. He then felt Kydd's forehead, laid his own head lightly on Kydd's chest, listening, and finally delicately sniffed the wound.

'I shall operate.'

'You'll put him under the knife?' Hollett asked, in amazement. 'Sir – the man is due to meet his maker very soon. What good can come of the pain?'

'Is that your opinon?' Gibbons retorted. 'I pity your patients, sir. Can you not see that he has a chance?'

'Really, Professor, your comments are quite uncalled for. Any can see that a probe and bullet-hook to this depth will shock the patient into a wretched stupor and death!'

'Which is why I shall leave those barbarisms for others. For a probe, my longest seton needle will serve, not requiring a dilater as it does, the depth it indicates being a sovereign pointer to where I shall make incision – afresh from the outside – direct to the object to extract.'

'Then I see I'm not wanted.' Hollett snorted and, beckoning to his loblolly boys, departed.

'Everyone to leave, if you please.' Gibbons took off his frock coat and accepted a black smock. 'That means you as well,' he snapped at Stirk.

'I'm not going,' Stirk said doggedly.

'Don't be foolish, fellow. I've got my two assistants who will—'

'I'm stayin' with the captain.'

Gibbons paused, seeing the stubborn resolve in his eyes. 'Well, I suppose another assistant won't harm.' Sizing Stirk up, he added, 'As can be relied on to hold the man steady.'

Poole's polished dinner table was prepared, lanthorns brought and chests opened with their racks of gleaming blades and lethal steel implements.

Kydd lay motionless but his eyes flickered open, steadied and stayed fixed on the skylight above with its promise of sunlight and air. It seemed even a blessed unconsciousness was being denied him.

'I'll have a crow's bill forceps, terebellum, the smaller bistoury knife and . . . and the medium bullet-catcher.' The surgeon's mate deftly produced them and lined them up.

'For now, the longest seton needle.' He leaned over the wound, considering, and instructed that the limb be manipulated to give the same line of travel for the bullet as when Kydd had been struck.

'Hold!' he commanded, and gently began inserting the long needle.

Kydd tensed agonisingly but the three men held him still. Gibbons went further and further. Suddenly Kydd gave a squeal of anguish through his gag as the probe prodded something and Gibbons swiftly withdrew it. He laid it along the outside of the wound channel and at the right point on the skin above drew a small charcoal cross.

The torment was not over, for as Stirk watched, unbelieving, Gibbons inserted his longest finger into the wound, calmly disregarding Kydd's writhing while he felt about, and when he withdrew it said to no one in particular, 'And it's not compound, praise the Lord, but there's something amiss with the bullet.'

He paused, regarding Kydd's pitiful form, then said, in a confident, medical tone, 'Sir Thomas, if you can hear me. You've no splintered bones or similar to compound the wound and I shall now draw the bullet out of you and then you may rest.'

Readying a scalpel he stretched the skin and made an X incision at the charcoal mark. In deft, swift moves he had the glint of silver rapidly under his knife. Kydd contorted and thrashed but was held by straps and the combined weight of three men.

'Forceps,' Gibbons asked levelly and, taking them, he eased them into the bleeding orifice, frowning in concentration as he felt delicately. In a single movement he plucked out the bullet, dropping it with a smart *ting* into a dish.

He picked it up, examining it closely and shook his head.

'I see rag has been driven into the wound. There will be a corruption of the flesh if it is not removed. Do you understand, sir?' But Kydd's eyes were closed in a merciful unconsciousness.

'Quickly, now – oil of terebinth and a number five syringe.' The two assistants were engaged in restoring Kydd's position so he directed the instruction to Stirk, who mutely shook his head.

'What's wrong with you, man? Get a move on or I'll see you disrated as a loblolly.'

'I ain't a loblolly – a gunner's mate only,' Stirk said, in a hoarse whisper, backing away.

A filled syringe was passed over and Gibbons irrigated the bullet passage with a sharp, careful stroke. Among the stinking debris washed out were dark flecks, pieces of Kydd's coat. Another treatment was given and Gibbons stood back, satisfied.

'A difficult one,' he said conversationally, to one of the assistants. 'The locus has a confusion of nerve and tendons. I had my doubts the man could take the shock. It seems he has a chance, even at the hands of that ignorant quacksalver.'

Kydd was gently washed down and dressings made ready.

'Who's to care for this gentleman?' he asked.

'It'll be me,' mumbled Stirk, coming forward.

'You? The man's as good as dead! It needs skill, understanding. I'll send someone more suitable.'

Back ashore, the admiral said sharply, 'How did you find the patient, Professor?'

'As to be expected after his barbarous treatment at the hands of their surgeon, whom I had occasion to chastise in his ignorance, the vain fellow.'

'My meaning was, will he live – or no?'

'Everything depends on the next few weeks, sir, and the diligent ministrations of his nurse.'

'To hospital, then?'

'To be candid, sir, in cases of healing and recovery it is often to be recommended that the patient be suffered to remain on his ship, where it's both healthier in the sea air and more congenial to the patient to remain in familiar surroundings. You may choose, sir.'

'Hmm. If I allow that it would be of convenience should Sir Thomas be conveyed to England without delay, can you say that he might survive the experience?'

'With the same reservations, there is a chance.'

'Very well. It's of no moment to me whether my dispatches are taken to their lordships by cutter or brig-sloop, so I shall send *Rattler* to England in place of the usual dispatch vessel – bearing in her the person of Sir Thomas Kydd.'

'Quite. A small suggestion.'

'Yes, Professor?'

'I would advise that if you value his arriving *in corpore sano* let another surgeon be appointed. I have in mind a student of mine who would think it a fine thing to make visit to England to extend his medical acquaintance in return for the temporary post.'

'Very well. Flags – make it so.'

Chapter 24

HMS *Rattler* put to sea in the teeth of a seasonal north-easterly, her mainsails double-reefed and four men on the helm. In her captain's cot lay Sir Thomas Kydd, still unconscious. Rigged fore and aft, it took care of the ship's rolling but did little for the pitching.

Rollins, the young student-cum-surgeon, gamely tried to stay at his post but after giving Stirk a steer on treatments was sent away until he'd gained his sea-legs.

On a rack among Poole's personal effects there was a row of bottles and packets and Stirk tried to remember what he'd been told.

Apparently it was of prime importance to keep the wound clean. Bathing in Ægyptiacum (brown liquid in red-labelled bottle) as a detersive and oil of turpentine (green label) as an eschar. Whatever that jabberknowl meant, he knew his duty. He was also instructed about the tube that lay under the lint pledgets covering the injured area. It was there to drain the wound but his task was to smell it – if it exuded pus that stank, that was bad. If it did not, it would be rated laudable pus and all might rejoice.

Along with Binard he was the only Tyger aboard, the others being left stranded in Halifax facing an uncertain future. The duty was not onerous, and in any event it was what he would do for any stricken shipmate. But this was for Kydd – Tom Cutlass, risen from being part of his own gun crew through all the thickets and mires of interest and preferment to the lost-to-sight eminence of senior post-captain.

Stirk had inspected the fatal bullet closely. It was grossly misshapen, swollen out to near double its calibre, the reason for the grievous wound passage. He knew why: this was a pure lead bullet, not stiffened with antimony as were military rounds. A hunter's bullet, with its ready expansion on impact, designed to inflict a serious wound with its inevitable blood loss that would cause a creature to stumble and fall. What kind of soldier was wielding this sort of weapon?

Days passed. Kydd's eyes were increasingly open, staring up, his face empty of expression. Stirk got no response to his cheery greeting. Was Kydd slowly sinking?

On the upper deck there was the brave sight of blue seas and white billows to hearten sailors who'd endured icy gales. And below, in his cot, Kydd endured.

Suddenly his eyes stared upward, his face contorted, and a single agonised word sounded above the rush of seas. '*Tyger!*' It was as if it had been wrenched from the depths of his being, loud and hoarse.

'Yes, mate?'

This time Kydd turned to Stirk, with tortured eyes that tore at his senses.

'*Tygerrr!* She's lost to us! Lost!' He gulped, convulsively gripping his blanket.

'Aye, Tom, that she is. But she did us proud, you has t' say.'

'She always would, though – wouldn't she?' Stirk bent over to hear the words, not much above a whisper. But Kydd was speaking now and he didn't care what was being said.

'A right dimber barky, that's f'r sure.'

'And I killed her! I killed her! With my hands, I sent her to hell with powder and fire!' he sobbed, looking at Stirk with eyes that pleaded for understanding.

'No, y' didn't, cuffin! Why, I wouldn't leave a dog t' die in misery if I had it in m' power to end it quick, like.'

Kydd stared at him for long seconds, then said, more steadily, 'Thank you, Toby, d-dear fellow.' He took a deep, gulping breath but another storm broke. 'She'd not be on the reef in the first place if I hadn't trusted that traitorous girl!'

'You had to, we not havin' a pilot as we had in the first 'un. An' she can't be a traitor if'n she was a-doin' it for her country.'

Stirk smoothed out the bedclothes and found his bathing cloth, feeling the feverish heat under his hands, but he could tell that Kydd was fighting for sanity and an emergence back into the world he knew.

'But who's complaining, b' God? We all got off an' away. Loss o' the ship? Why, if'n ye counts up the number o' other ships we lost on the rocks—'

'Thank you, Toby,' Kydd said, with an effort. 'Do leave me now, m' friend. I've a mort o' thinking to do.'

Dr Rollins was feeling better. No longer helpless with seasickness, he was often seen below on some errand of curiosity so it took Stirk time to find him and let him know of developments.

'All is not secure for the future. We've yet to see some laudable pus or any sign of incarning.'

'Incarning?'

'New fresh sweet flesh growing to fill the wound. But from what you've told me he has a harder battle to fight. First the body must be healed and then the spirit. With the flesh and blood we can ply our small skills sometimes to wonderful effect but wounds of the spirit are less amenable to our medicine.'

Stirk blinked in perplexity. 'Our Tom Cutlass is a hard horse, y' knows. I don't reckon he'd be troubled by a sight o' blood or such.'

'Believe me, it's got naught to do with how gallant or unyielding our man might be. If the nature of the peril touches him then he will suffer in ways we cannot know. Your Tom Cutlass has been made in an instant to take pain and suffering on an inhuman scale. He's been standing within a pace of entering death's door and he would know it, and it seems the experience has touched him in some unspeakable way – whether for all of the time on earth remaining to him or until it passes from him, medicine cannot tell.'

'So—'

'We stand by his side as he battles – and be prepared to forgive if his spirits are disordered and he turns on those who care most about him.'

Stirk nodded dumbly. He was out of his depth in these waters.

Rollins turned grave, his voice low. 'But only if he knows there are those about him who will stand by him, whatever assails his being, will he have a chance to mend and be restored.'

Chapter 25

Kydd's mind was clearing, rising above the depths of pain and despair that had cruelly seized him as he drifted in and out of consciousness.

He was taking in the world around him. This must be *Rattler*'s cabin, her captain's quarters. And the excruciating bar of pain down his side must be the wound he'd suffered when . . .

In disjointed flashes of memory, he put together what he could remember of those last hours of *Tyger*, now lost to him and them all. At his hand! A surge of grief threatened to unman him at the thought of her ashen carcass, a smoking ruin that no more would know Neptune's kiss as she won the open ocean, outward bound. She was now dead – but he was alive . . .

An almost unendurable spasm of pain clutched at him as he tried to ease his position and he cried out, bringing a worried Stirk to his side.

'What's t' do, mate?' he asked, smoothing the bedclothes as best he could. 'Can I . . .?'

'No, Toby. It just took me . . . no warning.' He tried to smile, to shrug it off.

He would always remember Stirk by him as he'd writhed under the knife, waking up in the night with mortal dreads, retching into a pan. He'd never forget what he'd done for him in his ordeal.

Kydd lay back, wincing again, and let the thoughts invade his mind. One stood out, demanded he notice, take it into his new world of pain and helplessness. He was no longer invincible, immune to the worst the foe could do.

He'd long ago come to terms with the notion that in a man-o'-war it was as much the duty of the enemy to kill him as it was his to do the same to them, and he'd faced the heat of battle with an acceptance of such that had become unthinking over the years. His successes and occasional failures had involved the malice of the enemy actually reaching out and touching him, and now he had been – without warning and in a single moment – thrown into this pit of agony. He was no coward but reason couldn't save him from the prospect that in the future he might shrink away when he found himself once more standing before an enemy.

It was a disturbing realisation.

Could he maintain for ever the image of a fearless commander in front of a warship's company as they closed with their foe? If not, what use was he on the quarterdeck? Would he – Heaven forbid – break down before them?

More thoughts crowded in.

It might not be over. He'd known others with such a wound as his go on to develop infections – gangrene even, which would mean at best an amputation of his leg, at worst a squalid death. As it was he stood a chance of that – especially with the unusually deep and tissue-gouging bullet that had struck him, of remaining a cripple for the rest of his life. And with a seagoing command then obviously not to be offered, it had to be a life of pointless existence on land.

And in a creeping realisation he had to face an even worse future: as an object of pity for Persephone, shackled to him, half a man who in company she would be making excuses for throughout the rest of his life. Or would her love simply fade and die, as she found herself no longer seeing in him the man she'd married?

Misery returned, but an inner voice reasoned. Better not to dwell on things out of his power to do anything about, to concentrate instead on . . .

He'd almost overlooked it. There was one thing more he had to face. As soon as he recovered sufficiently there was waiting for him a stern naval tradition – an accounting for the loss of one of His Majesty's Ships of War in unexplained circumstances.

First, a court of inquiry, which would make judgement on his actions at the time. If deemed inappropriate or negligent this would be followed by a full-dress court-martial, a public spectacle with unlimited powers. If found guilty he could find himself at the least cashiered from the Royal Navy in disgrace. And, frankly, there was much that a court of crusty and hostile admirals could find questionable in the events of that day.

Chilled, he knew he was looking at a monumental change in his fortunes that made the simple recovery from a wound a distraction only.

Stirk came again, pleased at his progress but puzzled at his lack of spirit. Kydd knew that this was nothing the honest foremast hand could help with, and determined to spare him the worry. 'Sorry to be such a burden, Toby. You see, I'm in a hurry to get up and about, on deck – you know what I mean, old fellow.'

Stirk's face cleared. Of course he knew what was meant and he'd have a word with Dr Rollins to see what could be done.

Rollins was cautiously optimistic and declared that Kydd might in some days' time sit in a chair on deck, provided the progress of the wound was satisfactory, but Kydd had other ideas.

'Toby, could you . . .?'

Three days later a gunroom chair was brought up on deck and Kydd installed in it, to his intense satisfaction. That he was made to have a knee blanket and be tucked in, like any common cripple, was infinitely to be borne for the sheer pleasure of having a keen Atlantic breeze in his face, the sight of the vast blue dome of the sky and the expanse of white combers as far as the eye could see. And be almost part of the watch-on-deck, who snatched glances at him as they went about their work.

Stirk came up bearing what he'd been asked for – *Rattler*'s carpenter had crafted a magnificent pair of crutches, leather shod and with ornate filigree in keeping with an implement worthy of a naval officer.

Kydd took them reverently, knowing the hours it must have taken in their making but then becoming abruptly aware that these very same could be with him for the rest of his life.

'Bear a fist, old chap,' he muttered at Stirk, who heaved him upright, like a child, passing him the crutches.

Kydd took one, positioned it, then the other. It felt fearsomely strange, even held as he was by Stirk, but he was determined to snatch this chance at freedom.

He steadied himself, intending to make for the bitts about the mainmast and ordered, 'Cast off there.'

Stirk hesitantly let go and Kydd took his first tottering steps.

It was a mistake. The familiar heaving of the deck turned into a malicious bucking that toppled him in an instant and sent him sliding helplessly into the scuppers just as Rollins appeared on deck.

'Hold him there!' he shouted, running to Kydd, who was near blinded with pain and writhed uncontrollably, his wound quickly suffusing with blood. 'Get him back below,' he commanded, after a hasty look at the result.

Out of sight of the deck he rounded on Stirk. 'You blind fool – he's not in any condition to stand, let alone walk!'

There would be no more attempts at freedom.

Chapter 26

England appeared in the form of the Lizard, emerging every so often from the grey misery of constant drizzle and rain-squalls from the south-east. It was a not unfamiliar vista for Kydd but now it had a quite different meaning: in a very short time he would be face to face with his nightmares.

The brig-sloop humbly made her number to the Mount Wise signal station and took up her moorings in Barn Pool, just as Kydd had done as commander of the sloop *Teazer*. In full-dress uniform Poole lost no time in going ashore to see the admiral with his report and startling news of a wounded hero, but for Kydd there would be no summoning yet to account for himself. In a poignant mix of longing and dread, he wanted only to go home.

'Two carriages, I reckon,' Stirk pronounced: one for Rollins and himself to go on ahead to prepare Lady Kydd, and another, much more sedate, for Kydd under the care of Binard.

The pair set off together, Kydd's conveyance at not much more than walking pace, the other at a smart clip for Knowle Manor. Rollins kept his silence before Stirk, the common seaman.

Their carriage turned into the little driveway and, with a snorting of horses, it ground on up to the front door.

'Thank you – I shall be returning presently,' Rollins told the driver and made to descend, but Stirk caught his arm. 'No, mate. She doesn't know ye, better I tell her first.'

Mrs Appleby primly answered the door. 'Your business, gennelmen?'

'Gunner's mate Stirk come t' see Lady Kydd,' Stirk said gravely, holding his shapeless hat before him.

Persephone appeared behind her. 'Why, Mr Stirk!' she said, clearly delighted to see him, but then she caught something of his manner.

'Please come in, gentlemen.' Her eyes never left them as they entered the little drawing room.

'M' lady, we've come t' tell ye . . . Well, it's like this, an' I can't put it any easier for ye . . .'

'It's Thomas, isn't it?' she blurted, her hand flying to her mouth, her voice shrill. 'He's – he's—'

'No, m'lady, he ain't. Just comin' behind in another carriage, slow like, seein' as how he's taken such a knock.'

As white as a sheet, she sat suddenly. 'Tell me! For God's sake, tell me all of it!'

'Well, we's on the Ameriky coast, see, and—'

'I'll explain, Stirk.' With a bow he introduced himself. 'Dr Rollins, for the nonce surgeon of His Majesty's Sloop *Rattler*, lately of the North American station.'

'Doctor?' Persephone said faintly.

'Yes. It grieves me to tell you that in an engagement with the Americans your husband lost his ship to the rocks and received a bullet wound that can only be described as severe. I'm further distressed to have to tell you that he is by no means recovered and it is not impossible, even at this stage, that an infection might become evident, which would require the removal of his leg. Nor is it out of consideration that lockjaw could intervene with what would normally be held to be mortal consequences.'

She heard it out with rigid control, staring at him as the words penetrated. 'Will he . . .?'

'It is now in the hands of He who disposes of all things, madam.'

'He must be in some pain.' Only a slight tremor in her voice betrayed her feelings.

Rollins gave a sympathetic smile. 'He is, but your diligent attention to his wellbeing will go far in easing his spirits.'

Accepting the offer of tea, he proceeded to deliver detailed instructions for the care and treatment of his patient.

As dusk drew in, Kydd's carriage ground to a halt outside. At the sound of its arrival Persephone ran to it. The men looked away as she wrenched open the door and climbed inside. After an interval she reappeared and, eyes glittering, whispered that her husband would be grateful for a lift into his home.

Stirk and Binard gently carried Kydd to the drawing room. The frigate hero had finally cast anchor in his own home and refuge, and must now begin his new life as he may.

'Well, gentlemen, shall we leave them alone to their reunion?' Rollins said, after a quick check of his patient, and departed quietly with the others.

'Darling!' Persephone said brokenly, and fell to weeping on his chest.

'Seph, dear sweetheart,' Kydd said, wincing with pain. 'How I've missed you!' He couldn't help it and, trying in vain to choke it back, wept as well.

They clung to each other for a long moment and then, with a light kiss, she smoothed his covers and looked at him lovingly and tenderly. 'We'll get you better soon, my love, and then you'll be as good as new,' she said bravely.

'It could be a long time I fear, dearest.'

'But we'll be facing it together,' she said firmly. 'And you mustn't take silly chances, now, will you?'

He turned away, a fleeting despair just visible. 'There's . . . a mort of grief ahead, Seph, believe me.'

'That's why it needs both of us. Now, the good doctor has instructed me well in what I have to do and I shall prepare it all directly.'

It was Kydd's turn to smile bravely. 'Yes, dear. Could you give Stirk a hail? I owe him more than I can say and the least I can do is . . .'

She left to find him but when she returned it was with Binard only, who told him, 'M'sieur Stirk, he leave with the *docteur* back to the ship. Say his job done, now.'

Kydd fell back. So like the bluff seaman – no fuss, whether it was triumph or calamity, as reliable as an iron stanchion and about as talkative.

Chapter 27

Binard and Mr Appleby manhandled the furniture, guided by Mrs Appleby in consultation with Persephone, and new quarters for Kydd were squared away in the drawing room to spare him the stairs. Outside a fine-mown path was made for his twice-daily hobble on crutches around the flower-erbed, and many delicious treats came from the kitchen, deemed to be necessary for an invalid cast up ashore.

One day Kydd opened his morning *Plymouth Dock & Telegraph*. Nestled inside was a familiar column which gleefully reported:

Our doughty spy, Lookout, once again mounts to the crow's nest in his tireless quest for items of value to pique our readers' interest. He raises his powerful glass and begins his search – and spies a lone shadow hobbling up from the Stonehouse Pool. He trains more carefully and sees something familiar about it, a noble and commanding bearing that betokens the presence only of a Hero of England. Can it be? It is! The far-famed Captain Kidd, whose sea exploits this journal has faithfully followed since his celebrated marriage to the beauty of the age, Lady Persephone Lockwood.

But what is this? We farewelled the intrepid Sir Thomas just months ago when he was dispatched to America to teach them a lesson in frigate handling. And now he returns — not to the customary huzzahs from the crowds of adoring spectators but a lonely figure on his way home. Lookout forswears rumour and hearsay and roundly condemns those who maintain that the good captain suffered a reverse at arms at the hands of the Yankees, together with a near-mortal wound that sent him home to the Lady Kidd. What we can allow is that his famous frigate Tyger *is no more, cast up on the rocks for reasons which the Court of Inquiry will no doubt be interested to hear. Other details your loyal scribe will report as they stand revealed.*

It was starting already. The only thing the crowd loves more than a popular hero, Kydd recalled from the court-martial of the conqueror of Buenos Aires, was a popular hero humbled. Even his welcome back by the village had been low-key, but he had put it down to their desire to allow him time to recover.

As his strength returned, he set about preparing his 'defence' – a report of his actions and his own account of the loss of *Tyger* to be forwarded through the port admiral to the Admiralty. Its mere existence would show him to be recovered sufficiently to stand before a court and he should expect to be arraigned soon afterwards.

Several times he thought of Stirk. He'd sent to ask *Rattler* what his situation now was and discovered that as Stirk was not on her muster roll he'd taken the opportunity to disappear without fear of being made a deserter. He could be anywhere. There was a chance they might meet again but possibly they never would.

One morning, Cecilia and Renzi, his sister and his best friend, her husband, breathlessly arrived. A tearful Cecilia inspected his wound, Renzi awkwardly commiserated on his confinement, and both offered their own home and estate for the purposes of convalescence. In the face of the trials of life that lay ahead he wanted to stay in the warmth of Knowle Manor.

Craddock appeared soon afterwards, bearing some very palatable vintages, which he was certain were just what were required to recruit the strength. He sat companionably by the fire with Kydd to hear his troubles, wisely proffering no advice of his own.

Kydd ruefully told him that without a ship he could offer him no position of any kind and, with his own situation so unclear, was unable to make promise of any in the future. Craddock's sympathetic acceptance only deepened Kydd's depression, which now was never far away. Even the joy at his infant son, Francis, wilted as he confronted a future vision of explaining that once upon a time he was a famed frigate captain but now he was no different from anyone else, no longer a hero.

He finished his report and sent it on its way. Almost by return he received a charmingly phrased note from the admiral wishing him a speedy recovery and at the same time enquiring whether he felt up to the disagreeable necessity of a court of inquiry in the near future.

There was little to be gained in putting off the dread day and he replied that he was able to attend at the convenience of the court.

A formal letter some time later informed him that his attendance would be required in five days aboard HMS *Monarch* at anchor in the Hamoaze. The presiding president of the court would be Admiral Winterton and a list of captains attending was appended. Kydd vaguely knew one or two but could see none likely to take against him.

Some naval officers had made many enemies among their peers and had, like Commodore Popham, suffered for it at court-martial. And politics often seemed to be lurking behind expressions of malice. Winterton, however, was an elderly but straight-line officer of the old school and would not wish to unnecessarily prolong the proceedings. But with the Admiralty keeping an ominous silence, the finding could go either way.

Dressed in immaculate full-dress uniform, the star and sash of his knighthood adding splendour to his appearance, he took carriage for Plymouth, and further on at Dock he was delivered to a jetty and waiting boat. With the help of a pair of burly seamen he was deposited in the sternsheets with his crutches and taken out to his fate.

Chapter 28

To Kydd's surprise and gratification his ordeal passed quickly – and he was home for supper. 'Discharged without a stain on my character, Seph! A fine parcel of sailors. Heard my evidence, Poole's deposition, and that of dear old peg-leg Joyce – that's our sailing master – about the hazards of the American shore. The ruling was that in time o' war it might be necessary to take chances in navigating for an important objective. None more so than privateers in that part of the world, you'll agree.'

'That's wonderful, darling! Were there many in attendance?'

'Not so many, it not being a public occasion, m' love. In any wise the Admiralty are saying to the world that *Tyger* was lost as a consequence of casting up on a rocky shore in a fog and light winds without we had fair charts and similar.'

'Yes, dear – as has happened to so many in this war.'

Kydd kept to himself that there was another factor, even more pressing to consider. That was the need, at this time of frigate losses to the Americans, of making clear that this was not the result of enemy action of any kind. The legendary Captain Kydd of *Tyger* had suffered a misfortune that any might encounter and therefore could remain an idol of the public.

And possibly his appearance – a decorated hero with crutches approaching the stand – had excited sympathy and support.

So, he was out from under that particular cloud. His wound was healing, the ligatures removed with no sign of mortification, and he could look to the less obvious support of a stick before long.

It was time to hope – what ship would then be made available to him? *Thunderer* was far from complete in her great repair but it was common knowledge that ships were lying idle for want of men and officers to man them. Kydd was a well-experienced known quantity, his fame as a frigate captain ensuring that volunteers would flock to join any ship he commanded. Would it be a frigate once more then?

Almost in the same thought a cold, betraying dread crept over him. He shrank from it, but it was cruelly insistent. If he was the commander of a frigate it was more than likely he would soon be back in action. Could he stand and face enemy fire knowing that he no longer had the unthinking mystic invincibility that had kept him invulnerable for so many years and countless adventures? That he was as likely to receive his death-blow through the chances of war just as the meanest seaman under him?

It was not the vapourings of a coward: he knew he would do his duty whatever the situation. Instead, it could be summed up in one word: he was flinching.

Whether at the sight of an enemy sail, a decision in the heat of battle or the cold-blooded planning of an expedition, if he shrank back at the prospect, he had lost the edge that had given him victory over the years. He was no longer the daring, thrusting young captain of the ballads. And he would be diminished in the sight of the seamen who fought and died for him, the cruellest cut of all.

This was not something he could talk about with Persephone. Only those who'd actually faced the enemy in war knew what he was talking about. It was his problem and his alone.

Chapter 29

Kydd had been able to move from crutches to a stick, a stout blackthorn with a neat brass ferrule finish at its tip and a broad top. He tried it in the house and on his flowerbed path – it felt odd, the rhythm being so different. 'Dot and carry one' was how he was taught by the wizened attendant at the naval hospital at Stonehouse and he persevered until he was proficient, feeling his body readjust.

The outside world began to lay claim to his attention. Napoleon Bonaparte had retreated from Moscow, his army, a shadow of its former might, had suffered cruelly from the winter weather. Although they were now out of Russia the wily Bonaparte was still able to win battles, the new coalition against him managing to lose engagements for lack of unity and agreement at the highest levels. The emperor had raced back to Paris to rally the nation and, incredibly, was in the process of raising a massive new army.

For England, the war stretched ahead wearisomely for years to come. The country was deeply in debt: sums in the millions were talked about and industrial enterprises starved of investment. Discontent now took the place of patriotic defiance.

It was as different from the eighteenth-century world that Kydd had known in his youth as it was possible to be.

And no offer of a ship came for Kydd.

Quite unexpectedly, however, a missive arrived from the Navy Board. This was unusual – the body that dealt with strategy and senior officer appointments was the Board of Admiralty. The Navy Board concerned itself with day-to-day issues – victuals, dockyards, transport, ordnance and so forth – and would have no other need to correspond with serving and active officers.

The letter was from a Mr Alleyne's secretary. Following a recommendation from the Admiralty it seemed Kydd was peculiarly suited for a post recently created by them – surveyor of projects to the inspector general of Naval Works. In this capacity he was to examine the various inventions, projects, contrivances and novelties that were increasingly exercising the Board, and render an opinion on their practicality from the point of view of an experienced sea officer. He would be entitled to an office and clerks with the Navy Board at Somerset House and could expect an emolument not less than his pay as a post-captain and subsequently a pension.

It was a considerable surprise but there was much to think on. Certainly it would be intriguing work. He'd been much taken by recent developments in industry as they affected his professional life but what did this mean?

The first thing that suggested itself was that his appearance in the court with the aid of crutches had worked against him – in a kindly way. Seeing his disability the powers that be of the Admiralty had shaken their collective heads at the sight and decided his days at sea were over. But instead of the usual arrangement – a generous encomium but reversion to half-pay for the rest of his life – he was being treated very well.

Half-pay was a mechanism that allowed an officer temporarily unemployed at sea to be kept on retainer until a post was open to him, the understanding being that he could take up a sea appointment at short notice. It was a charitable device in the case of a crippled sea officer, but by this letter they had moved themselves to find Kydd a position on full pay with all the respect this commanded.

It was touching but in accepting it Kydd knew that his sea days were finished. This was hard to take for a fighting captain, and the chance for the further glory if he were ever to be elevated to admiral had now gone.

They couldn't be blamed for taking the view that in his present state he would make a sad spectacle of boarding a hostile man-o'-war at the head of his men, sword in hand on a hostile deck.

No, it was better, for Francis's sake, that he make practical arrangement for the future. He'd take the job.

Chapter 30

Washington

In the American republic's capital, the centre of strategics and operations in this second war against the English, things were not going well: repulses all along the Canadian border, the military embarrassed by defeats in the field at the hands of Indian war parties, and the gloss wearing off the early frigate successes at sea contributed to a malaise working against the early enthusiasm for hostilities against the arrogant British.

It was hard for Lieutenant Gindler of the United States Navy. In the time of his country's need he'd been rusticated, denied a place aboard one of the out-numbered ships trying to break the hold of the Royal Navy on the ports and bases along the Atlantic seaboard, so crucial to the survival of the young nation. This was through no fault of his, but the working of the politics that pitted statesmen against each other in heated squabbles about the conduct of the war.

Gindler was making his way up Pennsylvania Avenue to see William Jones, the secretary to the Navy. He'd been selected by the re-elected President Madison to replace the previous, Paul Hamilton, an inebriate of wasted talents who'd been the one to refuse Gindler his destiny. Did he have a better chance with Jones?

It was a long walk but it gave him an opportunity to see how work was progressing on the grand edifices being erected to mark the capital's primacy, some even now occupied by the administration. The grey day and blustery drizzle did nothing to affect the swelling pride he felt to see them – each one the equal of any to be seen in Europe, he'd been told.

Jones saw him at once, moving around his imposing desk to greet him. A dry, abstemious individual, he was the antithesis of the loud and hectoring Hamilton, courteously hearing him out as he made his case. 'I do not deny you have every qualification for sea service, Lootenant. The problem lies in that we've precious few men-o'-war and they're nearly all kept bailed up in harbour by the English. I'd like to see you back at sea, but that would be at the cost of an officer who's won his place by . . . Well, shall we say I can't spring one just for your benefit, sir?' Meaning that all officers were political appointments and it was not worth the effort by Jones just for Gindler's sake. Did not his recent success against the British count for something?

'I wouldn't rely on topping it the hero here in Washington, Lootenant. There's rumours about how the ship ran on the rocks – and didn't they set her afire themselves, without help from you?'

The words were hard but there was no spite in them. The man had no experience of the naval service, his background, he'd heard, that of a merchant trading with Europe who'd lost much to the English. 'That's true enough, sir, but my purpose is to stand against the enemy however I may. I know them, and 'twould be a folly to underestimate their ability to choke off our commerce at will.'

Jones looked up sharply. 'You a New Englander, sir?'

'Connecticut, Westbrook.'

'I thought so. You're a Federalist, then.'

Gindler had never indulged in politics, the vacuity of its posturings annoying him, but at the same time he knew that almost all of the long-established families of the region detested what they called 'Mr Madison's War' and all it stood for, and supported the opposition Federalists.

'Never, sir. Or Republican. Stars 'n' Stripes says it all for me.' He knew, though, that he'd betrayed himself from the start to this Republican nominee by mentioning the economic cost of the war – a patriot of the Republican sort would rant about the impressment of seamen or the stopping of neutrals on the high seas.

Unexpectedly, Jones gave a snort of humour and clapped him on the shoulder.

'You're my kind o' man, Gindler. I can see right through you – and I like what I see. Leave it to me, and if there's any kind o' placing I'll let you know. Stay about for a few days, yes?'

Out on the broad avenue again, in spite of the grey drizzle, the world seemed brighter. If there was any kind of situation at sea he knew he'd have Jones to thank for it. But for now there were still feelings of intense frustration that he was doing nothing to defend what he believed was right.

In effect, he was putting himself forward to meet the Royal Navy face to face in the field, the most battle-hardened and legendary sea service in the world. Stretched as they were by the need to bring down Napoleon Bonaparte, they would eventually turn on the infant United States and wreak deadly havoc. Then he would be ready to answer his country's call.

In a twist of feeling he brought to mind the open and generous face of Thomas Kydd, the English friend he'd come to know before the war, facing the local politics of Exbury and by extraordinary means achieving a victory against the French. And then, years later, with him as a legendary frigate captain, seeing him cut down at American hands and choking his life away. He hoped that his friend did not suffer long . . .

He became aware that there was a figure to the right, to the rear but keeping pace.

Another appeared to the left, closer and with calculating eyes.

Gindler's hands instinctively fell to his sword but out of uniform he wasn't wearing one. With a snarl of triumph the man lunged forward with a vicious swing and Gindler remembered no more.

'Please! Please – speak to me!'

The pain was acute, sapping his fight to consciousness but the words were compelling. A female voice of pity and compassion.

'Er, I . . . was set upon,' he managed, realisation creeping in that he was sprawled in the gutter, his clothes torn and ruined.

'I know – we saw you in the road,' the voice above said in relief. 'Are you feeling better, sir?'

Gindler elbowed himself up. The evening was drawing in and, with it, the cold of the night. 'I thank you for your concern, ma'am, and I can assure you I'm all the better for it.'

A carriage of some opulence stood in the background but it was clear that the driver was not inclined to assist.

'Your wound, sir. It were better if it was treated.' Her hands strayed to the matted blood on his head.

'Um, yes, of course.'

Her figure came into focus. Young, fashionably dressed and with innocent, not to say adorable, features.

'You're a gentleman. This is not to be borne. You shall come home and be mended.' The voice now was commanding. 'Cole, come down and help the gentleman into the carriage.'

He hesitated, unsure. 'Er, my name is Gindler. Lootenant Gindler of the United States Navy.'

It sounded pompous but she smiled delightedly.

'My respects, Lootenant. I'm Miss Maybelle Ditler of Berkley.'

The carriage ground off, Gindler ignoring his pounding head for the delight of being seated next to the prettiest girl he'd ever seen. She sat primly, her hands in her lap, her glances at him covert and fleeting. They discussed the noble architecture going up around them, the improved skyline that resulted and the employment it was giving. Shyly, she allowed that her father was a Treasury official at some eminence whose work saw many famous names dropping by to consult and dispute and who no doubt would be pleased to see him attended to.

The Ditler mansion stood in grounds within sight of the Capitol building, its interior richly decorated.

Gindler found himself at ease in a high-backed chair in front of a vast marble fireplace, its warmth grateful to his aching body.

'It's truly kind in you, sir, to allow me use of these clothes.' It was unfortunate that Ditler senior was short and stout but he was grateful for the garments while his own clothing was stitched and cleaned.

'So you're a sailorman,' Ditler opened, his voice rich and commanding.

'Lootenant, United States Navy, sir.'

'What ship?'

'At this time I'm temporarily without one, sir.'

'Oh?' The shaggy brows lowered in suspicion. 'When we're tradin' blows with the greatest set o' villains unhanged?'

'He can't help it, Papa,' protested Maybelle, 'they don't have enough ships!'

'More ships – you're soundin' like Potter and his seventy-fours! What say you, sir?'

'It's only the Navy as will save the country, sir. Give it a few battleships, more frigates, and it'll take the war right out to the British.'

'Rubbish! In case you haven't noticed, this is a whole damn continent we're sittin' on – the sea's got nothin' to do with it.'

'I beg to differ, Mr Ditler. If we—'

'You've got an interest in a big navy, son. If you only saw the half of the accounts from the Navy Yard come my way every day you'd be a mite quieter about it. Now, you stayin' for dinner?'

Chapter 31

Somerset House, London

'Mr Alleyne, office of the inspector general of Naval Works.'

The officious functionary at the door raised an eyebrow.

'Sir Thomas Kydd. He's expecting me.' He was in plain clothes, well-cut but still feeling odd after the years of naval uniform.

'Very well, sir.' He beckoned for a messenger who ran up. 'The boy will take you.'

Kydd fell in behind the youngster and, while trying to keep up, marvelled at the buzzing confusion in this concentration of the great offices of state. The grand building he knew housed the Navy Office, the complex that ran the Royal Navy for the Admiralty, which itself resided in Whitehall. The only time he'd ever been within these splendid walls was as a candidate in examination for lieutenant those many years ago and apart from that knew nothing of its inhabitants or workings.

Alleyne was to be found on the opposite side of the building's entrance on the Strand, well placed up against the riverside. His office had a view but was small and crowded.

'A good morning to you, Sir Thomas,' the man said, rising to greet him. 'An honour to have you aboard, so to speak, sir.'

Kydd became aware that he was being keenly observed and met the gaze stiffly. 'As I trust I shall earn the honour, sir.'

'Pray sit, sir. It is not so often we see gentlemen of such report as yourself in our midst. Refreshment?'

'No, thank you. Sir, I stand in some puzzlement as to the exact nature of my position. As a sea officer I'm accustomed to a line of command originating with the captain and extending down to the lowliest foremast hand. How might this be realised in a civil appointment, I ask in all innocence?'

'Ah. As to the nature of your contributions I must leave it to your superior to instruct you. As to—'

'You are not in charge?'

There was a pained smile. 'No, Sir Thomas. I am the comptroller of the clerks-in-office. The one in charge is Major General Bentham.'

'Shall I—'

'Who is absent at this time.' Something of Kydd's impatience must have penetrated, for he softened and said, in a friendly tone, 'He's travelling more often than he's not, as no doubt you will yourself. Your appointment was advised and arrangements have been made – an office and a clerk detailed as your assistant. I will introduce you to him presently.' He noticed Kydd shift uneasily in his chair and, embarrassed, asked, 'Does your wound trouble you, sir? I know a—'

'It doesn't signify,' Kydd replied abruptly. 'I'm more concerned with learning of these arrangements.'

'Well, at your eminence you are entitled to quarters in the City. You're married?'

'Yes.'

'Then you shall reside at what we call Captain's Row in St Clement Danes, which is close by. If your good lady desires to make household in the City I'm sure in this she'll be well satisfied. Your emoluments, by the by, shall be issued quarterly by the Treasurer's Office in this building. Privily, of course and—'

'Yes, thank you. Then my work shall consist of the writing of opinions in this office to be passed to General Bentham?'

'In theory, yes. In practice there are . . . complications, which I'm sure the general will hasten to lay before you. He will expect your written opinions to be well informed and to date, and, above all, supported by evidence that no doubt you will gather as you investigate the matter.'

'I see.' There was a hill of questions he needed answering, not the least being the conundrum of why a major general was at the head of a department devoted to abstruse concerns of the Navy. That and the exact nature of what was expected of him it seemed must wait until the general returned.

'My office?' Kydd prompted.

'Certainly, follow me.'

It was handily just at the end of the corridor. It had no view and was very small. His clerk, one Godfrey, was wedged behind a diminutive desk.

'I'll leave you for now, Sir Thomas. Give you time to learn the ropes, hey!'

Kydd eased himself painfully into the severe, straight-backed chair behind his desk, now bare of anything except a neat pile of papers.

'And how long have you served, Godfrey?' he asked politely.

'Sir, you're the first in post as surveyor of projects.' The man was painfully thin, in featureless black, which gave his eyes behind the square-lensed spectacles a certain prominence.

'I meant in the Naval Works office.'

'Four years.'

'Then you'll know where the general's to be found,' he asked drily.

'The caissons in Portsmouth dockyard with Mr Goodrich,' Godfrey answered immediately.

'And he is?'

'Our mechanist, Sir Thomas.'

'I believe I'll call in on him. Would that be proper?'

'Sir, you are a surveyor to the office,' Godfrey replied in astonishment. 'The usual is to take the morning mail coach down, the expense to be borne by us. When will you be . . .?'

'Um, yes. I'll let you know.' It was becoming clearer. This would be his base. Therefore he'd arrange for Persephone to move into Captain's Row. While he was doing his travelling she could visit her parents, who would be sure to welcome their new grandchild.

Suddenly he felt the pangs of hunger. Until he learned the Byzantine customs and hierarchy of the civil service he'd prefer to find somewhere to eat for himself.

The Strand was at a decent level of civilisation and he moved into the crowds, looking for a suitable hostelry, and then he heard his name – distinctly, even against the grinding of carriage wheels and raucous shouting.

He stopped, fending off cross passers-by, and looking around, spotted a stout gentleman of some years waving a furled umbrella in pursuit of him.

'I say, Captain Kydd is it not?' he puffed, his red face creased in pleasure.

'It is. And you . . .?'

'Ah. You won't remember me, sir, but I do remember you! Andrews – back in the last war you kindly took my youngest as midshipman on his first ship. *Teazer*, brig-sloop. Came home full of himself, bless his heart!'

Kydd brought to mind the frightened, wispy child who'd overcome much to make a first-class seaman, if a little over-endowed with youthful zest and impulsiveness. 'Yes, I do recall, Mr Andrews. May I ask what's become of him?'

'Naught to set next to your fame, sir, but he's turned out well, second of *Ariadne* frigate no less. Speaks always of his time under you in *Teazer*, sir.'

'Then do convey my earnest felicitations on his achieving,' Kydd said, touched by the man's evident delight in their acquainting once more.

'Er, I'm on my way to take a small repast. It would gratify me beyond measure should you be my guest – that is if you . . .?'

'That's kind in you, sir. I'm not familiar with this part of Town and would be grateful to discover an establishment of repute nearby.'

'Oh? Do you have business here, by chance?'

'I do. For my sins I'm to take post in one of the Navy Office concerns. My first day,' he added modestly.

'Well, now! Somerset House is where I hold court as the commissioner for the Auditing of Public Accounts. We'll see more of you, it seems. Do let's get off the street – it's so damned noisy.'

The Quill and Ledger was old and snug but well patronised by those of a certain standing. Kydd inched himself into his chair, easing his leg before him and fending off the awkward concern.

The preliminaries over, Kydd felt able to enquire more of the noble building where he would have his being. 'A rare place – packed with a crew all pell-mell on their business. How many would this be, do you think?'

'Oh. I really don't think anyone's counted. Hmm . . . There's the Stamp Office, the Salt Office, the Pipe Office – that's the pipe rolls, of course – the Office of the Duchy of Lancaster, Auditors of the Imprest Office – or was, afore its name was changed. We've the Hawkers and Pedlars, Publick Lottery, Hackney Coach, King's Bargemaster and . . . and the Tax Office, of course, Duchy of Cornwall, surveyor general of Crown Lands . . .'

Kydd shook his head then added brightly, 'And the Navy Office, in course.'

'Certainly. The biggest of all. Your situation, pray?'

'At the inspector general of Naval Works, surveyor of projects. Mr Bentham.'

'General Bentham you must say, sir. And you're welcome to the entertainment,' he said, with a guffaw.

'Tell me.'

'Why, the man's a genius or charlatan, I'm not sure which.'

'And a philosopher?'

'Not as who should say. This is Samuel. You're thinking of Jeremy, his brother. They're very close but vastly different.' He signalled for the pot-boy. 'You should tread softly about your general. He's some original ideas concerning stipends – he insisted his post be remunerated once a year solely by an audited examination of the savings accruing to the Crown through his stewardship. And warmly recommends it be taken up by the world in common.

'He started out in youth as a shipwright apprentice in the royal dockyards. Did his time in full and I dare say knows the tricks. Feeling unappreciated, the young man goes to Russia – and I tell you as a measure of the fellow – he wins gratitude and favours from Empress Catherine and her paramour, Potemkin, for causing to be built all manner of devices and ships of war for use against the Swedes. They appoint him to the army and, after dishing the Turks in Siberia, create him a Russian major general before his return here from China. Remarkable chap – full of inventions and bright ideas but prickly with it. The Admiralty liked his style and assigned him his present position in 'ninety-five but he's made a mountain of enemies since as could bring him down, I'm persuaded.'

'Mr Andrews, if I might ask it of you – do you know aught about why I've been given the post? From the point of view of someone on the inside at Somerset House, as it were.'

'Well, that's easy enough. It's Admiralty against Navy Board all over again. The innovations and inspired notions need quiet scrutiny right enough but the Admiralty don't trust the Navy Board, only some of 'em with any kind of smell of the sea. They will rely on you to give them the plain word so there you are, set up to argue with the best professionals and philosophers the Board can conjure but must deliver what their lordships want to hear.'

'Then I should take care in what I produce.'

Andrews looked at him fondly, as at a child. 'You could say that, sir. It's a wicked world and you should know who are your friends and, er, the converse. I wish you well of the post, Sir Thomas. We shall meet again and I'd be delighted to give of my opinions, if asked.'

Chapter 32

En route to Portsmouth

The coach was nearly empty, allowing Kydd to rest his leg on the opposite seat and peer idly through the window at the countryside passing by. The three sailors on the outside were making the most of their last hours of liberty before Spithead and Kydd hadn't the heart to let them know who he was. In any case he was in frock coat and loose cravat, which he supposed he must regard as his uniform now.

In view of the jollity above, Binard had been grudgingly allowed the sanctity of the inside and, while sitting in a decorous silence, was clearly enjoying the sights.

Persephone had loyally fallen in with whatever he'd asked and was with her parents at the moment. Captain's Row had turned out to be a robust, simple but scrupulously clean set of mansions, and Kydd was pleased to recognise one or two of his neighbours. And, he noted wryly, each of them was a retired naval officer.

The well-known approach to Portsmouth along the Petersfield road saw the jolly tars subside, and at the final rise and crest, with the naval anchorage spread out before them, they fell silent.

'The George,' he told the driver.

Soon he and Binard stepped into the familiar surroundings of the inn that had rested Nelson on his last day in his native land before Trafalgar, and had done the same for Kydd many times since.

The dockyard gatekeeper knew where the general was and directed Kydd to the far workshops beyond the last dock, a trying good half-mile. With a pang he realised it was the dock his first frigate *L'Aurore* had been in. It was close to the remarkable block mills that he'd heard about but never visited.

Outside a grimy brick building, a knot of men appeared to be in argument. A slightly built older man seemed to be getting the upper hand, and before Kydd could reach them, one of the group stormed away.

Kydd approached hesitantly. 'General Bentham?'

'I am he,' the victor of the argument said. 'Sir, you're not here to try my patience over the saw-pits, are you? There's nothing I can do until—'

'Sir Thomas Kydd, sir. New in post as your surveyor of projects, come to make your acquaintance.'

His bow was returned with a touch of impatience. 'That is well, Sir Thomas, your presence is welcome but, as you may see, I'm devilish busy.' The voice was high and the delivery was excited.

'Then I shall make my excuses and seek your attention at some other time.'

'No, no. That won't be necessary. You're staying where? Not the Blue Posts, I hope.'

'The George, sir.'

'A good choice. Then we shall sup there together. At eight, shall we say? I'll bring Goodrich. You must meet him.'

'At eight, sir.' But Bentham had already turned away.

It was in fact nearer nine when a boy breathlessly announced the arrival of the general below.

There were two in conversation before the fire, Bentham, and a quiet, reserved character.

Kydd approached, hearing Bentham instructing the man on some point or other, a pencil flying over a large notebook.

'Ah, Sir Thomas. Shall we go in? I'm clemmed to a clinch. Oh, and this is Mr Goodrich, our worthy mechanist.'

They were found a quiet table and ordered a bottle of wine opened.

'So, you are what their lordships found for me,' Bentham said expansively, over his glass. 'I charged them to discover a man of undoubted probity but as well sound in his nauticals. I see you've lately been wounded, sir. No doubt in the service of His Majesty? I do hope it will not impede you in the performance of your duty.'

'Sir, I'm much desirous to know just what this involves.'

'You are, are you? Then it can be easily stated. Your opinion will be sought on any number of odd notions that projectors and speculators thrust at the Admiralty, some of which have a degree of merit, most of which are the work of lunatics. You shall satisfy yourself in the particulars of each, paying attendance where necessary and seeking advice from those in a position to give it.'

'To whom do I address the opinion?' Kydd said carefully.

'Myself. I shall make the decision as to whether the matter goes forward to the commissioners of the Navy Board.'

'The delicate question invites itself to be asked, sir. Upon what criteria do I base the opinion? My estimate of its effectiveness in a hostile sea setting or—'

164

'No. Not at all, sir. There is only one word that can adequately convey its nature.'

'Sir?'

Bentham didn't answer but looked meaningfully at Goodrich, who delivered the reply: 'Utility, Sir Thomas. The measure of all things.'

'Quite,' Bentham interrupted. 'As my heaven-gifted brother has shown in his Utilitarian philosophy, it is that quality which assures the greater happiness or the least pain to the subject. In this case, the ship considered an organism, or an action affecting one's subordinates.'

'The general desires you to make specific observation on the efficacy of the idea or scheme in promoting utility in a situation,' Goodrich offered.

'In all its subsequent guises,' Bentham said darkly. 'Let not the dead hand of custom smother the flowering of the human intellect, still less the barbarous iniquities of fees and rewards.'

Kydd blinked. If all he was about was philosophising for this odd character it was not how he wished to spend his next years. 'Sir, in my investigations who shall be my crew to stand with me? That is, who will share the responsibility for the findings?'

'None, sir! Your opinions shall be yours alone, evidenced how you may. You shall bear the responsibility but also the credit. No hiding behind a committee of anonymous creatures. You stand or fall by your own hand, sir!'

With some trepidation Kydd recalled Andrews's words about being entertained.

'Well, I rather believe the learning is in the doing. Tomorrow morning I shall have a project of some sort ready for your first assay into naval works and its undoubted tribulations.' Bentham seemed considerably enthused at the thought and raised his glass, then said loudly, 'To Captain Sir Thomas Kydd – may he be as victorious against the cavilling rogues at the Navy Board as he's ever been against Boney himself!'

Chapter 33

'Wh-what?'

The innkeeper who'd roused Kydd was insistent. 'A gent wants t' see you, sharpish like. Says you're expectin' him.'

Kydd threw on his clothes and hurried down the stairs in the early-morning half-light. Bentham was consulting his fob-watch by the fire, now coldly extinct.

'Good morning, Sir Thomas. You'll be wanting to be about your business without delay, and as promised I have your project.' A drowsy servant appeared with a coffee pot but was waved away. 'You will see it is in the form of an instruction to proceed under my signature. It is also an authorisation to incur expenses in the name of the office. You'll be aware of how to proceed in the matter?'

Kydd, who, as a captain, had signed away half his life to pursers and clerks without number, nodded.

'The line of budget is not to be exceeded, specifying in each item whether it be wear and tear, extra or ordinary expenses and rendered quarterly. Sir, I'm much engaged this morning. Have you any questions?'

'Er, not at this time, General.'

After Bentham had left Kydd inspected the papers. Hastily written, they told him to attach himself to the party engaged in trials of chain cable in the Hamoaze, there to begin observing and recording.

Chain cable? He'd heard it mentioned some years before but as far as he knew it had been dismissed as unworkable. Presumably he must learn all he could about the subject, then find reasons as to why this was so – or conceivably perceive its drawbacks and suggest a remedy.

His thigh was throbbing after the previous day's activity and he cursed as he adjusted his dress. So, now it was to be Plymouth as his place of work, leaving Persephone in London. It couldn't be helped, especially in view of the fact that he'd be judged on what he produced on his first project.

The coach trip to Plymouth was tedious, and what thinking he could do was not productive. The familiar hemp of heavy cable replaced by clanking iron chain? It didn't bear imagining.

The port admiral's office was obliging, digging out all mention of the chain-cable trials. It seemed they'd been undertaken in a sloop in ordinary moored in the Hamoaze, *Whippet*. The gentleman conducting them was a Mr Gardner of the Board of Ordnance, who could be found in a dockyard office located in the South Yard.

Gardner looked up in surprise when Kydd was shown in. He was in company with a somewhat stout and well-dressed gentleman enjoying a cigar.

'How are matters proceeding?' Kydd asked carefully.

'May I know your interest, sir?' The man was elderly, his voice tired.

The other kept his silence.

Kydd explained his mission, which caused Gardner to

stiffen and peer at him. 'I've not heard of such a thing from the Admiralty. My findings will as usual be made available to them in good time.'

'I rather think their intention is to secure an independent opinion by one in the sea profession.'

The other man stopped puffing his cigar and listened with interest.

'That's as may be,' Gardner replied. 'Pray tell me, sir, what is your understanding of the qualities of wrought iron – its strength in tension, its response to the interior inclusion of slag, its mechanical properties under load? You may be explicit. We're all authorities on the subject. No? Then this is why the Ordnance Board is conducting the trials as being thoroughly familiar with iron in all its strengths and limitations. If you desire, my findings will be passed to yourself for whatever purpose.'

'Sir, I mean to attend the trials. These are at the request and direction of the Navy Board, who will be dismayed if they learn you intend to deny me.'

'We have been encountering . . . difficulties that are proving hard to resolve. I can see no value in your attending, sir.'

'I shall be judge of that, Mr Gardner.'

'The trials will not resume for another week.'

'During which time I promise you my acquaintance with wrought iron will be considerably increased,' Kydd answered politely. 'Good day, gentlemen.'

Seething inside, he gave a curt nod to the other man and prepared for the long walk back. He hadn't gone more than a hundred yards when he realised the man was up beside him.

'Sir Thomas,' he puffed, 'forgive my effrontery . . . but I do believe . . . I can help you.'

'Oh?'

'Josiah Phipps, ironmaster of Broseley and, damn his blood, adviser to the trials-crew director.'

'How do you suppose you might help me?'

What he had to say was revealing. The trials were going badly and it was all the fault of the academicals, who had no grasp of the practicalities and were concentrating on the theoretics at the expense of reality. The advantages of iron cables were too numerous to dismiss lightly but the results of the latest round were sadly set fair to end in yet another abandoning. Should Kydd deploy his superior knowledge on the problem it might well prove advantageous to all parties.

'Mr Phipps, can I entice you to dinner with me? As my guest,' Kydd said pleasantly. An opportunity to learn of trial progress or lack of it and more, the state of the iron industry and the perspectives of an insider – the expense would go down as ordinary.

The meal went well and he warmed to the frustrated iron-master who'd been summoned as an adviser. It was obvious he wanted to be in front when bids were called to supply the entire navy. But it was equally apparent that the trials, like so many before since the previous century, had run into the sand with the same cause: handling on board ship, which was much different from that ashore.

Kydd saw it was necessary to unearth the secrets of shore use for himself. The only chain he'd come across of substantial size had been on industrial cranes and so forth where he'd seen no problems with their handling, so how . . .?

Phipps leaned back. 'Sir, you have a reputation. If anybody on this earth can get through the mire, it'll be you. I give you a proposition. Should you succeed and I prevail in a contract to supply, a substantial recompense will be advanced to you, sir.'

It brought Kydd up sharply. Was this how it was done

shoreside? An amicable *sub rosa* agreement that was nobody else's business, with no requirement for Kydd to do anything other than he would do anyway to forward the Navy's cause? It felt tawdry. If he took it up, was he therefore Phipps's hireling? On the other hand if he didn't prove cooperative there was no one else who could help him with the technicals, the practicalities.

'That won't be necessary, Mr Phipps. Chain cable has to stand on its own merits and my opinion must be my own.'

'We'll leave that aside for now, but this is what I can do for you. You'll learn more about iron by seeing, touching, feeling than ever you'll find in books. A few days in my foundry will see you well equipped in the article of iron-savvy – do please consider tarrying a while in Broseley, sir.'

It was too good an offer to refuse – there was no obligation, nothing implied by way of return, and his evidence for Bentham would be impeachable.

'Very well, Mr Phipps. I shall do so.'

Chapter 34

Shropshire

The ironworks were in the lower town, its smoky roiling at a distance from the rest of Broseley on the higher ground at the other side of the Severn.

Kydd wasn't detained by a detailed tour of the processes, merely a swift acquainting with the noise and blinding heat of the furnaces and channel-ways while Phipps explained that what he was looking at was the latest puddling process, infinitely superior, it seemed, to the usual finery forge.

Away from the reek and clamour Phipps got down to the nub of the matter. Over a hurried lunch Kydd was instructed in iron, its nature and uses. There were only two forms of iron-based metals, iron and steel, made from the same substance but varying in how much carbon they contained. And there were only two kinds of iron – cast and wrought.

'Here is your first lesson,' Phipps said importantly. They entered a well-lit building that contained several complex frames. He crossed to the largest, which appeared to be a strong beam, hinged at one end and with a rack along its other end. Midway it intersected with a protruding vice. He took a rod of metal an inch thick and handed it to Kydd, who hefted it wonderingly before handing it back to Phipps, who secured it in the vice. In the rack he placed some weights, then ratcheted up the beam.

'Stand clear – but watch the specimen.'

The beam fell and, with a vicious crack, the rod was snapped cleanly in two.

'And now this.'

Another rod was produced, to Kydd's untutored touch feeling somewhat smoother. It was secured into the vice and the exercise repeated, but this time the beam bounced off the rod with a dull ringing, resting inertly on the specimen.

'The first, cast iron, the second, wrought, the test common strength. In each case the impelling weight and the diameter of the specimen was identical. The cast iron is brittle and broke, the wrought iron is malleable and bent.'

'So wrought iron is the superior.'

'This is then your learning. If we repeated the test but as a measure of compression, the cast iron would prevail without a doubt. Iron in all its forms must be thoroughly known so that its properties are always matched to its uses.'

'In chain cable?'

'Wrought iron for its superior performance under tension. Would you wish to see this for yourself?'

It was another apparatus of beam and weight, but instead of a specimen there was a single link of chain cable of size, some two inches through. 'Here we have a cable suitable for holding a ship-of-the-line in a tideway, equivalent to your twenty-four-inch hempen cable.' The link was only two inches thick to the hemp of some eight, even if the closed link itself occupied more space.

Mounted vertically in a clamp, the beam towered overhead

and the weight racks were enormous, spread over twenty yards and manned by three workmen.

'Carry on,' ordered Phipps.

Staggering under their burdens, the men loaded the long tray with weights from their storage against the wall.

Mesmerised by the sight, Kydd was unprepared for the ear-splitting bang and crazy rearing of the beam as the link finally gave.

'A whisker over a hunnert an' ten,' called one of the men.

'You see?' Phipps purred. 'A hundred and ten tons before our link thinks to fail.'

Dizzy with impressions, Kydd followed him to an engineer's office. 'You've seen a mort of what wrought iron can do, Sir Thomas. May I entertain you for a period with a rehearsal of its further qualities?'

'By all means – and pray don't be offended if I take the precaution of noting it down.'

'Then I shall tell you of what you might expect should you ship chain cable instead of common hemp.

'First, its price. At current rates a hempen cable for a first-rate costs two hundred and forty pounds fresh from the ropewalk. My iron chain will be a hundred and ninety-six only and . . . it will never wear out.' This was a great saving with hard service overseas resulting in the need for new cables every three years or so.

'Then it is very easy to seize it to the inner end of its stowage and at the opposite end to the anchor ring. And of iron, it is fire resistant and proof against the worst of sea-beds – coral, rock and similar.'

A truly shining advantage in the Caribbean, Kydd mused, remembering the desperate times in the old *Trajan* lying to a single anchor on a coral bottom with a dreadful fate awaiting all aboard should the hemp cable finally strand and fray.

He scribbled furiously.

'This is not to complete all its virtues. When anchoring, the ship may lie to two anchors in the usual way but in its front part the chains are joined in one by a shackle that swivels and thence out to the two anchors, thereby banishing for ever the spectre of fouled cables. And then there's—'

'Mr Phipps. You've persuaded me, but I must believe there to be some dark reason why we're not using chain cable at sea. The gouging and splintering of iron over wooden decks?'

'Simple flat iron plates along its course.'

'Well, passing an iron chain around the wooden capstan whelps?'

'Fit adaptors. I can show you the drawings.'

'Stowing below?'

'Sir Thomas, these you can see for yourself on the trials ship. I'm not a mariner, still less a captain, but from what I've seen it may be that no more is Mr Gardner, and he cannot direct his sailors to a rightful success in its handling. Or,' he added, with a wry smile, 'the sailors are making difficulties on account of its novelty or weight, which admittedly is above that of hemp.'

Chapter 35

Aboard Whippet

'How unfortunate,' Kydd murmured smoothly, after learning from Gardner that the trials could not resume owing to the absence of Timmins, the lieutenant in command of *Whippet*. It had cost Kydd's conscience much in lying to the awe-struck officer that the trials had been postponed, and that he would certainly be sent for when they recommenced.

'But no matter. Out of consideration for your good self I shall take charge and direct the men. No – don't thank me. There's my time to take into account as well.'

Muttering inaudibly Gardner indicated a grudging assent and Kydd stepped awkwardly to the upper deck and along to the fo'c'sle. His eyes expertly took in the arrangements. In place of the hempen cable arising through the fore gratings there was the grey metal of a chain cable of some size – each link eight inches long and an inch thick. It made its way across the deck directly to the hawse over a temporary path of iron-plate. A clumsy arrangement at the bowsprit had the anchor suspended ready to be released in a simulated mooring in place of making use of the cathead. The net effect of the whole looked crude and industrial to Kydd's sensibilities.

He was aware that the idle seamen in the fo'c'sle party were eyeing him as he surveyed it but didn't care. This trial was going to be executed properly.

Painfully he went to the riding bitts. There'd been no effort made to take a pass around them, as was usual when riding to an anchor, the chain simply passing beneath them. Odd lengths of rope seemed to suggest that the cable was prevented from surging by tying off, a contemptible solution if permanent.

At the capstan he saw no sign of modification – but, then, if they were using a messenger as they did in big ships it would not be needed. He snatched a glance to where the links led through the open hatchway down to the hold and cable tiers. In the dim light below, all he could make out was an untidy pile of chain. He snorted – the tierers must be a sorry lot if this was their idea of flaking down.

On his way back he stopped and examined a link. Scuffed and with the gleam of the knocks of hard usage it looked nothing like a world-changing invention. He gave it a kick. It hardly moved, a mass of inert metal.

He stopped himself: he had to let the evidence guide his conclusions and he hadn't even seen it in action. Clearly this cable was over-specified for this class of vessel, but then again, they were trialling on behalf of the true man-o'-war.

The men stood about in something like dejection. One, plainly the boatswain, returned his gaze with a scowl.

'Your name?' he snapped.

'Wiley.'

'I'm Captain Kydd. You may have heard of me. Mr Timmins is unavailable at this time – I'll be in charge. Now, this chain cable has a chance of becoming a very useful piece of gear so these trials are very important. It would be a sad thing if we rejected the idea simply for reason that we did the job with a lazy crew of idlers or similar.'

The men's looks were now resentful.

'Mr Wiley, I'm going to be down on any shirker who thinks to skulk his duty and lays it on his shipmate to take his weight.'

'Sir.'

'Very well. We start with a simple moor. I presume at the order "Slip" the device forrard lets go the anchor, the tierers ready to render the cable?'

'Aye, sir.' There was an almost sly edge to his voice and Kydd bristled. 'Then post your men – we haven't got all day.'

'Ready forrard?' One of the men raised his hand wearily.

'Ready the tierers?' The question was shouted down and relayed back.

'Then stand by . . . slip!'

There was a delay punctuated by the sound of hammer on metal and then in a staggering avalanche of sound the heavy chain roared across the deck and through the metal-lined hawse, going on and on until, with a sudden quiver, it came to a stop, banging up and down once or twice on the deck plate, then resting unmoving.

In the unexpected silence Kydd gathered his wits. 'How much cable have we veered?' he asked.

'Seventeen fathoms.' Wiley's tone was neutral and he was looking past him. Kydd turned to see and saw it was Gardner, standing and watching, his arms folded.

'Seventeen fathoms only? Who gave the order to avast veering? I want at least fifty out!'

'Can't.'

Kydd advanced on Wiley in a dangerous mood. 'Pray why not?' he asked silkily.

'Tierers can't do it.'

'Stand fast on deck – I'll sort it out with those mumping lubbers below.'

Cursing at the pain of his leg he descended the ladders to the depths of the hold, nearly in darkness, a noisome, stinking hole. He'd taken the precaution of bringing the ship's corporal with his lanthorn and by its light he took in the sight – a monstrous, shapeless pile of chain cable with the end leading out from under the unwieldy mass. The men had chain hooks, long iron rods with the curl of a hook at the end. They were half-heartedly pulling and heaving at the links and, apart from a sullen heavy clink, were getting nowhere.

Kydd gestured that the lanthorn be brought nearer and, by its dim flickering, stared at the massive heap. It was tangled into a horrific snarl of iron.

'Give me that,' he muttered. The man obediently handed him his chain hook and Kydd went to the most likely of the links to give but he could not move it. He tried another, which slid over the pile and nearly crushed his foot.

It was hopeless. And it was not the fault of the tierers.

Gardner was waiting, his arms still folded, impassive.

'Mr Wiley,' Kydd said evenly, ignoring him. 'I wish to see the men weigh anchor. Roundly, if you please.'

The boatswain raised an eyebrow and sent the men to their stations.

'Heave in.'

This was no trifling task. Every man, including the boatswain, went to the capstan bars and began hauling in. With a hemp cable the capstan pawl would merrily click as the slack was taken in, but there was nothing except the slow and grudging *tink* as the chain cable was won.

Kydd took in the men's shirts stained with sweat, the trembling of muscles, the dogged looks. The sheer weight of tons

179

of metal was almost too much to bear – but he knew it wasn't this: the cable was not moving over the deck. Somehow it must have snarled yet again, this time at the anchor end.

''Vast heaving!' he ordered. 'Mr Wiley, what's happened?'

'Got 'isself in a tangle, ain't it?' he said, hoarse and panting.

'What do you do about it, then?'

'Get a boat out, grapple for the chain and haul the bugger sideways, hope it clears.'

So this was what was meant by 'men having difficulties with handling'. In a surge of emotion Kydd felt for them, this hopeless, losing fight against the alien iron.

He stood back, trying to make sense of it all. Chain cable in varying sizes was used everywhere ashore – cranes, bridge supports. It was even laid along riverbeds for ferries to pick up and haul themselves across. What difference was there between them and this pitiful charade?

The answer was simple. The instances ashore were all static, taking the strain in place and never trying to move before or afterwards. Here, they were attempting to do things a chain wasn't designed to do – twist, form a neat coil, stow in a small space.

He went to the cable and looked closely. There was nothing wrong with it: the chain was neatly interlinked as a long series of identical squashed iron circles. If laid out in an extended line it was fine, but if jostled together it became tangled.

He'd said he'd recommend or not as a consequence of the evidence, and the evidence was damning. By its very nature chain cable was well able to take the tension of tons' weight but not the handling necessary to deploy it in a ship. Gardner might or might not have seen this.

'I had it in my desiring to see you take in hand that sorry crew, sir. To see this ship at peaceful anchor. Is there any kind of difficulty, then?' Gardner's supercilious smile, which accompanied his words, infuriated Kydd but he held his anger in check.

'I've seen what I need to, Mr Gardner. The problem is self-evident and lies in the nature of chain cable.'

'Then . . . then your professional opinion is that chain cable is . . . *impractical* on board a ship?'

'My opinion is my own, sir,' Kydd said stiffly.

'Come now, sir, you will be made privy to my findings. I rather think I should be allowed to hear yours.'

'You shall have a copy when it is completed.'

It was galling to have to admit Gardner was right, but from where Kydd stood it looked as though he was. In a black mood he headed for his lodgings, the wording of his opinion forming in his mind. The sooner this depressing conclusion to his first project was over the better.

Chapter 36

A visitor was waiting for him, a mild-looking gentleman with thinning hair but dressed as one of quality. He rose to greet Kydd.

'Sir Thomas Kydd?' The voice was soft and hesitant.

'It is, sir.'

'The Navy Board gentleman seconded to the chain-cable trials?'

'May I know what business is it of yours, sir?'

'Sir Thomas – my card.' One Thomas Brunton of Maidstone. 'You've been having difficulties with the handling, I believe.'

'Sir, I'm fatigued and out of sympathy with the world. Please be brief.'

'I do beg your indulgence in hearing me for a few minutes only. It concerns a measure that will resolve these same difficulties.'

Kydd sighed. How he'd got to hear of the trials was one thing. That he was going to be pestered by this well-meaning fellow, with no appearance of industrial familiarity, was another. Still, he needed a few minutes' sitting down to settle the pain in his thigh. 'We'll take a noggin together,' he suggested.

'Oh. I'd rather not partake, if you don't mind.'

They sat together by the fire and Brunton wasted no time in setting out his case. 'I've had this idea concerning the propensity of chain to snarl at the least provocation and do believe it has merit.'

'Carry on, Mr Brunton.'

'I've drawings in detail and much description to support it but unhappily the Admiralty has not seen fit to entertain the idea. Or the Navy Board, who had the temerity of showing me the door the third time I visited.'

'How unfortunate for you. Perhaps Mr Gardner – he's our chief of trials – possibly he will hear you.'

'Regretfully, no. Like all the others he will not listen to a humble merchant without experience of the sea.' So that was who he was. It was hardly surprising he'd been ignored.

'Well, all I can say to you is keep trying. There may be one who will hear you. Is that all?'

Crestfallen, Brunton picked up a long bundle he'd been carrying. 'Do you think it's because I have only drawings? The cost of a full-scale example is beyond my slender purse and, of course, I couldn't carry it with me. So lately I've thought to produce a model. Do you wish to see it?'

'A model? Yes, Mr Brunton. A good idea, I'd think it.'

The man brightened. 'Do please excuse its appearance. I'm not very good with my hands.'

Opening the package he offered it to Kydd. It was a simple model in wood, a foot and a half long, clumsily finished but quite recognisable as a representation of a chain cable.

'How ingenious,' Kydd murmured, handing it back.

'You'll see what happens when I let it down.' He raised one end until it hung free vertically, then gradually lowered it. Exactly as Kydd had seen full size in the hold of *Whippet*, it slid and worked the links into a tangle.

'Yes, I've seen this kind of thing.'

Brunton gathered it up and turned away. 'Do excuse me for a minute.' When he turned back he suspended it in just the same way and lowered it slowly. Before Kydd's unbelieving eyes the chain obediently coiled itself into a perfect circle.

'Again?' He lifted the end and did it once more with the same miraculous result.

'Stop! Mr Brunton, how did you . . .?'

'A simple modification.' He held up one of the links for Kydd to see. A single pin had been inserted across the middle of the link, the whole chain served likewise. 'This is my stay, or stud. With it in place it is quite impossible for one link to ride through another.'

Kydd shook his head in open admiration. Simple, but effective.

'Actually, you're the first I've shown my model to. Do you think it answers?' he asked anxiously.

At a loss for words, Kydd was struck dumb for long moments before he spoke. 'Mr Brunton. You must never show it to any other.'

'Oh dear. How will I—'

'You'll be richly rewarded when this is offered to the Admiralty. Think of Mr Harrison and his chronometer! But if another sees it and claims the idea for his own you'll have no chance. No, you must move swiftly. The next stage is to obtain agreement in principle from an iron-worker that this can indeed be manufactured and at what price.'

He was floundering but knew the innocent would be fleeced of his idea the instant an unscrupulous projector got hold of it. They'd have to trust Phipps to give an honest opinion, and that rapidly, before the secret was out.

'And, Mr Brunton, I know one who can do just that for you.'

Phipps had returned to Plymouth and his post as adviser, and was quickly found. Sworn to secrecy he was handed the model.

He took his time, exercising its magic for himself but in the end handed it back regretfully. 'A pretty idea, right enough. But no one's going to believe that a chain cable will run smoother by slapping on more metal, and these studs will demand the same thickness as the main link, not a wee pin like this. O' course, the whole piece will then be so much the heavier and look damned ugly into the bargain.'

He hesitated, turning the model over and over, and added, 'And these studs, they'll have to be forge-welded – both ends. Means heating each link to white hot and hammering hard 'n' accurate while the chain is all the time extending across the floor.'

Rubbing his chin, he concluded sorrowfully, 'Good idea an' that, but this sort of work is going to cost a heap. No money left in it for anybody.'

'You're saying as it's all over for Mr Brunton,' Kydd prodded.

'Can't rightly see how it's to be done, except slow and expensive, so I'd have to agree on the grounds of it not being, as we'd call it, economic.'

'Good to see you, my friend!' Kydd clasped the hands of Craddock, still with his Spanish beard to hide the burns from the horror of the Balkan wars. 'How did you know where I was?'

'In course, at Knowle Manor you had a forwarding address for mail, so here in Plymouth on business I thought to look in on you. Your last letter mentioned a post in the

Navy Office that sounded most interesting. How does it fare?'

Kydd briefly told of his position and its challenges. 'And for my first project I find I have to condemn the poor fellow, even as his idea does work.'

'Really? Tell me of it – I do have a *tendre* for the underdog.'

'He's still here, his coach leaving at noon,' Kydd remembered. 'I'll ask him to join us.'

Just as Kydd had been, Craddock was impressed with a demonstration of the model.

'Who knows of this?' he asked shrewdly.

'No one of significance.'

He glanced at the long faces and grinned. 'Then I would say Mr Brunton stands in a very fair way of success, not to mention a hill of money.'

'Mr Craddock, I can't see how—'

'You thought to offer the Admiralty a chain cable of undoubted utility, then sit back and enjoy your reward. I'd suggest you'll still be waiting long after this odious war is over. No, sir, this is not the way.'

'Then—'

'As of this very hour you will set in motion the legal process that will lead to your being the holder of an unassailable patent for your, um, studded link chain cable.'

Kydd interrupted. 'Harry, we've spoken to an ironmaster whose opinion I trust, who declared that its construction would demonstrably be uneconomic – as would not be touched by any other either.'

'Not a difficulty.'

'But—'

'Let me trace the elements. Mr Brunton here is possessor of the sole patent for the idea. He goes to your ironmaster and makes a proposal. If he himself undertakes to devise a more economic method of production and outlays the necessary capital to produce a full-sized sample cable for the testing, in return he is granted the right to produce and sell under licence as many cables as he desires. Given that the whole world is waiting for such a one, I would suggest that the risk he takes he will think worthwhile.'

Chapter 37

Plymouth

'Well done, Kydd! A rare stroke indeed – as will see all parties well satisfied.' Bentham's handshake was sincere and vigorous.

'Then the Admiralty will take it up?'

'Should the trials prove successful, which I think we can accept will be so, they'll not waste a moment. They can see as well as any the savings to be made as a consequence of the advantages you so cogently argued in your opinion.'

They were sitting in a corner of the Lamb and Compass just down from the Hoe. Their view of the Sound was through grubby windows but Kydd was not put out and raised his glass to Bentham, who returned the gesture.

'Captain, to your continued success – but pray do not believe all will be so easily won. You have a different enemy to fight now.'

'Sir?'

'Politicoes, their lordships of the sainted Admiralty, all the tribes of man who put custom and venality before the stern principles of utility. If you'd been witness to the battles I myself have fought since the last century . . .'

Kydd said nothing, knowing that if he acted with the same uncompromising single-mindedness any chances of naval promotion would fade.

'Take my non-recoil principle for ship-borne artillery. A simple mathematical equivalence and they can't bring themselves to acknowledge it.'

'Er, non-recoil?'

'Certainly. Only now are guns of the fleet being fitted to my principle, and those merely carronades.'

'Do tell me, General. I can't recall ever hearing of this.'

'A gun. It fires and recoils until it meets its restraint. Then it comes to rest. At the moment we have an elaborate system of breeching that slows and damps the motion, but this requires precious space to accommodate and quantities of men to run out the gun again. If the gun did not recoil it would need half its crew and half the time to reload – and it still remains on its target. You see?'

Kydd swallowed. This was either brute ignorance or the delusions of a madman. 'Sir, everyone knows a gun recoils. How can you—'

'I agree with you completely, dear fellow.'

'Then?'

'If we believe Mr Newton, we must allow that every action has an equal and opposite reaction. If the heavy shot flies out of the barrel the gun desires to leap backwards in response, your recoil. What happens if we restrain it completely, such that it cannot move?'

Kydd recalled the ear-splitting thunder of a thirty-two-pounder and its maddened lunge to the rear and could not conceive of it in any other way. 'It breaks away for its freedom?'

'Saving your undoubted superior experience in these matters, Sir Thomas, I beg to differ. The cannon does not move. It cannot. So then . . .?'

'Er, something or other will be wrenched to splinters.'

'No, sir. All we are doing by checking its motion is to have the reactive forces transferred – to the ship to which it is securely bound. That is, the recoil is still there but instead of acting upon your several tons of gun the recoil attempts its thrust upon the *thousand* tons of the ship, achieving instead only a contemptible inch or two. Yet all agreeable to the laws of mechanics as before.'

In dawning wonder Kydd realised he was right. And he saw in his mind's eye an immediate use – in ship's boats about to face the enemy. In place of the present heavy carronade slide with its demand for room and danger when firing, a solidly mounted piece would transfer its recoil to the boat, which would probably do no more than dip backwards in the water.

'Sir, I stand amazed, as to say, in admiration. This surely must receive attention.'

Bentham slumped back in his chair. 'So you might believe.' He sighed. 'Yet I've hammered away for years of my life upon this very thing with pitiful results. There are so many notions of its ilk that I'd wish to see incarnated in the fleet, but languish unfulfilled.'

He looked at Kydd intently for a long moment. 'Sir, you're intelligent and stand for no humbug or flim-flam. Might I count you a friend?'

Kydd smiled. 'Most certainly, General.'

'Then we shall post up together to London on the morrow – and see what awaits us in the office.'

Chapter 38

London

It was not until the next afternoon that Bentham was able to rid himself of the supplicants, official visitors and assorted creatures demanding interview.

He called Kydd in apologetically. 'Dear fellow, a quick matter before we set you to a more taxing issue. One Upjohn of Rotherhithe seeks to draw the Navy's attention to his apparatus enabling a ship to distil fresh water at sea.'

Kydd needed no encouraging to take an interest: watering ship away from a harbour was a hard and lengthy task, huge leaguer casks needing to be taken ashore, filled and towed out again. In hostile seas it was a dangerous undertaking and was usually a limiting factor in endurance. If this project was as promising as the last it would transform life aboard for ships on blockade or far cruising – another advance in maritime science.

'You may wish to make use of our files. As I remember there's been a deal of fuss on the subject over the years.'

For the rest of the afternoon Kydd leafed through the

wisdom accumulated concerning the subject, even from the time of the Tudors. He noted that the famed Dr Lind had invented an apparatus in 1762 but had been overshadowed by a Dr Irving, whose own invention was so superior that he was awarded the spectacular sum of five thousand pounds by a grateful Admiralty. In all his time at sea Kydd had never seen an Irving fitted and soon found why. The famed explorer Captain Cook had taken one with him on his second voyage and in disgust had discarded it as worthless, falling back on a Lind, which had ended as dismally, rusting in weeks.

There had been occasional further attempts but nothing that could be termed a practical solution. Possibly this enterprise would fail with the others but he'd see it tested thoroughly.

Upjohn's letter was painfully written and, by its phrasing, clearly the work of one in humble circumstances. In Kydd's eyes that was no barrier to acceptance. What caused him to hesitate was the return address: Ratcliffe Highway. A well-known sailors' haunt in Wapping and not the kind of quarter a gentleman should be seen in. Was this therefore a sly seaman pitching a gammon – or was it a salty mariner now retired who'd reflected on the problem and found an ingenious resolution?

He'd find out soon enough. A polite noncommittal note suggesting a meeting at the Old Rose for ten the next day had him at the appointed time in a boat and alighting at Shadwell stairs.

The alehouse was on the corner of the busy highway but had a fine snug, and when Kydd entered, a slight older man with startlingly blue eyes rose respectfully.

'Mr Upjohn?' Kydd asked evenly. The man had the wiry ruggedness of a long-serving sailor.

'Aye, sir.' The voice was so soft as to be almost indistinct, the clothing faded but clean.

Kydd introduced himself. 'I've been asked by the Navy Board to investigate your claim of a water-distilling apparatus suitable for shipboard use. Is this your doing?'

'It is, Mr Kydd, sir.'

'Then do tell me about it.'

'Sir, ye'll understan' that I'm a-feared my idea'll be taken by another, so I has t' ask of ye that this is all m' secret.'

'As I shall assure you in writing if you desire it.'

'See, when I left the sea to go home t' my dear heart Annie all is well, an' then she gets the river fever an' dies. It all but sends me t' my own grave too but I tries t' find something as'll take my mind off of it. That's when I tumbles t' my idea, which I then thinks about all th' hours God gives to me.'

'A brave and worthy thing in you, Mr Upjohn.'

'Well, I has an advantage, m' father bein' a clockmaker an' all. I didn't take t' a life o' toil at the bench and run off t' sea, but remembered what he taught me, so when I gets to puzzlin' how t' go at it, I thinks as how I'll do it all different like.'

'Oh?'

'Instead o' distilling wi' a fire an' such, I use a engine o' sorts.'

This was an astonishing idea indeed and if . . .

'Mr Upjohn, have you tried this out? That is, have you any kind of working model?' Kydd asked earnestly.

'No, sir, I haven't no model, sir.'

Kydd's expectations fell away. Another hopeful, then.

'It do work, if that's your meaning – I built a real one, which I has in a barge downriver.'

His spirits rose as quickly as they'd fallen. 'Can I view it in action – see and taste the water it yields?' Kydd pressed.

'Um, if you wants to, sir. But when ye looks at it ye has to know that it's not b' way of fittin' in a lumpin' big man-o'-war. I can't lay hands on th' rhino as I can make it t' size. See, I've used up all m' cobbs as I saved an' now hopes that if the Navy's interested they'll advance me the coin t' make it so.'

'All things are possible – if it works as you say it does. For instance, what's its yield – how much potable water can it make per day?'

'Well, the one I has in the barge gives me a reg'lar five gallon an hour. That's as saying it c'n satisfy a brig's crew in drinking an' washing if we run it in two watches.'

This was more than adequate. It was spectacular!

'I'd very much like to see it in the near future, Mr Upjohn. I've not much time to spare.'

'What – now? Um, I'm not ready for 'un and—'

'Time presses, sir.' If any deception had to be set up before-hand, better to go without warning.

'Then we takes a wherry. Beggin' y'r pardon but the barge is downriver, an' I asks ye again t' excuse it as not bein' a sight f'r a gennelman as you, sir.'

The stink and reek of the wharves was a miasma that clutched at the throat, making Kydd gag, for men-o'-war never ventured into these regions where cargoes from the four corners of the world ended. He knew the area generally but had never set foot there, the nearest naval base being at the Deptford victualling docks, the opposite side of the Thames.

The wherry took them to a small and dingy wharf, with two or three barges tied alongside. Upjohn scrambled aboard the first, turning to haul Kydd after him. The barge, like the others, was old and had been decked over, undergoing conver-sion into a living space. It was clearly not in use for that purpose now, with quantities of rope, blocks and canvas laid neatly wherever there was room.

'I begs pardon f'r the raffle, sir, as I lets 'un stow tackle temp'ry, like.'

They made it to the forward part, and by wedging himself to one side Kydd could see what had to be the apparatus. It was the size of a ten-gallon anker cask, finished in polished wood and with fittings in brass.

'Here we is,' Upjohn said, patting it affectionately. 'Sea-water we gets in fr'm low in the ship, gives us pressure up so we've no need t' pump.' He indicated a pipe that led from down near the keel up to where it entered the apparatus at its base. There were other fitments, valves, metal straps, a small crank, none of which made any sense to Kydd.

'Comes in here, gets treated an' comes out here.' He pointed out a spigot on the side.

'Then can we see it work, Mr Upjohn?'

'O' course.' He reached for a china mug, then felt about a ledge above and brought down a large brass key of the kind to be found in winding chronometers.

'Are ye ready, sir?'

The key was carefully inserted at the back, and in strong, deliberate turns some kind of clockwork mechanism was armed. 'Put y' mug at that tap there.'

Kydd did as he was told, then was struck by an unwelcome thought. 'We're not taking water from the Thames?' God forbid he'd be tasting anything from that foul brew.

'Not t' worry, sir. The same as takes away the salt does the same f'r the nasties. You'll see it when it comes. Ready?'

He felt down the input pipe, found a valve and opened it, then cocked his head and listened carefully. At the right moment he leaned over and threw a lever. Immediately the space was filled with the sound of a clockwork machine, energetically rattling as it drove some mysterious inner mechanism.

'Y'r cup!' he shouted over the noise.

Kydd held his cup under the spigot and Upjohn swivelled it on. At first there was nothing, then a few drops and finally a cheerful stream of respectable strength and volume. The cup quickly filled and picking up on Kydd's wonder he reached behind and came out with a bucket, indicating that Kydd should use that.

He did and in increasing wonder saw the stream continue to gush until at half full the clockwork began to run down and the stream diminished.

'On a big engine we doesn't have to do this all the time,' Upjohn said apologetically, wielding his key. The flow resumed enthusiastically, and when the bucket was full, Kydd rested its weight on the floor with a rueful grin.

'I rather think that answers my questions. Now . . .' He retrieved his mug and, in the dim light, inspected its contents carefully. 'I'll go topsides before I drink this.'

In the open air the water glimmered transparent and pure, and Kydd took a sniff. There was nothing but the welcome waft of fresh water. He dared a taste. Beyond a slight tang of iron it was as grateful to the throat as any he would find in Knowle Manor.

'Mr Upjohn, upon my word, this is a fine drop. And you say the engine can be increased in size, fit to supply a ship-of-the-line, say?'

'Aye, sir, sure it can – but I needs coin t' do it.'

'I'd like to know how it works,' Kydd said hesitantly. 'Just so I can speak with the Navy's mechanists.'

'Y' knows it's my secret, as y' said.'

'Certainly.' The man was trusting him with something that would lift him out of this squalor for ever. He'd never betray him. He could see conflicting emotions chasing each other on his face – to keep the secret and lose his chances with Kydd or reveal his design and risk losing everything?

'It's all I've left t' show for eight years o' work.' His voice had grown so soft Kydd had to lean towards him to hear.

'I'll never tell a soul.'

'Ye're a gennelman, Mr Kydd. You'd never peach on me.'

'I wouldn't.'

'Then here's how it works. There's a chamber inside is free t' move. It spins around, drove by the clockwork but wi' a heap o' gears so it's going main fast. Water goes t' the top, the salt an' other separates out t' the bottom. Sounds easy, but cuttin' all those gears nearly sent me stupid, s' many.'

'But it works,' Kydd enthused. 'By glory, it works!'

'Remember what ye said,' Upjohn warned, worry returning to cloud his features.

'It's safe with me. Now, what is it that you'd need to start on a bigger?'

He brightened. 'Why, now, I'm out o' materials and then I'll need a workshop as I has room t' work in. And some gear-cutters as knows their trade and—'

'One thousand – or two?'

'Once I get goin' it'll need all the cobbs I can find. Say . . . four?'

Chapter 39

'Too good to be true? I thought so as well, Harry, but that was before I actually saw the water gush.'

Kydd lifted his whisky companionably, grateful to have Craddock still with him while he was in the City finalising Brunton's patent application. 'A rare sight in this old barge, water sparkling as if it was coming off a moorland hillside.'

'You saw it being distilled or whatever he claims it to be?'

'I saw him open the sea valve, start up his engine, and at the right time he opens the output spigot and into the bucket it goes. The spinning chamber and gears and so on he didn't show me, but he was mortally afraid I'd let out even this secret to a heartless world. Can't blame him, all his years of hard labour and perfecting.'

Craddock shook his head. 'After all this time and we're set fair to making our own water as we go along. Another modern miracle.'

'Just that . . .'

'A problem?'

'Well, not as who's to say. I think it a mort strange that while trying to impress me he never showed me the other end of his process – the foul particles and salt he must have extracted from the input. Come to think of it, I didn't see any kind of door or trap where they could be got rid of before they choked the device.'

'He must have some way or it wouldn't work.'

Kydd frowned. 'And when I'm asked for a written opinion, I'm on a lee shore to the truth. My own reputation depends on whether I'm recommending or condemning something I know about, have investigated to its right true end.'

'Ask him to show you.'

'He won't do that. He doesn't know me, and if he reveals everything, he's got nothing to hold back until he's been paid.'

'Get him paid, then.'

'Harry. If I cause four thousand pounds to be handed over and it turns out he can't do it, I'll be damned in spades.' Kydd stared gloomily out of the window at the chaos of traffic below. 'I'd just feel a lot happier if I could clap eyes on the workings. That's all.'

Craddock stirred awkwardly. 'There's only one way to get a sight of 'em if he won't show you.'

'Oh, what's that?'

'You're never going to divulge his secrets, you've promised him that.'

'No.'

'So if you returned privily to the barge one night and took a quick look, as your motive is pure you can steal away satisfied and the fellow none the wiser.'

Later that night a legendary frigate captain and knight of the realm took the oars in a borrowed skiff accompanied by a noted international merchant from Manchester – for all the world as if it were a deadly cutting-out expedition.

Near impenetrable gloom and ominous shadows along the

waterfront made their progress perilous close in along the bank. The Thames current was swift-flowing and treacherous, and the last thing Kydd wanted was to be carried out to mid-stream and be spotted.

It was hard work and Kydd's muscles ached from the unaccustomed exercise. He persevered, stretching out as, in years before, he'd done as a young seaman.

At one point there was shouting and a lantern flourished. A group of figures on the wharf shook their fists at them. Craddock gripped the gunwale and stared up at them but Kydd didn't pause. 'Scuffle hunters – they think we're rivals.'

Further on, children ran from a rickety tenement down to the peep of sand and mud, which was the foreshore, chanting and throwing stones at them.

'Don't mind those, Harry. It's the river police we've to think about. Come down hard on coves they find loitering around the docks with intent.'

'Perhaps not.'

'And why not?'

'As the name Bentham is imperishably associated with their formation and duties. It's quite possible that should you flourish the name of your employer another construction might well be found on your activities.'

They arrived at the spot but the barge was difficult to make out until Kydd remembered that it was the outboard one of two.

Carefully he came up alongside, boating the oars and resting as they listened.

No sounds in or out.

'Hop aboard, Harry, and then pull me in,' Kydd whispered.

His wound jolted abominably as he was hauled up, and he fell to all fours to make his way along to the cockpit and hatch. As soon as they were below decks Craddock eased open the dark lantern and in the sepulchral gloom they picked their way over the sea stores.

'There it is!' Kydd hissed, in suppressed excitement.

Its polished wood and brass banding reflected the golden light and Craddock regarded it with interest.

'Hold the lantern,' Kydd commanded, and squirmed right up to the apparatus. 'I just . . . want to get the top off,' he muttered, feeling over and around it. 'Should be a way . . .'

As his hands passed around the rear of the device he stopped, felt around for a space and said in surprise, 'And what the devil's this?'

Craddock lowered the lantern for Kydd.

'Well, I'll be damned! So that's how he did it!' He straightened slowly, shaking his head ruefully.

'What do you mean?'

Kydd said nothing but bent to the inlet valve and opening it, listened carefully. 'As I thought. Nothing. Harry, I don't need to look any further to find I was well choused by the shab.'

'Tell me!'

'This pipe is the inlet providing the seawater. And this one is where we get our fresh-made water.'

'Well?'

'The inlet is not open to the sea, nothing floods in when I open the valve.'

'Then . . .'

'Tucked away around the back out of sight is another pipe, which I dare to say leads straight to a hidden cistern of good clear water.'

'Ha! So what are you going to do about it?'

'I should have him taken in charge, the rogue.'

'Perhaps a tad harsh,' Craddock said.

'How can you be—'

'The part about him leaving the sea, then losing his wife. This might be his way of providing for his old age.'

'I can't let him go free!'

'A suggestion . . .'

A few minutes later the two noiselessly departed. They took with them a keepsake — unscrewing and pocketing the outlet spigot — and left in exchange a note.

It read simply: 'You are discovered, sir!'

Kydd was satisfied. The man would realise that his plot had been uncovered but he would not know what Kydd would do. His only course would be to run, never knowing when a hand might come on the shoulder.

Chapter 40

The Bentham residence

'Do offer our guest the cutlets. I vow they're quite the
most succulent this age,' General Bentham said to his
wife, who dutifully obeyed, taking the dish from a servant
and fussily serving Kydd.

'Is it true, Sir Thomas, you led an expedition to board and
challenge the villain?' she asked demurely.

'Not quite, Mrs Bentham,' Kydd answered, with a grin.
'Myself and a friend were all it took to bowl the rogue out.
No action to speak of, I can assure you.'

'But all to be expected of our doughty sea captain,' Bentham
said, with a chuckle. 'As being more than I'd dare contemplate,
Wapping docks after dark. Quite dished the scapegallows,
don't you think, Mary?'

Her well-bred admiration was followed by a significant
pause and Kydd knew an utterance of moment was about
to be delivered.

'Sir Thomas, your direct acting in the matter of the fraud-
ulent distilling apparatus marks you out as a formidable fellow.

Quite the man I'd wish to have upon my side when I move against the forces of ignorance and venality.'

Kydd waited.

'I'd be obliged for your views, sir.' Bentham delicately touched his lips with napkin. His expression was unreadable. 'On steam.'

'Steam?'

'Just so. As we find in mills and places of industry.'

'Steam engines.'

'Yes, sir,' Bentham said patiently.

'Why, I, er, have not had the opportunity to make my acquaintance with them.'

'You should, Sir Thomas. It's my unshakeable view that the future lies in our taming of these beasts.' His manner intensified. 'Particularly the Navy, which stands to be left well astern, as we might say, in the advance of these machines.'

'The Navy?' Kydd came back. 'You can't mean ships with engines and no sails!' The stories of such had been around and laughed at since he was a boy and he hadn't given it much thought.

'I mean just that, sir. My purpose and calling I believe is to direct the thinking of the highest at the Admiralty into a committing of funds and an aspiration to the great object of setting steam afloat.'

Kydd had once seen a steam engine at a coal mine when his father had been drawn by the wonder of it all and had insisted his son share the experience. All he could remember was its enormous size, the heat, a beam of green-painted iron dominating as it nodded and rose in stately cadence with spiteful hisses of escaping steam. And, above all, the mesmerising rhythm of impossibly shiny oil-burnished steel endlessly sliding to and fro. It had needed a three-storey building for its den and men to tend and feed it, a wonderful and fearful creature of another world.

But how was it going to find a place in a taut, ocean-going frigate where every space was spoken for? Every rope, spar and gun-deck was neatly positioned with purpose and refined by long tradition such that nothing aloft or alow could be spared for the housing of a mechanical beast.

'This could be a difficult object to achieve, I'm persuaded.'

'Which I'm determined shall succeed.'

His wife loyally chimed in: 'Samuel relishes opposition, Sir Thomas. You must know that he was the one who insisted that steam be introduced to the dockyard and himself laid down the specifics for its installing.'

'This is so,' Bentham acknowledged. 'I might be accounted as no stranger to steam in all its practical forms. Sir Thomas, your undoubted probity and, might I say, genius in the element of seamanship leads me to suppose that your insights and opinions in respect of its place at sea would be worth hearing.'

'Sir, I have not seen or heard of any usage of steam at sea in any wise. I have no views.'

Bentham smiled. 'Then this, sir, is your opportunity to remedy same. I desire for your next examination an opinion on the practicability of the usage of steam as applied to the maritime universe as will accompany my approaches to the Admiralty.'

'Sir, be this opinion opposed to yours, will you still accept it, allowing me to write what I will?'

'I desire only the truth, supported by evidence. If there is no future for steam upon the briny deep I must accept this, made easier only because it comes from a sea hero with no other interests other than the primacy of his country's navy.'

'As I said, sir, I know nothing of steam.'

'All to the better! Your views will be the weightier, being

unhindered by foolish preconceptions. As to lack of knowledge, I shall ask my mechanist Mr Goodrich to lay down the elements for you before demonstrating the same with such engines as we have here in the dockyard. Then I'm sure you'll want to make visit to some of the more illustrious of the breed.'

Chapter 41

Portsmouth dockyard

'Sir Thomas, the honour is entirely mine.' Goodrich was a quiet, composed individual, wearing a smock over his gentleman's day clothes and with a pleasant manner. 'The general has asked me to introduce you to the uses and benefits of steam. This I can do for you. Shall we . . .?'

Kydd followed him into an office towards the end of the immensely long rope-walk, his stick tap-tapping annoyingly beside him. Would he have to use it for the rest of his life? The regular shafts of pain told him that was probable.

'Now, sir. If you'll attend to me.'

Kydd sat in a chair opposite a well-used chalkboard and waited while it was cleared of its incomprehensible maze of diagrams.

Goodrich then neatly drew three boxes. 'All steam engines have these main elements. The first is the boiler, which conjures the steam. The second is a cylinder with a movable base, which we call a piston and which might be said to be the engine itself. The third differs in accordance with the use to which the steam engine is put – we call it the work. This may be pumping, a tool jig or any of infinite other uses.'

'What of all those long bars and gears?' Kydd wanted to know.

'Naught but the linking of valves by rods to allow steam to pass or no depending on the point of the stroke reached,' Goodrich said. 'But you'll be wanting to know more of the different species of engine you'll have to compare.'

This was not difficult: just three. The early but reliable Newcomen beam engine seen in coal mines around the kingdom, and the similar but improved Boulton-Watt, both relying on the pressure of the atmosphere to return the stroke. Last there were the modern high-pressure steam engines of the Cornishman Trevithick.

'And the work?'

'Only two kinds to serve every usage, Sir Thomas. One, the natural to and fro motion of the piston harnessed like a carpenter with his plane, the other, continuous rotation afforded by its connection to a flywheel and crank.'

'And that's all?'

'That is the sum total of what it is to be a steam engine.'

'There must be more.'

'There is, but only mere detail to hang on those elements. For instance, in your comparing you will be doing so by scale, the size of each, their efficiency at what they do – and, of course, their duty.'

'Duty?'

'How much work we can get them to do for a bushel of coal. Do be content that in all these things the elements will always remain the same, differing only in detail.'

'Thank you, Mr Goodrich. That was lucid and clear. Now I do hanker to see one of your monsters doing its "duty", as we must say.'

A dockyard shay was summoned, for which Kydd was grateful as it seemed the further reaches of the dockyard were their objective. It gave him time to appreciate the colossal scope of the greatest of its kind in the world, with its multitudes of docks capable of taking the largest ship-of-the-line, the best-equipped metal foundries and other facilities. It was familiar yet he realised how little he knew of it.

They stepped down outside a modest double building at the north-east corner of the Great Basin in the heart of the dockyard. Kydd counted six docks.

'You'll not be aware of it, Sir Thomas, but we're standing atop the old North Basin. It now serves a different purpose entirely. This way, if you please, sir.'

Around them were the hum and bustle of industrial working but beneath it all he sensed the subliminal calm pounding of some massive creature, its exhalations from a tall, square chimney drifting past them, grey and black, wreathed with the defining smell of steam.

'The engine house, sir.' He opened a small door, and immediately Kydd was confronted by the sight of a gleaming, steel-glinting hulk that moved – was alive!

It gave off a dull heat and seemed to radiate one compelling, overwhelming essence. Power.

Not wanting to betray his feelings he enquired, 'And what of the boiler?'

Goodrich went to a door and opened it with a gesture.

Kydd peered in and was at once assaulted by a suffocating heat, catching sight of a raging fire being fed with coal by filthy workers wielding shovels.

He hastily pulled back and racked his brain for something intelligent to say, ignoring the hypnotic endless gyrations of a twelve-foot flywheel and the grand rising and lowering of the immense beam. 'Er, what can we say about its work?'

'As we desire to extract the maximum duty from the engine, it must perform both kinds of work. You'll remember when you were standing atop North Basin? It now serves as a reservoir whereby dry docks fill and empty into it as they may, without recourse to the tides. The engine's pumps are brought in when needed to effect its emptying.'

'There was another kind of work.'

'Rotation.' He pointed to the flywheel and followed the crank along until the jointed shaft left the engine-house through an opening in the wall. 'There, sir. You will see a sight as shall perfectly amaze.'

By a roundabout route Kydd found himself on an upper floor. It was lined as far as he could see with machines, each one connected by a broad belt to a continuous long shaft running high above and industriously at work.

The noise was deafening but there was no doubt that much was being achieved.

'Machine-driven tools. Here in the Wood Mill we can keep many craftsmen working at their machines at the same time. If a new tool is brought in we add it to the shaft with its own speed and power determined by the diameter of the wheel being driven. This is the future, sir!'

It was an assault on the senses, a madness of purpose and uproar. All this grand fire and motion had no place in a ship of war and his opinion was fast hardening against it. Perhaps Bentham was right that steam might well be the future, but on the unresisting earth, not the live sea.

'You see? We run the machine tools in the daylight and in the night hours we change to pumping. Twice the utility, sir.'

Kydd was barely listening. If the Navy went with steam then not only the ships must change but whole crews, too. Mechanics to tend the beast, lower mortals to serve the fire – where would it all end?

'Sir Thomas?'

Goodrich seemed concerned. Kydd knew he hadn't been attending. 'Yes, do carry on, if you please.'

'I was saying that should we proceed past the smith's shop we shall discover another gratifying sight.'

This turned out to be steam-driven vertical saws on a metal bench that, with an appalling screech, were fed with tree boles that became long timber strakes for the hulls of ships. Kydd knew that the previous way of it were saw-pits the size and dimension of graves that required one sawyer above and another below, skilfully but with back-breaking effort doing the same.

And at another place these same lengths were then planed perfectly smooth and to a pre-set thickness, this time replacing teams of men with heavy jack-planes.

Kydd was dizzy with impressions. 'Mr Goodrich, your tour has been revealing and informative and I thank you for your time. If I might consult you at a later time, you will indulge me?'

There was much to think on.

Chapter 42

Washington

'Where've you been?' Ditler Senior said, in mock severity, holding back the plush red velvet curtain at the rear of the theatre box.

'Why, Pa, we wanted to know what's to see next.' Maybelle laughed, her arm still on Gindler's. In his well-cut dress uniform and she in sprigged muslin, they were an eye-catching couple.

The 'we' was not lost on her father who nevertheless chose not to notice. As they entered, a stout, whiskered man rose.

'Lootenant, you'll want to make the acquaintance here of the Honourable Jeremiah Howell, senior senator from Rhode Island. Jez, this is the lad I was telling you about.'

Gindler had no idea why he should meet the man but gave a polite bow and murmured a greeting.

'Mr Howell has a special interest in our navy, Lootenant. He'd be obliged to hear your views at some time on its manning and supply.'

'That's as may be,' boomed Howell, his eyes sharp and

appraising. 'Any opinion as comes from the sharp end of our war effort will be worth the hearing, I say. But for now let's enjoy the spectacle, hey?'

Maybelle and Gindler were placed decorously between her mother and father and they settled to their programmes.

The play was a comedy and the frequent bursts of laughter allowed them to glance delightedly at each other. Then it was time to retire for a light supper.

'So you've a record in the Quasi War, sir,' Howell said, sipping appreciatively at his champagne.

'Sir. And with Bainbridge in the Med.'

'But not in this war of victories.'

'Sir, if you know my record, you'll understand why,' Gindler replied carefully.

'I think I do, son. Something to do with Hamilton and his crew. While his cronies are out taking English frigates you're to be left to rot ashore.'

'Sir.'

'Well, new man at the, er, helm as navy secretary. Dry old stick and a mort slow to act but heart's in the right place, I guess. So you'd like a ship, Lootenant?'

Gindler looked at him directly. 'As I'd like to take my next breath.'

'Bad as that, hey?' Howell chuckled. 'Ease off, m' boy. I'll have a word with Jones. That's any kind o' ship, any position as officer?'

'Any.'

'See what I can do. No promises but we can't let a fine officer like you go to waste when the country's in dire need of such.'

Chapter 43

The crisp spring morning felt like a new beginning as Gindler strolled down the avenue, Maybelle on his arm, and the exciting crackle of his new commission in his waistcoat. To sea again! And to the very forefront of the action – as captain of his own ship. Admittedly, it was only a war schooner and he was a lieutenant in command rather than the grand master commandant he would be if he commanded a frigate, but he was now one of the tiny number of officers in the United States Navy who would be walking the deck of his own ship. There was, however, the reality that it would not be ranging the ocean for prey: he was appointed to *Prospero*, part of the forces in Lake Erie under Commodore Perry for whatever duty this demanded.

Beside him Maybelle was uncharacteristically subdued, walking slowly as though to delay the inevitable.

'It's not as if I'll be gone for years, my sweet,' he soothed. 'And I won't be thousands of miles at sea, either. Lake Erie is only in our north.'

She stopped and looked at him, her eyes brimming. 'Jasper,

it's not that. You're going out to face the enemy – and I know you. You'll charge straight at them and – and . . .'

'As I must, dearest. I can't let the Navy down and hang back, now, can I?'

She sniffed into her handkerchief.

'Besides, there can't be many enemy on a lake,' he answered reasonably. 'And isn't it in the middle of a country so wild it has naught but the Indians and other folk?'

'Indians? Oh, my dear Lord, you're not going in among they?' she asked miserably.

'No, Maybelle, I shall not. I'll be sailing about all the time in the good ship *Prospero*,' he said. He hadn't heard of any threats from the British in that benighted part of the world and wondered why a commodore had to be appointed. To show the flag against the far shore in Canadian territory?

His orders made it clearer. He was to attach to a convoy of stores that was going to cross overland from Pittsburgh through the Alleghenys to a settlement on the southern shore of Lake Erie called Presque Isle Bay, where apparently the building of the first craft under an American flag was taking place. It would be an exciting trip through the raw wilderness as an overture to his first command and he was letting nothing spoil his mood.

His departure was not long in coming, Maybelle, in the presence of her parents, curtseying shyly to him.

'You will write, Jasper, won't you?' she whispered, as he briefly pressed her hand to his lips in farewell.

'It's the only thing that can connect us, Maybelle. Of course I will!'

Mounting his horse, he waved gaily and trotted away.

Chapter 44

To Gindler's dismay, after a long and difficult journey Presque Ile turned out to be little more than a glorified slipway, even if a large one, whose workmen paid no attention to the new arrivals. He eventually found someone who pointed out where the naval party was quartered and he made his way to the first of the huts where he was redirected up the hill to a larger one set away from the others, bravely flying the Stars and Stripes.

It was the office of the commodore, Lake Erie – Oliver Hazard Perry.

'Come in, old chap, and sit yourself down. A bracer?' The voice was soft but had an unmistakable element of strength.

'The hour's a little early for me, sir, but a cordial would be welcome.'

Perry was young but had a patrician aloofness and a steady gaze. Not one to cross, Gindler reflected.

'You know why you're here, Gindler?'

'To take command of *Prospero*, armed schooner.'

'And what of the enemy?'

'Take, burn and destroy wherever they may be found.'

'Come with me.' Perry beckoned, and went to the window overlooking the sea. A small peninsula curved out from the land and back on itself, holding a bay in perfect defensive topography. Inside it was a clutch of small vessels but Perry wasn't pointing to them. He was indicating away to the left, near the horizon. In the crystal air Gindler could see in flawless detail a ship – a full-rigged, three-masted vessel hardly seeming to move at that distance but plainly drawing across before them.

'There. There's your enemy. What are you going to do now, Mr Firebrand?'

'Sail out in challenge, of course.'

Perry gave a slight smile. 'A brave plan. But with a number of fatal flaws.' He returned to his desk and sat down. 'Not as you'd be expected to know of them.

'The first: over yonder lies not just your ship-rigged sloop you see but a whole squadron. The British were first on the lake and are at the moment masters of it, but time is not on their side. It's a war of ship-builders – whosoever can out-build the other and with the better craft will undoubtedly prevail.

'The second: the reason we're safe here is that we've a substantial sandbar at the entrance to our little bay. This is why we're not to be troubled by Commander Barclay coming a-visiting with all guns blazing – his ships draw too much. But on the other hand we're at a stand. That same sandbar allows us to proceed to sea only singly, and if this is so, he has only to position his squadron all together at the entrance to swat us as we emerge one by one.'

'Then, sir, we are comprehensively blockaded, are we not?'

'Quite. But, you see, we have a line of supply from our own country to the south and will never lack for stores and victuals. Mr Barclay is himself faced with a hostile shore and long, vulnerable supply lines, and must retire at some point, leaving us then to make sally to the open sea.'

'Sir, dare I ask it? What is our mission? Why are we here?'

'Easily answered. Mastery of the lake – and with it the priceless ability to transport unhindered an army of invasion from Sandusky to fall upon Upper Canada.'

'Ah.'

'And necessarily recover Detroit and lay siege to the British yards thereabouts.'

'When this blockade is broken.'

'Quite.' Perry stiffened. 'You'll be wanting to see to your ship?'

Trying to hide his eagerness Gindler took his leave and hurried down to the waterfront. The navy craft were moored together and he greedily took in the sight.

There were two substantial brigs and a smaller, a tiny sloop. Clustered to one side there were five schooners. Heart in his mouth, he strode towards them. 'Ahoy, there! Which of you is *Prospero*?'

To his satisfaction an arm rose languidly in the largest.

'Lootenant Gindler coming aboard,' he hailed importantly, and crossed to the sleek schooner, at least a hundred tons and some seventy feet at the waterline. With both masts wickedly raked she gave a convincing appearance of speed. The deck looked narrow but what caught the eye was the armament in plain view. Respectably-sized twelve-pounders – not short-range carronades but full-sized long guns. And for the first time on an American vessel he saw weapons fitted on the new non-recoil principle from England. These were in the form of an iron band and massive pivot set into the deck with one on the fo'c'sle, another two between the masts and one aft, a handsome fit for a vessel of her size.

The man who'd waved was still sitting on the fore-gratings, contentedly whittling an Indian in a war bonnet. 'What c'n I do for yez?'

'I'm your new captain.'

'If y' says it,' he rejoined casually, continuing his carving. 'What happened to Mr Holmes?'

Curious heads popped up at various points on the upper deck, drawn by the visitor. Gindler held his temper: these were backwoodsmen, unused to the proud discipline on the quarterdeck of a frigate.

'He's gone on to other things,' he replied neutrally. So, someone had been bumped off the ship to suit a political move. He squirmed inside. 'Why don't you tell the hands I'll be mustering 'em all in ten minutes?'

They duly appeared, warily falling into some sort of line, and awaited his words.

His little speech on taking command fell a trifle flat, he had to admit after he'd dismissed them. This wasn't the blue-water navy but he'd seen some likely hands – tough, with a direct gaze, answering without prompting and loping away in a sailor's sea gait. But more than a few had the smell of the hayseed about them.

Twenty-eight in all, and he the only officer.

Borden, master's mate, was rangy and with far-seeing eyes, his boatswain-cum-second-in-command. Samson, the gunner, seemed oddly evasive and restless. Coltrop, a midshipman and older than Gindler, was doleful and reluctant.

He made acquaintance of the others, right down to Isaiah, the African cook.

The success of his command depended on his knowing their strengths and weaknesses and bringing them together as a regular ship's company.

By evening he had the measure of his little world. Trim and taut though she was, it was dismayingly cramped below, his own cabin being little more than a cupboard, divided by a table, with a sleeping bunk on one side, domestics on the other.

He inspected the ship's books, brought to him by the slow but methodical seaman clerk. The entries were terse but revealing. *Prospero* was in effect a tender to *Lawrence*, the large brig that was Perry's flagship, which would sign off on all his indents and statements of condition.

Gun drill was a priority and he would keep them at it. Sooner or later there would be the crash of guns echoing around the bay as they faced the English. *Prospero* under Lieutenant-in-Command Gindler was not going to be accounted slack in stays.

Each dawning day saw sail at the horizon, sometimes two. On occasions these were replaced by a different rigged vessel, proof that a whole squadron lay offshore. While it remained they were going nowhere.

Then, one morning, the seascape was bare, empty of sail in any direction.

Perry's reaction was an instant summons of all captains to *Lawrence*.

As soon as the shuffling of chairs in the great cabin stopped, he rasped, 'Your attention, gentlemen. The sainted Barclay has chosen to retire for the moment. Presque Isle is open. We have our chance!'

It was not going to be easy. The enemy squadron could return at any moment, and if they wanted to make open water in anything like fighting order, a single-ship exit was asking for trouble. It had to be a substantial move to get the bulk of Perry's fleet out in a very short time. Once this was achieved they could form up as a squadron and take their chances.

Leaving aside the usual fighting instructions, signals and manoeuvres, Perry gave detailed direction on how they were to put to sea in short order.

With the wind in the north-west the schooners with their fore-and-aft rig could exit rapidly but the square-rig brigs, the largest, were another matter. It would be necessary to haul them out, by brute force if required.

The ship's companies of all the vessels under his command were mustered and made ready. *Lawrence* and *Niagara*, the two square-riggers, were set a-swim opposite the entrance and their guns removed. They were swayed out by yardarm tackle into a succession of pontoon barges, while a doubtful sailing master watched the draught decrease. It was not enough. Stores and water were landed next and still they grounded.

'Camels,' Perry ordered. Barges, pontoons, anything that could be put to use were filled with water and ballast until near sunk, then brought to the big ships' sides and secured tightly. Then they were emptied and rose higher in the water, the ships with them. Towed by anything with oars, the ships were finally floated over the bar and quickly restored to fighting trim.

It took a short while only for the war schooners to join them and gloriously the Lake Erie Squadron was whole once more. Sail was clapped on and they went out to meet the British squadron in battle – but they were not there.

All looked to Perry for what to do next. To sail north back to the safety of the American stronghold of Black Rock or west, to the Detroit River and the British ship-building centre?

He chose west.

Gindler was both exhilarated and fretful. *Prospero* was showing every sign of being a flyer, easily staying with the brigs and, in the light airs, hissing along famously. But play at the guns would largely decide the match. And he knew nothing of these new-fangled pivot guns apart from the little drill he'd been able to witness. They were also at least half a dozen men under strength, with only enough to man three of the guns.

Arriving at Sandusky to the south they were lionised. Commodore Perry had succeeded in breaking the blockade without loss, bringing his squadron to the lonely army outpost that faced the British in Detroit across the western end of the lake.

At a council-of-war Perry laid out the stakes. 'I'm going to take the lake from the British,' he began, with an intensity that was unsettling, 'then transport the army to Detroit. After we've cleared it of the enemy, General Harrison will advance to Niagara Falls to meet our columns coming up from the south – to descend on York together. Canada will fall into our hands like a ripe plum!'

'How in Hades do we achieve this?' Elliott of *Niagara* put in acidly. It was common knowledge that Washington had passed him over for his commodore's pennant in favour of his rival, Perry.

'In a word – blockade,' Perry answered instantly. 'Barclay is refitting in Detroit. I'm to find a base within a few hours' sail of the Detroit River and throttle it, letting nothing pass. He's an army and Indian allies to feed, and the only way he can do that is by coming out to meet us, and then . . .'

The rest of the meeting was taken up with the usual fighting instructions, signals and storing priorities.

This was how to conduct a war! Rapid, vigorous activity to confront the enemy directly. Gindler's spirits soared – he was going to see action, even in these distant waters.

Perry found his base just fifteen miles north. South Bass Island had a pretty, enclosed stretch of water known as Put-in Bay. It was just eight miles short of the Canadian sea border.

Anchors were cast. Men were set to bringing their ships to battle-worthy condition while boats brought stores, ammunition – and more men. Volunteers came from General Harrison's army and even from USS *Constitution*, refitting in Boston. All to be forged into a single weapon with one purpose: to gain mastery of Lake Erie.

Chapter 45

Perry's squadron put to sea promptly, bound for the enemy coast less than a half-day's sail to the north. There he paraded his squadron in full sight of the English base, flying all the flags and pennons he could muster in a show of arrogance. It brought no response.

First one, then several store-ships and victuallers were taken. Unless Barclay acted, he and his Indian allies, including the legendary Tecumseh, would be starved out, so why didn't he contest the situation?

The American squadron fell back on Put-in Bay, frustrated but exultant. The tables had been turned and the blockaders were the blockaded – unless they wanted to dispute it.

Then, on an unusually warm and hazy morning, from out of the north a crowd of sail was made out. There could be only one explanation: the English had put to sea. This day would decide who prevailed to rule Lake Erie.

In Commodore Perry's flagship, *Lawrence*, the signal was thrown out that had his squadron eagerly prepare to sail and, minutes later, the command given to make for the open water.

The British came on slowly, the light airs not in their favour.

It gave time for Perry to imitate the naval hero he most admired – Horatio Nelson. 'Form line of battle!'

Prepared for the order, the Americans proudly obeyed. Two schooners led out the flagship *Lawrence*, Perry's commodore's pennant jauntily a-fly. With *Niagara* under Elliott as his second-in-command several places down, it was a brave sight: nine vessels in line ahead, the centre three sizeable brigs, and the remainder schooners bearing fearsome long guns. *Prospero* was next to last in the rear.

Gindler saw the British, coming in from the right, were in a similar formation. Only six vessels led by a schooner, their line nevertheless was powerful, the bulk of Commander Barclay's flagship *Detroit* dominating. Another ship-rigged sloop was astern of her, which had to be *Queen Charlotte*, the first British ship on the lake at the beginning of the war, with two brigs but only another two schooners. The British were outnumbered and therefore out-gunned! Before sunset there would be a decision – and Gindler had every trust it would be theirs.

Frustratingly the wind was skittishly light, in the west, then veering northerly – not what was wanted in a fight to the death under sail. Both commanders held on, however, the lines now converging at their head. Barclay's *Detroit* manifestly made the ship bearing Perry's commodore's pennant her particular mark, closely supported by *Queen Charlotte*. The breeze fluttered sail, stirred flags and left playful ripples in the bright morning waters but did nothing to urge a hot charge against the enemy.

The first shots were from *Detroit* – her guns out-ranged *Lawrence* and she began a devastating attack on Perry, ignoring the schooners and firing all they carried at *Lawrence*, whose reply was faltering and ineffective. *Niagara*, trailing astern in the light winds, was not in a position to come to her aid, and then, in the slowly rolling gun-smoke, the venerable *Queen Charlotte* loomed close by, joining in the battering.

Gindler knew that Perry's intention was to get his bigger ships rapidly within carronade range of the British but this was not happening. At the rear of the line, he could see ahead what was developing and felt helpless. His orders were the same as those of the other schooners, to stay in line and harass the enemy with their singly mounted long guns. However, it was proving damned difficult to land hits, with the long range and spirited motion of his little craft.

It was not his first taste of gunfire but he had never experienced an occasion when the stakes were as high as this. As his guns banged away his feelings wavered between exaltation and despair.

'Go to it, you devils!' he roared at the men at the midships' guns, in a tangle of haste and fear.

Coltrop was standing irresolute, staring at the mountains of gun-smoke, shot through with flashes, that was the head of their line. The boatswain, Borden, was with others forward, dousing a heap of canvas that had been their foresail and had taken a shot high in the rigging. He was growling loudly at them to double their efforts.

Gindler couldn't make out where Samson, the gunner, had got to, but his mind was crystallising on a course of action. Unauthorised, dangerous, but necessary. And one, he realised with a pang, Thomas Kydd would have taken in his situation, the direct inheritor of Nelson that he was.

While he watched, *Lawrence* was being reduced to a total wreck and could no longer fight, but she was under the guns of the two biggest English ships, whose captains were determined on her destruction. And yet another crawled toward the terrible sight, a brig double his own size no doubt intent on sinking the American flagship and ending the contest.

'Borden, get yourself here on the instant!' he bawled.

Loping aft, Borden seemed mystified. 'Mr Gindler?'

'I'm falling out of line and making for that English brig as is going for the flagship.'

Borden gave a devilish grin and instantly wheeled about to turn all gun crew into sailors, setting every rag they could in the race to get to the fight.

Gindler's heart sang. This was what *Prospero* was built for and the schooner surged ahead, like a racehorse given its head, even in the light airs finding what she needed to reach out to her destiny.

The American line had grown long and straggling and Gindler sailed past schooner and brig, loyally staying at their place in the line, then *Niagara*, hardly moving in the calm.

Prospero passed into the fighting, the towering, reeking clouds of gun-smoke, the hellish din, the confusion and terror of close combat. The little schooner racing past was largely ignored and she neared the tangle of ships untouched.

'Sir, may I?'

Gindler handed the telescope to Borden. 'As I thought. That big 'un is *General Hunter*,' he said calmly, indicating the vessel they were heading for. 'Brig, but smothered in guns. Seen her before.'

The talk about guns made Gindler pause. His plan of standing off at point-blank range to draw fire away from the flagship and conceivably maul it with his own was now in doubt. He glanced across at *Lawrence*, a hulk at the extremity of suffering. He couldn't let the Englishman bring the *coup de grâce* to Perry and his ship.

The breeze was fitful and treacherous, but as they went in he suddenly saw what he could do. The two British ships were close together as they approached, and *Hunter* nearby was turning slowly to meet the impudent schooner. It was not fast enough. *Prospero*'s handy fore-and-aft rig told, and in a wide sweep she found herself ahead of the bigger ship and, not a hundred yards distant, she opened up with her guns straight down its throat.

It was a master-stroke: through the rolling clouds of gun-smoke the out-of-control brig fell to starboard, towards the two British pounding *Lawrence*, and in the smoke and confusion all guns fell silent as the two tried to claw away from the drifting vessel. It ended with the one falling a-foul of the other in a hopeless tangle of wreckage.

The whoops and shrieks of *Prospero*'s crew – his crew – resounded even over the thunder of the guns. They'd made their mark! Now Commodore Perry could do whatever was needed to save the honour of their flag.

Some hours later, weary, smoke-grimed but exultant, Gindler left the evening deck to Borden and found sanctuary in his cabin. Trimming the lamp, he reverently drew out paper and began his letter.

> *My dearest Maybelle,*
>   *I write this to you in the blazing light of a wonderful victory, in which I can say that this humble soul has done his duty. I'm so tired that this has to be a short letter – enough to tell you the news. Well, you see . . .*

How to convey that at daybreak their feeling was one of trepidation but resolution, going off to battle with a fearsome enemy; by evening they had won their fight and in a most handsome and complete manner. This morning the British had sailed Lake Erie as its master, tonight the lake was American.

And the firing was prodigious, my love, and to see poor Lawrence *lying dead in the water and being smashed to pieces would wring your heart. We did what we could to draw their fire away, for as you must understand, the British concentrated all their fury on our leading ships even as they received a smart reply you may be sure. Then the most courageous and imaginative thing. Commodore Perry in* Lawrence *has himself rowed in an ordinary ship's boat to the rear of our line where* Niagara *lay not yet engaged and therefore undamaged. He takes command and directs her to make for the British big ships, badly damaged in the contest, and orders the schooners to hunt down the rest. By the end of the day they were ours – all of them!*

He paused, suddenly overcome by the vivid memories of what he'd seen: blood-driven decks, appalling wreckage and corpses still below decks where they'd breathed their last. They'd found that in every British ship, save one, the commander and second were killed or wounded – but they'd fought like heroes.

So now we're preparing to take General Harrison and his army to Detroit and by the time you receive this we might well be hearing of another success to American arms – and after that – the road to Canada lies open.

Laying down his pen he felt waves of fatigue overtake him, but his letter to Maybelle would be going with Perry's dispatches to Washington in the morning.

He would be left with the undying recollection of his hand being taken by the commodore for his action, which had resulted in gunfire being lifted from *Lawrence* for just the time needed to make his daring transfer to *Niagara* and all that resulted.

And now . . . rest.

Chapter 46

London, Captain's Row

'What's troubling you, my love?' Persephone asked softly. 'These last few days you've been so quiet.'

Kydd put down his evening whisky but continued to stare at the fire.

'Is it your wound? I'll send for the doctor to call.'

But he knew it was not something that a physician could remedy. It was a soul sickness – the shrivelling of spirit since his alienation from the element that was most natural to him: the sea.

It was not that he could do anything about it. It was what he'd become. The world was not to blame. The wound he'd suffered, like many others before him, was the risk that every warrior took, with so many killed in their prime. He'd been left with the consequences, however, the worst of which was being denied any future on the quarterdeck at the very crest of his manhood.

He knew it was hard on Persephone, her love continuing as it always had, strong, caring, passionate.

His mind shied away from the implications as he told himself he should be grateful that he was alive. His position at the Navy Board had given him the security of a useful income and it was being made clear that he was of distinct service to his country.

It was just that . . . The sea. He was missing it: the heave of a deck, the hard ocean breezes, the knowledge that a ship of a thousand tons was obedient to his will, heading for adventure and fulfilment just over the horizon.

He downed the whisky in one and coughed apologetically. 'Oh, Seph. I was just thinking about this devil's brew – you know, the steam business. My interim report's gone in and it caused a bit of a fuss.'

'Oh dear,' she said fondly. 'Not another bothersome fellow objecting to the cut of your jib.'

'Not this time. The first is I've sadly let down Bentham who's greatly taken by anything steam, and there's been more than a few at the Admiralty quoting me as a reason to dismiss it all out of hand.' It irritated Kydd that his position was so misconstrued. He'd been careful to point out that while his conclusion was that steam had no place at sea, it was based on the evidence of what he'd seen. He'd given solid reasons of practicality that made it unsuitable, such as the insanity of having continuous roaring furnace fires in the bowels of a wooden ship when at night in any well-found frigate the galley fire and even all candles were doused in respect of the danger of fire.

This thought brought on a fit of longing for the uncomplicated and satisfying life at sea and he doggedly steered his mind back to the present. What fresh ingenuity would he be presented with next? It was extraordinary what the human mind was capable of and possibly he himself might come up with something – what about that wire rope he'd seen on bridges? It would be a sovereign replacement for backstays and shrouds, presumably never rotting or stretching and—

He heard a knocking at the door and shortly afterwards a servant appeared with a note. He recognised the hand immediately. It was from Bentham and was hastily scribbled.

While aware of your objections to steam I rather fancy you will be intrigued by developments in the north, Glasgow. I would take it kindly should you journey there and make yourself known to the gentleman detailed below who will take care of the details. I beg you will not delay. The matter is well afoot.

Apparently Bentham was not going to hold Kydd's report against him and was prepared to trust him on further work, presumably steam. So, another huge reeking industrial beast to admire and detest? He'd go, if only to show impartial.

Chapter 47

Glasgow

It was not as he'd expected. No industrial works, no drab manufactory. Instead, he'd received a polite welcome from a Mr Hurley, chief clerk at the headquarters of the Helensburgh Hotel and Baths.

'Oh, Mr Kydd. So pleased to see you. We've been advised you wish to stay and take the waters at our Helensburgh chateau downriver.'

'Er, that's as may be. I believe there's been some error, sir. You are Mr Hurley?'

'I am, sir. You're accompanied? No? Then we shall endeavour to make your stay as comfortable as possible. You'll be availing yourself of passage in our tender?'

'Sir, I'm not sure I'm—'

'Yes, of course you will. Most people do, their only chance to ride in a genuine steam-ship at all.'

'I— What did you say?'

'An authentic steam-ship.' Gratified by Kydd's thunder-struck look, he went on, 'Yes, sir. A craft urged on by the power of steam alone. None of your sails and ropes and similar – our tender makes the river voyage of twenty-five miles in no more than three hours or so, whether the wind be fair or foul. And only here, the first of its kind. So, shall we say one ticket?'

In a daze Kydd allowed himself to be taken outside and shown the direction to the quay.

It was at the Broomielaw, the legendary last piece of Scottish soil trodden by generations of emigrants now settled in faraway lands. And now he was apparently going to take a journey made possible by the very steam engines he'd come to despise. As he strode towards the busy dock he tried to picture one of the massive beam engines ponderously nodding as it drove . . . what exactly? How was it mounted in the vessel without causing it to capsize under its weight?

He cast about, looking for a strange-appearing vessel towering over the others with a smoking chimney and a brickwork house on deck but couldn't see one.

Then he spotted a gathering crowd near the end of the quay. They were looking down at a small and undistinguished craft that had a tall but thick single pole . . . from the top of which smoke was lazily emerging.

Surely not! But then Kydd took in the jaunty house-flag and realised that this was what he was looking for.

He quickly joined the crowd and stared down. It was so small! He took in that it was only some fifty feet long, say a twenty- or thirty-ton burden vessel, not much more than twice the length of a man-o'-war's launch, but very different: a flared bow in place of the usual honest bluff sturdiness, a squared-off stern and a plain deck that ran at a level fore and aft. Dominating each side was a long rectangular green box and a dismaying lack of anything like rigging. No masts and spars, the only concession a single shroud and stay each side supporting the chimney. Even more unsettling was the complete lack of gear to enable rowing or the use of multi-manned sweeps. This ship – this boat – had to proceed by steam or not at all.

Her appearance was smart and well kept, her hull a bright black set off with yellow striping around the boxes. She had the pretence of a bowsprit but with a plain scrowling in place of a figurehead. Her name was there in gilt proudly across her transom: *Comet*.

'All aboard who dares come!' bawled one of the crew, emerging from below with a well-polished speaking trumpet. 'Ten minutes!'

There was an awed ripple of comment in the crowd and Kydd felt a stab of alarm. He'd heard of boilers exploding, and if the mechanicals of this vessel exerted themselves more than the ordinary to move it, could this produce a calamity?

Two or three of the onlookers went down the stone steps to board, followed by Kydd whose stick caused a couple of crewmen help him clumsily over the short gangway.

He guessed Bentham had chosen to handle things this way as he didn't want any fuss made that could affect his findings. Therefore he would not disclose who he was or the reason for his interest, and confined himself to a mildly curious inspection of the fitments. Aft there was a tiny cabin with seats concealing a pair of beds and a diminutive table. Amidships he found the well that contained the engine, forward the crew quarters.

It was the engine that would tell him the most. Even with his new-won knowledge from Goodrich he found it perplexing, but noticing his interest a coal-blackened seaman offered to point out the main features.

It seemed that there was no great nodding beam, just a single upright cylinder with a throw of only sixteen inches connected to a six-foot flywheel and crankshaft running across the craft. These in turn would be rotating a pair of opposite paddlewheels to send *Comet* along allegedly at anything up to seven knots – the speed of a frigate full and bye in light airs.

The boiler was pointed out, set in brickwork, the opposite side occupied by the coal bunker. Already there were three crewmen in the confined space heaving coal into the maw of the boiler, heat coming up in oven-like waves; the others around the deck seemed to be there only to handle the mooring ropes. A better-dressed individual standing impatiently next to the tiller was doubtless the captain.

There was a sudden hiss and a proud hail came from the engine: '*Steeeeam ho!*'

'All aboard?' the captain demanded.

'Aye!'

'Bear off forrard.'

Lines were quickly thrown aboard and the bow of *Comet* was poled out. Another cry was heard from the captain. 'Both ahead, a half-oh!'

A faint squeal came from one of the ladies standing near Kydd as, with an iron clanking, levers were thrown and, with a fearsome breath, steam was admitted to the engine. An increasing pounding rhythm began and, with much heavy splashing overside, *Comet* made her way out through the vessels at anchor ready for their cargo handling.

Kydd was mesmerised – horrified and fascinated by turns.

All this captain-cum-helmsman needed was to show the boat the way with his tiller. No necessity to try the wind, work out the set of the sails to cast to the right side, send the men aloft to loose them, then stand by to go about mid-river.

It was done in minutes with no fuss and the barest effort.

A man at the steering, several at the engine, perhaps five or so in all?

His world spun.

As *Comet* straightened for the run downriver he pulled himself together. Time to take measure of this – this phantasm.

He couldn't ask questions as it would give him away but he could observe. The vessel was proceeding at a steady rate, well up to the seven knots quoted, and it was in complete disregard, even ignorance, of the stiffening north-easterly, normally a fine wind outward bound. The tide was against them and Kydd knew that their speed through the water might be seven knots but speed over the ground would be less – no steam advantage.

Remembering Goodrich's stern comments on 'duty', he crossed casually to see into the coal bunker. It was some twelve feet long and three or four deep. Later he would convert this volume to bushels of coal. With nearly a quarter used already, by the amount remaining he could calculate its consumption for the voyage. Voyage? It was passing strange to be thinking in these terms.

Lost to speculation he watched the banks of the Clyde slip by in regular progression – if he was in *Tyger* and the breeze was more in the west he'd be at stations to put about by now. Hundreds of men would abandon their work to close up for the manoeuvre with officers to command them through experienced petty officers, overseen by the wise and all-knowing sailing master – and the same again when they'd made the other side.

The biggest mystery was how the monstrous engines he'd seen working before had been reduced in size to this one. It could all be contained in a box a fathom square!

He sauntered up to the 'captain' and complimented him on his fine vessel.

'Aye, she is that,' he replied, completely at his ease.

'Does she answer the helm well?' Kydd ventured.

'She does. Take her – yes, like this,' he said condescendingly, to the man who'd fought the tiller of a naval cutter in the madness of a Caribbean hurricane.

Kydd held the tiller firmly and with his thigh pressuring slightly nudged the boat to starboard. It had an odd, dead feel to it, quite unlike a ship under sail. That had a liveliness resulting from its characteristic weather or lee helm, always resisting the wheel's attempt to deviate from the vessel's set balance of sail and rudder pressure. He put the tiller over and, without argument, the boat altered to comply. It was alien, giving no indication of how the craft liked it, and all the time the engine pounded on, endlessly driving into it cared not where.

He yielded up the helm, trying not to notice the man's curious gaze.

By the time the river widened the boat was beginning to feel the rising chop from seawards, rolling awkwardly and uncomfortably, the steadying pressure of the sails not there to damp the alien twitching and jolting, but he now had what he needed written in his notebook.

The owner and designer was Henry Bell. *Comet* had been built locally at a Clyde shipyard and was powered by an engine with the strength of four horses.

The coal bunker had emptied at an alarming rate and would need replenishing before the return run, and *Comet* could easily take twenty-five passengers if they stood for the whole three-hour journey. Water for the steam was provided by a condensing chamber and the iron paddles could be disengaged, then coupled such that one or both could be regulated in terms of speed and even reversed to send the vessel astern.

His careful inspection told him that *Comet*, while odd-looking, was put together with materials and techniques common to any timber-built craft, the only novelty its engine and paddle-wheels, but he hadn't the knowledge to make any further judgement until he had spoken to one who had. And Bentham had recommended to him a master in steam, a Cornishman by the name of Richard Trevithick.

Chapter 48

London

'Cap'n Dick? Of course I know him! He's a firm friend to all who love steam – and should you wish to meet him, I do believe he's in Town at the moment.' Goodrich had lost his usual weighty expression and it was now wreathed in reluctant smiles at some recollection. 'A gentle giant, knows his mechanicals more than any man alive.'

He shook his head in wonderment. 'Has a mind as fertile as would stun any philosopher, believe me. In the year one, if I remember rightly, he wonders why a steam engine should be fixed in place and decides he'll make one to roam about. Calls it his "road carriage" as it's naught but a common coach fitted with one of his engines for driving on the roads. To test it one Christmas Eve he invites a party of his intimates to board the jolly craft and heads up the steep hill out of Camborne. They reach near to the top and to celebrate the feat they dash into a tavern and carouse, forgetting to draw fires. Outside, his wondrous carriage proceeds to explode.'

Kydd grinned, drawn to this picture of the man.

'And more recently, his Steam Circus?' Goodrich continued. 'Do tell.'

'Here in London, the Euston Road. Erects a huge circular stockade, and within lays a pair of tram rails. On it he places a locomoting engine he calls "Catch-me-who-can", which draws behind it a number of wagons, and invites the public to ride with no horse in sight at a shilling a head.'

'A sovereign idea.'

'Unhappily, no. The public was seized with terror at the unknown snorting beast and wouldn't ride, rather watching from a safe distance.' Goodrich gave a sad smile. 'A man of ideas, not one to trouble seeing them through to perfection. And cruelly hounded by Boulton and Watt for patent infringement on their original design as they saw their profits dwindle in the wake of his ingenious contrivances. I could not suggest a better to provide you with a picture of where steam stands now and what of the future.'

The stews of Limehouse were not where Kydd expected to find such a titan of invention, but the careworn soul who answered the door at the address given admitted to being Jane, his wife, but not before he assured her that he was not a bailiff.

At the moment it seemed her husband was to be found at the Dog and Duck with his friends.

The afternoon was grey and dreary, spatters of rain obliging Kydd to draw his grego close, which at the same time enabled him to conceal his gentlemanly dress.

In the brightly lit interior of the hostelry one table in particular was in lively debate, centred on a large man in an ironworker's smock. He was loudly regaling some tale to the others who laughed and slapped the table. At the end one of them interrupted: 'It's easy for you t' say, Dick. You've put y' mark on the world. How are we to do the same, then?'

'Well, if that's what you're after . . .'

'Don't flam wi' me—'

'. . . then I'm sure I can help ye!' With a grace that belied his size the large man shot to his feet and lifted the man bodily out of his seat, then, neatly rotating him to a dangle, thrust his legs sharply upward to leave two muddy footprints on the whitewashed ceiling. 'There you are, cuffin!'

The roars of laughter included Kydd's. 'Mr Trevithick?' he managed.

'Aye?' He was well-built but his generous open face was lined and worn. 'And who's you?' The Cornish accent was marked.

'I'd like to hire your services if I may. To talk steam with me.'

'What's your game, cully?' The expression changed in an instant to a pinched suspicion.

'I need a cove as knows his steam to give me a steer, is all. Shall we say five guineas for the evening?'

A sudden hush descended.

'To talk steam?'

'Just so.'

'Seven guineas!'

There had to be a budget line for this kind of thing, Kydd reflected. 'Done!'

Mrs Trevithick welcomed him doubtfully. Their home was tiny, the living room dwarfed by Trevithick's bulky frame, but it was neat and snug. 'Settle y'selves down, then, and I'll fetch you a bite,' she said, and brought an oil-lamp to set on the table.

'So what do ye want to know, Mr . . .?' The expression was guarded, with a hint of suspicion.

'Kydd. Thomas Kydd. I want to know about steam, Mr Trevithick. Should I put my trust in it, or is it a passing fancy of projectors? You're a master in steam – what's your answer?'

'Steam? Cully, anywhere you sees horses I can put an engine. Anywhere!'

'That's all very well, sir, but—'

'And that's anywheres – pumping, tool-shaping, smelting, dredging—'

'Quite. But what of its future?'

'Future? Nothing short o' golden, Mr Kydd. An' that's because o' two things it has: mobility, and strong steam.'

'Oh?'

'Mobility – I've myself shown as how an engine can be carried in anything with wheels and it'll go like a good 'un. Strong steam – your Newcomen, even the latest Boulton an' Watt only uses atmospheric pressure. With them, if y' wants a more powerful beastie, all you can do is increase the size o' the cylinder. Why, you can go out now an' find one with a twenty-foot cylinder, as I can replace with a six-inch job.'

'How, pray?'

'As I said, strong steam. Means steam admitted at many times atmospheric pressure. Stands t' reason, it can move mountains.'

He watched Kydd closely, then sat back. 'M' friend, steam comes in many ways. Unless you tell me who's sending you I can't give you any more words on the matter.'

'My— Our interest is in . . . the sea. Steam in ships.'

'Ah. Maritime. You've made visit to see *Comet*? Well, she's the one and only boat in steam I can point you at – none I should say have tasted salt water, actually gone out on the high seas.'

This was a blow to Kydd. Bentham would want evidence,

and if *Comet* was the only one and she not seagoing, what could he say?

Trevithick brightened. 'But I likes you, Mr Kydd. Have a friend in Leeds who asked me to furnish him with one o' my engines as will allow him to ply for hire on the River Yare. Wants strong steam and a tight engine, so I provides him with an eight-inch double-acting job, which'll give him a full eight horses' power. So there you are, yes?'

'Meaning?'

'Well, if he's in Leeds an' wants to work on the Yare, doesn't it mean he'll have t' take the ship out the Humber into the North Sea and around to Yarmouth to deliver 'un? Open sea all the way, and if you take passage with him you'll see how a steam-ship works against the waves an' all. Come to think on it, shouldn't be surprised if he's the first to do it, b' Gob.'

Kydd breathed deeply. It was coming together! Whatever his feelings about steam there was now a chance to see it matched against the majesty of the ocean – and his opinion would then take form and substance with unanswerable backing.

'Mr Trevithick, I thank you most sincerely. I'm leaving now for Leeds and if you give me his address I'll think your guineas right well earned.'

Chapter 49

Yorkshire

Kydd soon found himself well inland in Leeds, a mill town of rapidly growing size in the industrial landscape that was changing so much of Britain's central countryside. Oddly, while being so far from the sea, it had a port. Blessed with deep-water rivers it could reach the sea by following the Aire and the Ouse to the Humber, then a further fifty miles to the North Sea past Spurn Head.

Kydd took this in, remembering the near-invisible sand spit finality from seaward.

The address he'd been given led to a modest, red-stone building in the centre of the town.

'Mr Wright? Would that be Mr Richard or Mr John?'

'Er, the one dealing with the steam-ship.'

'They both do, sir, but I believe Mr Richard will answer. Your name, sir?'

Mr Richard Wright was small in stature, comfortably rotund, and with creased, twinkling eyes. He greeted Kydd effusively. 'The Navy!' he spluttered. 'As I stand and stare! What, sir, can we do for you?'

Trevithick's introductory note smoothed the way. 'Well, you do come at a propitious moment, sir. Our fine vessel stands ready for the voyage south and you may bid her adieu on Thursday next.'

'Sir, I have an interest in what you propose in this venture and it's my earnest desire to see through the passage at sea – to be aboard as she sails . . . or, um, leaves.'

'A singular request, Sir Thomas.' His air became defensive and grave. 'Sir, you're not to be numbered among those who turn their face against marine steam?'

'No, certainly not.'

'Then I will speak with Captain Woods. If he concurs, you'll take passage.'

Kydd stood by the docks as *L'Actif* was readied for sea. A curious feeling stole over him. The vessel he was seeing close to was unquestionably a French privateer – the typical three-masted lug rig of a Brittany *chasse-marée*, the generous lines that kept her draught down, the retracting bowsprit for tucking into scarce space alongside cargo-handling wharves. And at this size it would be twenty guns shipped at least.

He caught the captain as he approached from a wharf office with a bundle of papers. A heavily built, no-nonsense seaman of the old school in a long frock coat of another age and shabby tricorn, he glared at Kydd as though he was the source of all his troubles.

'I've a note from Mr Richard Wright begging you'll allow me passage in *L'Actif* as you'll be delivering her to Yarmouth.'

'No room f'r passengers!' Woods growled, and made to push past Kydd.

Kydd held his ground. 'I'm no passenger, sir. I'm here to see how your fine craft behaves in the open sea.'

'Get out of my way! Short-handed, the last thing I needs is a dandy-rigged lubber to fuss over.'

With a saintly smile Kydd allowed that as a post-captain, Royal Navy, he was hoping that it would qualify him to ship out as an able seaman in his fine vessel – of which he could claim a trifle of acquaintance off the French coast.

'Bear a fist at the ropes? Forrard some hauley-hauley at the winch?' His lip curled in something like contempt.

'Any lawful order under the Articles,' Kydd replied evenly.

The man's eyes dropped to Kydd's stick but when he looked up it was with a touch of humour. 'Well, an abled-bodied seaman you ain't, but if you needs to go that bad, I'll take a chance on ye. Kip in a 'mick with the others, ship's vittles, keep out o' the way, specially them engines.'

In the evening Woods mellowed over a beef pie at the Seven Seas, and Kydd learned much. It seemed that the vessel had originally been taken by one Lieutenant Hancock of *Blazer* sloop after a smart action off Flamborough Head. It had duly gone on to the prize-court auctions, to be snapped up cheaply, given the number of other victories the Navy was achieving at sea.

All guns had been removed and the engine fitted by mill-wrights from a Leeds yard. And at the moment *L'Actif* was storing for the voyage.

It turned out that at first the Wright brothers had put money into an extraordinary hydrogen-explosion-powered engine but after it proved unreliable had fallen back on one of Mr Trevithick's high-pressure engines of eight horses' power driving a pair of side paddles. It had recently been tested in the river and had reached the astonishing speed of six and a half knots, faster than most merchant ships could do with a favourable wind. She was unlike *Comet* in that she had not been built for steam and still retained her full rig of sails, which, being fore-and-aft in nature, wouldn't obstruct the working of the steam engine.

They had their hopes in the venture, the vessel able to carry above a hundred passengers at a shilling a ticket to ply the Yare from Yarmouth inland to Norwich.

What he said next brought Kydd up short. 'In course we'll sail her down to Yarmouth. Can't get insurance on a voyage in steam out to sea, seein' how nobody's ever done it afore. As it is, the beggars are making me take the paddles off and lash 'em on deck and douse the fires to show I didn't do so.'

'Captain, how will you know her ways under mechanicals without you steam her there?'

'The voyage is over when we pass Gorleston pier into the Yare. I'll then set about re-shipping m' paddles and firin' up, so we'll give everyone a show.'

'In the river.'

'Can't be helped.'

Kydd was on the edge of abandoning the trip but realised that even a river run would give him valuable evidence. 'Then I'll see you Thursday, Captain.'

It was a long run to sea – inland waterways thirty miles to Goole, then the Ouse to the much wider Humber. Woods went by steam only a small part of the way out of respect to wear, for *L'Actif* would be spending her working life as a commercial vessel later. It gave Kydd another chance to experience being afloat in steam, this time in an allegedly sea-going craft. It was the same rattling, clanking, waterwheel-splashing progress – a never-ending busy hiss and snorting, but with a wheel as helm in place of the smaller *Comet's* tiller there was still that same disturbing dead feel.

After a snatched four-hour sleep while tied to the riverbank they were off at daylight and headed into tidal waters. The flat, marshy banks fell away each side as the river imperceptibly turned into an estuary and the first sea winds came bustling in. Woods didn't hesitate. This was Spurn Head, the seaward end of the river and he had no intention of risking his insurance. *L'Actif* obediently set her bow for the lee of the sandy foreland and gently nudged into a tiny fisherman's pier.

'Rig y' stay-end tackles and we'll have the paddlers out o' her.' The crew of nine found the going hard until the vast sized paddle-wheels were securely in place on deck, the boiler fires damped down and extinguished. *L'Actif* was now a sailing ship and would stay so until Yarmouth.

'She's a good sailer,' said Woods, patting her wheel. But it was singular for Kydd, a square-rig sailor, to see how sail was bent on near vertically and let loose by turns to meet the wind. With long practice he faced the wind and sniffed, and saw that as a respectable north-easter it was fair for leaving.

They showed some sail at the fore, which set the privateer out from the pier. Neatly catching a workmanlike breeze, they took in all lines and fell away in a long sweep for the open sea. Following the channel past the Binks, *L'Actif* made good speed but in respect to the north-easterly it would be necessary to keep a decent offing from the shore in their lee.

Kydd saw that with the tide on the ebb the wave progressions were being countered by the wind. The result was irritable, choppy waves that sent spiteful lashes of salt spray into their teeth.

'I mislike that boldering weather t' the east, Cap'n,' Woods growled at Kydd. 'Mayhap have t' make more of an offing, I reckons.' It was a question, really, and Kydd was pleased that he was being recognised as a brother captain.

He raised his eyes and had to agree. The horizon in the wind's eye was lost in white-grey murk, with a dismal leaden backdrop behind, as plain as a written label that the North Sea was in a sullen mood that could turn savage later.

'A reef, at all?'

'Aye.' Kydd's suggestion was to reduce sail in preparation but Woods kept on until after several angry gusts the wind veered easterly and strengthened.

'Bugger this,' Woods spat. 'In a fore 'n' after, less sail the safer, but y' get carried t' leeward.'

It was a wicked part of the east coast with its offshore banks and low, near-invisible shoreline. The wind's chop to more in the east meant that his move to make an offing was in doubt. His only option now was to shape course more to the south and attempt to round the bulge of Norfolk without being headed or driven ashore.

'But I'll do it!'

The wheel went over, the sheets eased and *L'Actif* took up to the south-east. They continued for only a while before Kydd's instincts sounded an alarm. 'We're not getting our offing – wind and current against us!'

There was nothing in the seascape that could prove his words, only the direction and angle of the marching waves matched against the dancing compass card. The situation was, however, getting serious.

'Yes,' shouted back Woods. 'We needs t' get somewhere out of this.'

Kydd knew little of the east-coast inshore shipping routes, with their haven ports, for his usual track from there was for Scandinavia and the Baltic.

'An' I know where,' Woods declared positively. 'Helm up an' its west-nor'-westerly, lads,' he ordered the two at the wheel, and the fine-lined privateer seethed away downwind.

It couldn't last, and within the hour an anxious lookout reported land right across their course.

Woods leaped to the shrouds and stared out. 'Thornham church!' he threw back. 'We needs to sight it as gives us clearance o' the Threddlethorpe overfalls!'

Kydd joined the others in a frantic search for anything that looked like a church. Woods suddenly pointed and jumped back to the deck to take a bearing. 'I've got 'un! Fine up more t' the nor'-west.'

The coast neared, with its border of white surf, but Kydd could see nothing that even resembled a shelter and this a dead lee shore. Only the calm faces of the crew eased his fears and he watched respectfully as, closer to, he could make out a break in the white to which they were heading.

Without comment Woods brought *L'Actif* through a narrow waterway into inner and calmer waters.

It was no place to anchor and, without any hesitation, he had the privateer curving around, then driving hard aground on the muddy foreshore to her rest.

They were safe.

But the tide was not in their favour. It was busily on the ebb. *L'Actif*, though, settled happily to the mud as a 'tide-chaser' was designed to do.

'This is not getting us to Yarmouth,' Woods said, after an hour had passed. 'They'll think us worthless fussocks, we taking our time.'

Kydd commiserated but knew that with the wind firmly in the east and probably shifting to the south-east they had little choice. 'Batten down and wait?'

Woods's features turned ugly, pugnacious. 'Because the wind's turned agin' us? I've a mind t' do something about it, Cap'n Sir Kydd.'

'What can you do, sir. I counsel—'

'Bosun!' he roared. 'Get those paddles rigged. Top o' the tide in two hours – and, you stokers, get that fire up. I'm steaming off.'

L'Actif floated off and the engines started their clanking, hissing chorus.

'I've lost my insurance but saved her from wreck,' Woods snarled defiantly.

It was a colossal gamble. He was defying traditional practice and no court in the land would approve of his action.

The long bows of the privateer turned and faced the fury of the open ocean, taking each comber as it came.

The winds now were flat and hard from the east and had every sign of veering more to the south and heading her, but *L'Actif*, with her sturdy mechanical heart thumping away, headed directly into them, shouldering the vicious seas aside to win her way seaward.

For Kydd, it was against all the vital instincts of years: the wooing of Neptune in his bad moods, the easing and clawing that were the way of a sail-ship to stay with a storm. The tricks and strategies that saw the vessel and her trusting crew through to the other side, the deep relationship a captain had with the creature that was fighting for him: was this all to be made extinct in the same way that hand weavers had seen their life and livelihood lost to the power loom?

The seas were murderous, short but vicious, driven by a savage gale, foaming in from the North Sea – but *L'Actif* showed no canvas. All gear was frapped in and a vessel with the same canvas aloft as one idly alongside was nevertheless making her way out to the deep sea. It was hard to take – but he was here to give a fair report of what he saw.

She kept her course. The helmsman was not fighting the wheel, but throwing the bow into one roaring sea and easing back to take another on the shoulder before swiftly putting on wheel to meet an ugly cross-sea. And then Kydd understood: there was no strong, steadying sail to keep her on track through all these frontal assaults. With mechanical steam each wave progression had to be fought separately and to its conclusion. Without feel at the helm it would be a hard and skilful trick at the wheel.

He grabbed a line and hauled himself forward to the engine-well. He looked down and saw the crew feeding the boiler. Fighting to keep a foothold, with a long coal-slice they unerringly projected their load into the maw of the fire, hooking back the iron door closed with a metal claw. On the engine side the levers and sliding rods were playing in precisely the same rhythm whatever the ship's motion, to and fro. Endless pulsing movements, mesmerising in their unvarying motion in a whirl of gleaming steel and oil, wisps of steam instantly carried away.

And in the little cabin below there was the usual chaos of a tempest but as well there was something else. A thumping rhythm more felt than heard, as precise as a clock ticking and as calming, a protecting mother's heartbeat, an assurance of security. As long as the engine continued its mechanical pounding, kept up its beat, they were safe.

He went back on deck. This was past a topsail gale – they'd be bringing in canvas hand over fist if this were *Tyger*, and decisions would have to be made before night fell.

Yet it could not be denied that they were successfully thrashing their way out, directly and deliberately into the angry seas, with no regard to wind direction. Their offing was being won by brute mechanical force. If not now, in the future steam would surely triumph.

Chapter 50

The Atlantic

The broad swell from out of the west urged them on. Lieutenant Gindler felt bound for both adventure and destiny.

He was under no illusion: he was captain of a seagoing man-o'-war because his impulsive act in throwing himself at the enemy ships in the Lake Erie battle had been taken as a cool calculation of chances by Perry, his squadron commander. He'd seen him placed in this brave little bark as master so Gindler thus joined the select few that were captains of a real warship in the United States Navy.

USS *Kestrel* was a brig-sloop and accounted a flyer by her many admirers. She was no leviathan, the smallest in the fleet to be trusted to cross oceans, but in his eyes the most spirited. Her yellow-varnished hull boasted a full nine gun-ports a side, each covering a twenty-four-pounder carronade, with a pair of long twelve-pounders on deck. Gindler had found the means to ensure her bulwarks inboard were in scarlet, her spars black and the figurehead of a bird of prey picked out in gold and colour.

When asked by a sympathetic secretary to the Navy what operations he had in mind for his first cruise he had answered instantly: to follow in the wake of his childhood hero, John Paul Jones, and fall on the English shipping in their home waters. And now here he was, tasked with taking the fight to the enemy, about to raise the southern tip of Ireland, the focus of English shipping making for their home ports after long voyages.

Looking forward he could see Davis, his first lieutenant and only other officer, hazing the hands as they worked. If his behaviour in battle was as fierce as this Gindler would be well satisfied. Next to the mainmast his master's mate Borden in his capacity of boatswain was instructing some seamen. Along with Coltrop, the midshipman, and Samson, the gunner, he was among those who'd transferred into *Kestrel* from *Prospero*. And with the pick of the Boston waterfront Gindler had got together a crew of blue-water sailormen.

'Deck there!' called the foretop lookout. '*Laaaand ho!* Fine on the weather bow!'

Gindler tried to hide a smile of satisfaction behind a professional frown. Making landfall on the nose after all those thousands of miles of empty ocean: this was what it meant to be a deep-sea mariner.

There was an instant buzz of anticipation about the decks that always followed the miracle of raising land, but for him it was a different matter. They had safely crossed the Atlantic and were now in hostile waters where every sail was an enemy – and they were utterly alone. It was up to him to bring them to an action and justify his cruise, but if he blundered onto a powerful Royal Navy warship the glory would turn to ashes. The essence of his orders was simple. He was to station himself at the mouth of the English Channel and cause havoc to the merchant shipping that passed, meaning almost all of Britain's foreign trade.

He could expect opposition. This was the most sensitive, most vulnerable of sea-lanes, where all must converge. England would deploy defences in depth against marauders in their home waters and he must be prepared. And as a prize-taker he had another problem. He still hadn't resolved the issue of prize crews. In his small man-o'-war he wasn't in a position to supply an endless stream of hands to man each prize, not as it would be in a large privateer. He'd take it case by case. And water, victuals – this was an enemy coast and his resources were limited. He must make their time in the field count.

At noon this fine day he could get a precise latitudinal fix. As it turned out the hazy foreland on the larboard bow was Mizzen Head, a well-known signalling station where merchant ships would let their owners know that their voyaging was safely over. There would be much prey about here but with the fatal drawback that a strike against the enemy within sight of the signal station would bring retaliation about his ears in short order.

He'd try his luck elsewhere. The Royal Navy had their base in Cork, to the south-east of Ireland. He'd venture further around the west coast, perhaps towards the busy Shannon River.

'English colours, Mr Coltrop,' he ordered. Under an enemy flag *Kestrel* bore away innocently northwards, remembering as she passed to dip her ensign in respect to the King's colours ashore.

It was almost too easy. There were more than a few sail in sight for this would be assumed to be a safe but longer passage north-about Ireland to Liverpool. But Gindler was aware that at the first prize he took an alarm would be sounded up and down the coast that they were no longer safe. He'd better make it a good one.

Through his powerful telescope he surveyed the vessels and one in particular stood out: a fat brig in the process of rounding the point before them into the startling green of Bantry Bay.

His victim was selected and he had only to pounce but a long chase was not what was wanted at this stage.

'Easy at the helm,' he cautioned. No point in frightening him off by altering towards, and he had a better plan. Just as soon as the vessel had disappeared behind the point, *Kestrel* clapped on full sail in a glorious charge that once around found them just a few hundred yards astern of their prey. A gun was fired and the brig brought to with gratifying haste.

Gindler himself went in the boat and boarded with pride. *Kestrel*'s first capture!

With the Stars and Stripes now a-fly over his command he demanded papers of the sullen captain, quickly discovering that the ship was English, with a cargo of wine and ceramics for Limerick, undeniably enemy trade and therefore prize. But he was now confronted with the problem he knew he must face – detach some of his precious crew to man the brig and sail her to the nearest prize court, now the other side of the Atlantic or . . .?

There was really only one answer and soon after the last of the dejected crew had been taken off, flames began licking up the hatchways, a fortune in prize cargo going up in the blaze acknowledged by long faces among the Kestrels.

International law required any prize to be first condemned in a prize court. Gindler knew he was in contravention of this but felt justified in his action. This was war and he was doing more than taking an enemy ship: he was spreading alarm and despondency among his country's enemies to their cost, if only in the raising of insurance rates.

Leaving their bonfire astern, *Kestrel* re-hoisted English colours and moved on to take another, a barque close inshore with a hold crammed full of cheeses and hornware from Ireland's rural west bound to Liverpool, and yet another further out with ironmongery for Galway. It was becoming impossible: even taking and burning were leaving him with prisoners that outnumbered his own crew. The nature of the latest cargo suggested a way out: all prisoners were set to throwing overside the tin pans, saucepans and griddles in a steady stream and then the empty ship took aboard all his prisoners, told to make for the nearest port.

It was all he could do but it guaranteed their presence was known. A predator more dangerous than the occasional privateer, nothing less than a unit of the United States Navy with a mission to cause the utmost harm to the English. Intelligence of *Kestrel*'s name, her size and armament, even down to the name of her captain would now be spreading rapidly, the forces of retribution angrily gathering. He had to do what he could before they closed in.

Here on the Atlantic side of Ireland he'd go no further than the Shannon, knowing it would be sure to harbour some kind of naval presence but at the same time be a-swarm with merchant shipping.

When they rounded the Dingle and then Kerry's Head at the entrance, he had the pick of at least fifty sail. The word had not yet been passed. There was no terrified fleeing and, under the English flag, he brazenly joined the tide of inward-bound shipping, gazing left and right to choose his victim.

This was a sizeable full-rigged foreigner, which with contraband bound for an English port was certainly prize-worthy, and Gindler, after dousing his British colours and hoisting the American, sent his first lieutenant to take possession. It was a rich haul – Indian luxury goods and eastern spices – but it couldn't be helped. The flames spared nothing and uncountable thousands were dashed from English hands.

But a sharp-eyed lookout had noticed something. On the highest eminence of Kerry Head there was a low structure with an adjacent mast, a signal station. They'd seen everything and now had furious hoists of flags aloft, a minute gun demanding attention.

It were better they departed the scene as quickly as possible. Should he return to the United States after an admitted success in setting alight the seas around Britain? If he turned south and rounded Cape Clear he would be in the Celtic Sea, the busiest and richest sea highway he'd ever get the chance to see.

He'd sustain his cruise by confiscating all victuals and stores aboard his captures and sending in the occasional cargo-stripped item with his prisoners.

Here there was sail aplenty so he took and burned two more, but he knew his luck would run out sooner or later.

As they shaped course up the coast an eager lookout spied a curious thing. A rakish schooner closely pursued by a cutter and a brig-of-war. Gindler could see it all – a Boston schooner sent to add to his mission being run down by the British.

'We'll join the party!' he announced, and gave orders that saw them throw over the helm to intercept.

It wasn't long, however, before it became clearer. As one, the three came across the wind and made straight for *Kestrel*. It was some sort of trap and Gindler wasn't to be caught. Abruptly coming about tight to the wind and making for the open sea he fled the scene.

For all of seven hours he maintained his course and only as the day faded could he stand down his exhausted men.

After a night under easy sail he resumed his hunting. For some reason the calmness of the seascape was unsettling. Counting on *Kestrel*'s light-sparred build for escape, even in light winds, Gindler knew he should not have been disturbed but he was.

There was hardly a ripple and a languid sun rose slowly from a misty horizon, which hour by hour thickened into a broad fog-bank. *Kestrel* was now past Cape Clear. This was the confluence of the sea-lanes that led to Bristol and Liverpool and by rights should have been alive with merchant shipping but there was nothing in sight.

Closing the white blankness at a mere walking pace, Gindler froze. Emerging from the fog were the indistinct silhouettes of not one but three sizeable vessels. Before he could react another four had come into view, all heading directly for him.

A fleet! And in these waters no need to guess under whose flag they sailed.

'English colours,' he snapped. 'Helm down, and pass under their lee.'

If they altered to follow he would know the worst but the truth dawned quickly. This was no fleet – it was a convoy, by its course homeward bound. His reflex was the right one: he was giving best to the river of ships that now passed them, an escort not bothering to investigate *Kestrel*, for Gindler's action had been the conventional thing to do in the circumstances.

He counted twenty, thirty, or more, resuming their lines and stations after the confusion of the fog-bank, thinning out as the stragglers and fearful tried to catch up.

It dawned on him that, far from tamely letting the convoy go, there was something he could do. 'Into the fog,' he ordered, 'and I'll have one hand in the fore cross-trees.' High enough to see mastheads protruding up through the fog.

His plan was simple. In the fog, he'd curve about the rear

of the convoy and come up on the last one or two before the escorts or other ships could see what was going on.

It was dangerous work, with visibility down to yards, but a large barque was firming up ahead. There could be no betraying sound of gunfire and Gindler made his point by hauling alongside and, at his order to heave to, running out his guns. It was a rich haul of indigo and joggaree sugar but, as with all the others, pitilessly set to the torch. Handily a last straggler was nearby and *Kestrel* off-loaded her prisoners.

By this time the fog was lifting, revealing two ships alongside each other, never normally to be seen in a convoy and a ship afire close by, leaving little to the imagination as to what had happened.

'Cut loose!' Gindler yelled. He'd seen a powerful 38-gun frigate towards the van of the convoy and, no doubt attracted by the smoke, it had put about and was under full sail, charging back.

Tearing herself free *Kestrel* wheeled and promptly disappeared into the fog. Gratefully, Gindler felt its clammy chill enfolding them, embracing him with the blessed anonymity of its depths.

A sharp turn had them plunging ever deeper on a different course and after yet another to confuse further they could be accounted as having got away with it.

'Stand down the men?' asked Borden.

They'd been at a knife's edge of readiness for weeks now, had been mercilessly driven in chase after chase, and in these deadly hostile waters had had no chance to relax and rest. They'd done very well – for their size, very well indeed – and they'd fulfilled their orders to create a hullabaloo where it counted.

'No, Mr Borden,' he answered. 'Set 'em to rig all plain sail – we're going home.'

Chapter 51

London

'So I'm t' be hauled out o' my ship just t' hear a tale of
the sea?' Commander Edmund Bazely harrumphed in
mock disgust.

'As I happen to know, old trout, *Mermaid* is at Deptford
stairs in a state of idleness awaiting a new fit of carronades,'
Kydd replied, affronted with his old friend in equally feigned
measure. 'And this I promise will be worth your attending.'

Bazely slouched comfortably in his chair, feet towards the
fire. Kydd's naval apartment was not large but well fitted out,
and the whisky was on an ornamented side-table nearby. His
gaze turned to the elaborate painting above the mantel of a
long-ago battle of another time, darkened with age. 'Last I
heard you was struttin' the quarterdeck of a two-decker like
that'n. What are ye—'

'Another time, old chap. This is more interesting, I fancy.'

'Do stand on, then.'

Kydd couldn't help a pleased grin. This much-weathered
sailor was a staunch friend of his early days as an officer, and

261

later, as Kydd had advanced in society and his profession, had been the rock of plain-speaking and practical sense who had stood by him. When he'd seen him in the street earlier, he'd felt that Bazely was just the one to help cohere his racing thoughts to some sort of conclusion.

'Not so many days back I was in a humble barky in the North Sea, taking a bad-tempered nor'-easterly straight on the bow.'

'You – in a squiddy packet? Can't quite see that!'

'As a passenger.'

'Oh?'

'With Spurn Head under our lee, trying for an offing.'

Bazely took up a heroic pose. 'And so our Tom Cutlass springs up and roars, "Shiver me timbers, an' we has t' put about!" and orders more sail clapped on.'

'Not quite. See, we has no sail. At all.'

'Crack on, man. This is getting interesting.'

'Instead the helm's put down and we head directly into the seas and gale and that way makes our offing.'

'Um, not quite gettin' your drift. Without sail . . .'

'None. You see, dear fellow, our ship was no ordinary of the breed – it was a steam-ship.'

Bazely blinked. 'You mean you had one o' those clanking monsters on board an' it was . . . was . . .'

'I do. Now, old friend, I want you to think what it feels like, standing forrard watching as, without a stitch of canvas abroad, the ship bowts her way into the blow while we win our offing. Then helm over, and just point the beast in whatever direction as will give a good course, be damned to the wind.'

Bazely was struck dumb for a space, then shook his head slowly. 'As if it were by a spell o' magic. How . . .?'

'Not so hard to fathom. Your steam gives power to wheels

of paddles like oar-blades, only they keep turning in a circle, never stopping to rest.'

Slowly, as if in a trance, Bazely lifted his whisky and downed it in one. 'This needs thinking about.'

'As I'm trying. And not much time.'

'How so?'

'I took a knock from our Yankee cousins as nearly did for me. As I've been recovering these damned long months they thought to make me a surveyor for the Navy Board – of inventions and notions that might help the fight or save money.'

'You?'

'Well, I'm a junior in the ministry that does just that, taken aboard as I've a few thousand sea miles under my keel as will inform my judgement on its usefulness. This last task was given me by the inspector general himself – to look at steam as it could affect the Navy, then write a report all about it, with evidence.'

'What will you say to 'em?'

'He's a lover of steam himself and I'm devilish sure would like me to cry it up, but while there's been a few boats punting up and down canals this is the first one dares put out to the open sea. So, while I've proof it can be done, because it's the first there's nobody else to point to.'

'An' would it be wrong t' say that you're in with steam?' Bazely asked, fixing Kydd with a gaze of uncomfortable intensity.

'Er, I'm not saying that. I can quite see the advantages but . . .'

'I'd think hard afore you says anything, cully. You make out that the Admiralty should fit a steam engine in every crack frigate and ship-of-the-line and they'll think you either a hare-brained ninny or in the pay of a steam jobber. You've a fine future, which you'll lose if you go up agin' them.'

'You're assuming that the Admiralty will immediately take against steam. Once they see for themselves what I did, there's no doubt they'll want to get started, and that main quickly.'

'No, there you're wrong, my friend. Every man jack of your sacred Admiralty is old an' with habits settled in Vernon's day. They'll not—'

'If it's presented to them properly reasoned, every advantage explained as will appear in my account, they'll be brought to reason, I believe.'

'And if not? Think on it! They'll—'

He was interrupted by a hurried knock. Before Kydd could get to his feet the door burst open and Bentham, his cape streaming with rain, strode in.

'Ah, Kydd – I do hope I don't intrude?'

'Why, no, sir. Do meet my friend of years, Commander Bazely. This is the inspector general of Naval Works, Sir Samuel Bentham.'

'My honour, sir,' Bentham allowed, with a hurried bow and turned to Kydd. 'My dear fellow! I heard you were just returned after a startling adventure and I must know how you did.'

'Let me take your cape, sir. There – and I'm to tell you that I have conclusive proof that a vessel powered by steam is quite capable of riding the ocean billows where it will. I know, for I've seen it with my own eyes, sir.'

Bentham's eyes glowed. 'Well said, sir. Pray do tell me all of it.'

With Bazely silent but attentive, Kydd laid out the circumstances of his unlooked-for drama, realising as he spoke that his experience was propelling him into an eagerness and passion that part of his being was rebelling against. There had to be a deal of thinking about the implications of it all.

'Then their lordships can no longer ignore its existence.

Sir Thomas, I ask that your report with its conclusions and recommendations be upon my desk as soon as it may. I intend the world and his dog shall hear of steam and the sea!'

Bentham left as abruptly as he'd arrived.

'Tom – don't let it seize hold on ye,' Bazely said, in a low voice. 'It's only the latest fancy, new an' who should say dazzling to the senses. I beg you don't offend their lordships with matters as will only confuse 'em and set their faces against ye.'

But Kydd's mind was racing. Who knows? He was now the first and only naval officer seagoing in steam, and if there was to be a leading figure in a colossal push to bring the Navy to some sort of age of steam it would not be unreasonable to think it would be offered to him. If he was being denied a ship this would be a remarkable compensation.

'I hear what you're telling me, Bazely, but I must do my duty and get on with it. Do excuse, but I've a mort o' work to do.'

Chapter 52

Kydd's leg had been throbbing painfully lately, a red puff-iness becoming more than a little distracting. There were no more ligatures to pull out but the wound channel should have healed by now. It could well be that grave meas-ures would need to be taken soon. But now, sitting at his small desk, it was more irritating than threatening while he addressed himself to the crucial task of rendering wandering thoughts into incisive persuasion.

The first thing to settle was his real feelings in the matter, those he would stand behind as he argued.

Sucking his quill he tried to bring order to his reasoning.

Was he being unduly swayed by what he'd seen? Certainly he was impressed – more than that, he'd been viscerally moved by the shocking reality of something that went against all he knew of sailoring and the sea. But was this enough to condemn the old ways and insist on a navy of smoking chimneys and filthy coal?

Or was the whole thing, as Bazely had it, a passing novelty, a fad – much like Trevithick's steam road-carriage that had taken to the streets more than a dozen years ago now and which, for all its wonder, the world had not seen fit to accept?

If, on the other hand, he moved cautiously, it could conceivably result in a quicker-reacting Napoleon Bonaparte at the head of an invasion fleet of ships of steam, 'sailing' into the teeth of foul winds while . . .

All the time it was hammering in on him that this was no airy *proposed* theory. It had happened and he had been there to see it as a solid fact. Nothing could change that.

Yet was he, deep inside, prepared to contemplate service in a navy whose ships no longer moved under a glorious tracery of masts and sails, to be allowed to go only where a mechanist said he could? Shipmates with a clanking monstrosity he could not be expected to understand? All the little tricks and subterfuges he'd learned in a lifetime in sail now entirely useless and cast aside?

A surge of feeling left him in no doubt of his true devotion. That soaring monument to man's creating – a full-rigged ship under sail – was where his soul lay. The sweet curve of a sail's edge, the barely sensible changes in a ship's motions under the caring hands of a seaman, the exhilaration of a fresh gale and the barky held to a bowline: this was what it was to be a mariner, and this was where he belonged.

As swiftly as a striking snake came the retort: he must be true to his present position and commitment and make appraisal purely on the evidence. In essence, to expand on what he'd seen.

He began listing the advantages.

A battle squadron putting to sea in the teeth of a foul wind, never more to be embayed in its anchorage. The power at Admiralty level to know that a ship would arrive at its destination on a precise date, given the entirely predictable speed to be expected from steam machinery. In stately line-ahead a fleet able to keep station merely by setting the same speed by means of some valve. And with no complexity of mast and rigging, dozens of sails and so forth, far fewer seamen required to man a ship.

There was more but those were the main heads.

He began writing, keeping in mind the odd vagaries of Admiralty style – not omitting to keep his prose solemn, weighty and dignified. And setting out the conclusion as his own: that all steps be taken to introduce steam into the Royal Navy as soon as possible before other nations saw their chance to challenge its primacy at sea.

He read and reread the piece. Not so long, only three pages in his own bold hand, notionally addressed to his senior, the inspector general of Naval Works for the Navy Board.

It would go off by messenger in the morning and he would hold himself ready to answer any point at issue. Then it crossed his mind that it would be of value to get another's informed perspective, in particular that of an old acquaintance responsible for more than a few innovations of his own – from catamaran torpedo launchers to the very telegraph code the Navy used to this day. He would surely have views of his own, and he hurriedly penned a copy and placed it inside a cover addressed to Commodore Home Popham, Royal Navy.

Within days he had his response – and not the one he expected. Letters came, first singly, and then by dozens. From naval officers, Admiralty functionaries, notables of every stripe, even retired admirals.

They had much to say, with vigour and venom in equal measure. Most took against him for venturing to advocate a navy of iron and coal when the one in existence was so splendidly keeping the seas. One or two gave cautious backing, but in the main it was a tidal wave of hostility. Kydd could not understand where it was coming from in such a short while. Bentham himself was unable to account for it as the report and his covering note had only just been forwarded, but he promised Kydd that he would be making a personal visit to the Admiralty in support.

It had to be that he'd touched a nerve, given so much opposition to a logical treatment.

When Bazely called, Kydd was no further forward in explaining the reaction. 'So quick, damnit! As if they were all waiting for it.'

'You can't say as I didn't warn ye,' his friend rumbled.

'But why—'

'Outside of y'r chief, does anyone else know your views?'

'Er, I sent a copy to Popham. You know the fellow – I was at his court-martial after the South American affair. I wanted his slant on steam. He hasn't yet returned on the business, though.'

'Popham. A poisonous creature, I'm believing. You didn't take his part at the court-martial as is my recollection?'

'Well . . . no.'

'A clever an' ruthless beggar.' Bazely looked thoughtful for a moment, then said softly, 'As I wouldn't put him past a mort o' hookum snivey if it suits him.'

'He's a right ingenious cove,' Kydd answered loyally. 'I've seen him—'

'Who quickly made hay out of an innocent like you.'

'I can't see how!' Kydd retorted stiffly.

'No, you wouldn't, brother, but I detect his hand in all this.'

'In what way?'

'He gets his eyes on your words and sees how you've got a right advantage there, you a public figure and with a real

269

experience at sea in steam. He knows the Admiralty and such and makes sure a copy of y'r report or whatever gets to everyone who hates the smell o' steam. You're well overborne in the debate, mistrusted as a novice dabbler, and he stands fair to play the wise and steady hand at the tiller.'

It was by no means impossible, Kydd was forced to acknowledge. He knew Popham and, while respecting his undoubted superior intellect, there were elements of ruthlessness and ambition that made it all more than a little believable.

'So – the shab. What's to do, then?' Kydd said thickly, realising now that this did in fact explain everything.

'That's easily said,' Bazely said soberly. 'The damage is done. You're damned for a steam lover. You can do one o' two things, an' only two.'

'Tell me.'

'Haul down y'r colours, let 'em all know that on reflection ye see how you're mistaken.'

'The other?'

'Fight. Find some friends, get all the solid facts you can scrape together and defy 'em to say you're wrong. A long haul, a lot o' bruising an' bad blood, but if you're sure o' where ye stand, the only other way.'

'I'll fight,' Kydd came back.

But first he must hoist in as much he could about the subject, and that in a very short time. He needed peace and quiet as the battle would be with words, not swords. He'd get hold of every book published on the subject and make sure he knew as much as any.

His office was too noisy and distracting. He'd demand leave from Bentham and rusticate in Devon while he got on with it.

Chapter 53

Knowle Manor

It was no good. He slammed the book shut and stared unseeingly into the glorious greenery of his garden. At a table under the shade of a tree he was trying to assume the mantle of a sage of steam and it was not happening. It was not the fault of the weighty tomes he'd been studying – his heart was not in it.

The gulf between the simple village life and ways he'd grown up with was at such a stark contrast to this new dark world of steam and iron. And the fashion of reasoning employed by these mechanists was alien to Kydd – it seemed that for every discussion of crank and fly-wheel there would be an interminable laying out of mathematics and arcane proofs.

He sighed and took another pull at his lemon cordial.

In his mind a vision of the loveliness of a well-found sailing ship cleaving the seas in a willing coupling with the elements was replaced by another, the spectacle of stolid rows of frigate-sized vessels, each with its belching chimney and thrashing paddles.

Bonaparte was on the defensive now, beaten by the Russian weather and consequently at his most dangerous. If the secret of the conquering of wind and waves fell into his hands, would he hesitate to use it?

There was no alternative for Kydd but to do his duty. He picked up a book and wearily found his place. Out of the corner of his eye he regarded the inexpressibly touching sight of Persephone softly cooing at Francis in his baby carriage. She knew what he was trying to achieve, what it was costing him, and tried to help, but she hadn't seen what he had, and hadn't the experience to envisage where it was all leading.

A personal letter arrived, forwarded by his office. It was from a Vice Admiral Sir Arthur Lindsey, correctly addressed to Kydd in his situation as a servant of the Navy Board, brief and to the point. Would Kydd be so good as to attend on him at his office, the Board of Admiralty at Admiralty House? This was the home of the near mythical lords commissioners for executing the office of Lord High Admiral.

Kydd didn't know him, still less his function at the highest professional level the Navy possessed, but he would wager a sack of prize-money that it had to be concerned in some form with steam.

Returning to London, Kydd found himself being solemnly greeted, then ushered up grand steps to an upper floor and the admiral's office.

'Kydd. So pleased you could come. You'll have work of your own, no doubt, so I won't detain you for long.'

Lindsey was of an age, greying but with an uncompromising upright carriage and flint-like eyes that caught and held his.

There was a single visitor's chair and Kydd lowered himself cautiously into it.

'Sir Thomas. I've asked you here at the request of their lordships. They're concerned at the reasons behind your making public of views, that are, to say the least, singular in nature.'

He made much of extracting a newspaper from a drawer and holding it up. A headline spluttered, 'Navy hero demands steam!' and under it a smaller, 'Orders Admiralty to set a new course'. Without comment he found another publication of a more sedate appearance but with similar sentiments. It seemed Popham had cast his seed far and wide, and clearly the Admiralty had taken offence.

'There are those who would consider that you may well have violated the limits of the authority granted you as a consequence of your office under the Crown.'

'Sir. It was not my desire to see this note of appraisal be made public, or for its contents to be taken as anything more than my own opinion and—'

'Your opinion, sir, that we should immediately undertake a scheme of replacement, all ships under sail to be altered to steam.'

'Not as who should say immediately,' Kydd said uncomfortably.

'Your situation with the Navy Board you believe entitles you to make comment on the deliberations of their lordships, many times your senior in years and experience?'

'Sir, my assessment is based not on argument but on what I saw happening before me in the open sea, from the deck of a ship urged on by the power of steam.'

Lindsey gave a cynical smile. 'So I understand. This, then, is what you believe gives you the right to dictate the course of action of the entire Admiralty?'

'The implications are undeniable. Bonaparte is dangerous and if he's not checked or—'

'Implications? I do believe you have no true understanding. Neither have you explored their consequences.'

'Sir! I must protest! In the inspector general's office we do value evidence above all things in framing any conclusion and—'

'Then what, pray, do you consider a valid appreciation of the role of coal, inasmuch as its price now is above belief while our sailing navy is powered by the wind free of charge to His Majesty?'

'Coal?' Kydd said carefully. 'This, sir, is no more than the price we must pay for our freedom to move as we will.'

'And?'

'If you're referring to the larger issue—'

'I am.'

'Then we need have no concern, sir. As I mentioned in the report, this country is possessed of more than enough coal to power any number of steam-ships.'

'This is not the larger issue,' Lindsey said silkily.

'Then, sir, what is?'

'What amount of coal is consumed in one hour by your steam-ships, pray?'

Before Kydd could answer he went on, 'Consider a voyage of several weeks requiring therefore a burden of so many tons of coal to be shipped to cover the consumption. At what cost to provisions and stores will this be and to what requirement of ballast to replace its consuming? I will not speak of metacentres or other architectural matters at this stage or passages of months in duration.'

'Yes. Well, in this case—'

'The steam-ship you journeyed in was not much more than a boat. If we increase its size to a more useful dimension, say that of a frigate, we must proportionally increase the coal consumption. I believe we will now be speaking of so many tons each *day*.' He picked up a pencil and idly fiddled with it, smiling with a certain humour. 'Which implies that this single vessel is turning into smoke the winnings of a whole team of coal miners for every twenty-four hours it proceeds on its way. Where then is your mountain of coal kept to provide for this consuming?'

'The ship will be designed bigger to provide for the need,' Kydd replied stubbornly.

'A bigger ship, a bigger engine, more coal necessitated. Really, sir, this is getting out of hand. And we're not finished . . .'

'Um . . .'

'Come, come, Kydd. That which must lie at the forefront of all thinking by their lordships at a time of peril to our nation!'

'I – I do not follow you, sir.'

'Of course not, and neither should it be expected of you, a brave and gallant tar standing before the King's enemies on the high seas. Rather it should be left to your seniors who have won their place through qualities of sagacity and penetration to the strategicals.'

Kydd smouldered but remained silent.

Lindsey leaned forward, fixing him with a hard intensity. 'You are commander-in-chief of the Channel Squadron. You receive sudden orders to proceed to Cádiz to confront the enemy, a distance of some thousand and more miles. You arrive to find they have not yet sortied, so you lie off in blockade. Where are you going to find some hundreds of tons of coal every day to sustain your fleet?'

Kydd held his gaze but knew there was no answer.

'The Admiralty gets intelligence that in Toulon an enemy fleet is massing to break out and your squadron must be instructed to proceed on to enter into the Mediterranean without delay. But they have no knowledge of how much coal the distant fleet has left in its lockers. Can you so order them? No. Of course not. All is thrown into doubt and confusion at that remove, and any thought in headquarters of planning some bold strategical move is thereby rendered futile.'

Lindsey gave a sigh and eased back. 'I can conceive how attractive it must be to an eager commander to contemplate the motion of a ship into a foul wind but at what cost? The establishing of immense piles of coal all over the world where it is conceived that our ships might one day be brought to action far from home?'

'A way will be found,' Kydd answered thickly.

'No answer? But we've only touched on coal. There are many more questions. Perhaps you feel now that you might like to revisit your conclusions, agree that a corn-grinding or cess-pumping engine is not to be seriously entertained as a direction to be taken by His Majesty's fleet. Yes?'

'Sir. I admit that my study has its limitations but I stand by my findings – that we must take to steam before others do.'

'And be damned to the cost . . .'

'It has to be done!'

'Have you any idea how many millions we need each year simply to keep our present ships afloat? No? Then this explains why you cannot see the rank impossibility of replacing everything we set to sea with a new. Even should we so desire, it is out of our reach during the span of this war.'

'But—'

'And the need to raise a tribe of mechanists, artificers if you will, to tend your mechanisms. So many more men to accommodate within each hull, to victual and pay. And where shall your press-gang roam to secure such?' The admiral straightened some papers on his desk. 'I won't detain you further, Captain.'

Kydd stood up and reached for his stick with as much dignity as he could muster. 'I thank you for acquainting me with the thoughts of their lordships but I beg you to know that my own views remain unaltered. Good day to you, sir.'

Chapter 54

Knowle Manor

Kydd realised he had burned his bridges. He was now to be known as a supporter of steam, and his acquaintances would divide into friends or enemies and battle would be joined. It was not a fight he wanted to pick – especially as the only one on his side who could in any way be said to be a powerful ally was Bentham.

He was still notionally on leave and saw no reason why he shouldn't resume, particularly as his need for quiet and reflection was essential. What was now clear was that he hadn't thought it through as he should. Admiral Lindsey had shown the kind of thinking that he should be doing, and the level at which to be countering objections.

Persephone had been pleased to see him and fussed about with his wound, which was now giving him increasing pain, but he had more important matters on his mind. The stakes were too high. If he was successful in swaying the majority at the Admiralty the others would be obliged to fall into line and this would place him at the forefront of the move into steam. Was this how political advantage was won?

The key to it was in knowing what he was talking about. More books? In the long term, perhaps. Right now he needed practical, workmanlike experience to get the feel, explore the possibilities, the potential, the limitations.

Persephone had the answer. 'Did Mr Goodrich not take you in hand to introduce you to steam? You told me how he divided a steam engine into three parts and you understood it immediately.'

Kydd decided he'd spend a little more time at Knowle Manor to increase his strength, then go back to the office for as long as it took to answer the admiral's questions. And there were other matters. Would it be readily possible to scale up the size of an engine with the eight horses' power of *L'Actif* into the presumably fifty or a hundred needed to pull a frigate? And how would it be possible to protect boilers and delicate machines with their giant furnaces from the kind of broadsides he'd endured in ferocious combat?

It would be hard going but he'd do it.

Chapter 55

London

As he entered Somerset House, Kydd was surprised by how busy it seemed to be. Not with clerks and managers but workmen, with tools and bags, some man-handling furniture. It was disturbing and when he reached his office not one of his familiar staff was on hand to greet him and the department itself was in the process of some sort of upheaval.

'What the devil are you doing in my office?' he demanded of one worker.

'Your office, y' say? I don't reckon on it, cuffin.'

A beadle hurried up, one Kydd didn't know. 'An' you be Sir Thomas?' he puffed. 'Then I has a note for ye.'

Kydd took it and recognised Bentham's scrawl. It was brief and to the point but helped little. In essence it informed Kydd that at appallingly short notice the inspector general had been sent to Russia to negotiate the building there of a number of ships-of-the-line and he expected to be absent for some months. In the meantime Kydd was to ensure the work of the department be carried on as usual, taking in new work as he saw fit and rendering the usual forms to the Navy Board as were from day to day required.

So what was all this disorder and upset about? After some questioning, the awful truth emerged. For reasons not known, after Bentham had gone the department of the inspector general of Naval Works had been abolished in its entirety. Neither was it clear what the subsequent status of its officers was to be. Kydd's office had been emptied, like all the others, in favour of its new inhabitant, the Land Registry.

Bewildered, Kydd tried to make sense of it all. One possible explanation fitted only too well: their lordships had rid themselves in one stroke of the two biggest irritants against their 'do nothing' steam policy.

He hurried to the Admiralty to beg audience.

'Admiral Lindsey is engaged but finds he can spare you five minutes, Sir Thomas.'

He was ushered in and the two left alone.

'Ah, Captain Kydd,' he said smoothly. 'Always pleased to see you. You have something of an urgent nature you wish to discuss?'

'I desire to know the meaning of the dismissal in his absence of General Bentham's office of state.'

'Oh, yes, of course. You'll necessarily be involved. In fine, the work remit for the department is being subsumed into that of a larger, that of the surveyor of the Navy. A simple and inevitable evolving, I'd have thought.'

'And the officers?'

'Sir, you can't think me responsible for high matters of state. Like you, they'll be free to seek whatever employment they so desire. Now, you'll please excuse me – I have a deal to attend to this morning . . .'

Chapter 56

It was neatly done, and with nothing the public could take exception to or Parliament register objection about. And with his wound becoming more troublesome there was no prospect of a return to sea – even if he *was* forgiven for defying the Admiralty in all its wisdom. At the moment, however, all Kydd felt was a world-weary fatigue and a detestation of all that higher politics stood for. There was only one place he wanted to be – one that he yearned for with all his heart.

Back at Knowle Manor it all came out to Persephone. The shocking swiftness of the move, the sudden transition into inactivity, the removal of purpose from his life.

She hugged him close and murmured reassurances, but it was something for which he had to find his own way ahead.

Without an office to forward his post he began to worry he was falling behind but then caught himself: it was all over. He had no connection to steam in any form. He'd done his duty and rendered his report so he had no more to do with ugly machine-powered contraptions. On the one hand he could see how steam would prevail eventually, but for now he was free to return to the world of the sea as he'd known it, the towering canvas and rope to be hauled, weather to be sensed. And, as the Admiralty had refused to have anything to do with steam, the future was safe – the handsome ships of sail would continue to roam the seas.

But he wouldn't be going back to sea. A pall of unhappiness descended, remaining even when his dear friend Nicholas Renzi visited and did his best to cheer him, pointing out that his standing with the people of Britain was never higher: even if he had now to retire from the sea he would take with him their whole-hearted respect.

One morning, as Kydd was alighting from the trap, the horse jibbed at the noisy flare of a bird out of a bush, sending him sprawling and landing heavily to excruciating pain.

Some days later, his leg swaddled and splinted up high, the local doctor broke the hard news. An abscess was spreading in the wound. Unless it could be relieved the only safe course was to remove the leg.

The blow plunged Kydd into misery. Compounded with the wrenching loss of his calling, he fell into a state of unspeaking despair that even Persephone couldn't penetrate.

She had to find someone to help, but as she'd just heard that Renzi had been called away, who was there? She knew Kydd would not want to burden a fellow naval officer so she sent an urgent call to the only other in the world who was close to him – his friend and former confidential secretary, Lucius Craddock.

He quickly assessed the situation. 'I myself will go to Harley Street and discover the most distinguished physician of our age, whom I shall instruct in the issue at hand. We will not notice the expense in this matter.'

Days later a carriage swept into Knowle Manor and delivered Dr Sir Benjamin Lowe, physician to the Court of St James, with a colleague, a Dr Ferdinand Ballasteros.

'Your patient, honoured sirs, Sir Thomas Kydd, late of His Majesty's sea service,' Craddock introduced.

Lowe, the senior physician, began the examination. A ponderous, jowl-hung man with an old-fashioned wig, his bright eyes scanned the wound, taking in the quantities of bandages, the ominous seeping, and making much of sniffing about the site.

Exchanging incomprehensible medical cant to Ballasteros he yielded his place and the younger man bent to take a look. The bandages were unwound, the thickening crust as it was broken and pulled away visibly causing Kydd much pain. As blood mingled with purulent matter it was obvious that only a serious intervention could be in contemplation.

'Do excuse us,' Lowe muttered. 'A consultation is required.'

They left the room but returned quickly.

'Sir Thomas,' Lowe said, in grave tones, 'I cannot in all conscience hide it from you. In the natural course of events, the evil in your leg will in time spread about your body and will finally occasion your death.'

Kydd, pale with shock, barely registered it but croaked an acknowledgement.

'My instinct and training both urge me to prevent this unhappy occurrence by the removal of your leg above the wound, in this case to the hip.' He paused, stroking his jaw as though reluctant to complete the thought. 'But I have with me Dr Ballasteros whose experience of severe lesions in military hostilities is in my opinion unparalleled. He brings experience of a novel mode of treatment, which he declares in many instances can spare the patient an amputation.'

284

'Does he believe it indicated in the case of Sir Thomas?' Craddock asked, in a low voice.

'He does, but warns that the procedure is . . . unusual and may cause distress.'

'I'm sanguine Sir Thomas will bear it with due fortitude.'

'Very well, we will begin. If you'd fetch hot towels and boiling water? The patient and yourself only in the room, if you'd please.'

Persephone was last to leave, her face a pitiful mask of enduring.

Carefully and deliberately Ballasteros drew from his medical bag a metal container with a glass lid. To his horror Craddock found he was looking into a slowly squirming mass of maggots.

'They consume the putrescence, leaving untouched the flesh that is whole.'

Patiently, Ballasteros began dropping the live maggots onto the wound. Immediately they started to devour the pus and decaying black matter.

Chapter 57

Boston Harbor

'She's adorable, Jasper,' breathed Maybelle, clutching at Gindler's arm. 'So warlike but so . . . beautiful.'

Gindler swelled with pride at the fine sight *Castine* made. The full-rigged frigate was ready for sea below them at the Navy Yard.

'And you're to be the captain,' she added, awe-struck.

'Her master commandant, dearest,' he corrected gently, squeezing her hand.

It had been almost casual: a personal letter from Jones, the secretary to the Navy, alerting him of the intention of the administration to break the strangling British blockade with a force sufficient to cause disruption of the Atlantic trade, therewith obliging them to reduce their numbers in the necessary protection.

As recognition of his successful predatory cruise in British waters he was being offered command of *Castine*, not as weighty as the big frigates, like the *Constitution*, but rated as a 32-gun and the equal of most British frigates. And there she was, from the leaping Indian of her figurehead, the trail-boards wreathed in green vines and picked out in vermilion blossoms, down the elegant sweep of her black hull, with its broad ochre stripe, to the oddly neat stern-quarters. His home for who knew how long in this ocean cruise.

'You see there, right at the top of the mainmast, the middle one,' he pointed to the tiniest glint of silver at its peak, 'guess who put that there.'

'I'm sure I don't know, Jasper, dear.'

'No other than Paul Revere! It's our lightning rod and he made it for us. The tip is silver over a copper forging.'

'Oh! Then *Castine* has been honoured, dear love.'

'Not above what she deserves. Did you know she's been the first United States warship to double the Cape of Good Hope – and the first to cross the equator?'

They stood for a moment, hand in hand. Then Gindler gently turned to her and said quietly, 'You'll bear our separation kindly, my love? It's my chance for glory and distinction, and I plan to make my fortune in her.'

'Yes, sweet love,' she said softly, looking tenderly at him. 'And I'll be here for you when you return.'

He held her tight, almost brutally, and kissed her.

Chapter 58

Aboard Castine

'Come!'

Hanson, the first lieutenant leaned through the cabin door. 'Moxey,' he growled. 'Knockin' the toplights outa Sanders again. You want I should bring the bastard up afore you tomorrow, or leave him to me?'

Gindler winced. Although a fighting seaman of the front rank, the big Virginian was crude and forceful, qualities that didn't endear him to Gindler's more refined New England sensibilities.

'You deal with it. How's the storing?'

It had seemed endless, the humping on board of everything from coils of line to casks of dried peas, all to be found somewhere in the rapidly diminishing space below decks. His orders told him to prepare for an extended mission of indefinite duration, and Commodore Bainbridge would not tolerate any excuses that spoke of slackness in the fitting out of his frigate.

'Well, I reckon. Leavin' the watering for last, there's only the powder.'

That meant sailing in, say, three days. It would do.

Time passed all too quickly: he concluded his letter to his intended with the tenderest expressions of feeling before he folded and sealed it to catch the post on its way ashore.

Ignoring the clamour and uproar of a ship preparing for sea, he took a last look at the chart and the scribbled notes he'd made at the base indicating the best intelligence of the dispositions of the British blockade outside Boston. They were close and included at least one two-decker. There was every possibility he'd have to fight before he won the open sea – did his ship have it in her?

He was new to *Castine* and her crew: there was precious little time to earn their respect and loyalty before he could be yard-arm to yard-arm in mortal combat with the enemy.

They put off in late evening, the better to keep their departure from traitorous loyalists, who were said to alert the blockaders of any attempted run to sea. With the dark shadows of islands slipping past in the night, under topsails they descended the Delaware out into the wide bay, doubled lookouts straining to catch the first heart-stopping sight of an English man-o'-war.

Then, mercifully, slowly drifting rain came in and with it a westerly. In the increasingly brisk wind and rain *Castine* set her prow for the Atlantic. By daybreak she had sunk the land and was well out. With a clear horizon Gindler had the chance he so badly needed: sea-room to test the mettle of his command and his men.

He drove them hard and they responded. First, in this useful west wind there was an opportunity to discover her best point of sailing. *Castine* it seemed favoured a quarterly above all, and without setting stunsails Gindler determined he could rely on at least eleven knots, with eight and one half more to be expected close by the breeze, and all with relatively little leeway. Sailing large was acceptable but her fine lines forward made her a wet boat, pitching with rather too much spirit across the swells.

Of just as much importance was her armament. No less than forty of the largest carronades to be seen at sea in any navy, the thirty-two-pounder, as well as six long twelve-pounder carriage guns, a broadside of near a third of a ton of cold iron. More than enough to subdue anything that swam short of a heavy frigate but with the usual penalty of requiring a close-quarters fight.

Gun practice was every morning, sail handling in the afternoon. Laggards were set to work into the dog-watches.

As it was, it turned out they'd be stretched by more than anything he could devise. The useful westerly, driving them out into the broad reaches of the Atlantic, firmed into a spiteful blast, and before long into a full-throated gale that had the ship at her worst, seas breaking inboard from astern, her bow snorting into the rearing combers. Hands were quickly aloft on the wildly jibbing spars, handing sail to a double reef, while their ship fought the seas beneath them.

But by morning the blow had settled, and Gindler set about his mission in earnest. His orders were to throw his vessel athwart the enemy's shipping lanes and cause mayhem. The greatest river of trade before the equatorial latitudes was somewhere in the central vastness of the ocean: rich cargoes in Indiamen from China, India and ports all over the east, curving from the mid-Atlantic to the Channel. This was a worthy quarry for an ardent warrior.

And then a rendezvous at the Cape Verde islands with Commodore Bainbridge in *Constitution* for further orders.

He'd cut across the north-easterly trade-wind belt down to the south-east, which would take him through the sea lanes and end up at the Cape Verde rendezvous. If he couldn't lay hands on a prize or two he wasn't worth his salt.

As the days turned into weeks it became clear that while many ships plied the seas the ocean was so vast, distances so extreme, that they would be swallowed into it without trace. In one fit of discouragement he took a pencil and made some calculations. Given a height-of-eye at the foremast lookout's position of a hundred feet it would imply a range of vision no more than a dozen miles all round to find ships that could be anywhere within a four-thousand-mile bubble of existence.

After a week of steady progress into the Atlantic, sail was sighted at first light.

It was close – on a course to cross their bows and a considerably smaller two-master. It immediately tacked about, suspiciously swiftly and efficiently – a naval crew?

The chase was on.

Then some sort of signal, probably a challenge, jerked up with British colours, but *Castine* did not reply. In the streaming winds with her broad sails she had the advantage and began hauling in the stranger.

'T' quarters?' demanded Hanson, with a savage grin.

'I'd think so,' Gindler replied. 'But stand fast the great guns – don't want to disfigure our pretty little prize, do we? Instead, each man to take a musket.'

As they drew closer, their quarry did everything it could to get clear but inexorably *Castine* drew up and Gindler hailed her. 'Lower your topsails and heave to or I'll fire into you!'

The brig was not about to give up and in a spirited move fell off the wind and swung around in a tight circle with the object of crossing the stern of the bigger ship and raking her with what guns she had.

Gindler was ready for it. 'Helm hard down!' he ordered and, with the enemy even closer to leeward, yelled, 'Fire!'

Nearly a hundred muskets crashed out, the storm of shot a hail of death taking its toll. Before they reloaded, the British flag was reluctantly lowered and the ship was their prize.

They had happened on the Post Office packet *Plympton* homeward bound from Brazil.

'Your mails,' demanded Gindler. He would have no hesitation about ransacking their haul for intelligence of sailings. Official sacks were dragged up from the hold but then he remembered something he'd heard. 'Clear the ship, Mr Hanson, and then make search. A damn good search, and you could be astonished!'

It took some time but then a shout came from below. Triumphantly into the sunlight a chest was hoisted. It was heavy with promise and was soon broken open revealing silver coin with several rolls of gold. Gindler had recalled that these handy fast packets were often freighted with specie in preference to the slower and more vulnerable merchant ships.

Gleefully the haul was counted. They were now richer by twelve thousand pounds, the property of the English merchants of Rio de Janeiro.

The cruise had started in the best possible way.

The rest of the passage across the Atlantic was disappointing. One or two Portuguese merchant brigs in the Brazil trade came into view but they were untouchable since, while allied with the English against the French, they were otherwise neutrals. Any information they gave had to be treated with suspicion and their vague reports of an English squadron nearby could mean anything. Nevertheless, in these far waters it was much more likely that a strange sail would turn out to be hostile. But with fellow marauders of the size of *Constitution*, it balanced out, and Gindler sailed on to the archipelago of Cape Verde to join the rest of the squadron.

These were scattered islands well off the African mainland, anciently held by the Portuguese, a lazy, dreary place to Gindler's eyes. The rendezvous was set for Porto da Praia, a small but snug harbour in the southern tip of Santiago, well sheltered against blasts from the Atlantic by overtopping volcanic peaks and ridges.

Comfortably in time *Castine*, under easy sail, opened up the bay but there was no squadron to be seen.

This was no calamity. Bainbridge might have come and gone after a rich prey, or had been chased away by a powerful British squadron. He'd had the forethought to specify another rendezvous but just possibly he'd left a message with the port authorities.

He recalled the Portuguese seaman on board. 'Mr Hanson, take Pereira, go to the fort and see what's happening.' Gindler needed facts: the other rendezvous was off the coast of Brazil, weeks away.

The fort was near the entry point of the harbour, a dilapidated edifice that spoke of the quiet decay of Portuguese rule over the centuries.

Soon Gindler's first lieutenant was back with no message or news of any American squadron ever touching at the port. What was welcome, however, was the invitation of the governor to refresh and resupply at leisure. It gave time to await the squadron and to refit spars and rigging that had suffered in the storm.

It was tempting to delay in the area, well placed at the

intersection of shipping lanes that went broadly north and south, but orders were orders. Fernando de Noronha in Brazil was the alternative rendezvous and, after a final watering, *Castine* spread her wings and stood across the broad ocean expanse.

This was an entirely different matter from their previous destination. One main island not much more than half a dozen miles long and a few uninhabited offshore islets, it was an almost impossibly remote location – perfect for a penal colony. Gindler knew that it was a Brazilian dependency and under the direct rule of the Portuguese Royal Family who had been rescued by the Royal Navy just before Napoleon's march of invasion into Portugal. Given this, their loyalties were obvious.

He would enter under British colours. With a blue ensign aloft he eased around the northern point and hove to offshore. As before he sent Hanson and Pereira ashore, and this time they returned with news.

'The British have been here not ten days afore.'

'In what force?'

'He says a 44 an' a sloop o' twenty-two guns.'

Completely out-classing *Castine*. Would they be lingering about, waiting for the Americans? Or simply using the tiny island as a rendezvous the same as they?

'An' the governor said as how he's a letter from the commodore as needs to be carried on to Halifax by the next British ship chancing by.'

They'd been taken in by their British colours right enough, but then Gindler stiffened. Here was a chance to . . .

But it didn't sound right. There were very few 44s in the Royal Navy and certainly none that he'd heard about in this area. Could these be Bainbridge also flying British colours and using the letter as a ploy to deliver a message to him? There was only one way to find out.

A basket of cheese and a brace of porter were taken ashore

as a gift for the governor, Gindler allowing it would be convenient for him to forward the letter as Halifax was where he was returning.

It worked!

The letter was eagerly examined: it was a dispatch from a Captain Pearse, HMS *Southampton*, to the Royal Navy commander-in-chief, North America station, giving ordinary details of recent events on station.

Disappointed, Gindler read it again. Was it in code?

'Bring a candle.' He'd heard that Bainbridge, while in captivity in Tripoli in the war with the Barbary States, had used a clever method of communication. And here it was, faded brown lettering appearing out of invisibility as the heat of the flame did its work on the lime-juice 'ink'.

And it was indeed from Bainbridge. Realising *Castine* was probably wasting time tracking about looking for him, he was herewith releasing Gindler to roam at will until the end of his cruise.

It couldn't have been better! He was in command of a well-found frigate, free to go wherever he chose – in fact, anywhere in the world that offered victims. They were well stocked with provisions and warlike stores, and could sustain a long cruise without retiring, so what was not possible?

A thought took hold, a wonderful vision – that *Castine* could add to the lustre of her honours by being first once again, this time as the first man-o'-war of the United States Navy to stalk the Pacific Ocean!

It would mean rounding Cape Horn but then he'd be loose in a vast sea that had not known anything of this war, English ships that had been at sea for months or years that were ignorant even that a state of war existed.

In rising excitement he knew it was possible – it could be done!

Chapter 59

Knowle Manor

'You'll never guess, darling!' Persephone said softly, reluctant to disturb Kydd in the garden in his special chair with its extended leg rest, an unread book put aside. 'It's Mr Craddock come to see how you are.'

'Save I'm half bitten alive by those maggots . . .'

She hurried off. Kydd had not agreed to see any visitors since he'd lost his post with the Navy Board. With his painful wound and lack of prospects, he'd been hard to handle – there was nothing any could do for a legendary sea-dog fallen on harder times.

Craddock had been waiting out of sight and stepped forward. 'Ahoy there, old fellow. Just wanted to know how things are for you. No, don't get up. I'll sit next to you.'

Kydd went to say something, then thought better of it, obstinately gazing ahead.

'How's the leg?'

'After your pintle tagger with his maggots has done with

me, well, I have to say the thing doesn't smell so bad, must be half good.'

'That's very encouraging,' Craddock said brightly. 'And, um, have you had any thoughts of where you'll be going next?'

'Damn it!' Kydd exploded. 'O' course I have! Have you taken thought yourself what's out there for a sad wight who looks to losing his leg and knows aught but how to throw out canvas in a fresh breeze?'

'Yes, so unfortunate about your position on inventions. Is there any chance of—'

'None,' Kydd ground out. 'I've fouled my nest by telling 'em what they didn't want to hear and my name's not to be mentioned by their lordships or their lackeys. They've the very excuse – this leg gone rotten – to keep me from a sea appointment for ever.'

'And—'

'Mr Craddock,' Persephone interrupted in a brittle voice, 'can I show you what I came across in Tavistock market the other day?'

Catching on, he followed her inside. 'You're disturbed by Thomas's condition.'

She hesitated. 'It must be admitted.'

'Do feel you may confide in me, dear lady.' He was startled to see her eyes suddenly glisten, then witness a racking sob take her.

'He . . . he's not himself, I know that. It's . . . It's that he said to me that . . . he wasn't the man I married so . . . so . . .'

'My dear. Don't take on – he doesn't mean it!'

'Harry, he does – and he's right. Thomas is crippled but I care not a fig about that. It's just that his mind has been altered. He's surly, bites at the maid, wants to be left alone, stares out of the window for hours, and – and believes I don't understand.'

Her hands clasped hard together. 'But I know what it is. I married an intelligent, confident, trusting, loving man of the sea. It was all of life for him and he was surpassing content with his lot. Until he was struck down and the fates conspired to keep him from it. The poor, poor dear – how I feel for him and he doesn't know it.' She buried her face in her handkerchief while sobs again took her.

'I'm sure there are others in the Navy who've been winged, as they say.'

'He knows of some, but they've all been retired from sea service. You see, by this he means active service, leaping on an enemy deck and so forth. He couldn't bear to send away his men on some hard mission without he's at their head – you know him.'

'Yes, my lady, I do,' he said sadly. His face furrowed in concentration. 'And I fear I have no ready nostrum to offer. He's still, as the world might say, a young man but the prospects for a sea hero on land are by no means attractive I'd surmise.'

His brow furrowed. Then he brightened. 'There is one small thing I could do for him.'

'Anything!'

'My business firm has dealings in a land not so distant that's bathed in the most salubrious sunshine and is far from the clamour of war. I must attend to the agency from time to time. Should I offer the use of the company villa for you both, then the removal to a lazy climate to allow the passage of time to do its healing may go somewhat towards an amelioration of spirit.'

'Perfect!' she breathed. 'As will get him interested in new things and people and food and – and— Where is this, pray?'

'Madeira.'

* * *

'Madeira?' Kydd grunted, pushing away his dish. 'A god-forsaken island off Africa, swarming with Portuguees and with a rum idea of what makes a good breakfast? Not my idea of paradise.'

Craddock frowned. 'Take my word on it, my friend, it's a wonderfully fine place to take one's ease. So many come to be cured of their ailments for the climate is—'

'I've been there,' Kydd said cuttingly. 'Before the action at the Cape. I can't remember we topped it the Brighton seaside folk at the time.'

'Darling,' Persephone reproved, 'Mr Craddock is our host – he'll know where we might go to make the best of our time there.'

'Sitting about all day, nothing to do save getting as red as a new-baked topman,' Kydd answered, with gloom. 'Not for me. Here's at least quiet an' comfortable.'

'Oh, Thomas! Don't be so grumpy, please. It's a wonderful island, and all for us, my love.'

'Then leave me here. You go,' he replied sarcastically.

Persephone looked at him, stricken, and fled the room.

Craddock paused, then addressed him gravely. 'It does strike me that your lady has her heart set on such a respite, dear fellow. You said you don't want to be a burden to her, but are you not, if you forbid this species of travel to her in any way?'

Moodily, Kydd stared at the fire without replying.

'And it may well prove most beneficial to your healing.'

Kydd looked up ironically. 'She's been speaking to you.'

'Only to tell me how worried she is about your health and thinking the stay an excellent purgative of humours. Can I not urge you in your wife's name to accede to her wishes?'

Chapter 60

Plymouth

The *Castelo de São Jorge* was at Mill Bay docks, taking aboard her final provisioning for the voyage to Madeira. No stranger to the port town, Kydd could remember her from some convoy he'd escorted in the past, a reasonably well-found barque with passengers, which usually meant cautious ship-handling and obedience to regulations.

Her flag was Portuguese but her master was English, a jovial Yorkshireman by the name of Whittier, who welcomed him aboard with respect.

'This time o' the year, we'll have some fine nor'-westerlies to Funchal, an'. . . ' He tailed off at Kydd's look.

They had the best stateroom, tastefully made up in polished mahogany and brass, and Persephone took to it with glee, instructing Esther, the maid, with all she knew about sea travelling.

Kydd left them to join Craddock on deck. It was as busy as expected in a ship outward bound and he knew exactly what was going on. The final formalities, the pilot aboard, men at their stations. No salutes, however, no notice taken of a foreign barque putting to sea, one of thousands that season, soon to be lost over the horizon.

Seeing Persephone come to join them, Craddock bowed politely. 'M' lady, and pleased to see you on deck. Have you ever . . .?'

'Once before, sir.'

'It always seizes me – the moment when a ship quits the place of her birth and joins with her true love, Neptune.'

'Yes, that's what sailors . . .' Persephone recovered quickly, 'Look – over there! That's what they call Devil's Point for all the contrary currents to be met with past it. And at our back there's Plymouth Hoe.

'And the new breakwater – ah, there it is, ahead of us. They say when it's finished it will shield Plymouth from the worst a southerly can throw at it.'

Castelo hauled to the wind, making spirited way for the open sea, the slap and hiss of incoming waves from the Atlantic now felt. Rame Head reared and passed them by as the ship shaped course for the open ocean, widening in an immensity of living sea before them.

Craddock suddenly looked around. 'Er, Thomas?'

'I can't see him – perhaps he's in the cabin.' Persephone left and went below. He was sitting in an easy-chair but staring into space with the most desolate bleakness she'd ever seen.

'Thomas?'

She knelt at his feet, looking up into the stricken face and understood. The last deck he'd trodden, lively with sea, was the famous frigate he'd so recently commanded. And in her he'd proceeded to sea from here so many times, now for ever denied him.

She couldn't help it: with wrenching sobs she joined his misery.

Chapter 61

The cry of the masthead lookout did not stop Kydd. It was going to be thirty of the strengthening leg raises and that was that. He soldiered on in his accustomed chair on *Castelo*'s quarterdeck, puffing at the effort, his wounded leg rising then gently lowering, restoring something of the muscle tone at the cost of an eye-watering bar of pain each time. He had no need to do as the others did and rush to the side to catch sight of land, for he knew it was Madeira, and moreover it wouldn't be visible from the deck for some time in these light airs.

'Done.' He smiled triumphantly at Persephone, who impulsively kissed him.

'And when we get to be on land you'll be able to walk about, darling,' she said happily.

By the time they raised Funchal he'd completed his squats and, stretched out in the chair, claimed his reward – a lemon cordial spliced with gin.

'Ye must've been here more'n once, Admiral.' The kindly Whittier had come up to share the morning with him. He had insisted on addressing Kydd as such, saying that he was sure to hoist his flag in the future and then he'd be so grand he wouldn't be allowed to speak to him, so while he had the chance . . .

'Never ashore much,' Kydd admitted. There was the one visit to the odd but very ancient yellow and brown fortress São Tiago for a council-of-war before the descent on the Cape of Good Hope, which didn't really count, it being right on the waterfront and he being otherwise distracted.

'It's British territory nowadays,' the grey-muzzled captain declared, 'since we relieved the Portuguee of the worry in aught-seven. That is, according to m' papers.'

Both Kydd and Persephone had been separately involved in the flight of the Portuguese Royal Family to Brazil. He felt a peculiar pang, part guilt, the rest pure pleasure, for in the end it had brought them together.

The anchor went down in Funchal roads among the many other merchantmen that gave the lie to Napoleon's claim that his continental system had ruined Great Britain's trade.

'So we step ashore after the quarantine examination,' Craddock said breezily. 'And I know what I'll be first to tuck into.'

'Oh?' Persephone said, curious.

'*Espada com banana,* black scabbard fish with banana. You'll adore its unique flavours.'

Kydd knew he couldn't manage the side-steps into the boat and, cringing, accepted a boatswain's chair like the ladies.

Despite himself, he remembered the place well. Green with verdure of all kinds, warm, ancient, interesting. It was odd, though, having his wife with him in this place of martial memories.

Craddock took charge. After a messenger was dispatched a carriage appeared. It took but minutes to clop away up the volcanic slopes to reach a substantial villa perched on a rise to give the best view of the ocean. 'Your *residência,*' Craddock announced.

It was cool, colourful and most comfortable, with quantities of servants and cooks. Persephone declared herself entirely satisfied and wondered whether Craddock would stay to show them the sights, but he excused himself with the need for an early arrival at his business house.

Kydd could sense the silence and scented warmth working on him already and closed his eyes.

The few weeks at sea had seen his wound heal into a long, tender but clean seam. The exercises had built up his body and he'd felt it return to more of a balance as his muscle tone improved.

He decided that if his future was going to be something like this there were worse fates and he shouldn't pine after what couldn't be at the cost of Persephone's distress.

So the Admiralty had set their face against him. He'd never command at sea again but his honours and distinctions were enough for most men.

Throwing off his mood, he declared, 'And I for the town, Seph! Will you step off with me?' The villa would be brought to rights in their absence by his manservant, Binard, and Persephone's maid Esther.

Funchal was the only town of size in Madeira, sparsely furnished with shops but with a quaintness that won over Persephone's romantic eye. Intensely Portuguese, the houses and narrow streets were medieval, their vivid terracotta colours of quite another character to English dwellings.

There were no docks and quays. Shipping lay offshore, boats plying the Atlantic rollers with ease.

Along one stretch the houses gave way to a south-facing bench-lined avenue with a view open to the sea and there Kydd rested, enjoying the sultry warmth of the sun.

* * *

In the days that followed they wandered through the old town, taking in the sight of a fine old cathedral, a spirited market and several stout fortresses of another age. They found the actual house of Christopher Columbus and, in an alcove, a charming bust of Philippa, daughter of John of Gaunt and mother of Prince Henry the Navigator.

And then they were noticed. The governor's aide-de-camp had alerted his master to the presence of a notable: the governor duly invited Sir Thomas and Lady Kydd to a reception at the resplendent Palácio de São Lourenço.

Kydd had brought one set of evening wear, which in its simplicity but immaculate cut was well suited to the quiet display of his knightly adornments.

The evening was warm and gracious, less than a dozen dignitaries at a spacious candle-lit table, their jolly host Governor Robert Meade at one end, his pale-faced wife to the side.

Sitting at the other end Kydd was flanked by an exquisitely mannered Portuguese gentleman of years who turned out to be the prefect of Funchal, as well as other gentlemen of society with their ladies. It was diverting to see Craddock noted as a visiting personage in his own right and flanking him to the left, next to Persephone.

The food was delectable and Kydd and Persephone learned much of Madeira. Able to trace its first colonisation to 1420, its nature and ways had changed but slowly over the centuries, the Madeirans only finding lasting prosperity in the producing of their famed Madeira wine and the victualling of passing ships. Volcanic, the interior was nearly impenetrably mountainous, but the south side was of a gentler cast and well sheltered from the winter northerlies.

Kydd's words of thanks were greeted with murmurs of sympathy at his war wound as he held his stick to stand.

The governor's speech was in like tenor, brisk and

welcoming. It had Persephone blushing with pleasure and the room abuzz with happy conversation competing with a small orchestra. When the gentlemen retired to the drawing room, Kydd was in a contented mood.

Almost immediately Governor Meade came across to him. 'Dear fellow, so good to have you here!'

He held out his hand in a familiar way, which took Kydd off balance. This was a major general who'd taken over some years ago from General Baird in the occupation of Madeira by the British following the flight of the Portuguese Royal Family to Brazil. He must have been here since, in possibly the quietest military station there was.

'Oh, er, distinctly my pleasure, sir.'

'Sicily!' crowed Meade. 'You saw off Cavaignac's invasion in fine style. Left us naught but the sweepings to settle, even if they left me with a gammy arm.'

'Of course,' Kydd said pleasantly, although he couldn't bring to mind from the confusion of the day this particular figure. It was clear, though, that after being wounded the man had accepted an agreeable post to see out his military career, even at the cost of chances for distinction.

'You came by packet, I see,' Meade remarked. 'With your lady wife? Not as it were a professional visit, I'd venture.'

'Not at all. For my health alone. This damn leg nearly had to come off after the Yankee militia objected to my presence.'

'Then you'll take another ship – when you're well enough, o' course.'

'Er, possibly not. There's a time when the sweets of the land can no longer be resisted, I'm persuaded,' Kydd answered carefully.

'I see. Well, do enjoy yourself in our little sea kingdom as will speedily mend your ills, sir.'

* * *

It was time to take in the country. The lower slopes had their farms and settlements but often the upper peaks were lost in ragged mists. A wicker sled pulled by a pair of oxen was their conveyance up the steep slopes but the spectacle in the interior was breath-taking: precipitous ravines and waterfalls, everywhere iron-hued crags and windswept, mist-enshrouded mountain tracks, utterly empty of human presence.

Persephone was entranced at the bold, dangerous romantic vision and filled sketchbook after sketchbook with wild imaginings that would keep her happily creating at her easel for hours on her return. Craddock, attending to his business, nevertheless found the time for a personal tour of wine production. In the warehouse, the vista of so many huge barrels stacked in rows in the dimness, slowly taking in the seasoning of years, was a singular sight.

Kydd was coming to terms with the fact that this was to be his future: slow, measured, and with the sea no longer his to challenge.

Chapter 62

Aboard Castine

'No, it ain't!' yelled the foretop lookout.

'I tell you, I saw it!' came back the maintop lookout, shading his eyes to somewhere over to the larboard beam.

Master Commandant Gindler wasn't worried. In these vast wastes of the Pacific a sail would appear and disappear as the deep half-mile-long swell experienced by *Castine* and itself went in or out of synchrony – it was there well enough.

'Course to head him off,' he ordered.

It was rare to find any vessel so far out in this limitless ocean and the odds were it was British, one of the South Seas whaling concerns. With voyages as long as three years, it was unlikely they'd any word that a state of war existed between Great Britain and the United States.

Castine obediently bore away, the picture of another whaler wanting to speak to a stranger, pass the time, sight new faces.

The other vessel took the bait, coming to in the languorous scend of the swell, probably trying to make out their identity which, as they were approaching bow-on, would be near impossible.

It had been almost too easy – there were no British warships in the Pacific to spoil the fun and already eight whalers, their cargo and crew prisoners, on their way to Coquimbo to be condemned.

In this one foray west of Cape Horn Gindler's prizes exceeded that of any other United States man-o'-war to this point. And he'd only just started.

After this cruise, however, his ship, sea-worn and with so many of her crew away in prizes, needed to rest and repair, re-store and prepare for the next voyage of predation. The problem was, where could this happen? There were no other United States warships in the Pacific, let alone naval bases, so he would be obliged to enter a South American trade port. The problem there was that the entire continent was under Spanish rule, the colonies notionally owing allegiance to the Spanish Crown, which at the moment was in amity with England in its ferocious war in the peninsula against France.

Touching at any port might lead them into a trap that would stop his victorious cruise.

The strange sail was indeed a British whaler. Her faded tar-black sides and well-patched sails told of a long and gruelling time at sea, her hard-won cargo of oil probably near completion. The name *Success of Maryport* could just be made out across her plain sternworks.

In well-practised movements the scene played out. Coming close alongside, Gindler hailed the other, conveying the dread news. Before the stricken ship could make sail to flee, *Castine's* broadside was run out and simultaneously a swivel gun cracked on her fo'c'sle, sending a ball pluming before the whaler's forefoot.

It then just needed Hanson and a party of armed seamen

to take possession and, after ransacking for any charts, revealing logs, or other, send her in as prize.

It didn't take long and Gindler was back to his conundrum. He would try the same trick as before and go in under a British flag, lying offshore away from close inspection. The question was, should it be a distant and isolated small haven where he should not be disturbed by any hypothetical British squadron looking for him but at the cost of not being able to supply his wants? Or one of the big trading ports that had all he needed but might offer unwanted attention?

He'd take the last – he could always make a swift exit to sea should his welcome prove disagreeable.

He considered his options on the west coast of South America. The vice-royalty of Peru, the provinces of Bolivia, Chile, Peru itself? Probably as distant as possible from the populous north would be advisable – Valparaíso, for instance, a prosperous seaport in the dependency of Chile and not too far distant.

'Thirty-three south, Mr Hanson, we're going to take our ease for a space.'

As the eight-mile expanse of Valparaíso Bay opened up, every eye was on the inner shipping roads: were there any lurking British or, more likely, Spanish men-o'-war at anchor? Or sloops and gunboats on their way out to dispute their presence officially?

All seemed quiet and lazy in the noonday sun. Their anchor tumbled and splashed among the outer craft, no notice given to the newcomer. A boat was readied: Hanson would go ashore and test the waters.

He was back promptly. 'Couldn't be sweeter, Mr Gindler. They've gone an' had some sort o' revolution, don't hold with Spanish rule any more. Say that we Yankees threw out our English masters, and they're doing the same with the Spanish – we're brothers.'

And the proof was immediate. Beef, flour, poultry, potatoes and beans to last six months. Fruit, wine, fresh bread by the cartload. And an invitation for the captain to dine with the governor.

This was not the official Spanish *corregidor* but José Carrera, the young and fiery figure at the head of the Junta La Patria Vieja that had taken the city.

'Republic, liberty and revolution!' Toasts were loud and insistent, and as the feast progressed, fine wine was displaced by a more martial aguardiente, the ills of the world dealt with in true revolutionary style.

Castine was taken in hand and readied for her next cruise but Gindler was uneasy. The reality of an American presence on this side of the continent would inevitably come to the ears of the British and without doubt some kind of squadron would be sent to hunt him down. What should he do?

A week more – liberty for the crew, relaxation for all, care lavished on the gallant *Castine* and then away. The Pacific was an immense body of water and the chance of any hunter finding them, a tiny speck in an area half the size of the planet, was highly unlikely. They would continue their voyage of destruction.

Chapter 63

Madeira

The afternoon sun, taken in the fragrant shade of a peach orchard, was warm and beneficent, as Kydd in his native hammock pondered on life. By degrees, slowly and reluctantly, he had come to accept that his future would be very different from his past. He'd dismissed the thought out of hand, even if it was made possible, for him to take naval shore employment. It would probably not be unthinkable to stay at sea with a merchant-service command but he knew he'd always suffer from the memories of what had been.

He put down his cordial and addressed himself to the weighty tome that promised to explain the situation in the peninsula but became aware of the flustered maid running towards him in some confusion.

'Oh, sir! This jus' came b' hand o' messenger – from the governor hisself!'

It was a note, folded once but not sealed, nothing like an official invitation.

Dear Sir Thomas, it would oblige me greatly should you feel able to attend on me at your earliest convenience at which my impertinence at interrupting your rest shall be made clear.

Most unusual, not to say perplexing. Any approach on official lines would be in a much more formal style, and if some kind of friendly communication between governor and visitor, whatever the rank, a certain decorum would have been more the case.

'Er, fetch the carriage, Esther. I'm to visit the governor.'

General Meade immediately rose at his desk. 'Dear fellow! So good of you to come! Sit down – a bracer for your trouble?'

'No, thank you, sir.'

Meade took a chair to one side of Kydd and, dismissing a hovering functionary, laid out his quandary. 'I need help,' he said quickly. 'As I'm a military man and have no idea what to do for the best.'

Earnestly he went on to lay out the essence of the problem. Not two hours previously a British frigate had come to moorings and one of her boats had arrived bearing her captain, gravely ill. Her first lieutenant had sought audience and explained that this had occasioned a crisis he felt the Madeiran commander-in-chief was the only authority able to resolve.

It seemed that the frigate had left England under Admiralty orders on a critical mission, the details of which the first lieutenant had learned from secret orders kept by the now helpless captain.

In confidence, Meade had been told that they detailed word that had come from Halifax of an American frigate known to have been loosed on the valuable shipping south of the Brazils. They had been tasked with the object of hunting it down with the utmost dispatch.

Kydd wondered why the South American squadron based on Buenos Aires wasn't dealing with it, then realised that this intelligence had come with the frigate and they would have no knowledge of the situation. It was still peculiar that the Admiralty had seen fit to send a frigate on a detached mission when warships were available locally.

'My difficulty arises, old fellow, in that this first-lieutenant Johnny desires that in view of the urgency of the orders, he be made captain on the spot to carry 'em through. Now, you being Navy and all, can you say I've enough authority to do that, me being an army general and so on?'

To send back for a replacement captain would lead to months of waiting – quite unacceptable.

'Yes, an awkward poser,' Kydd agreed. 'And not forgetting that even if you did, you'd have to find another first lieutenant as well.' He pondered, imagining the irate questions later being raised – a major general trespassing against the prerogative of the Board of Admiralty in promoting a lieutenant to the august ranks of a post-captain, then to be sent on a vital commission.

At the same time there was the very real problem of whether the individual was of the calibre to go up against one of the American super-frigates, if it were one. Another loss of an English frigate to the Yankees would probably result in the fall of the government.

'Sir, I really can't advise that . . .' He tailed off, for a stupendous, blinding thought had burst in on him. What if he volunteered his own services, it only requiring that a theoretically active genuine frigate captain on hand be asked to take acting command in respect of the urgency of the situation? It had happened many times before in sea service. And being a commander-in-chief Meade would surely have the authority for such an act.

Yes!

'On the other hand, I find there may be a course that . . .'

In a fever of excitement he reviewed its feasibility. In the first instance, he owed it to his country to step forward in this emergency for there was most certainly no other available to Meade.

Other compelling thoughts were flooding in – decidedly more personal. He would get back to sea, if only for a short while . . . but was that the only imperative? The Admiralty had been able to keep him ashore on the pretext that, wounded, he was no longer fit to be a fighting captain. Should he succeed in putting down the Yankee they would be left with no argument as to why he shouldn't return to command at sea.

There was a roaring in his ears as he tried to fault the reasoning but could find nothing. Even if it were a borrowed frigate he sailed to victory it would prove to all that he was the Sea Devil of legend, the Tom Cutlass of public adulation.

Only if he was victorious.

Returning in a rush of memory was his last action. It had left him a cripple, destroyed his unthinking sense of invulnerability that had strengthened over the years and had taken him into legendary fights, to emerge on the other side whole and exultant. Would he now flinch in the face of the enemy? Would fear of wounds and pain freeze his vitals, affecting his judgement at the cost of men's lives? Was he still a fighting captain that he should dare to take command again?

'Er, you were saying, sir?' Meade's face came into focus, concerned.

'Um, yes. My thought was that . . . that in this case, in the absence of others being available, I should offer my own services as acting captain in the matter.'

He had said it.

The governor's face cleared in relief. 'That's right handsome in you, sir. Most noble. I take it there'll be no objection from your Admiralty?'

'In your official capacity you command both the land and sea forces in your territory, which must be said to include the ship lately entered. You have no need to disturb the command structure, merely appoint me acting captain.'

'Certainly. Er . . .?'

'The form of appointing is a warrant that shall be read on the quarterdeck to all hands. I shall provide a species of wording.'

In a daze of mixed feelings Kydd returned to the villa, his thoughts racing.

It didn't take long to announce the news.

'No! No! You're too ill – you can't!' Persephone, white with shock, clung to him, unbelieving, pitifully bereft.

'I must, Seph.'

There was something in his voice that made further discussion pointless.

Craddock came over to her, took both her hands and whispered, 'This will be the making of him, dear lady. Don't stand in his way and I dare to say you'll soon be getting your old Thomas Kydd back.'

She blinked, sniffed just once, then went to Kydd. 'Darling, I understand. Do go to your ship with my love. What's her name at all?'

'Do you know, sweetheart? I forgot to ask.'

Chapter 64

The boat put off from the small jetty, the midshipman at the tiller abashed at the sight of the fierce, upright figure in gold lace, decorations and fine sword sitting in the stern-sheets. Not entitled to either an accompanying officer, or to be piped aboard a ship not yet his own, Kydd concentrated on his first sight of His Majesty's Frigate *Active* of 36 guns lying at anchor. He was satisfied with what he saw: rather plain and workmanlike due to her wartime construction, it had to be admitted, but British-built with bulldog lines.

As they came in closer his eyes roved over her rigging, the set of her spars, her general seaworthiness. Not so very different from *Tyger*, he saw, with satisfaction: eighteen-pounders in the line of open gun-ports and what looked like nines on the quarterdeck and fo'c'sle, with the odd carronade additional. The ratlines needed attention but the sails, still bent to the yards, were in a snug, professional harbour stow. A good start.

Kydd wore a borrowed uniform, its lace and baubles hastily sewn on. Hauling himself up the man-ropes was painful but he was pleased to find he could do it, and in due form he appeared over the bulwarks. He doffed his hat to the quarterdeck, then strode towards a thick-set, dark-featured officer waiting by the wheel.

'Sir Thomas Kydd? Happy to see you aboard, sir. Tyler, first l'tenant.' There was something wooden, defensive, about the words delivered in a northern accent.

Fighting down a rush of emotions, Kydd told him, 'Call the men aft, if you will, Mr Tyler.'

It had been only a few hours since their captain had been stretchered ashore and here was another coming to take his place.

He took out the warrant and addressed the sea of anonymous faces before him. '"By virtue of the Power and Authority to me given, Sir Robert Meade, Commander-in-Chief of His Majesty's forces in and about the territory of Madeira, do hereby constitute and appoint Sir Thomas Kydd acting Captain of His Majesty's ship *Active*, willing and requiring you forthwith to go on Board, and take upon you the Charge and Command of Captain in her accordingly . . ."'

He was now captain. Did the hands need a speech of some kind at this point? He rather thought not and told Tyler to let them carry on, then allowed himself to be conducted to his great cabin.

Like the rest of the ship it was plain but sturdy, two armchairs planted exactly at forty-five degrees opposite the stern windows, a stout table occupying half of the deck, the whole still smelling of liniments. A few discreet miniatures of an unknown woman and one or two other ornaments were the only indications that an individual had recently owned the space. The bed-place had a cot, but its rumpled appearance indicated that it might be a good idea to change the linen and bedclothes.

'This will do. Officers to attend on me in one hour.'

Tyler left without a word and Kydd sat, his mind in a whirl. Was it morally right to thrust himself, damaged in body and mind, into a situation like this, responsible for the several hundred men on board?

Binard arrived, all a-splutter with something or other not to satisfaction, and then it was Craddock.

He'd insisted on accompanying Kydd, saying that not only did he deserve at least one friend at hand but in the event his leg needed treating it could be done discreetly: *Active*'s ship's company need not know of Kydd's disability. In any case it was not to last for more than a few weeks and would no doubt provide a splendid yarn at the next company dinner.

Craddock was sitting to one side, taking notes, as the officers came to present themselves, one by one.

Tyler was first, in keeping with his station as deputy to Kydd. It seemed the bluff Yorkshireman had served in *Active* some three years, seeing some action, and before that a sloop in the Baltic. A straightforward service history, significantly with no interruption to be on shore. Clearly competent and reliable, his manner was still stiff and defensive, which Kydd put down to the awkwardness of the circumstances.

Second lieutenant was a Matthew Denby. Slender, well-spoken and diffident, this was his first frigate after a series of ships-of-the-line of the Channel Squadron. How he would perform in the very different environment of a single-decker remained to be discovered.

And the third was Bartlett, a wary youth with a cultured accent, who stood back from Kydd as though intimidated. *Active* was his first ship as lieutenant, he having spent most of his time as midshipman in a 74 on blockade. Softly spoken, he would need to be kept under eye.

'Well, what do you think of 'em, Harry?' Kydd asked mildly, after they'd left.

'Save the last – rather young, I thought – a passable crew. Your premier seems to have reservations of some kind, I believe.'

'Ah, the usual tale probably. Restless at not being made up to captain, I'm supposing. He'll just have to get over it. The rest of our brave company I'll learn about in due course.' It was indeed a pleasant thing to have a friend on hand, so much easier than his first acquaintance with *Thunderer* had been. 'You'll want to make your number with the purser and his books, old fellow. I'm to get the barky to sea at the run.'

There was no reason for delay and no tide to consult, and before the bell rang out for the first dog-watch, *Active* was well under way for the south.

By the evening Kydd had made measure of his ship and her company.

Not a beautiful craft, more a willing soul, but in good condition. She'd seen her share of sea-time and it showed here and there, but he was in command of a perfectly respectable specimen of the breed, able to face anything the French could put up against him. Then, with a surge of feeling, he reflected that her eighteens were no match for a big American frigate's twenty-fours. He quashed the thought but it left a lingering trace of something like fear. Was he flinching at the prospect?

The boatswain, Parnall, was short but well-muscled and had an easy way with his men. Moffett, the sailing master, was the opposite: tall, quiet and almost scholarly in his studied, careful perusing of any chart. There were others – the gunner, his mate, topmen – strangers, yet those he had to know very quickly.

Every ship had her quirks and *Active* was no exception. A fast sailer, but unsteady going large, a tendency to corkscrew. Close-hauled to within six and a half points, which was acceptable but not outstanding. A disposition to shy while staying about, a hesitation that was asking for sail to be held on longer than usual before 'mainsail haul'. And an irritating amount of griping that would probably respond to a re-stowage of the hold. But, in all, a stout and reliable vessel.

The men, as they swarmed aloft about their business, appeared capable, the topmen loose-limbed and agile, working like a team. In the afternoon at the guns he saw good practice being made even if shortage of men meant only one side of guns could be served at a time.

As far as he could tell, their mood was cautious and without the signs that he knew were indicators of trouble. This was an everyday ship's company, who were content with their lot and could be relied on. For, after all, he was not taking on a new crew for a fresh commission, and these had been together long enough on the voyage to know each other and their officers.

He reached for the orders and read them again. It was all very well for the nameless Admiralty official to direct *Active* to find and destroy the unnamed American frigate but where in Hades was the thing?

The answer came to mind quickly – he would make rendezvous with Rear Admiral Dixon's squadron off Buenos Aires and there pick up the latest intelligence. If they had spotted nothing, the whole thing was likely to be a false alarm.

In the week or so on passage there didn't appear to be any fearful moves to flee among the ships on the busy sea-lane, no sign that they were alarmed at the presence of an American raider. The Halifax intelligence seemed distinctly uncertain and when they finally raised the squadron off the River Plate Kydd was prepared to accept that no Yankee marauders were at large. It was a blow, for a fruitless jaunt in a frigate would not count in high places to set him back at sea in his own ship.

The 74-gun *Montagu* flew Dixon's flag, an elderly ship that must have seen service in the original American war. She was under easy sail in the grey-tinged chop of the Plate estuary, courteously backing sails and heaving to in answer to Kydd's request to come aboard.

'Well, well, Cap'n Kydd,' rumbled Dixon. 'Pleased to meet you at last. Come to see how we do things on this station – or is it to add to our merry band?'

'Sir. My orders.' Kydd handed over the folded pack.

'So. You're after a Yankee frigate. Said to be in our neck of the woods.'

'Sir.'

'And you think I've had word of such,' Dixon said shrewdly.

'Just so, sir.'

The bluff-featured admiral leaned back, regarding him steadily. Then he spoke, in a quieter but more serious tone: 'Why do you think, sir, that their lordships have seen fit to dispatch a frigate for this affair, rather than leaving the extermination to me?'

'I really can't say, sir.'

'Let me explain, and allow that it concerns your mission in no small measure. Since that absurd descent on Buenos Aires by Popham, we've had open access to the Spanish colonies for our trade. This is a valuable market indeed for our manufactories, which must be protected at all costs.'

'I see, sir.'

'But what you will not know – and this in the utmost confidence – is that the ancient shipments of silver and treasure in galleons back to Spain, which ceased with the present war, are now resumed. But in British vessels, to be held in trust for the Dons until the peace. My mission here, Sir Thomas, is chiefly the safeguarding of this and the larger silver trade.'

Kydd nodded in understanding. There were few enough ships in Dixon's squadron and to send them off in all directions looking for a reported American would put everything to hazard. The Admiralty recognised this, and it was why a detached frigate had been sent.

'Now as to your chase. I can say for a surety that there's been no Yankees here since *Constitution*, which headed off for the Azores some time since.'

'Ah.'

'Yet here's a thing. Only a day or so ago, our consul – who is a first-class source, let me assure you – received some interesting news from across the mountains. The Spanish are all in a tizz because some American frigate has suddenly appeared from nowhere and is making friends with the insurgents. In the absence of your man on this side of the continent it does rather seem he's decided to go against us where we're not. My man says too that, on the side, the devil's sent in half a dozen of our South Sea whalers as prize. What do you think?'

Whalers were valuable, with the refined oil going into all kinds of uses, from the brightest kind of lighting to vats of the stuff into which Kydd had seen forge workers plunge their hot steel.

Apart from that there were the usual trade routes, but what about far to the north, the Canadian border? There must be fighting of a kind going on even there in the wilderness – a full-sized frigate on the scene would be able to dominate the waters and tip the military balance any way it chose.

'I've a notion he may be on his way north to the border to set our colony there to blazes. A clever move,' Kydd responded.

'With only your own good self to go after the beggar,' Dixon said delicately.

Active was a fully outfitted frigate with a warrant for its destruction from the Admiralty and, commanded by a proven ship-killer, free to go anywhere the enemy happened to be.

'I think I must.'

'Stout fellow! If I can be of any kind of service . . .?'

'It'll mean a passage around the Horn and some time at sea without chance of watering and victualling. If I could top out our stores to the deckhead I'd be grateful, sir.'

'You shall have it, and the best of good fortune to you, sir!'

Chapter 65

Active stretched ever south. Kydd knew that in not much more than a week they'd be off Cape Horn, with the worst weather in the world waiting to fall on them. Only he and two others aboard had doubled the Cape, few Royal Navy ships ever venturing into the Great South Sea in these war years. And his own experience had been as a young quartermaster and the passage had been from the west, going with the gales. Here, he was contemplating beating his way against the monstrous winds and seas to win through to the other side of the continent.

By great good fortune *Active* had stowed a suit of heavy-weather sails, in keeping with her recent service in the North Sea and Baltic. And Kydd had laid hands on as much foul-weather gear as he could for his men, remembering the awful shrieking blasts tearing across the deck, stinging ice spicules, freezing spray.

But he was going after the Yankee, meeting his destiny like a man with everything to win – or lose.

He stood abruptly and made his way to the wheel where,

used to his ways, with his cocked hat under his arm, he was studiously ignored.

Active was taking it well. Before they left he'd re-stowed below to give more of a bows-down posture and therefore grip when close-hauled, essential when plying to windward but at the cost of slowing their tacking about. But they were not likely to meet any adversaries in those latitudes.

Looking out, he saw how the seas were already greying. Turning from the blue of mid-latitudes, by degrees they were now changing to the unfriendly tiger-clawed combers of the higher. Rushing forward, mounting up, becoming the malevolent fiends Kydd remembered.

The heavy-weather canvas was roused out and the ship readied for the battle ahead. Life-lines were rigged and old hands competed to terrify newer with tales of ships capsizing under monster waves, men lost overside with barely a cry and giant ice-islands looming out of the darkness.

At fifty south latitude *Active* left the Falkland Islands to larboard and the blustery discomfort and cold of the grey seas turned now to a livening malevolence, the seas rising to slap and bully viciously as they headed for the very tip of the world. The sky clouded, then ominously lowered, with endless scudding of cloud rack, a dismal and continuing sight. The chill now was permanent, the driven spray a freezing lash, and a watch-on-deck a shuddering trial.

The wheel was now manned by two helmsmen, a weather cloth spread on the higher side to give some kind of relief from the wind-blast. All scuppers had been freed: before long *Active* would be trying to rid her upper decks of tons of seawater flooding aboard as her bow cleaved rampaging waves driven by the merciless westerlies.

A lookout's cry drew attention ahead, to a dark, mountainous mass spreading across their course, one of the many islands that infested the seas south of Tierra del Fuego. It had been quite some time since they'd been able to take a satisfactory noon sight and therefore it needed dead reckoning navigation, calculated guesswork. With a formidable easterly current and squall-ridden winds chopping around without warning it was a fearful art with the penalty for misjudgement a night-time death on desolate rocks.

There was one contrivance that was left to them: take careful observation of one of the islands, its main features, bearings and pattern with relation to others and match this to the best chart they had. If successful it would provide the priceless secret of an exact location, one that would give them the means to move forward the dead reckoning another step in confidence.

They were approaching fifty-six degrees south, the point where it was clear to set *Active*'s bows westward, into the five-hundred-mile gap that was Drake Passage. There, the great man had found his way to glory and the annals of history by doing exactly what they were undertaking – winning their way through to the other side of the continent.

Now they were taking the streaming gales in their teeth. The Great Southern Ocean was the only body of water to encircle the earth completely, with nothing to temper its onslaught. With these winds hammering out of the west it was going to be hard on the men and on their ship, under sail into the wind close-hauled and clawing every foot to windward they could, day after day, night after night.

Every wind-shift, every change of conditions, had men going aloft into a howling wilderness of cold and bluster. Iron-hard canvas, ropes bar-taut and always the furious gyrations and roll accentuated by height, which usually ended in a jerk that threatened to toss an unfortunate off the foot-rope.

Kydd found his eyes growing red-rimmed with salt spray

and muscles aching; only a manic grip on a stay could prevent slipping. But at the same time he was aware that a feeling was bursting through – of elation and heightened mood. He was at one with the sea – its wild majesty, its passion, its overwhelming power over all creation.

Some were in terror of their lives as the fight went on. Others, like him, revelled in it and were known in the Navy as 'foul weather jacks'. What he'd dreaded taken from him had not been.

Four days passed. They caught a snatched glimpse far to starboard of the peak of Cape Horn, its ravaged slopes with dark fissures plunging into the sea, only for the awesome scene to be swallowed by drifting murk.

It should have been a triumph of navigation, but out of the night whirled an ill-tempered snow-filled flurry and the winds turned implacably against them. Given a slant, any angle of wind bluster other than directly from the west, they could conform, tacking about to give a longer board on that side, but if not, then it was a monotonous tack by tack into its blast, making little headway against the streaming fury. The worst was the sight after another three days of the same Cape Horn. Despite their efforts they'd been carried back to the eastward, forced to start their unequal fight again.

The gods of winds and war were against them. There had to be another way.

Kydd held conclave in his wildly lurching cabin. From this it became clear that there was only one other option, and it came from Kydd's reading of Captain Cook's Antarctic exploration.

It was to go south, close to where the ice-islands were spawned, to the unexplored polar desolation that was the finality of the world. Cook had mentioned that calmer weather could be expected there, out of the circuit of the Great Southern Ocean.

The sailing master was not so sure. 'From the Roaring Forties to the Furious Fifties is enough to try a man, but to think to make the Screaming Sixties is askin' for more'n this barky could take, I'm thinking.'

Tyler gave a cynical smile as he intoned the old Cape Horn refrain, 'Below forty south there's no law – past fifty south there's no God.'

There was no amusement on the others' faces but Kydd had made up his mind and *Active* lay over and headed even further south.

Cook had been right: the winds eased to a fresh gale and then to a sullen stiff breeze and they made good way – but there was a price to pay. The cold was severe: ropes, canvas and even the spars covered themselves with hoar-frost and spray froze even as it flew. The deck became a slippery rink, and movement fore and aft was only possible with lines stretched along.

It was a deadly, alien and desperately lonely place.

A fog materialised out of nowhere – first, a frost-smoke arising from the sea, then a suffocating silence as it thickened and spread until visibility dropped to yards. Its clammy embrace was cold and repellent but in mercy the accompanying calm meant the ship lost way to a walking pace. As long as they stayed on the course they'd plotted ahead, clear of hazards, they should be safe.

Then a disbelieving shout from forward, taken up by others: '*Breakers* – I hear *breakers* ahead!'

'Silence on deck!' Kydd roared above the instant babble and strained to hear.

It had no meaning – as far as Cook and indeed others that had passed this way had reported, there was no land in the deep south. Without noon sights, *Active* had only the vaguest idea where they were and their charts were next to useless. There was no mistaking the sullen, heavy boom and endless swash of the swell ending its world-girdling run against some stern bluff.

Kydd volleyed out the orders that had the ship heaving to, quickly followed by a cast of the lead.

'No bottom with this line,' was the first call, followed by more of the same. The water was very deep – no anchoring possible. Out there must be a near vertical coastline lying in wait for them to pile into it.

In an agony of indecision Kydd felt the first stirrings of a polar zephyr. The fog must be lifting and all aboard waited to see what would be revealed.

Directly ahead, the size of a mountain and no more than a few hundred yards distant, was a gigantic ice-island. Rearing impossibly up, it was shot through with emerald and sapphire, breathtaking in its size and majesty.

The sound of seas breaking on the opposite side continued, and Kydd saw that where they were on the leeward side the huge ice mass was taking their wind. He'd be satisfied with what ground they'd won to westward, rejoin the world of boreal madness and leave this frightful place of bitter cold and ice-mountains.

By some freakish twist of nature they were met with a rare fresh easterly gale, which in short order took the frigate under its wing and ran with it in an exhilarating charge to westward. If they could keep with it for several more days, then throw over the helm to stretch northward they might find themselves past the crucial seventy-fifth meridian, indicating they had progressed to the other side of the continent and could safely go north, their travails over.

In three more days the wind had veered but in the process

had momentarily cleared the skies, at just the right time to wield sextants and determine their westing. They had achieved it, and could now reach up for the South American coast and beyond.

Chapter 66

A modest bay opened up as they warily passed the first point. It was deserted and perfect for restoring the craft for its mission north. The anchor tumbled down and Kydd called Tyler over. 'Tell the bosun to take all the men he needs to fettle the barky after our little jaunt. The master and purser to report on our victuals and water.'

'Aye, aye, sir.'

The first lieutenant now treated his captain with respect. Kydd wondered whether this was due to what he had seen of his seamanship. Or was he counting on promotion out of the ship when they successfully brought down the American?

In the privacy of his cabin Kydd pondered his next move. The quarry could be anywhere within the half of the planet occupied by the Pacific Ocean, some sixty-four million square miles, vastly more than that occupied by all of the land area added together. If he was going to come upon the intruder it needed guile, not long endurance.

He'd not attempted to search the lower half of the continent above its tip, that jumbled sprawl of islands offshore between the wild Fifties south and the more civilised Forties, as no one in possession of their senses would think to plunder such a place of desolation. Added to which the constant fierce westerlies around the Horn were deflected north by the mountains into a most useful wafting lift up the coast, where they now lay.

The trade ports were further on, dotted on the coast all the way north to the tropics, each under the sway of Spanish colonial masters, some well known, others raw settlements. If their prey was an American, he would be careful not to upset these people: his war was against the British. Conceivably he could be intercepting southbound merchantmen on the chance that they carried goods destined for the British but this was a paltry employment for a full-blooded frigate. What was there, then?

A whaler having spent years at sea without news would be easy meat, but these would be scattered over the entire South Seas and, while valuable, would be tedious in the finding. It wasn't that tribe – but what was as profitable?

He brought to mind his earlier suspicions. A frigate could create havoc in the wilderness at the Canadian border, reducing the forts put there to safeguard against the United States turning the western flank of Canada to fall on its lines of communication over the mountains.

This was the only thing that made sense, an effective and devastating incursion by a single frigate.

'How does it, Mr Tyler? I mean to weigh for the north without a moment's delay.'

It would be a straightforward reach northward without bothering to search inshore, cutting weeks off their passage.

They put to sea, course due north.

As day followed day *Active* took advantage of the reliable

southerly, ticking off the exotic ports invisible under their lee: Concepción, Pichilemu, Valparaíso, Coquimbo, Antofagasta. None held any interest for Kydd.

As they made progress northward, the weather improved: grey seas to blue, storm rack to soft clouds, heaving swells from the westward to well-behaved seas conforming to the southerly winds.

And then from the balmy mid-latitudes to the edge of the tropics. Sails were shifted to light-weather canvas and—

'*Sail ahoyyyy!*' bawled a lookout. It was just a smudge on the horizon, fine on the bow.

Kydd debated whether to stop and board to ask for news of the Yankee frigate at the risk of alerting its captain to the existence of a pursuer.

The advantage to be gained in knowing even to a hundred-mile square the location of the chase was worth the risk. 'Course to lay us alongside,' he growled.

In hours the vessel could be made out by a telescope in the tops: eastward bound, of modest size and homely construction, her rig was stout but not in any way built for speed – a whaler. And it was taking flight, hauling around for the north. A suspicious move for an innocent. Could it be English, mistaking *Active* for the American? If so, it meant she must have heard of it and could therefore give details.

There was no question of a whaling ship out-running a frigate and well before evening they closed with it and *Active* lay off to windward.

'British colours, sir,' reported Tyler, noting the splash of colour mounting up its mizzen. 'And if she's not Hull-built I'm a Dutchman.'

'English ship, ahoy!' roared Kydd, across the intervening seas heaving between the two. 'Have you word of an American frigate in these waters?'

A figure near the wheel replied, the faint words nearly overlaid with the sound of the swashing seas, but there was no mistaking the relief in the words: 'Aye, I have an' all. Thought you was it, Cap'n!'

'So, tell me what you know, if you please.'

Suddenly, right forward in the ship, an arm protruded out of a side scuttle. It held a handkerchief that was frantically shaken – and Kydd understood.

'I'm coming aboard you,' he bawled.

'No, don't yez bother none. I've nowt to say as will help and . . .' The voice tailed off as *Active*'s seaboat briskly descended from its davits. Kydd and four armed marines were carried smartly across.

'Who's the captain?' he demanded, looking around the weather-beaten vessel and the rather sulky crewmen standing about. 'Well?'

There was no response until an older man with a lop-sided grin stepped forward and answered, 'I guess that means m'self.'

It was quickly uncovered: this was a whaler right enough, and English. But it was also a prize of a United States Ship – and now recaptured.

From its original crew Kydd heard how the Yankee under English colours had tricked them. He also had intelligence they'd gained in overhearing their captors that they were not headed north to relieve Fort Astoria at the Canadian border or any other, preferring to concentrate on the British whaling fleet in mid-latitudes. The ship's name was *Castine* and could be easily identified by its full-dress Indian figurehead and a characteristic silver lightning conductor at the mainmast head – and had a large crew.

Most gratifying of all, however, was the nugget of information that they'd been so warmly welcomed when they put into Valparaíso that it could almost be regarded as a base of sorts.

The odds were suddenly reduced.

Putting the frigate about, Kydd had days to review plans. And all started with the same step: go to Valparaíso to discover what he could of the enemy.

After that, it depended on what was revealed.

Chapter 67

Valparaíso was well to the south and by the time its latitude had been reached Kydd was ready for anything
– that his intelligence was false, that there was more than one
enemy frigate on the loose or that the Spanish colonial authorities were going to make it hard for him, the British having
taken up most of the homeland's trade for themselves.

Prudently at quarters, they eased around the nondescript
scrubby point that marked the entrance to Valparaíso Bay,
which opened up before them, a broad vista with minor bays
and headlands further to the east. The city nestled under the
last foothills of the Andes, with a modest seafront area shel-
tering no more than half a dozen ships, some at a small
wharf and others lying at anchor in Valparaíso Roads a small
distance offshore.

Kydd decided to join them and send Craddock ashore to
see what he could uncover about the Yankee frigate.

'Hands to moor ship!' *Active* prepared to cast anchor just
astern of the largest and—

Three or four seamen saw the inconceivable sight at the
same time. There, within easy gun-shot, was a frigate, quite

as large as they and lazily flapping in the warm breeze a huge, brazen American flag.

Their arrival, shocking as it must have been to them, none-theless brought a response, a mass howl of defiance, of insult, of patriotism. Fists shook and yells of anger and righteous-ness split the air. It was returned with equal force by the Actives who began roaring, 'God Save the King', taking to the shrouds to be seen the better.

Kydd gathered his thoughts. This was a neutral port – Spain, although side by side with England against the French, was not a political ally. The international law concerning bellig-erents in neutral waters strictly applied: any might take shelter in the neutral port but were not permitted to undertake any warlike act against another flying the flag of an enemy. *Active* was thus free to enter the port but could not lay a finger on *Castine*, and vice versa.

His eyes flicked to the mounting disorder on the American ship. They were hoisting some kind of bunting up to her fore-topgallant masthead with writing on it: 'Sailors' Rights and Free Trade'. Other slogans rose but an ugly mood was building and ominously guns were being manned, with hoarse shouts that carried clearly across the water.

It only needed some fool . . .

If he withdrew to a safe place it would no doubt be construed as a retreat. 'We anchor right where we are, Mr Tyler,' Kydd ordered.

A bower anchor plunged off her bow and *Active* came to rest, directly opposite the Yankee frigate. They were now within easy gun-shot, each side glaring down the muzzle of a cannon at the other while the insults and taunts flew. Kydd had one object: to get the *Castine* to fire first and be condemned for breach of neutrality as well as giving the chance for a full-scale engagement here and now.

But the canny American captain, while giving full rein to his crew, kept them from the last act.

And so it remained – neither making any significant move.

Kydd was not going to be cowed and soon had a boat in the water with Craddock and the purser aboard to secure victuals and to see what the situation was.

They were back before dark with fresh beef, greens, beer. Access to water had been granted and every courtesy shown. It was a measure of how the situation ashore had changed since *Castine* had been made so welcome. It seemed that their hosts of before, the Carrera family, were now languishing in jail, their insurrection having been put down and the colonial Spanish reinstated. The American frigate was now seen more as a threat to trade, hostile to the English interests who kept commerce going, and as only a single ship, hardly a power to wield sufficient influence to think to change sides. As well, news had arrived that the British had faced a Yankee frigate in Chesapeake Bay and won out, bringing an end to the Americans' legend of invincibility and restoring the Royal Navy's reputation.

All in all, a satisfactory situation for the British.

Yet all came down to the one matter for Kydd: he was there to do a job and that was to put an end to the American.

With a powerful telescope he'd surveyed the enemy ship, noting the guns, probable sail area, expected performance at sea and the size of its crew. It would appear they were closely matched and, given equal skill of the captains, it would most probably be the fortunes of war that decided the victor.

It was odd indeed. Here, in perfect safety, a few hundred yards off an enemy ship, he was taking his fill of her power and strength, which in the course of time would be brought to bear on *Active* – and himself.

The thought turned by degrees dark and menacing. Even

muskets at this range would cause slaughter and if just one of those thirty-two-pounder carronades was loaded with grape or canister he'd be facing far worse than he had with the militia who had dealt him his near-death wound.

A tight, cold ball began to form in his stomach. Could he face it all again, knowing that as trivial a matter as a human eye sighting down a musket could in a single stroke end in unendurable pain and the finality of death?

He was flinching. His concentration was now on the dread of what might be, not on what must be – and too many lives hung on his fitness for command.

How had he coped before? He hadn't really thought about it in all the din and excitement of battle. Now he was older, and as he considered the consequences of actions, an appalling and very real prospect was sapping his manhood. In hours or days he could be a corpse, dead and unfeeling. Should he—

'Sir? Sir?' It was a midshipman. Who was it? It was Dingle, the young and lanky lad who so desired to be a frigate captain like him.

'Yes, Mr Dingle?' Kydd responded, his eyes focusing.

'Er, umm – Mr Tyler, that is the first lieutenant, sir, sends his er, compliments and . . . er . . . er . . .'

The child had been terrified by Kydd's unreadable expression and failed to pass the message.

Kydd softened. That the young lad had been put out of countenance by his own weakness had to be made right. 'Sir!' he said, drawing back in mock horror. 'Is Mr Tyler so advanced that he stands above myself?'

'S-sir?'

'The senior pays compliments to the junior and the junior sends due respects to the senior. Now, do correct yourself and rehearse to me your message.'

'Oh. Yes, sir. Then, Mr Tyler gives his respects and desires to send the last dog-watchmen to quarters for exercise an' requests your permission.'

'That's better, younker. Please inform the first lieutenant that I cannot think of a better employment for the hands.'

Chapter 68

That night Kydd slept badly. The reality of the enemy's presence in such a stark way brought on the nightmares he'd hoped put behind him.

As soon as it was light, the noise and hullabaloo began again with 'Yankee Doodle' competing against 'Rule Britannia' all through the morning. It couldn't last: a gun might go off and, irrespective of international law, they'd be at each other's throats.

But there was another, more compelling, element. International law required that should a belligerent put to sea, a clear twenty-four hours must pass before its enemy might sail after it.

If *Castine* quit her anchorage it would leave *Active* in Valparaíso, giving her a full day's start. The most immense ocean in existence would be enough to hide in and *Active*'s searching would have been in vain.

But there was another way. If it was turned on its head, quite another picture emerged. *Active* put to sea – so *Castine* had to delay for twenty-four hours. If *Active* lay to, just outside neutral waters, she could keep a watch on *Castine* and be in a position to lunge when the enemy ventured outside these waters.

It was fine in theory, but what if there was nothing to force *Castine* to sea?

Kydd made the first move and *Castine* saw their opponent loose sail and depart, leaving them unmolested.

'Lie off – line of sight Punta Angeles sou'-west b' west,' Kydd ordered. In view of their quarry but in international waters. That was the distance a country might enforce their neutral rights by fire from a fortress, namely gun-shot range. Not a precise definition but workable by an officer-of-the-watch. In effect *Castine* was now in forced blockade.

And it deferred the time when Kydd would have to face the enemy's guns. He crushed the thought and turned to face the open sea. *Castine* would think they'd come out the winner in the confrontation and take some time to see how the tables had been turned on them.

How long would they lie idle while *Active* lurked offshore? If they believed that *Active* must eventually sail away for lack of provisions or water they were wrong. With the sympathy ashore that Craddock had been able to generate, they'd simply resupply by boats, so the wait would be indefinite. It was time for patience.

Day followed day, still no movement by *Castine*. Was there nothing Kydd could do to lure her out?

Perhaps there was! That night Craddock and the purser went ashore as usual but with a singular errand in view. In his customary price negotiations the purser rewarded the chief merchant for his considerations in the matter with the information that *Active* was the first of four frigates and when they arrived shortly he would recommend his own good self for provisions' supply to them.

The word would get through. The American captain would

soon feel the pressure: he'd be trapped in port facing an armada. The fuse had been lit: Kydd had only to lie quietly in wait for whatever motion *Castine* would contrive.

It was not long in coming but in a form that was completely unexpected.

From the inner harbour a number of boats put out towing a small ship and heading for the centre of Valparaíso Roads, the civil anchorage.

'Good heavens,' Tyler said faintly, raising his telescope. 'Whatever are the rascals up to?'

The ship flew British colours but proudly above them floated the Stars and Stripes.

'It's one of the *Castine* prizes,' Kydd said in surprise. 'They've come to flaunt it.'

Having the entire attention of *Active*, the boats cast off their tow and presently, first from the waist and then the stern, thin wisps of smoke began rising.

'They're firing it!' spluttered Tyler.

But Kydd saw through it. What the Yankee captain needed was for Kydd to lose his temper at the calculated insult and be the first to fire in a fight that would take place in the harbour, favouring *Castine* with her forty close-range heavy carronades.

He wouldn't be gulled. 'Let 'em go – and give them joy of the prize-money they're burning.'

They watched the whale-oil soaked timbers catch and flare until the entire ship became a fiery spectacle visible for miles. As it subsided to a red and black ashen wreck it listed over and quietly disappeared from view.

'An entertainment, but at their expense,' agreed Tyler, and life went on as before in HMS *Active*.

A little over an hour later Kydd was summoned on deck by the officer-of-the-watch who indicated a boat approaching.

Over its transom was an enormous flag, Spanish, but sewn with ornaments and decorations that Kydd didn't recognise.

'The governor of Valparaíso,' he guessed. 'A side-party, I believe.'

In the privacy of his cabin Kydd heard him out with the assistance of Craddock, whose commercial Spanish sometimes wilted under the strain.

'This is intolerable, not to be borne by civilised nations and most assuredly not by me!' the governor spluttered.

'Sir. What is it that we have unwittingly done to incur your anger?'

'Not you, honoured sir. These *bucaneros*, the *Americanos* who defile our neutrality with acts of destruction, pollute our waters with—'

'*Gobernador* Lastra, I do comprehend your righteous distress at this flagrant act but I cannot see why you have come to me.'

'*Ah, ya veo*. It is this, Sir Kydd.' He paused, allowing a theatrical expression of stately gravity to settle. 'I come with an offer of my own making. In my position as the highest officer of the Spanish Crown in Valparaíso I hereby absolve you of any consequences should you proceed against this villain where he lies.'

'He's in neutral waters.'

'Of which I undertake not to notice. *Comprendes?*' This was no doubt at the behest of the local merchants who wanted a quick resolution to the contest that was keeping their ships cowering. It was, as well, a telling indictment of how far the Americans had fallen out of favour.

Kydd considered. The fort guns would be silent as he moved on the other ship, but if he did, it would certainly give the United States good and valid reason to protest whatever the outcome, a complication not to be welcomed at the

345

Admiralty. And then there was the more practical objection of the dangers of a full-scale engagement in a crowded anchorage.

'I do honour your offer, sir, but must give more thought to the military questions it presents.'

The governor doubtfully took his leave, giving Kydd time to ponder.

It was plain that the pressure of expecting a British squadron without warning was getting to the American captain. It was better to be on doubled alert – this commander was cunning and driven by circumstances.

The weather was not in Kydd's favour. What wind there was came from offshore, the last fading breeze of a wind born on the slopes of the Andes and dying to a whisper out at sea. *Active* hardly moved over a listless, glassy sea but Kydd knew that in with the land there was still quite sufficient of a breathy warm wind to take *Castine* out. Worse, the reigning current was northerly and strong, carrying *Active* away and off position. And there was a mist along the shoreline that could well thicken to fog, cutting off all sight of the enemy.

All he could do was keep within the bay, if possible, at what passed for the windward end, and await events.

As the day wore on it became obvious that they were losing the battle with the current. Windless, they hung there, the faint ripple at the forefoot entirely faded. It meant that they were held unmoving in a mass of water as it drifted with the current, unable to make way against it.

For hours the calm held. Lookouts were doubled and doubled again and placed in every position of advantage. The wait and watch went on.

And then, later in the afternoon, there was movement, firming through the mists – masts, sails, then a more substantial hull, heading for the open sea – at the other end of the bay.

It was *Castine*. Her captain had correctly read the conditions that held *Active* motionless and was taking the opportunity to break out by staying within the band of offshore breeze and making up the coast, then away.

They had lost the race and the enemy was now free to continue his voyage of predation. The scene was not lost on *Active*'s decks and a dismal silence descended.

But the day was not ended. In a quirk of nature, not unknown on those coasts, the cool of a sea breeze touched Kydd's face. From out to sea some stray zephyr was playfully rippling the surface from the opposite direction. It strengthened fitfully and decided to stay with them. Gripped by a wind that was this time born of the ocean, *Active* took it and ran. Still with the favourable but slight shore breeze *Castine* was slower and it became increasingly obvious that somewhere in Valparaíso Bay there would be a conclusion.

The hours and days of tedious blockade at last were over! Kydd smacked his fist into his palm in delight but then those betraying doubts crept in and his brow furrowed. Out there wounding or death could be waiting for the destined moment to strike and there was nothing he could do to ward off the judgement.

'Quarters, sir?' Tyler asked eagerly.

Kydd gulped, taking a handkerchief to his mouth to conceal his betraying expression. 'Beat to quarters, then.'

The martial thunder of drums and impassioned shouts only added to the sick dread that was building in him and he fought against it until a measure of calm had returned. He had a battle to fight and his cool judgement was needed – where, for instance, should he position *Active* for the first crushing broadside?

The range was closing, *Castine* was manoeuvring. First one of her guns fired, then another.

'To her larboard quarter,' he croaked.

'Aye aye, sir.'

Then, for no apparent reason in the strengthening breeze, *Castine* fell off the wind and wore around in a tight circle.

'Makes no sense,' muttered Tyler, raising his glass. The frigate's new course set her back in the direction she'd come from.

Then he burst out, 'She's running, by God! Back to her hidey-hole!'

Others on the quarterdeck saw it and loudly agreed, shouts turning to cheers. But Kydd suspected there was another reason: the Yankee wanted no damage to his precious frigate and his intentions were to continue with his voyage of destruction.

He left his officers to their exulting. There was little more he could do.

Chapter 69

One afternoon, several days later, the petty officer of the watering party asked to see Kydd. He'd picked up information from a friendly merchant that he'd seen the purser of *Castine* step ashore and place a substantial order for beef and bread. The frigate was storing for a voyage rather than taking on smaller amounts of fresh victuals day by day. And with beef to be slaughtered, bread to be baked, it was an indication that the sailing could not take place for a day or two.

It was tempting for Kydd to stand down the ship's company and take *Active* to some secluded bay for repair and rest, both in dire need. The Yankee captain, however, was brazen and clever and could be relied on for some kind of trickery, so there would be no diversion or ease. The watch would be maintained.

Nightfall saw *Active* at the windward end of the bay, Punta Angeles, and under slight sail. The wise birds aboard all promised a blow before long. Kydd allowed no slacking at the lookouts even if it wasn't likely that *Castine* would stir from her moorings.

Midnight passed, and apart from the glimmer of cabin lanthorns among the anchored ships, now nearly all doused, and beyond them the shore lights twinkling, there was nothing to disturb the tranquillity of the watch-on-deck. Then one, several, of the lookouts hailed. 'Blue lights, t'other end of the bay!'

Kydd was sent for and instantly snatched a night-glass. There they were: three blue flares in the darkness in the form of a triangle, which was the usual substitute for the Blue Peter flag of daylight hours. It was the signal to other vessels that one of their number was putting to sea and to clear their way of stray boats.

Castine? Showing betraying lights? Ridiculous. Then an explanation crystallised. What if one of the loyal British merchants wanted to indicate that *Castine* was making a break? And under cover of darkness slipping to the other end of the bay, Punta Gruesa, giving her the chance to get away. Daylight would find *Active* at the wrong side of the bay and reveal an empty berth where *Castine* had been.

'Shake out more sail – he's getting away around the point!' But for the trusty merchant concerned, in the darkness they'd have lost the chase.

Raging downwind it wouldn't take long to close with the Yankee as it made its dash for . . .

Dash? To reach down to Punta Gruesa he'd have to be close-hauled on the larboard tack, and with the curvature of the bay, he'd be headed well before he reached there, having to go about and lay over on the starboard tack to weather the point. That would place himself directly across *Active's* patrol line, a fearful risk that the kind of captain Kydd thought him would never take.

Then what . . . It was a trick! A beautifully executed decoy to lure him to the wrong end of the bay, leaving *Castine* the opportunity to get away in the opposite direction, well to windward.

'Damn the fellow! Wear ship this instant. Get us back,' Kydd snapped. They had to beat against the wind to reach their previous station off Punta Angeles with the probability that *Castine* would take advantage of the windward end of the bay to round the point swiftly and be away.

Active responded nobly and, in the stiff blow that was developing, leaned into it, her bow heaving and smashing through the seas until she had found her position again. There was no sign of the Yankee. All that could be done was to wait for daylight and look into Valparaíso Roads.

The weather worsened, squally blasts coming out of the night with no warning, and Kydd kept sail to a minimum, an exhausting, tedious fight with the sting of failure, waiting for the dawn.

As the light extended over the raging seascape it was difficult to make out the seafront and anchorage to establish whether the American had stolen away. But between two rain squalls they saw that the Yankee frigate was unaccountably still at anchor despite the success of its decoy.

With a lurch of the stomach Kydd knew there had to be a reckoning, and soon.

And almost as if presented by a gift from the gods the chance came.

It was now blowing a fresh gale from the south-west, off the land and, even as they watched, *Castine* lost her anchor cable and, unable to recover, found herself carried seawards. Smart seamanship saw sail hastily set and the frigate, clawing into the wind hard on the starboard tack, made to round Punta Gruesa, still just within neutral waters.

Kydd saw how it would develop: *Castine* would stay within neutral waters until he found a congenial retreat where he would rouse out another cable and anchor to ride out the storm before resuming his seclusion. All he could do was follow the American's movements from out at sea.

The winds turned boisterous, gusts and squalls and sheeting spray as *Castine* closed dangerously close to the rocks and reefs of the point. Then in a sudden flurry it could be seen that *Castine* had been near driven over by a murderous squall, and then on rising, the strain had been too much and her main topmast had given way, tumbling down in a tangle of rigging. As this was cut away, and by a singular feat of seamanship, the vessel wore around with the obvious intent of returning to the safety of Valparaíso Roads.

And it was nearly successful, but the gale was offshore and she was headed and fell off the wind, blustered around to face the way she had been. She was lucky: to have the filthy weather driving her away from the rocks allowed the injured vessel to round the point safely into a small bay a mile or two beyond.

Even as Kydd sailed in parallel up the coast the rough and volatile weather was easing and *Castine* could be seen anchoring a bare mile from the shore, her seamen visibly at work already on the topmast wreckage.

Still some way to seaward Kydd knew he had a decision to make. A final and decisive one.

There were no fortifications within sight, no habitations.

Should he throw himself at *Castine* where she lay or strictly observe the laws of neutrality and continue to lie off? All in his being shouted at him to close with the enemy and finish it, but again the insidious thoughts came pointing out that the American had a slight wound, was anchored, and could sight her guns with all her crew available to serve them.

But his years as a frigate captain obstinately replied with a robust plan. If he sailed in boldly the Yankee would be at his mercy. He would position *Active* off her quarter while anchored and reduce the frigate by close bombardment.

'We're going in.'

'Sir?' Kydd realised he had spoken softly to himself and repeated it louder.

Tyler's expression changed from grim to delight. 'Capital!' he chortled, slapping his thigh. 'We've got 'em where we want 'em!'

'Then shall we move?' Kydd asked pointedly.

Chapter 70

It must have been obvious in *Castine* what was under way: work stopped on the topmast and shifted to the bow. Kydd didn't concern himself with that. There was the complex resolution of the elements of the falling wind, current and the changing orientation of *Castine* relative to *Active* to reckon as they made their approach. If he got any of it wrong, his ship would career away past the American.

However, the correct position would enable them to close in off the quarter of the stationary Yankee and pound away to a conclusion in a killing rake.

But as they neared it became clear that *Castine* was prepared. Unmoving she might be but springs were being passed to her anchor cable to aim whole-ship broadsides and guns were being ranged aft, long guns, not carronades. This was not going to be an outright conquest.

Active closed, but again the wind-gods intervened, and instead of anchoring off *Castine*'s quarter to pound her into submission, *Active* was sent askew by a squall, her broadside unusable. *Castine*, however, opened fire on her with nine- and twelve-pounders, which had been brutally man-handled aft, her marines beginning vicious musketry play.

It told immediately. The howl and *whuup* of missiles, the crunch and skitter of hits filled the air as Kydd's mind raced. This was not a typical frigate action in streaming seas and open ocean and he could not rely on experience. The damage mounted – stays unstranded and sails cut about, and then, as the twelves firing from the quarterdeck of *Castine* found their range, there were savage blows taken to hull and upperworks. A shriek pierced through the din, mercifully cut short. Shouts followed but Kydd had to keep his head to give *Active* victory.

The wind veered and dropped to a slight breeze – and *Castine* was heaving in on her springs readying her first broadside of thirty-two pounders, the same bore as the heaviest guns *Victory* carried.

This paradoxically brought Kydd a cool vision of the solution presenting itself to him even in the fury of battle. He'd conjured a plan in the face of the worst the enemy could do and the realisation came: he hadn't flinched – he was no longer fearful and full of dread.

In the chaos and violence of combat he had fallen into the age-old way of battle he'd unconsciously built up over years of success at sea – the hotter the fight, the cooler the mind. At any given point he could be mortally wounded – but before that happened there was a victory to be won, which wouldn't come about if he was skulking in fear.

There were too many depending on him to have it any other way – those who'd set him on the quarterdeck in the first place, his ship's company sharing the same dangers as he and doing their duty and, of course, dear Persephone, who would trust him to be her knight in shining armour.

Suddenly energised, he seized his thought and followed it.

The Yankee was expecting him to come on as the English always did, close in for a man-to-man battering, broadside to broadside until the better ship won. And this was precisely why, in this fluky and treacherous weather, he'd got into difficulties.

Earlier, in the harbour, Kydd had been granted sight of his opponent at close quarters and had noticed something. *Castine* was armed with no less than forty of the largest thirty-two-pounder carronades, giving her the edge in weight of metal – but only at close range, for the stubby short-barrelled gun lost accuracy and hitting power at distance.

Active's guns were long eighteen-pounders, with a lesser bore, it had to be admitted, but carried further and aimed true.

Instead of closing and grappling he would stand off and carry out a systematic bombarding of the stationary vessel with no real risk of return fire.

There was no time to lose. 'Wear ship!' he bellowed above the din.

Men turned to gape at him, for this would turn *Active* away from the enemy, disengage her from the battle.

He rounded on his first lieutenant. 'Get those men moving, Mr Tyler,' he barked savagely. 'We've a battle to win!'

Active's guns fell silent as she braced around, the slight breeze taking her away steadily downwind while in *Castine* a mighty roar and cheering arose.

Kydd gave a grim smile. 'They think we're retreating, the loobies,' he grunted, easing his sword. 'We'll soon hear what they've got to say.'

At just the right point, *Active* rounded to and opened up with her long eighteens. A rolling broadside, each gun a short space after the previous, one by one down the length of the gun-deck, the gun captains making the most of the indulgence of aimed fire in place of the usual madness of point-blank broadsides.

The result was hideous. Even from their distance, cannon strike could clearly be seen: leaping deadly black splinters, spars shivered in two, bulwarks hammered flat, bodies flung into the air.

'It's murder,' Tyler said in a low, uncomfortable voice.

'This Yankee captain won't give up easily,' Kydd replied woodenly. 'It has to go on.'

And still from *Castine* every gun that could fire was blazing away regardless of how ineffectual it was at the range. Then the angle between her masts altered.

'She's cut her cable,' Kydd murmured. 'I do believe she's trying to board, the villains!'

But while the wounded vessel fell off the wind, her shattered and broken topmasts prevented her completing the wearing manoeuvre and she drifted back, helpless.

Kydd wasted no time – the vessel now without springs on its cable was unmanoeuvrable and was at his mercy but he was not going in to finish the job. This fighting captain would do his utmost to thwart anything he could bring to the fight and therefore his only recourse was to persuade by force.

'Lie off her stern – she's got to strike!'

In the light airs *Active* slowly and deliberately turned and took position. One by one her guns took up the battering again, *Castine* now unable to resist but, heroically, spread torn sail and the frigate turned towards the shore – the rocks and currents of the point itself. She was going to wreck herself to prevent being taken as prize.

Cruelly, even that was denied her, as the gleeful breeze shifted back to an offshore south-westerly and into *Active's* guns.

It was the end.

Kydd patiently kept his glass trained on the wreckage that passed for her rigging, hearing the last of her guns hopelessly thundering. He was unable to make out her colours, and realised that by now they'd probably been shot away.

'Cease fire, all!' he ordered, and waited.

There were one or two sullen thuds and *Castine* finally fell silent. She had given her all and now must surrender to the victor.

Chapter 71

It had been as hard-fought an engagement as any Kydd had been in. Later he'd have to confront the backwash of the frenzy of violence, the butcher's bill of good men sent to their end, the horror and pity of it all – but now he felt only the leaping exultation of the triumphant warrior.

And nevermore would he suffer fear and flinching – he'd also won that particular battle.

The crowning prize was that the news of his frigate victory over the Americans would reach England, and it was as certain as day followed night that the Admiralty would be obliged by public clamour to set the hero of the hour on his own quarterdeck once more, the wounded but demonstrably recovered sea legend.

'Call away my barge. I shall take possession,' Kydd said firmly, eager to meet her captain – if he lived.

On the way the breeze picked up, its warmth suffused with shore fragrances as the powder-smoke dissipated and Kydd regarded *Castine*.

Active's eighteens had done deadly work, ruin and blood fore and aft, unstranded lines hanging from aloft, ominous black pockmarks where balls had savagely torn into her belly with untold devastation and ruin within.

In respect, Kydd had not worn his knightly honours and was still in his dress for battle, a plain captain's rig, which bore the grey smears of gun-smoke and the odd tear. He was glad, for as he mounted the side-steps to the frigate's waste-land of a deck, crewmen were standing sullenly, exhausted but defiant among all the evidence of mortal combat. It would have been tactless to lord it the glittering conqueror over such brave souls.

He looked about until a slight figure came into sight from further forward. It hobbled, dragging a foot and using some sort of pole as a crutch, the head bandaged to one side, the whole heavily smudged with the same powder-smoke grey.

Kydd waited quietly as the man approached.

Quite suddenly he stopped – and straightened to stare at him. 'Y-you . . . you're Tom Kydd! How . . . how . . .'

Kydd froze. Jasper Gindler. Friend. Enemy.

Memories jostled: images of a preposterous attack on a French privateer those years ago; sharing clam chowder at his boathouse; working together on the ingenious contrivance that saved the day– and, much later, the final pitying look of the one who'd commanded the men who had felled him.

'Yes, Master Commandant,' Kydd said slowly.

It was an impossible situation – he was being asked by hallowed tradition to take the sword in surrender of not only his friend but the bravest man he knew.

'You're . . . you were sore wounded, the last I saw of yourself.'

'Thanks to your kindness and the devotion of Persephone – that is, my wife – I made recovery.'

Gindler moved forward awkwardly. 'I'm . . . happy to hear it.'

Kydd hesitated and, trying not to see the bandages and crutch, said impulsively, 'Do you . . . that is to say, have you any who now waits for your return?'

There was a soft smile, which turned wry as Gindler answered, 'There is, sir. Her name is Maybelle and . . . and . . .'

His lot was to be taken prisoner, sent to England to the bleak prison on Dartmoor until the end of this war. Maybelle must languish.

There were men about the deck, waiting for what had to come, and Gindler, sensing it, stiffened. He unbuckled his sword-belt and held it out, his expression unreadable.

Kydd kept his hands to his side. 'No, sir, I will not take the sword of one who fought so well for the honour of his country's flag.'

There was a murmur around the deck as the gesture was noticed, but he hadn't finished. Leaning forward so none could hear, he said evenly, 'Jasper. As you granted me life to return to *my* lady, I now pay back the kindness. Should you give me word that you will abstain from arms against His Majesty it would give me the greatest of pleasure to land you on United States territory as soon as I may.'

Emotions worked on Gindler's face before he answered firmly, 'That I do swear to you.'

With a roguish grin Kydd slapped him on the shoulder. 'Well, take care of Maybelle, Jasper.' His face softened. 'And may our next meeting, my Yankee friend, be at a time of peace between our two great nations.'

Glossary

anker cask	cask of ten gallons capacity
athwart	crosswise as opposed to fore and aft
bistoury	a surgical knife with a long, narrow, straight or curved blade
Boney	derisory term for Napoleon Bonaparte
bowt	where a ship stoutly confronts waves and smashes through them rather than rides over the top
calibogus	Canadian: a bracing mix of rum, spruce beer and molasses
carronade	a short, handy gun firing a large ball but with reduced range and accuracy
cataplasm	type of poultice
cobbs	coin, specifically the Spanish reale
copper sheeting	copper sheathing applied to the underwater parts of a hull to deter marine infestations
Cousin Jonathan	friendly British term for an American
dark lanthorn	lantern with shutters that can be closed to conceal the light
dispart	the differing diameter at the breech and at the muzzle; a dispart sight allows for this in aiming the gun
doldrums	an equatorial region between the trade winds renowned for its continuous calms
driver gaff	if fitted, the uppermost triangular sail above the driver, the aftermost fore-and-aft sail
erysipelas	an acute infectious disease of the skin, characterised by fever, headache, vomiting, and purplish raised lesions
fine on the bow	a sighting ahead, slightly to one side
fore-course	a course is the lowest level of sail on a square-rigger

frap	brought together and lashed to keep from moving
fussock	north-country term for fool letting things go
horse latitudes	that region between the regular westerly winds of temperate latitudes and the trade-winds, notorious for sudden calms. Named for the practice of throwing the corpses of horses dying of thirst overside to float for days next to the ship
in corpore sano	in good health
jabberknowl	spoken nonsense, not understood
keelson	inner length of timber laid above the main keel to act as notched securing for frame timbers going across the hull
lee	the downwind side
middling repair	that class of repair of a damaged ship that does require a dry-docking but not a major dismantling and replacement, a great repair
mizzen	the aftermost mast in a ship-rigged vessel; viz. fore, main and mizzen-masts
oil of terebinth	purified medical turpentine
pintle-tagger	sea term for doctor
pledget	a small flat mass of lint, absorbent cotton, or the like, for use on a wound
private signal	that flag hoist of identification raised in response to a challenge, which is known only to those having the key
quacksalver	charlatan
raking	cannonading down the length of a ship instead of into its side; a devastating blow
rhino	ready cash
royals	the topmost sails in a conventionally ship-rigged vessel; viz. course, topsails, topgallant and royals
scantlings	the dimensions of a finished element of a ship
shay	slang for chaise carriage
stopper	length of rope used to stop a line moving; in battle a stopper prevents a shot-torn rope from unravelling
terebellum	surgeon's exploratory auger
toper	noted drinker
truck	circular cap finish at the top of a mast; often with sheaves for signal halyards
trunnion	two opposing projections either side of a gun at the point of balance
wear about	to stay about stern to wind; as opposed to tack, slower but more sure
weather quarter	that direction out to the upwind side but past the beam
windward	the upwind side

Author's Note

It was with mixed feelings that I began this book, the twenty-fifth in the Kydd Series. From my earliest times at sea I've never been far from the United States Navy. Two years with the Australians in the Vietnam war based at the big US naval base at Subic Bay in the Philippines; serving as a Royal Navy liaison officer to COMTHIRDFLT at Pearl Harbor – and even a morsel of sea-time in the legendary World War II carrier USS *Midway* – have all informed my respect and liking for the tribe.

How could I write about the Yankee 'enemy' after the warmth of my various encounters with the USN? And to make things harder, I've had many American friends since, to name just three – Ty Martin, the retired captain of USS *Constitution*, who helped out in more than a few ways; George Jepson, inspired editor of *Quarterdeck* magazine; and Howard Libauer USNR, who taught me the American way of irony.

I've always been intrigued with the story of HMS *Java*, with which I opened this book. Captured only months before from the French, she not only carried the newly appointed lieutenant governor of Bombay but the plans for an upgraded version of the famous *Leda* class frigate to be built there – *Trincomalee*.

A sister ship to *Shannon,* which prevailed against *Chesapeake* some months later, the vessel survives to this day, beautifully preserved in Hartlepool. I believe that after *Java* was defeated her helm was taken out to replace *Constitution*'s, which had been destroyed in the battle. Does the twenty-first-century *Constitution* still sport this?

The action at Pettipaug (now Essex) seems a sacrilege to any visitor today. A lovely New England town, it retains much of its bucolic charm. The Bushnell Inn, now the Griswold, is still there, and tales of the days when the British landed are ever to be heard.

The campaign of the Lakes is to me extraordinary. In an age when the American settlements had not yet begun their pioneer migration westwards, a full-scale modern war was being waged even before the age of Davy Crockett, in a vast wilderness of Indians and bears and on those continental-sized inland seas.

Incidentally, the man offered the job before the hapless Captain Barclay actually refused it on the grounds that it was an impossible assignment. I suppose it was a shipbuilders' war as much as anything else, and it culminated in HMS *St Lawrence*, a great ship-of-the-line larger even than *Victory*, Nelson's flagship at Trafalgar, being launched on Lake Ontario.

The regular reader of my seafaring tales will be familiar with the torturous scenes in the cockpit of a man-o'-war. Today's preconceptions may lead us to overlook the fact that in Kydd's day there were no specialists, each physician was expected to know the whole of medicine. If he had his own ideas or made errors the patient was the only one who suffered.

This book was probably the right time to bring in the fascinating aspect of the birth and development of technology as it applied to the Royal Navy. Today it's inconceivable that innovations are not scientifically derived but in that era all increments were slow and mostly brought on by private individuals. And what characters they were!

Bentham – Samuel, not his famous philosophic brother Jeremy – was certainly one. Just in his twenties, with the rank of general, he took two army battalions through Siberia to the Chinese border with instructions to find new lands, make alliance with the Mongols and open trade links with Japan and Alaska.

On his return to Britain he built up a pioneering technology development section in Portsmouth dockyard that set the stage for the Navy's future. His impatience in a leisurely age ensured his downfall and the shameful artifice to be rid of him saw his inevitable eclipse.

Not as characterful but certainly world-changing was the diffident Thomas Brunton and his studded link cable. It's not much realised that today, without exception, the entire maritime world of deep-sea ships is equipped with a Brunton-designed anchor cable, unchanged from then to now.

A *truly* characterful man was Richard Trevithick, the Cornish gentle giant, more at home in a tavern than a boardroom. He was never a businessman but paid his debts always, gleefully tackling at heroic scale all matters engineering. He was, at various times in his life, a soldier under the revolutionary Simon Bolivar; a circus entrepreneur; a wharf labourer in Limehouse – and finally the genius who freed the world of the tyranny of the lazy motions of the patented Boulton and Watts atmospheric beam engine. And thus we entered the fearful and exciting age of high-pressure steam.

The years I portray in this book were really the stepping-off point for the whole era of maritime steam. In 1812 the *Comet* was by herself; by 1814 there were four others on the Clyde alone and by 1819 a steamer was a common spectacle there. I'm happy to say that her single-cylinder engine may be seen on display at the National Science Museum, and there's even a faithful replica of the craft on public view in Glasgow, if now wanting a little care and attention. As far as I can determine, the accidental voyage of *L'Actif* in 1812 is the first open-sea passage of any vessel under steam, a world record that was hardly known about then, or now.

The period in which this book is set was dizzying in its contrasts and advances. People of those times cannot be blamed for not seeing into the future any more than, in these days of robots and artificial intelligence, we can. If anything, it was even more baffling and obscure in those days, for there was not a profession of mechanics or anything like it, or even the vocabulary to describe matters technical by people in general. Installing steam engines, for instance, was the province of millwrights, for windmills were the largest machines about at the time. It was a matter of when in doubt take the thing to the village blacksmith: he'll be sure to fix it.

The Admiralty has been pilloried for their delay in introducing steam but in my candid opinion they were right. Not until the advent of true reliability in engines, a massive development in their power and endurance and the ready availability of competent mechanics in the population at large would it have been prudent to move, and that didn't really happen until half of the century had passed. As well as the objections mentioned earlier in this book there was the fundamental question as to whether the premier naval power in the world should scrap its entire war-winning fleets and start all over again – if ever that could have been afforded after a ruinous war.

The final part of the book is obviously based on the *Essex* incident. I couldn't employ it in its full historical verisimilitude for that's really a vast ocean-spanning saga, which would deserve in all its sprawling detail a book on its own.

As usual, my sincere thanks must go to the whole of Team Stockwin – my agent Isobel Dixon, my editor Morgan Springett, designer Larry Rostant for his stunning cover, and copy editor Hazel Orme. And, of course, a big shout-out to Kathy, my wife and literary partner.